Maya Blake's hopes of becoming a writer were born when she picked up her first romance at thirteen. Little did she know her dream would come true! Does she still pinch herself every now and then to make sure it's not a dream? Yes, she does! Feel free to pinch her, too, via X, Facebook or Goodreads! Happy reading!

Clare Connelly was raised in small-town Australia among a family of avid readers. She spent much of her childhood up a tree, Mills & Boon book in hand. Clare is married to her own real-life hero, and they live in a bungalow near the sea with their two children. She is frequently found staring into space—a surefire sign that she's in the world of her characters. She has a penchant for French food and ice-cold champagne, and Mills & Boon novels continue to be her favourite ever books. Writing for Modern is a long-held dream. Clare can be contacted via clareconnelly.com or on her Facebook page.

Also by Maya Blake

Enemy's Game of Revenge

Royals of Cartana miniseries

Crowned for His Son
Out of Office Nights
Snowbound and Royally Forbidden

Also by Clare Connelly

Billion-Dollar Secret Between Them

Royally Tempted collection

Twins for His Majesty

A Greek Inheritance Game miniseries

Billion-Dollar Dating Deception
Tycoon's Terms of Engagement

Discover more at millsandboon.co.uk.

A GREEK 'I DO'

MAYA BLAKE

CLARE CONNELLY

MILLS & BOON

All rights reserved including the right of reproduction in whole or in part in any form. This edition is published by arrangement with Harlequin Enterprises ULC.

This is a work of fiction. Names, characters, places, locations and incidents are purely fictional and bear no relationship to any real life individuals, living or dead, or to any actual places, business establishments, locations, events or incidents. Any resemblance is entirely coincidental.

Without limiting the exclusive rights of any author, contributor or the publisher of this publication, any unauthorised use of this publication to train generative artificial intelligence (AI) technologies is expressly prohibited. HarperCollins also exercise their rights under Article 4(3) of the Digital Single Market Directive 2019/790 and expressly reserve this publication from the text and data mining exception.

® and TM are trademarks owned and used by the trademark owner and/or its licensee. Trademarks marked with ® are registered with the United Kingdom Patent Office and/or the Office for Harmonisation in the Internal Market and in other countries.

First published in Great Britain 2026
by Mills & Boon, an imprint of HarperCollins*Publishers* Ltd,
1 London Bridge Street, London, SE1 9GF

www.harpercollins.co.uk

HarperCollins*Publishers*, Macken House, 39/40 Mayor Street Upper, Dublin 1, D01 C9W8, Ireland

A Greek 'I Do' © 2026 Harlequin Enterprises ULC

Keeping a Greek Secret © 2026 Maya Blake

Blackmail to White Veil © 2026 Clare Connelly

ISBN: 978-0-263-41816-3

02/26

KEEPING A GREEK SECRET

MAYA BLAKE

MILLS & BOON

CHAPTER ONE

Prologos. Parados. Epeisodion. Stasimon. Exodus.

The stages of a Greek tragedy according to the great Aristotle. Nelios Petralis boarded his private jet at London's City Airport half-hoping he was at the denouement: exodus.

The finale of a decades-long plot was close but not quite close enough. He hadn't asked for his life to turn out this way. He'd been plunged into a harrowing drama by those who should've made better choices. But, while he hadn't started it, by God he intended to finish it on *his* terms.

Cradling his favourite tipple—aged whiskey that cost more than the average man's monthly salary—he stared over the crystal glass at his right-hand man, Andreas Barbieri. He and Andreas had found each other at possibly the worst moment of their lives: cornered in a filthy alley with half a dozen bullies twice their size baying for their blood, all because they'd stolen a loaf of bread 'on their patch'. They hadn't perished that day, obviously, but they'd come far too close.

Nelios eyed Andreas's Brioni suit, Savile Row tie and sleek Ulysse Nardin watch with a heartening sense of satisfaction. The outer trappings of success clawed out of the gutter, literally and figuratively. He didn't ask the question bristling on his tongue—whether Andreas had ever imagined they would be here today—because he didn't crave a trip down memory lane.

The three-hour meeting he'd just come from, one peppered

with hoarsely voiced anguish and crocodile tears mingled with the stench of fear—from his opponents, never him—had been enough revisiting of his history for one day. His only regret was that another of those opponents had slipped his net through death some years ago—and, infuriatingly, remembering that fact still sent a lance of rage-tinged, wholly undeserving grief and regret through him, but that couldn't be changed.

He took another sip, savouring the exquisite taste, just as Andreas looked up.

'The meeting with the architects will start as soon as we take off. Would you like to go over the blueprints beforehand?' he asked with a trace of the Sicilian accent he'd never lost, despite having been dumped in Athens decades ago, just like Nelios.

'Not just yet,' he murmured. The low, dark throb in his voice echoed the rumbling within him. The rumbling he had every intention of ignoring because it always went away. Whiskey and a little distance always put him back on an even keel. Although...this *stasimon* might take a little longer.

He hadn't quite accounted for the little extra drama this afternoon in the form of the young woman full of fiery temper and righteous indignation. Definitely hadn't expected the heat stirring through him when in the boardroom she'd defiantly hurled her, 'I'll make sure you regret this if it's the last thing I do!'

'How is the other matter unfolding?' he asked now, with an extra-punchy layer of anticipation he didn't quite care for, and yet couldn't seem to discard. 'Is she on her way?'

Eyes so dark they looked black, and vicious in some lights, glinted at him as Andreas's brow quirked. 'As predicted. Our spies came through. She is walking through the terminal as we speak. Guess she intends on carrying through with her threat.'

Neither of them even glanced out of the window at the VIP terminal where more drama was unfolding. Andreas shook his head. 'It's shocking how very little money it takes for nos to turn into yeses when your name is dropped.'

Nelios smiled wryly. 'It's not just my name—yours too.' Although he knew his was weighty enough to swing things his way when required. 'And economies everywhere are in the toilet. People do what they must to get by with a little incentive.' *Like we had to.*

A sage nod from Andreas concurred that they'd both been there and done that, right before his phone pinged with an incoming text. His friend's satisfied grunt said everything Nelios needed to know. He hadn't set the trap, but he'd known about it almost the second it'd been created. And he intended to make full use of it.

He drained his glass as Andreas rose and headed for the front of the plane. In low tones, he informed the pilot and crew that they were ready for take-off—complete with their cheeky little stowaway. They'd been informed, on Nelios's orders, not to raise the alarm or do anything about it.

For the better part of two decades—ever since he'd ditched the name given to him at birth by undeserving parents who'd turned out to be faithless and cruel, and dragged himself and his new name from the gutters of Athens—he'd planned every corner of his life with lethal precision.

The woman who was sneaking her way onto his private jet with the sole purpose of somehow disrupting his plans to take over her hotel—an all but done deal with very small fry indeed—shouldn't have mattered this much, yet somehow…

He shifted in his seat, wondering just why she mattered to him. Was it because she was now connected to those who'd wronged him all those years ago? Because those scant minutes when she'd stood up to him in their meeting earlier replayed in his head with a vividness he couldn't dismiss?

Because her earnest desperation and flaming determination had struck a chord with him?

Whatever. He hated unsolved puzzles. That was all she was, he assured himself. And, by placing herself within his orbit, he could be done with this silly conundrum by the time he stopped to refuel. And, hell, maybe he could learn a thing or two about his enemies while he was at it.

A full hour later, long after his plane had taken off and levelled out over the clouds of the Atlantic, and his meeting with his architects had been satisfactorily concluded, Nelios rose from his club chair.

Andreas's teeth bared as they did whenever he scented a conquest. Sometimes it was hard to believe anyone on earth was more bloodthirsty than Nelios, but here he was, witnessing the stark truth on his friend's face. 'Happy hunting.'

Nelios grunted. 'The hunt was over even before it began, my friend. The real question is, what to do with my unwanted prey?'

His friend's low laughter echoed in his ears as Nelios strode to the back of the plane, entered his bedroom, stretched out on his bed...

And waited.

She'd done it.

Dear God.

Vayle Lancaster couldn't stop the shivers from unravelling through her, despite the adrenaline having fled her system hours ago. She was grateful for the tight closet bracing her back and knees otherwise she would've collapsed into a pathetic heap long ago.

From the glow of her phone screen she watched the countdown: another five long hours of being stuck in this closet. Then she could enact the next part of her plan. With any luck, she could be back home by the end of the day tomorrow.

Argentina was still hours away, though. No way would she make it all the way there hiding in Nelios Petralis's wardrobe. Especially when the scent swirling around in here made her even dizzier.

God, how did he smell so good?

By being filthy rich and having parfumiers and other rich people's accessories at his fingertips, that's how.

She shook her head. True but not entirely. She'd noticed, with much annoyance and alarm while caught in that one-way verbal spat—because Nelios Petralis hadn't lifted even an eyebrow when she'd let loose the volley of anger at his treatment of them—that the other guy, his right-hand man, smelled good too. But Vayle hadn't fixated on his scent the way she had on Petralis's.

Fixated? A rather strong word. But no other word accurately described how she couldn't get it out of her senses. How she wanted to keep breathing it in as if it was vital oxygen...

Enough. Concentrate!

She wrapped her arms around her knees. It was a good thing she was neither claustrophobic nor afraid of the dark. That she was used to contorting herself into tight spaces.

Distressing memories tried to crowd her brain but she shook her head free of them and glanced back at her phone. She wished for a split second she'd thought to pack her earbuds, before she snorted under her breath. This wasn't some jolly jaunt. Bopping to her favourite music wasn't an option when she needed to remain alert. To listen out for her chance with Nelios Petralis when he came into his bedroom.

Would he be angry or display that fathoms-deep icy indifference he'd basked in all through their meeting this afternoon? The meeting, she recalled with horror, that had devolved into tears from her surrogate mother and a shocking lack of decorum from Vayle herself—but who could blame her? Far from meeting with Nelios to come to an agreement about a possible business agreement regarding her hotel, as she'd thought, he'd informed her coldly that he was stealing her inheritance right from under her nose!

Vayle wasn't even sure which reaction she'd prefer. Both were terrifying. But, fortunately, not enough to dissuade her. She knew her subject matter inside and out. Knew like the back of her hand the hotel he was trying to annex. It bore her name, for heaven's sake. Just as she knew that what she had to offer was everything he'd refused to accommodate in this cruel hostile takeover he seemed bent on pursuing, despite her hotel being ludicrously below his radar.

Four hours, forty-five minutes, then she could state her case, calmly and concisely and hope he listened and didn't do anything drastic, like fling her out of his aeroplane from forty thousand feet into the frigid Atlantic.

Breathe, Vayle. Breathe.

Stowing away on his private jet had been a bonkers idea from the start but the potentially scary part—in which she'd imagined she would be caught before she boarded and thrown in jail—had gone surprisingly smoothly. Which didn't say a lot for aviation security, but she would lament that observation another day. The second, scarier part was still ahead of her so she needed to stay calm for a little bit longer.

She dropped her forehead onto her knees, practising the yoga breath-control she'd striven to master through turbulent years when the slightest misstep could set tempers flaring. Banishing her to the dark.

Thankfully, those years were behind her. She just needed to do this one last thing for Agnes Adamis—her 'surrogate mother'—the woman who'd opened her heart and arms to Vayle when she'd needed it most.

Bonkers or not, it was the very least she could do. Agnes could've returned to Greece after her husband Tolis's death, as she'd strongly hinted at doing, but she'd stayed with Vayle and helped her through her own complicated grief after she'd lost the father with whom she'd had a fraught relationship. Even Agnes's confession immediately after the meeting that Nelios's treatment of them was her fault—that their past history had led to this—hadn't dissuaded Vayle from pushing back against this billionaire's bullying tactics. Hell, it'd only spurred her on. She knew a thing or two about bullies—her father had been one, hiding behind illness to make everyone's life an absolute misery.

Whatever Nelios Petralis was hiding behind to treat Vayle and the woman she held dear like this—the woman who, shockingly, also happened to be his mother—she would hold him to account, if it was the last thing she did.

Purpose reasserted, she eyed the timer. Many more hours yet.

It wouldn't hurt to close her eyes, stay calm and just breathe. Breathe. Breathe...

She wasn't sure what woke her but the sound was far too close. Adrenaline roared through her system, making her jerk and... *Argh!*

'Oh...oh crap! Oh God!' The deadly cramp gripped her hamstring like vicious teeth sinking into her flesh and had her crying out a second time.

She scrambled out of the wardrobe on her hands and one knee while desperately trying to straighten her other leg and flex her foot to ease the wildly spasming muscle. It didn't budge. Hell, it got worse...

'Ah, there you are. I was wondering how long you intended to nap.'

Vayle froze, her stunned gaze falling on a set of feet. *Bare masculine feet.* Dry mouthed, her eyes moved up, inch by inch to bare, thick hair-roughened calves...bare knees...

Oh my God.

She should've averted her gaze then, and stopped this comedy of errors dead in its tracks, but no. Her stupefied gaze kept climbing. *Climbing...*

The tiniest layer of tension punched out when, thankfully, her gaze met the edge of a pristine white towel. But that dissipated quickly as another savage spasm ripped through her leg. She dropped and rolled over at his feet, her hands scrambling to grip her muscle.

'What is wrong with you?' the dark, unfortunately familiar voice bit out.

She winced. 'Cramp. Help, please!' Vayle couldn't believe the tears that sprang to her eyes. She never, ever cried, no matter what. So what was this? Maybe she was more sleep-deprived than she'd thought.

No; going without sleep was another talent she could claim to possess. She'd always needed to keep one eye open in case George Lancaster—the vicious half-man, all monster, who'd biologically fathered her, and the man with a temperament trickier than mercury—had decided to torment her while she was asleep and unguarded. She'd learnt to withhold her tears and her protests, her silent defiance and lack of engagement eventually outlasting his sometimes hours-long rants.

She'd been through some of the worst emotional torture a human being could withstand without shedding a single tear, and yet here she was, crying over a cramp.

Teeth gritted, she dropped onto the plush carpet, noting that he hadn't moved a single muscle to help her. *Bastard.* Lying on her back, she lifted her leg and tried to massage the spasm out of her calf but the more she tried, the worse it seemed to get.

'Are you serious right now?' The words were muttered incredulously.

Her eyes opened, helplessly drawn back to him, and she was granted an even more disturbing sight.

Nelios Petralis's entire body, clad in just a towel. His wet, damp hair fell over his face as he glowered at her. His unshaven jaw clamped tight. And his far too sensual lips were thin with disapproval.

Even upside down he was beyond spectacular, virile in a way that left zero doubt as to his rampant maleness, his dominance at the top of the food chain.

She rolled onto her side, as if that would dissipate both his overwhelming presence and the tearing ache in her flesh. Neither happened. Another cry tore past her guard and Vayle wanted to disappear. To find the strength to get up and fling herself out of the nearest opening.

Because this was mortifying... And agonising. And possibly her own fault for not hydrating enough. But she'd been too nervous to eat, never mind drink, once she'd made up her mind about her contingency plan for tackling Nelios Petralis.

'I'll do whatever I can to get his attention,' she'd said to Agnes. 'Even stow away on his plane if I must. Actually, that might be the only option. He's building his latest hotel in Buenos Aires and he's flying there tonight. I'll have several hours of his undivided attention to make him see sense.'

Agnes's tear-filled argument against Vayle's wild plan had nearly dissuaded her. But the other woman's clear anguish when she'd insisted that she deserved everything Nelios Petralis—her own son—was doing to her had filled Vayle with a deeper purpose. Intensely hot billionaire, with a body carved like the best of Greek gods or not, Vayle would not let him get away with this.

So here she was, sprawled on her back, contemplating her choices and writhing in agony while... Her breath punched out of her when a strong pair of hands gripped her flailing leg.

'Stay still.' The instruction was cold and terse, the very

opposite of the warmth that bracketed her when he planted her bare foot against his abs. She froze, less in line with his command and more in reaction to the sensation of the searing skin-to-skin contact. Captive, she watched as, with two fingers, he dug into her calf muscle, right at the epicentre of her agony. Vayle gasped as her muscles spasmed in opposition…for several seconds…then gave way beneath the pressure. Her moan of relief was unguarded, bouncing above the sound of the humming aeroplane engines to fill the room.

The muscles beneath her foot clenched and unclenched, his dark gaze narrowing on her face as he continued to tend to her. She couldn't help herself. Another moan threatened as relief poured through her, her agony subsiding. But with the lessening of one trauma came the resurgence of what she faced. Why she was here.

Nelios's deadly gaze told her that reality would come with a great reckoning. She attempted to remove her foot from his skin, but one hand dropped over the top of her foot, keeping it flush against him.

'It's a little too late for retreat now, Miss Lancaster.'

Several things fell into place then. His comment about her taking a nap when she'd tumbled out of his wardrobe. His lack of surprise.

He'd known she was here all along.

She tried once more to free herself. Displeasure flashed across his face as he held her still. 'Your cramp hasn't subsided. And, as entertaining as it is to watch you flop about on my floor, I have better things to do. Stay still,' he repeated, 'And let me finish.'

Dear God. The rumble of his voice… The power behind it… The towering magnificence of him… He was indeed a Greek god come to life, complete with all the bells and whistles of furious thunder and incandescent lightning. She was shocked she hadn't been incinerated beneath the force of his wrath.

And yes, he was angry. It was there in the stiff shoulders and clenched jaw. Or…was it something else? Because beneath the arctic gaze there was something mesmeric, shimmering with heat, with awareness. Striations of white-hot heat. Of attraction…?

No. Absolutely not.

Pain, and then the beginnings of relief from it, was addling her brain. She dragged her gaze over his shoulder, pinning it to the ceiling as she tried to ignore everything but the countdown to tackling her task. To letting him know unequivocally what she thought of him and his bullying tactics. Then, maybe, to striking some kind of deal. Because she couldn't lose.

'That's how you're going to play it?' he mused dryly. 'Pretend I don't exist? That's going to make it difficult for you to achieve your ultimate goals, is it not?'

Her gaze darted to him. 'What do you know about my goals?' she asked hesitantly, feeling him out.

A muscle twitched in his cheek. 'I'm assuming you didn't stow away on my plane for the sole purpose of taking a nap in my wardrobe and inconveniencing me and my driving need for a shower for over two hours?'

The apology on the tip of her tongue dried when she realised he was mocking her. Had he truly needed to shower hours ago, he would've taken one. He'd showered exactly when he'd needed to, all the while being aware she was hiding amongst his clothes.

A flush built in her face but Vayle refused to look away. 'If you knew I was in here, then why…?'

'Why did I not do something about it? Where would the fun have been in that?'

She flinched and stifled another gasp when his thumb

dug in deeper and slowly worked its way to the top of her Achilles tendon. Goodness, he might be a monster, but he was an expert at unknotting muscles. Why that thought suffused her with several waves of heat, she absolutely refused to contemplate as she attempted to remove herself from his grip again. And failed...again. But the movement dislodged the object in her pocket.

His gaze trailed to the right. She followed it to her phone screen: the timer displayed in bright red. 'And what is that clock counting down to? You locating your courage?' he taunted. 'Or rousing yourself from your beauty sleep?'

Irritation zipped through her. 'Neither. It's for when we took off again, after refuelling.'

'I see. At which point you'd believe I would be unwilling to turn back the plane or take steps to eject you entirely?' he enquired silkily.

Vayle squirmed beneath the incisiveness of his gaze. She knew her nerves and lack of a decent poker face gave her away but, she told herself, since that was exactly what she'd hoped, why hide from it? 'Yes.'

'Hmm.' It was very perturbing that this man was so livid with her, yet he continued to tend to her as if he had all the time in the world. As if she were a person in need he cared about.

Which was a vicious lie. Kindness and consideration were the last things he was capable of. For the better part of a year she'd watched him decimate the hotel she co-managed with Agnes, stealing contracts and clients right from under their noses and not even bothering to disguise what he was doing. He was systematically driving them out of business so he could scoop up what remained.

So this had to be a trick. An apex predator toying with his prey. His hands wreaked magic on her body while those eyes continued to flash hot and cold, keeping her guessing as to his true emotions.

With more power than she'd thought herself capable of, considering her insides veritably quivered with the nerves eating her alive, she yanked her foot from his hold.

This time she succeeded. Or he let her go. She scrambled back until her spine hit the side of the enormous bed. And he watched her with sizzling focus as she tried to compose herself, flex her foot and with relief note that the throb had substantially decreased. She curbed the urge to check the hair she could feel unravelling from its neat knot, or the grey pencil-skirt and jacket that she'd cobbled together to pass muster as one of his flight attendants. Glad when she managed both, she darted a glance at him and saw his folded-arms stance, the eyebrow raised in rigid expectation.

She licked her lips. 'You know why I'm here.'

His gaze slowly raked over her, the tiniest escalation in his breathing telling her he wasn't as supremely cool as he projected. 'Do I? Or should the more pertinent question be, why the hell should I care?' Before she could launch into the spiel she'd practised repeatedly since their meeting, he continued. 'You're adequately intelligent enough to know you've broken several laws. Shouldn't you concern yourself with navigating that dilemma before anything else?'

She opened her mouth to speak, then a cold shiver washed over her. 'So you knew I was onboard, and you deliberately let me hide in here just so you could get me into trouble? Is that your idea of fun?'

His head tilted. 'Let me get this straight. Are you attempting to make me somehow responsible for your crimes?' he mused, then every hint of amusement evaporated. 'I shouldn't be surprised, considering who reared you, and yet...' The hard edge embedded in his voice abruptly cut off, leaving her short of breath.

Because in those last words she'd witnessed a complex

mine of emotions, every single one of them containing ferocious charges set to detonate at the smallest friction.

Who reared you...

Whether he was referring to George Lancaster, or Agnes and her late husband Tolis, she wasn't sure. Both Tolis and her father had died within weeks of each other, eighteen months ago, the former from a stroke and the latter after a short and violent illness that had screeched in like an evil wind and taken him with it. It was a shockingly apt metaphor for how he'd lived his life and the anguish he'd left behind. And, while Tolis hadn't been as affable as his wife, Vayle was in the dark as to why his son was so bitter.

But acrimonious family history wasn't why she was here. She was here to save her inheritance, regardless of the despair shrouding it. Or maybe it was *because* of the despair that she fought so hard. Because all these years of suffering surely would have been for nothing if she couldn't turn Vayle Hotel into a happy and welcoming place.

'We're getting off on the wrong foot,' she started, only to halt when he barked out arid laughter.

'No, Miss Lancaster. You and I will not be getting off anywhere—ever.' The words hovered, dark, ominous and... curiously electrifying, before he added, 'We will be touching down on Ascension in the next hour. You will be handed over to the authorities with a full account of how you lied your way through the airport by pretending to be a member of my crew to gain access to my jet, then hid away with the intent of...doing me harm? Attempted poisoning, suffocation or strangulation? Which is more salacious, do you think?'

Her mouth gaped as her mind spun. 'I was right, wasn't I? You...knew and you let it happen.'

'I knew,' he confirmed with zero inflection, as if he were confirming a menu selection. 'Every step of the way.' He shrugged. 'I may have even eased your way just to see if you'd go through with it. Your commitment in the face of possible arrest was quite...something.' Again his eyes seemed to sizzle over her, his brows pinching faintly before he shook his head, as if freeing himself from a thrall.

She swallowed, ignoring her own elevated temperature. *Now* she knew why it'd seemed so easy to saunter past all the checkpoints that should've been more rigorous. He'd been watching, the ultimate puppet master as she'd strung herself up. She experienced a futile nanosecond of unadulterated fury with him before she wised up.

This was no one's fault but hers. Even if she actively detested his *where's the fun in that?* she'd willingly stepped into this trap. And, as she knew from years of torment at her father's hand, it was entirely up to her how she dealt with it. Curling herself into a ball and wailing was not an option.

Slowly she straightened her no longer spasming leg, flexing it again to test that it was indeed cramp-free before she manoeuvred onto her knees. Just before she rose to her feet, something hot and lethal flashed in his eyes, but it was gone far too quickly to decipher its origin or purpose. 'You said we have an hour before we land?'

He didn't answer, but his eyes narrowed that extra fraction, warning her that whatever she was about to demand wouldn't be well received.

She ploughed ahead because...she really had no choice. She hadn't done all this to back down now. 'That thing you said about the way I was reared...' Her heart lurched and she almost lost the power of speech when his eyes turned several degrees more arctic. 'You couldn't be more wrong. Because, while not my blood relatives, your mother, Agnes—and Tolis when he was alive—were more loving and generous to me than my own parent ever was. So, no, I wasn't *reared* like some wild and unruly farm animal, as you so insultingly implied, and...'

Vayle stuttered to a stop as the man before her turned into a statue. But, while his body froze, the complex mine of emotions cracked and fizzled through his eyes like the most devastating fireworks. The blood rushed from her head, making her stagger back one step, then another, until the back of her legs met the bed and she couldn't retreat further.

Still caught in the vortex of his eyes, she watched him pivot to face the wardrobe that'd been her hiding place. And, with zero warning, Nelios Petralis dropped his towel.

She told herself her knees weakened because of the deadly currents flying through the air. And while that was very true—dear heaven, why had her words triggered such an intense reaction from him?—she didn't even equivocate about her body's searing response to being presented with the most visually magnificent man she'd ever seen. A man whose body belonged in the annals for mortal men and women to study those mile-wide shoulders and the muscles that moved beneath them; the olive-hued perfection of his skin; the tight glutes that formed his gloriously impressive ass; the tree-trunk legs that could down a lion with stupefying vigour.

This was a man who had zero compunction about being naked in front of her. Did he want to scandalise her, perhaps? No, Vayle concluded as her fists bunched in the high-thread-count sheets; she was almost certain that wasn't the case.

The simple truth was that her words had triggered something in Nelios Petralis. Something so primal, raw and lethal, he'd momentarily acted purely on autopilot.

CHAPTER TWO

You couldn't be more wrong.

A string of impassioned words meant to sway him. To alter his goals, perhaps view the chessboard from her angle.

Not blood relatives... Loving and generous...

Something thick, noxious and near-terrifying locked in his throat, roared in his ears and hazed his eyes. For a full minute he couldn't see, feel or hear anything but those words.

He'd never once in his life felt as if he could hyperventilate into unconsciousness, not even when he'd been cornered by thugs and terrified out of his mind as a weak, malnourished boy of thirteen. And yet, standing there, stark-naked with his towel at his feet, Nelios wagered that he might be as close to doing so as he'd ever been. Because every cell in his body was locked in bitterness and acute disbelief...

He couldn't be more right. Because he'd lived that torturous reality. He knew down to his very marrow how it felt to have his every last hope dashed, his world turn to ash just for the hell of it. No, not for the hell of it. For thirty pieces of silver; a loftier position in life. To elevate oneself regardless of how it affected others. Oh yes, in his case it had been all of the above for the two people who'd callously tossed him away. Sure they'd debated the toss for a handful of days but it'd been more a circling of wagons than opting for a different path—a path that didn't involve the ruthless abandonment of their only child.

He sensed her behind him, wondering if and why her words had turned him into a seething mass of ice at the side of a mountain, waiting for the smallest trigger to unleash the raging avalanche he could feel just beneath the surface.

He owed her neither his agita nor his explanation. But with every breath he took, those handful of words reverberated through him, demanding a response, an outlet.

This afternoon he'd seen the evidence of what she'd so passionately proclaimed. At first, he hadn't wanted to believe it. He'd thought his eyes were playing tricks on him. But then he'd caught the warm, fond smile Agnes Adamis had slanted her and had wondered whether she'd received the same from Tolis when he was alive.

He'd seen the wide, encouraging smile Vayle had returned and he'd marvelled at *how a monster could smile*. How the woman who'd given him life, then turned her back on him, could project *fondness*. He had indeed skated to the edge of that abyss he'd stared into many times in years gone by and wondered if *he* was problem. If he'd sinned so egregiously in a past life that he'd deserved to be punished in this one.

Then he'd reminded himself that even *he* smiled on occasion. Usually right before he crushed his enemies beneath his polished Italian leather shoes. Certainly he and Andreas had smiled over the years as they'd bested every single person who'd wronged them. And, with each billion they'd added to their bank account, he'd *marvelled* and *smiled* through being screamed at and being cursed and cajoled for mercy, usually by the very people who were the epitome of mercilessness.

So, yes, he had put that smile between Agnes and Vayle out of his mind. But now, to hear Vayle putting her spin on it, urging him to believe it was for other reasons besides being utterly monstrous… The sheer gall of that was the abomination, not him.

'Say something.' Her husky entreaty chiselled the tiniest crack in the dense ice.

His emotions, locked down tightly and buried beneath the filthy alleys somewhere back in Athens, groaned beneath the weight of it. Fingers convulsed around the forgotten scrap of fabric he'd grabbed, he turned back round.

Her eyes, wide and luminous with a flurry of emotions, frantically searched his face. Then, her cheeks growing pinker by the second, those eyes dropped down his naked body to his chest, his abs, his groin...

And, to add absolute insult to injury, there in the cabin that she'd invaded with her unwanted presence, her loathsome views and unfounded judgements, Nelios felt his traitorous body react to her nonplussed, wide-eyed scrutiny. He felt the stirrings that had begun in the conference room this afternoon, and had risen to a low simmer as he'd waited for her to sneak onto his plane, then spark into an unconscionable blaze, stunning the hell out of him.

A growl built in his throat as he shook out the boxers he clutched and, daring her with his eyes to utter one word at his blatant erection, he yanked on his underwear.

Her cheeks puffed with the strength of her audible exhale as he once again pivoted to drag a pair of chinos and a T-shirt from his wardrobe.

Finally dressed, after what felt like hours after he'd first exited his bathroom, Nelios faced her once more.

Say something, she'd said. He approached, arms folded across his chest, his eyes pinned on her so there would be no mistaking his words.

'You want me to say something? I know exactly who she is, what kind of man my father was before he died—and, yes, I *will* speak ill of the dead. I know the evil they're capable of. You may have been fooled into putting on those rose-tinted glasses you're proudly wearing but know this:

that woman will throw you away like unwanted garbage the second something better comes along.'

His mouth twisted and he chuckled past the constriction in his throat. 'What am I talking about? She already has! She's thrown you at me, at my mercy, without a second thought to what I would do to you when I discovered your intentions.'

'No…no she hasn't. She didn't. Coming here was—'

'Of your own free will? Or were you manipulated? Perhaps even cajoled with a well-timed tear or two? An entreaty that you were a last hope and therefore needed to do the right thing?'

He watched her pale, her expression spout suspicion right before she vehemently shook her head. 'No. If you'd just let me speak, I'd tell you it's not like that. This was my idea and mine alone. In case you haven't noticed, mine is the name on the hotel. I have a horse in this race too. As for Agnes, she's kind and decent, no matter how much you want to think otherwise. Look, I don't know what happened between you and your mother, but—'

Another growl rose and her head snapped up, her apprehension gone.

'You won't trick me into denying what I know to be true. Besides, how would you know?' she challenged. 'Your own parents rarely mentioned you in all the years I've known them. And you haven't been interested in them in return. You weren't even at Tolis's funeral. And yet, in the past year, you've been intent on tearing up our lives from the comfort of your plane, or your mansion or wherever monsters like you ooze from. So where's your proof that you know them at all?'

He stalked towards her, aware his teeth were bared. That years of locked emotions strained to explode from him. He wasn't at all surprised when she shrank back onto her elbows, her breathing choppy as he stopped mere feet from her. Yes, he was monstrous. But then wasn't he a product of monsters?

His arms dropped to his sides, his fists curling. 'Where is my evidence? Open your eyes. Take a good look, Miss Lancaster. I was theirs too, once. But, unlike you, I was the child Apostolis and Agnes Adamis actually conceived. The son they reared from birth until I was twelve years old. The child they tolerated like a low-priority pet. Until a shiny new prospect was offered to them. And then, with neither kindness nor consideration, they threw me away. So, yes.' His fist slammed his chest in an act far too emotionally reminiscent of the *stasimon* he wished to be done with, but no matter. 'I am living, breathing proof of exactly what I'm talking about.'

From some dim corner of her brain Vayle examined the veracity of his words. Debated whether he was accomplished enough to spout such vicious lies with a straight, albeit breathtaking face. Because they *were* lies; they had to be. And yet the majority of her reasoning took in the complexities of elevated breathing and the bleak rage in those eyes fixed so ferociously on hers. Took in the stern brackets around his thinned lips and the jagged roughness of his voice that blared the evidence that he'd been pushed into confessing. Pushed to the edge—by her.

Vayle knew she would have to come up with something unassailable to refute what her senses screamed at her was the truth. A *horrifying* truth.

'I know you're their son.' Those brown eyes, which were a shade darker than Agnes's, and the male version of her mouth made it irrefutable. And she supposed his jet-black hair matched Tolis's, although his father's had turned more grey than black in the few years before his death. 'Even though your surnames are different. And... I've known them for nearly two decades. Agnes had told me a tiny bit about you, but only that she'd lost you. I thought you were...'

She pursed her lips, not wanting to repeat or recall Agnes's anguish when she'd spoken about her son. For years Vayle had believed 'lost' meant 'died', until she'd recently learned differently. 'There has to be a better explanation for what happened than they threw you away.'

She couldn't wrap her mind around what he was saying about the couple who'd arrived to helm her father's flagship hotel after the banks and doctors had declared George Lancaster unfit to keep managing his own affairs.

Over the years they'd become like parents to Vayle, protecting her from her father's many torments until his death, while co-managing the hotel with her after she'd finished university, and mentoring her to take over her inheritance one day.

While Tolis had had his moments of obstinacy and mild misogyny, he'd been miles better than her own father. Definitely not the parent Nelios had described.

Nelios took a step back, his emotions rapidly wrestled under control so he could stare down at her with something strongly resembling pity.

'Is that the only straw in your sinking raft, Miss Lancaster?' he mocked. 'I changed my name at the first opportunity because I couldn't abide the stench of it a second longer. Those people abandoned me and I renounced them legally on what was one of the best days of my life.' The thick vein of satisfaction, victory and loathing in his voice said he was reliving the memory with much relish.

She shuddered, still unable to reconcile the two realities. One *had* to be a distortion.

'You keep saying they threw you away, abandoned you. How...how is that even possible?'

His eyes narrowed. 'What were you told?'

She licked her lips, her pulse jumping when he followed the movement. Scrambling, she tried to recall what Agnes had told her about the son she found painful to talk about.

'Tolis, your father, rarely talked—' She stopped when he snarled under his breath. 'Agnes said they left you in Greece so you could continue your education. But that something happened, and they lost track of you…'

His teeth set harshly, his nostrils flaring for a moment before he turned away. She thought he would ignore her but surprisingly he spoke.

'Of course they would couch it in such vague terms.' He shook his head, his voice gravel-rough as he continued, 'I came home from school on a normal day to find someone my father claimed had been sent by a friend of his in our home. A friend who happened to run a foster-care agency. I was told I had to be placed with this stranger for a while, while my parents pursued a rosy future for us in England. What she didn't know was that even if we were destitute, I would have been prepared to live with them on the streets instead of being left behind.'

He stopped, clenched his jaw and exhaled. 'As I said, I knew they were lying. We weren't rich but we certainly weren't destitute. And they'd forgotten how thin the walls in our house were—that or they didn't care. I overheard them discussing it the night before but hadn't fully understood what I'd heard, until the foster carer arrived. It was my father's idea. My mother put up a token fight but she didn't hold out for long.'

His mouth twisted. 'And, yes, I said so to the carer. Gave her the real reason my parents were throwing me away. It was so they could make a better life for themselves in England, unencumbered by a child. She immediately marked me down as a troublemaker who liked to spin tales about his parents who were doing the right thing by seeking a better future for them and their child. The carer took their side, of course. Smiled approvingly as Tolis looked into my eyes and outright lied that they would be back in a year, when I'd heard them committing to at least three years in their new job the night before.'

His head snapped towards Vayle when she gasped.

His smile was a caricature of blinding white teeth. 'Oh yes, I know that means something to you. I know you recognise the stipulations regarding your father's guardianship. That the banks wanted whoever took over management of the hotel to be given a minimum three-year contract to ensure a stable tenure. And, yes, I know your father's extremely lucrative offer is what lured my parents. An offer which included the small but significant clause that whoever took the position should be *without encumbrances*. An offer they accepted.'

His body followed his head and he faced her once more, a towering pillar of icy control. 'So, given the circumstances described to you, do you not think I was well within my rights to denounce them as they once denounced me?' His question was a silky blade slicing through her jumbled senses.

Her fingers twisted in her lap. 'But Agnes said she tried to keep in contact with you. She never forgot about you. That something must have gone wrong. Have you tried speaking to your mother about what happened, instead of causing all this destruction? Because there's likely a good reason for it...that they... There has to be.'

His frozen face turned grimmer. 'Does there? Why? Because it would suit your rosy outlook? Your fairy-tale imagination where you think you've been rescued from a fate worse than death, only to discover your fairy godparents were the real monsters all along?'

Something clogged in her throat. Something like horror... A sob... She swallowed it down and shook her head. 'I know nothing I say can...will...change your mind. But the truth is, I know what I know.'

His teeth bared again. 'Good. Keep believing what you wish to believe. If you're saving me all the melodrama by admitting you can't change my mind then we're done here, feel free to return to the wardrobe until we land, if you prefer, but I won't save you from another cramping episode, so bear that in mind.'

Vayle jumped up when he strode to the door. 'Hold on. I never said I wasn't willing to... I still need to talk to you about my hotel.'

He slanted her a mocking glance. 'You mean *my* hotel, seeing as you have no choice but to accept my offer? The simple answer is nothing. You've had a wasted journey and may well have an upcoming stint in jail to look forward to. Congratulations.' He pulled the door open and walked out.

Knowing she would have to follow him, and show herself to his crew, made her cringe and seriously consider taking his offer to dive back into his wardrobe. It took a monumental effort to lock her knees and reheat courage gone cold at his devastating revelations. Revelations she would need to unpack later because right now she simply could not reconcile the two realities. There *was* a missing link somewhere. Until then, though...

She staggered one step forward and, realising she'd lost her shoes somewhere in her mad, cramping tumble, glanced at the wardrobe. But Vayle knew the second she approached it she would take the cowardly option and dive back in. Return to yet another dark cupboard, but this time of her own volition.

So, feet bare and courage woefully tepid, she hurried after Nelios Petralis.

She found him in the jet's dining room—after several wrong turns and encounters with sharply dressed crew whose lack of surprise at an additional passenger's appearance proved they'd known of her presence all along. And that, in sharp contrast to their flawless attire, her poor imitation must have made her stick out like a sore thumb all through her doomed escapade.

She hovered in the doorway and watched Nelios and the other man with whom he'd attended the meeting this afternoon converse in low tones while devouring sumptuous-looking steaks. She knew that they were both actively ignoring her, and a spark of ire warmed up her courage. But, before she could speak, her stomach took charge, growling fiercely enough to stop them mid-conversation.

Dear God, could this get any worse?

Apparently it could. Because the conversation stopped once her belly finished its demanding aria. Nelios turned his imperious head, eyes scouring her as if she was the trash he had just informed her he'd been treated as by his parents. Trash *he* intended to throw away the second they landed.

So do something. Don't just stand there.

'Mr Petralis,' she started, only to stop when he held up an imperious hand then lowered it to drum on the table, his stare penetrating.

'I cannot think or eat to the unsavoury accompaniment of your stomach's soundtrack.' He yanked out the chair next to him. 'Sit down,' he snapped.

Annoyingly, since she had no leg to stand on, Vayle sat. A button was pressed. An attendant appeared. Lavish choices were offered. Within minutes a large prime steak, salad and the prettiest potatoes she'd ever seen on a plate was set before her. And, because she'd been programmed to never look gift horses in the mouth, and despite her face flaming when another discordant melody surged from her middle, she picked up her cutlery and ate.

She was aware they were both watching. Aware that, after a full minute, the other man murmured something in Greek to Nelios, reigniting their conversation. Which dragged a rake of irritation across her senses, ruffling them until she couldn't stay quiet.

'You know it's impolite to conduct a conversation when one party doesn't speak the language, don't you?'

Derisive brown eyes turned on her. 'By all means, tutor us in the correct etiquette of conversation while you breathe my air and eat my food, Miss Stowaway,' Nelios drawled.

The other man smirked. Vayle attempted a glare that bounced off his wide shoulders.

Let it go. Let it go. 'I'm just saying...'

'Here's a word of advice: know when to quit,' the man said, cutting a square of steak and chewing it.

Her gaze moved to Nelios and she saw a flash of something close to irritation in his eyes before he too resumed eating. Silence reigned, self-consciousness aggravating her already ragged senses.

She was setting down her cutlery when an attendant approached. 'We'll be landing to refuel in ten minutes, Mr Petralis.' The man, who looked more like a bodyguard than an attendant, darted a glance at Vayle before returning to his boss. 'The pilot wants to know whether you still want the authorities on standby as you previously requested?'

Without glancing at her, Nelios nodded, picked up his wine glass and drained it. 'Tell him nothing has changed. I want Miss Lancaster off my plane and handed over as soon as—'

'No, wait. Please don't. Look, I'll... I'll do anything!'

'Rookie mistake,' Andreas muttered under his breath five minutes after Vayle Lancaster had blurted that unexpected response, and he and Nelios had left her in the dining room without replying. 'I'm not sure whether I pity her or am amused by her. Either way, you're better off cutting her loose asap. I'll go grab the security. She'll be someone else's problem within the hour, my friend.' He walked away.

Outside, the flurry of activity rumbled on, including the squad car and two policemen waiting patiently to board with Nelios's permission.

He rolled his shoulders with a combination of irritation at his friend and the knowledge that he needed to heed Andreas's warning and cut her loose. He didn't need this drama. Didn't need the flare of heat across his skin whenever he looked at her face, at her mouth, heard the breathless quality of her speech or observed the way her damn eyelashes fluttered when she was agitated. He didn't need to remember how firm and supple her body had felt beneath his touch.

His latest creation, the Nelios XV hotel, was in the final stages of construction in Argentina and needed every ounce of his attention. It would be the milestone to mark the many he'd accrued over the years, and it was his first foray into South America, a place he'd fallen in love with.

A place where he'd also witnessed the kind of hardship that ravaged his soul. Which was why, alongside his hotel construction, he was also building special housing for desperate children, as he and Andreas had once been. Both projects were ambitious, with varying challenges, the kind he fully relished. But also the kind that needed his full attention. So why the hell did he hear her *I'll do anything* plea on repeat in his head?

He'd already let himself down in that bedroom by revealing truths he'd excised from his life. Yes, her words and blind belief in his parents had riled him like nothing else had for a very long time. He'd barely managed to snap that, contrary to her belief, he had attended his father's funeral. He had stood beneath a tree thirty feet away and watched the man who'd discarded him get put in the ground. Then he'd waited until everyone had departed, and he had stood over his grave—bitter, bewildered, angry and, much to his deep chagrin, a little lost.

Maybe it was that last sensation that had triggered this end game, the need for answers before time cruelly stole them from him.

Whatever.

And, yes, he'd concluded the quicker he ripped those rose-tinted glasses off Vayle's face, the better for them all, because he wanted her to know exactly who Agnes Adamis truly was. Who Tolis had been. Wanted there to be no crumb of compassion left for them by the time he was done.

If Vayle cared enough to take the trouble, verification would only take her hours, days at most. Nelios had never bothered to hide his past. Hell, his first business venture had been one street away from that alley in which he'd nearly lost his life after he'd run away from the final foster home he'd been placed in. A home where flying fists and verbal abuse had been as commonplace as the stale, infested oatmeal he'd been expected to choke down at the breakfast table, or the freezing showers he was forced to take just so his foster parents could save the euros they'd greedily accepted from the government and kept for themselves.

Approaching his bedroom now, to where she'd marched off to rescue her shoes and whatever else she'd brought aboard on her little stowaway adventure, Nelios fully expected to toss her out and let the authorities charge her with whatever crime they saw fit.

Seeing her distraught expression when he entered, though, he hesitated. Not because he felt for her; absolutely not. But part of him wanted to understand how she could be so conclusively fooled. How her belief in Agnes and Tolis could be so unshakeable. *He* had known his parents were lying that day. And, true to their lies, they'd never bothered to come back for him. Not the year after, and not in the two decades since.

And yes, Vayle's knee-jerk offer to 'do anything' also intrigued him far more than he should've allowed. Even now, all the possibilities of how he could wield those two words in his favour seductively stirred through him.

His late father had had a gifted tongue, able to charm the very birds from trees. What lies had he and Agnes spun on this woman? Was it even worth his time to try and disabuse her of her beliefs?

No. It wasn't. This interest was akin to a scientific experiment he wanted to comprehend, so he could actively avoid its deficiencies.

She was staring out of the window, at the hive of activity below. At the authorities who would shortly cart her away.

Nelios leaned against the doorway, a sliver of interest piercing his rigid guard. Her hair had almost fully escaped the knot at the back of her head, several heavy strands of rich chestnut battling with gravity to stay put. It drew attention to the sleek line of her neck, her slim shoulders and the tiny movement of her throat as she swallowed.

She sucked in a breath through parted lips and Nelios recalled her unguarded expression when he'd turned. The tiny flicker of her tongue ignited that same spark low in his belly, his jaw gritting as the spark gravitated south. No. He was absolutely not attracted to Apostolis's and Agnes's deluded little charity case.

And yet, when she took another, deeper breath, his gaze followed it to her firm breasts straining against the cheap suit she'd attempted to use as a disguise. Nelios cursed as the spark flamed higher.

'If you've come here to gloat, just get on with it, will you? You're running out of time.'

She kept her gaze on the window for several more seconds before pivoting to face him. The sight of her fighting tears while her chin lifted in clear defiance should have been laughable. But he wasn't laughing. He was wondering why the words he needed to utter remained locked in his throat.

Why the two reasons continued to clamour ever louder as he slowly approached her.

Step aside. Cut her loose. Be done with this. Nelios shook his head, his brow furrowing tighter.

She blew out a breath, half-relieved, half-puzzled. Then, still eyeing him, she attempted to sidle past him. He would probably not understand why his hand shot out then, any time soon. Why he gripped her elbow to stop her taking another step. And why he gave life to the words that fell from his lips in that moment.

'I will stay your execution—not because of your entirely foolish offer to do anything, although we will revisit that later.'

Her eyes grew wide and, this close, Nelios saw the ocean-blue held green and gold specks that sparkled and dimmed at will. They could almost have been considered mesmerising if one were foolish enough to succumb to their allure.

'What do you want in return?'

A science experiment. That is all this is. Information gathering too. Knowledge is power, right?

'You're coming to Argentina with me. Make no mistake, your dilemma hasn't changed. With a single phone call I can have you thrown in jail and then deported, a process that could last weeks or months. You'll be in no position to help Agnes then. Or I will offer you an alternative: for the next forty-eight hours, you'll tell me everything I wish to know about them. And you will leave nothing out. Agreed?'

On the one hand, it felt like the easiest thing in the world to agree to. But Vayle knew that, scratch the surface, there were all sorts of traps waiting for the unsuspecting. Traps that could well give him the ammunition he sought against Agnes, the mother he believed had wronged him.

If she was going to agree to this she would have to play

this very carefully—and from the appearance of Nelios's right-hand man in the doorway, she knew her time was up, just as she knew prison in a foreign country was the very last thing she wanted.

'Why do you want to know about them? I thought you didn't care.'

His jaw clenched tightly, once. 'That is my business, not yours.'

She searched his features for some humanity. Vayle was reminded that he'd helped her with her cramp, despite coming across as ruthless and unfeeling. He'd fed her when he could easily have had her removed from his presence. But a trap was still a trap, whether disguised with flowers or lined with barbed wire. So she pushed just that little bit harder. 'Your illusions were shattered so you want mine shattered too? Because what—misery loves company?'

'Should it be an illusion to expect the people who decided to sire you to give you a modicum of care and consideration?'

The memory of being locked in a dark room for hours on end threatened to upsurge her already rollercoaster emotions. 'No, it's not. But expecting me to view my history through your warped lens is equally inconsiderate.' She raised her chin. 'But I will accept your deal. And, by the end of it, you'll see nothing you say can sway me about Tolis and Agnes.'

His mouth twisted, along with a hint of angst crossing his face, swiftly stifled. 'Tolis. How benign you make him sound. When exactly did he start calling himself that?'

The bitterness in his voice shook her to the core. 'I always knew him as Tolis. And I wasn't quite finished. I will accept your deal on condition that nothing I say will be used in this...vendetta against Agnes.'

The snort came from behind him, from Andreas. But Nelios raised his hand before his friend could put his clearly incredulous feelings into words. 'You're very bad at your job if you believe I'd need a lowly marketing and PR manager of a three-star hotel to give me the dirt I need to best my enemies. No, Miss Lancaster, I will not give you my word because it isn't needed. Agree without conditions or get the hell off my plane.'

Time ticked loudly and ominously in her head. Andreas levelled a narrow-eyed gaze at her, almost daring her not to take the deal. It was clear the other man despised her, that he wanted her gone.

In some abstract part of her brain she wondered what his story was; what exactly the two men had been through together. But she corralled her wayward thoughts. She was on the brink of buying herself two days, which was much longer than she'd anticipated when she'd hightailed it to London City airport half a day ago with her passport and a leaky plan with more holes in it than Swiss cheese.

She refocused on Nelios, on the laser beam gaze fixed squarely on her.

For better or worse... 'Yes. Agreed.'

CHAPTER THREE

HE REMAINED STILL, watching her for another taut stretch before he turned and nodded briskly at Andreas. The other man left without another word. And mere minutes later the police were gone, the refuelling truck had pulled away and the pilot had reboarded.

From her very shaky position as a stowaway, Vayle was elevated one tiny rung to unwanted guest, Nelios barely glancing at her as he instructed the head attendant to show her around. After a five-minute tour around the jaw-dropping double-floored aircraft, she was ushered into a tiny cabin.

'Mr Petralis advises you to rest for a few hours. You'll be summoned when he needs you.' The same attendant who'd brought her dinner hesitated for a moment before he pointed to the button. 'If you need anything, you can call me on that.'

He started to turn away but, cringing, Vayle stepped forward. 'Is there a way to make a phone call?'

'There is a way but Mr Petralis wishes any calls to be made in his presence.' Vayle opened her mouth to enquire why but he beat her to it. 'He says it's "part of the deal".'

Her lips pursed but she nodded. She suspected Nelios would trot out many more conditions in a bid to get her to back down, withholding her ability to contact Agnes probably high on the list.

Alone, she dropped down onto the single, perfectly made bed and glanced around her. Like everything else, it was top notch with bespoke accents and Nelios monograms stamped on the sheets and furniture. Trailing her finger over the silver jacquard coverlet, she once again wondered who was telling the truth in this scenario. If Tolis and Agnes had indeed abandoned their own child, could she cope with that knowledge? One tormentor for a parent was bad enough, but another two who had pulled the wool over her eyes...

No. Knowing she couldn't rest without letting Agnes know she was all right, she searched for her bag—because Nelios and his rules could go hang—only to remember that she'd discarded her phone somewhere on his bedroom floor. And regaining entry would be impossible this time round.

With a huff of impatience, she tossed off her shoes and climbed into the bed. While she hated to admit he was right, exhaustion sucked at her limbs, the tumultuous few hours she'd had suddenly weighing down on her. Tugging the coverlet off the high-thread-count sheets, she crawled under the covers and within minutes she fell asleep, the sound of the engine lulling her.

The firm knock on the door dragged her out of sleep what felt like only minutes later. Jerking upright, she stumbled out of bed and went to the door. The same attendant waited on the other side, his impassive face not drawing attention to the fact that she must've looked a horror.

'I suppose Mr Petralis wants to see me?' she asked.

'No. I came to tell you we will be landing in ten minutes, so you should put your seat belt on.'

'What? But we've only been flying for a couple of hours.'

'We've been in the air for seven hours, Miss Lancaster, and you've been asleep for most of them.'

She frowned at the darkened windows, expecting to see sunlight if what he was saying was true. Then she paused when he reached for the little nub next to the light switch, pressed it and the window shades changed.

'The windows are regulated to maximise rest.'

She bit her lip, knowing it wasn't his fault she'd been so tired she'd slept like the dead in the best bedding she'd ever experienced in her life.

'Thank you, I'll be ready,' she said.

With a brisk nod, he left again.

Knowing her restful state was temporary and would most likely be reversed the moment she was in Nelios's presence—because the man only needed to breathe to remind everyone in his vicinity that he was an apex predator—she went into the adjoining bathroom. There, presented with an array of luxurious products that probably cost more than the entire stock of accessories at Vayle Hotel, she set about freshening up as best she could.

Done, she pulled open the door to find the attendant waiting in the hallway. She took a closer look at him and realised he looked large and intimidating enough to double up as a bodyguard. And, come to think of it, every member of the crew looked different from the run-of-the mill ones she encountered on a normal commercial flight.

She was wondering about that when she was led into the main cabin. Her belly did that crazy somersault when she zeroed in on Nelios. He too had freshened up. His slightly damp hair was styled off his forehead, his clean shave throwing his square jaw and dimpled chin into relief. The suit he wore to the meeting had been swapped for a navy version, the dark shirt underneath making his warm, olive skin glow in a way that made her fingers tingle with the urge to touch… Was she insane?

She realised the thought had frozen her whole body when his eyes slid from Andreas to rest on her, one eyebrow quirked. 'Do you plan to break a few more rules by remaining standing while we land, Miss Lancaster?'

Galvanised by his electric voice and her own impatience

with herself and her behaviour around this man, she hurried to the nearest available seat as she spotted the tops of buildings just outside the window. She'd barely clipped herself in when the wheels touched down.

Moments later, Nelios followed by Andreas and the crew disembarked like a well-oiled machine and headed for the fleet of cars awaiting them. Feeling like the ugly duckling in a veritable gaggle of swans, she hurried to keep up, darting towards the tinted-windowed SUV the attendant indicated. Hugely relieved not to see any sign of the police, she slid into the back of the vehicle...and lost the breath she'd just taken when she came face-to-face with Nelios.

Of course he wouldn't want her out of his sight. Her heartbeat further escalated when she realised they were alone, with the privacy partition fully in place.

'I'm guessing you want to start your interrogation right away?' she said into the tense silence.

'Considering you've had what accounts to a full night's sleep? Yes, I do believe I should make hay before you whittle away all my time.'

She licked her lower lip, then tensed when he followed the action with narrowed, heated eyes. 'All right, then, what do you want to know?'

Silence reigned. Her heart thumped loudly in her ears. When full minute had passed, and his nostrils had flared once, twice, as if he sought control, Vayle forced herself not to squirm.

'You claim they are your "surrogate parents".'

'I'm not hearing a question there.' She was hedging for time. She shouldn't have been surprised he'd plunged right into the deep end. Yet she'd been unprepared to have her anguish over her father's illness, known only to a handful of people, pried open so starkly.

'Did they *unofficially* adopt you?' he went on coldly, his

sneer over the word making her heart lurch. 'Was it part of the bank's terms when they took over?'

A wave of light-headedness washed over her. 'What do you know about the...about that?'

His speaking look questioned her reasoning, mocking why she would ask it in the first place. 'The bank's terms were private.'

'You truly believe there's such a thing as privacy when you're in the thick of a hostile takeover?'

'If you have any semblance of humanity, yes.'

He delivered a cold, hard smile that froze her middle. 'And, as we've established, I have none. So answer the question.'

'And if I refuse?'

'Then I would deem you extremely foolish for backing out on a deal you've made with me. You're not an ally by a long shot, but you definitely don't want to become my enemy. So for starters, and for wasting several hours of my time, I'll drive you to the police station myself.'

She swallowed, partly glad her frozen status had halted her squirming. It was also easier for her numbed senses when she answered. 'Yes and no. Yes, there was no official documentation, and no, it wasn't a specific requirement by the bank. But it was approved by the doctors who...' She paused, pressed her lips together and watched his face for signs that he knew more about her past. About the true reasons that had necessitated Tolis's and Agnes's stable presence in her life.

'The doctors who first diagnosed your father?' he finished, much to her horror.

He knew. Nelios knew at least something about her father's condition. The condition George Lancaster had point blank refused to have treated, subjecting her and anyone who encountered the Lancaster family to needless distress.

It was only after her father's diagnosis of depression and

acute mania had been discovered—an extreme version of his bipolar disorder—on the request of the bank who held the mortgage on his precious Vayle Hotel, and their subsequent insistence on his receiving treatment and donating power of attorney that he'd agreed to seek help. And, even then, he'd defied the recommended treatment at every turn.

She dragged her gaze away because she didn't want to know if Nelios knew more. Did he know the extent of her father's neglect of her—the distance between father and daughter that Vayle had never been able to close following her mother's death when she'd been ten? George Lancaster had fallen apart in the aftermath, his grief and depression driving him into bouts of careless cruelty and unreliability.

Gritting her teeth against the surge of rough emotions, Vayle exhaled. 'Yes.' It was a mere whisper, but she knew he heard it.

His piercing gaze didn't relent. 'What were the bank's conditions, precisely?'

'Don't you already know?'

'Not yet,' he replied. 'But I will once I own Vayle Hotel.'

She chanced a glance at him and saw the rigid control he'd fastened over his emotions. Whereas only a handful of hours ago she'd marvelled at it, Vayle now wondered how much effort it took for Nelios Petralis to keep all that willpower in place.

'So you're really going ahead with this takeover? Do you care who you hurt in the process?'

His jaw rippled and her thought deepened. *Why did he need to exert so much control? What was buried beneath his glacial surface?*

'Everyone involved besides you and Agnes will be offered compensation and a position elsewhere. And you, as owner, are being paid more than market value for a crumbling relic. I'd hardly call that hurting you. What you're really asking is if this is personal to Agnes Adamis. The answer is yes, it is. So, as agreed, you will tell me what I wish to know,' he tagged on silkily. *Like the cobra said to the mouse.*

Vayle considered refusing; considered using that information to strike a better deal. But if felt...sleazy to use her family trauma, *her very personal* trauma, as a bargaining tool. Besides, as he'd so arrogantly announced, if she failed in this task—and that hope dwindled by the second—he would have the sordid details presented to him on a silver platter anyway.

'My father had a condition that went undiagnosed for years.' She curled her fists in her lap, the admission tunnelling to the very heart of her painful memories. 'Severe mood swings that arose out of nowhere, lingered for hours, then disappeared. My mother, when she was alive, was the only one he'd listen to. She would cover for him—pacify the guests he offended.' A bitter smile twisted her lips until she forced it away. 'Unfortunately, after her death, he...fell apart. And with social media, and information now readily available, word started to spread about Dad's condition and the hotel started to suffer. As you probably know, we were mortgaged to the hilt.'

'Why didn't the bank foreclose straight away if it was a losing business?' he asked curiously.

She shook her head. 'The bank manager was Dad's friend. He kept giving him a chance to turn things round. And, at first, he would. When he wasn't feeling...himself he would let the junior staff take over, that sort of thing. But inevitably things would take a turn for the worse...until eventually the bank gave him an ultimatum. He could stay on as the owner and proprietor on the condition he hired a manager and assistant to run the day to day.' Her gaze darted to him to catch a wave of bleak bitterness.

'And did the bank insist that these people your father hired were to be childless or did he come up with that condition on his own?' His voice was tinder-dry and bitter.

Her heart lurched again and, although she suspected the awful answer, having lived with George Lancaster almost all her life, she answered with the truth. 'No bank has the right to order that. I think it was my father. I had no idea that stipulation even existed before you mentioned it today.'

Again those dark-brown eyes bore into her, digging out her hidden depths. Staring back, she caught a shadow of what he felt. It wasn't enough to trigger a sense of kinship but it... eased one tiny knot inside her.

'Continue,' he said, his tone back to that chilled edge with the many complex emotions weaved in.

'As I said, it wasn't official, but they were a great help—they taught me everything they knew about running a hotel.' She shrugged. 'I had a father who was indifferent to whether I was sick or healthy, fed or hungry. They...saved me from the worst parts of his neglect.'

A sound that was part-growl part-scoff rumbled from him, freezing her words. 'The documents show you're the rightful heir to Vayle Hotel. That your father dying without a will means you would've inherited it after the issues with the bank were resolved.'

She didn't hide her glare. 'Are you insinuating that the only reason your parents helped me was because they wanted the hotel I would eventually own?'

'They are *not* my parents,' he delivered acidly through his teeth. 'And no, it's not an insinuation, it's a fact.'

She opened her mouth to hotly refute that. Only to startle when her car door was pulled open and she turned to find a doorman standing attention with a welcoming smile on his face.

They'd arrived.

Amongst the stylish gems littered around the impressive Recoleta neighbourhood of Buenos Aires, including the Four

Seasons and other high-end hotels, the Rosa Corona was a cut above the rest.

But even it couldn't hold a candle to the nearly finished hotel right across the street from it. Nelios XV, the soon-to-be crown jewel in Nelios Petralis's collection, had been whispered about on the luxury hotel circuit for the better part of three years. It was rumoured that the elite suites didn't just come with butlers and top chefs, but that the experience would include a private jet, a yacht and chefs flown across the world at a word. Put simply, to live the Nelios XV experience would be to inhabit a world where every single whim was catered for without exception—at the kind of price tag double the GDP of most small countries.

Vayle stood at her hotel room window in the suite adjoining the one Nelios had disappeared into the second they'd stepped off the lift. Looking across at the breathtaking architecture of the nearly finished hotel, she found herself once again wondering if the kind of motivation it took to birth not just one but fifteen masterpieces so far—and counting—was part of Nelios's DNA or a characteristic formed out of the trauma he'd undergone.

If it was true.

But...why would he lie? He'd all but succeeded in his plans to destroy Vayle Hotel and force a buyout. They'd already been on the back foot for a few years, barely making the payments to the bank after the deaths of both her father and Tolis, before Nelios's new hotel had sprung up directly next to them—all glitz and elegance, sucking the life out of the woefully-in-need-of-refurbishment Vayle Hotel. Their bookings had taken a steep dive, requiring them to take out emergency funding from the bank just to keep their heads above water.

While Vayle's marketing ideas had seen a few surges in bookings, to her horror their rival had immediately countered their efforts, even going as far as to drastically slash their prices. She'd been puzzled as to why they would do that, until Agnes had tearfully confessed her relationship with Nelios. Things had gone steadily downhill from then on.

She shivered in recollection at his icy loathing when he'd seen Agnes at that meeting yesterday. No. That sort of reaction hadn't been manufactured. Which meant…something had gone drastically wrong somewhere.

Her chest tightening at the implications, she turned away from the view of the hotel even she couldn't deny was simply extraordinary. Like its namesake hotels across the world, the front edifice was sculpted in glass, grey stone and steel around the distinct Roman numerals, making it stand out, while also blending into the historical architecture. It was a soaring building that would repeatedly draw the eye with the promise of discovering a new feature with each glance. Vayle grimaced at the bite of envy of whomever would get the privilege of working within its walls when the ping from her phone refocused her attention.

She'd tried to call Agnes the second she was alone but she hadn't picked up. Snatching up her phone now, she read the text from Agnes.

Are you okay? I'm worried about you. Text an update when you can.

Her heart warming, and roiling emotions settling, she immediately dialled again. Then frowned when it rang and went to voicemail.

The time difference was only three hours ahead in England. Vayle wondered why she hadn't picked up. Clearing her throat, she left a message, attempting not to sound as perturbed as she felt. She decided that probing deeper about why Agnes had lost touch with her son, the man actively trying to destroy them, was a conversation she would prefer to have in person. She knew there was a measure of shying away from the possible truth but she grasped at the distraction when a knock sounded on her door.

Setting her phone on the coffee table, she went to open it, to see the head attendant from the plane, now dressed in a sharp suit with a visible bulge at his waist that confirmed his dual role as bodyguard.

'Hello,' she offered tentatively. 'I'm sorry, I don't know your name.'

'It's Capaldi,' he said. 'Mr Petralis would like you to join him for dinner in an hour.'

'Oh...um, sure.' She glanced past him then grimaced at the futility of it. 'Where?'

'In his suite. One floor up. I will come and fetch you.'

'Thanks.' She shut the door, then glanced down at herself. She looked and felt grimy. She'd intended to shower, but she couldn't stomach wearing the same clothes she'd been wearing for twenty-four hours straight. Recalling the shops she'd seen downstairs, she made a quick decision and grabbed her bag.

Funds were scarce, and she'd taken a drastic income cut from the hotel when their troubles had started, but she'd barely touched the rainy day savings from the small inheritance her mother had left her. And, while she was severely on the back foot when it came to her interactions with Nelios Petralis, she could at least continue from a place of better confidence.

Vayle blew out a relieved breath when she made it downstairs without encountering either Andreas or Capaldi. She'd been half-afraid they'd appear like a nightmare and inform her she was to stay in her room until Nelios gave her express permission to leave. Was he so confident she'd stay put—that he had her exactly where he wanted her?

Yes. Unfortunately.

Mildly grumpy at the thought, she entered the hotel boutique and just as quickly exited when the eye-watering prices and disdainful looks told her she was out of her league.

The warm sultry air, even at that time of the evening, was welcome as she hurried towards the brighter lights that, thankfully, produced shops in her price range.

Within fifteen minutes she'd secured dark indigo jeans, stylish enough to pass muster as smart-casual, and two tops: one a sleeveless black satin peplum and the other a flowery lilac billow-sleeved blouse she could wear during the day. Her kitten heels would work with both. Adding a couple of accessories and paying quickly, she hightailed it back to her suite and into the shower.

She tidied her hair into a loose bun with a compact hairbrush, and she was halfway through pulling on her clothes when the knock sounded. Buttoning her jeans, she caught up the hook earrings and managed to secure one, only to get flustered when the other one refused to situate in her lobe.

The knock came again, more insistently.

Stifling a curse, she rushed towards the door. 'I'm coming!'

Still attempting to do up the side-zip of her top *and* slide one hoop in her ear, she gave up with the earring, turned the handle and immediately turned away. 'I'll be another minute, Capaldi. Sorry, time got away from me.' She tried a second time, blew out a breath when she got the hoop into her ear, then tackled the zip once more.

At the taut silence, she frowned over her shoulder.

Nelios stood tall and imposing in the doorway, dark-brown eyes fixed squarely on her. A shudder slammed out of nowhere, rippling through her body.

Shock—it was shock—*not* sizzling awareness with a heavy dose of electricity that gripped her very core and rattled it mercilessly.

'Oh, I thought you were Capaldi.'

'That is apparent.' His searing scrutiny and biting tone froze her as he stepped into the room and shut the door, her hand still on the zip of the top that half-gaped, displaying the side edges of her bra. Face flaming when his gaze tracked her from top to bottom, she twisted away and tried to finish what should've been a simple task but had instead become an arduous challenge.

'Are you in the habit of letting men into your room while half-dressed?' he asked.

She snorted. 'Hardly. And you didn't have to come in, did you? Or be so impatient?'

Her answer clearly didn't please him. His eyes narrowed, the expression in them blazing to life at her continued wriggling. 'What are you doing?'

Was his voice raspier or was it just the buzzing in her ears? Another wave of heat washed over her as she was forced to admit, 'My zip is stuck. I think.' *Damn it.* If it didn't budge, there was no way she could get it off. And she could hardly go to dinner half-dressed, could she?

Cringing, she faced him. 'Could you...could you help me?'

One brow quirked, and he said nothing for uncomfortably long seconds. Then, prowling closer, he nudged his square chin at her. She released the pull tab and kept her arm aloft. Did she wish the ground would open and swallow her? Very much so.

Somehow she managed to keep her chin up and he studied her.

'I'll have to insert a finger to protect your skin.' His voice was lower, definitely with a deeper rasp, and she dragged her gaze up to find his rising from her side to rest on her face. This close, his brown eyes didn't look so dark and ominous. They looked...warm; heated, even, with dark-gold specks that made them glint as he waited for her response.

'O-okay.' *Dear heaven.* Could she sound more breathless?

The sight of his large hands and elegant fingers tackling her delicate zip shouldn't have been erotic. Shouldn't have made heat pool low in her belly or simmer between her legs. And yet there she was—dying and praying he would mistake the tiny shivers coursing through her for something else. Nelios's knuckles brushing the skin over her ribs shouldn't have been more than a ticklish sensation. Instead, Vayle became abruptly aware of an erogenous zone she'd had no inkling of before today.

She bit back a moan as her very skin jerked and shivered. Her peaking nipples were unmistakable through the shiny satin. The rise and fall of her chest blared her agitation.

'Easy. You need to remain still, Vayle,' he murmured.

Oh, God. It was impossible, she wanted to protest. Between the deeper gruffness of his voice, the faintly accented way his voice curled out her name and the new sensation of his masculine scent filtering through her senses, she had to shut her eyes to contain her wayward reactions.

'It is done,' he said curtly.

She took a giant sidestep as she opened her eyes, attempting to blink reason into her sluggish brain. 'T-thank you.' Another step. 'I'll be...' She looked around for her phone and, spotting it where she'd left it on the coffee table, rushed across to snatch it up. A quick glance showed Agnes hadn't returned her call. Stemming another tendril of worry, she sucked in a breath and faced him. 'I'm ready.'

Again he watched her for several more seconds than was strictly polite, his aura deceptively calm, a technique she was learning was very effective in disarming his opponents. Thank goodness she would not be in his orbit for very much longer.

Then, without a word, he turned and strode for the door. She followed him, watching him activate the lift with a special keycard and, when it arrived, he stood to one side to let her enter.

Still wordless, they rode up one floor.

Vayle was stunned all over again by the plush surroundings. But, before she could take in any specific details, Andreas walked towards them, a neutral expression that belied the mild censure in his gaze as he exchanged words in Greek with Nelios before he eyed her.

'Enjoy your evening,' he said with a distinct lack of sincerity that made her grimace.

'Is it even worth asking why he dislikes me so much or should I save my breath?' she asked Nelios once the doors had shut behind Andreas.

He paused in the wide, exquisitely decorated hallway. 'We share a dislike for wilful blindness,' he delivered, before striding deeper into the suite.

Ouch.

On slow feet, she followed him into the lavish suite past groupings of sofas and an extensive bar area, through an alcove to an elegant dining table set for two. It wasn't lost on her at all that through the floor-to-ceiling windows, displayed in perfect lighting, was the Nelios XV.

At every turn he meant to remind her who he was, what their association meant. As if she could forget, when her every breath, her every erratic heartbeat, shrieked how far out of her comfort zone she was.

He pulled out her chair and she sat down. She startled a little and earned herself a narrow-eyed look when his hand brushed her bare skin.

'Why so jumpy?'

She shrugged. 'Guess I'm waiting for the hammer to fall. Or for the interrogation to resume.'

He took his own seat, his mouth turning down with mild

derision. 'Hardly a hammer when I let you roam freely in the streets earlier on, shopping without a care in the world.'

'Let me...?' she echoed, then frowned. 'How do you know where I went? Are you having me followed?'

'You're here in my care. Besides the fact that I and anyone in my group are required to use a security team, and you traipsed out without so much as a whisper to anyone, you have already proven not to have the best judgement with your stowaway antics. Do you truly believe I'm not within my rights to keep tabs on you? Let's not forget that you're also in this country illegally and I will be culpable should you be discovered.'

'Does it make you feel powerful to list everyone's weaknesses or it a safeguarding crutch?' she enquired softly, ignoring her sprinting pulse, which she was one hundred per cent confident was fully derived from anger, not hopelessness.

He stiffened so hard, he resembled marble. 'Excuse me?'

She sighed. 'My use of the word "hammer" before wasn't an exaggeration, it seems. You Hulk-smash when a scalpel is needed.'

One dark brow arched, drawing her attention to the sinfully silky length of his sooty lashes. 'Are you accusing me of lacking finesse, Vayle?'

'Maybe I am... Nelios.'

His nostrils flared—because he was irritated, right? Not because he was reacting to the cursed breathlessness that had made her sound like a cheesy movie siren when she'd said his name. The live wire that seemed to need no encouragement at all to zing to life writhed through her. Fiercely combating it, she picked up her napkin and took her time spreading it over thighs that had grown far too hot, scaldingly aware he was staring at her. About to snap at his rudeness, her breath stalled as a door opened to the side and a man dressed in chef's whites accompanied by a butler bearing wine pushed in a sterling-silver trolley.

'Good evening, Mr Petralis, Miss Lancaster,' they both greeted.

She blinked. Had Nelios bothered to tell the chef her name? She murmured a response then listened as the chef rattled off the mouthwatering menu he'd prepared. Spoilt for choice, she picked the first thing she remembered and was presented with a sumptuous Greek salad drizzled with olive oil. Then she proceeded to stifle moan after moan while she ate the most glorious melt-in-the-mouth empanadas she'd ever tasted, accompanied by sublime red wine.

Surprisingly, Nelios didn't grill her over dinner. But she saw his gaze repeatedly linger on the phone she'd placed on the dining table. Etiquette-wise, it wasn't strictly polite, but Vayle hadn't wanted to miss a call.

He waited until she was done with her decadent dessert before he struck. 'Have you been in touch with Agnes to report your progress?'

'What progress? All you've done is threaten to have me thrown in jail.' She bit the inside of her cheek, because that wasn't strictly true. Yes he'd threatened her, but he'd also given her a choice. And she'd accepted. 'What I mean is—'

'I'm well aware of what you mean. You're much more comfortable listing all the bad things perpetrated on you and blithely ignoring the good.'

She flushed, then was inexorably drawn to study him when she heard the underlying bleakness in his voice. But his face was shut tighter than Fort Knox. And, since she was swimming in a shallow pond of her own disingenuousness, she remained silent.

Until, 'Answer the question, Vayle,' he insisted firmly.

And, yes, this time she couldn't deny that she shivered solely because of the way he said her name with a gravelly bite that seemed to rake over her jittery senses, sending waves of heat and awareness through her body.

'No, I haven't spoken to your…to Agnes. She texted. I tried calling back but there was no answer.'

His gaze bore into her. 'What exactly did the text say?'

'To find out how I am because she hadn't heard from me and is worried,' she answered unequivocally.

Something darted across his face, hot and fast as quicksilver. It was indecipherable then gone…but not forgotten. It was visceral enough to strike her hard in the middle.

'That wasn't all, though, was it?' came the hard, sardonic rejoinder. As if he needed there to be more.

She lifted her eyebrows. 'Because you want there to be? Something that justifies your beliefs?'

He didn't rise to her bait, merely levelled his incisive gaze on her and waited until it wore her down, leaving her no choice but to respond.

'Yes; she also asked if I had any updates.'

And then that mocking smile appeared. It was full-bodied, labelling her ten kinds of a fool for believing that the warmth and affection she'd treasured for years had been genuine. That the surrogate mother—who'd kept her aloft when she'd thought she would drown in her father's cruelty and disregard, both before and after his diagnosis—was not who Vayle believed her to be.

That his smile was devastatingly gorgeous shouldn't have factored in at all. And yet her runaway heartbeat howled and said otherwise—that her inability to look away from his magnificent face or to control the sizzling heat rising within her was a big problem. Huge. Because she intensely disliked the narrative Nelios was attempting to force her to face. *And* he warped her brain with this chemistry between them that she couldn't deny.

Tossing her napkin on the table, she snatched up her phone

and marched into the living room. There she stopped and spun round...to catch his fiery gaze on her backside.

Her heated demand dried up. *What the hell had she been about to say?* So she stood there, caught in that insane vortex of awareness as he slowly rose and sauntered towards her. A clutch of words peppered her sluggish brain as she tried to stop staring at his raw, masculine body. 'Where do you want me?' she blurted.

His stride hitched a tiny fraction, and he inhaled sharply. 'What?'

Oh, yes. She truly wished for a lethal lightning bolt instantly to destroy her.

'For your interrogation. Where should I...can I...sit?' she amended.

'Dangling you from the ceiling by your fingernails so soon after dinner is too tedious, so by all means, yes, sit down, Vayle.' He gestured at the nearest group of sofas.

She chose the furthest sofa, ignoring the twitch of mockery on his face as he sat at the other end, suavely crossing one leg over the other.

The butler approached and Nelios turned to her. 'Night cap?'

She started to shake her head, then at the last moment she nodded. 'Please.' Glancing at the butler, she smiled. 'Surprise me.' She'd learned very early that hospitality staff loved demonstrating their skills and, from the butler's pleased nod, she'd guessed right.

He returned minutes later with an amber-coloured drink for Nelios and a bright-yellow drink for her. He hovered as she took a sip, blinked and took a larger sip.

'This is lovely; thank you so much.'

His broader smile warmed her like the clementine-based alcoholic drink in her hand.

'If you're quite done?' Nelios drawled.

She eyed him as the butler left. 'Clearly you don't believe that when you make people feel valued they repay you in ways you might not expect.'

He set his glass on his raised knee. 'Another lesson from… those people?'

'Yes, as a matter of fact.'

He looked poleaxed for a flash, then openly sceptical. 'Next you're going to tell me they hung the moon,' he drawled in a voice coated with acid.

'I'm not going to volunteer anything you don't emphatically ask for, because I'll be wasting my breath. So…' she took another sip of her drink then cradled her glass in her palm '…fire away.'

CHAPTER FOUR

IT WAS ALMOST laughable how unequivocal she was in her beliefs. How intransigently she clung to her well-disguised monsters.

Almost.

As Nelios examined this strange woman—who should've been easy enough to dismiss but somehow clung burr-like in his head—he wondered why he was even bothering. Clearly, she'd been brainwashed to slavishly fall for the lines she'd been fed. A coating of sugar disguised the poison pill.

He'd read the thorough report his well-paid sources had provided on the history of Vayle Hotel and its owner. He knew George Lancaster had been a living nightmare: a minor aristocrat clinging doggedly to what remained of a family estate he'd whittled away through careless dealings, and an arrogant refusal to seek help with a condition that could've been managed with a little care and attention.

Equally careless was the child he'd dragged into the middle of his tumultuous, woefully mismanaged life. For a while, Vayle's mother had helped, but she'd died too soon, leaving her child in the clutches of yet another monster.

His mouth twisted. This was one of the many reasons he wanted neither a wife nor children. Hell, it was why his rigorously controlled policy of seven days of dinner, sex—if both parties were willing—and a fond, tasteful, gift-strewn farewell was so successful. A policy he'd *never* once strayed from, long before he'd made his first million. It was why he'd even contemplated having a vasectomy, to remove the last risk of ever parenting a child and passing on the monstrous strain of cruelty Apostolis and Agnes might have bequeathed to him. Nelios wasn't entirely sure why he'd allowed Andreas to talk him out of that decision. But, no matter, with his system firmly in place, there would be no risk anyway.

Apparently, though, Vayle's treatment from her father had driven her into his parents' arms, them readily providing the saviour status they'd needed to trap her into a long, lucrative arrangement. No other explanation made sense.

So why are you digging any further?

He ignored the voice and watched her sip the drink his pleased butler had made her. Shifting in his seat when another wave of disgruntlement attacked his spine, he prodded the scab he was sure hid no festering wound. It couldn't. It'd calcified a long time ago. As he'd told himself before, this was merely a matter of him learning his enemies' ways.

'How old are you, Vayle?'

Luminous blue eyes landed on his and blinked, searched. 'Why?'

'You earned a scholarship and have a degree in hospitality and marketing from a respectable university.' His gaze moved over her, attempting not to recall how smooth her warm skin had felt beneath his fingers when he'd helped her with her zip. How her repeated breath-catching had threatened the edges of his control. *How much he wanted to touch her again.* 'You seem old enough to have taken over the helm of the hotel which bears your name. Why haven't you?'

'First of all, I'm twenty-six. And why don't you ask me what you really mean—why haven't I tossed Agnes out onto the streets like you claim they did to you?' She shook her head and, while his gut clenched hard with each utterance of his mother's name, heat pooled lower when his attention was drawn to the mouth pursing then twisting with displeasure at his questions.

Maybe this was truly a fool's errand. Maybe he should just leave her blind and naively trusting, waiting for the buy-out to reach its final and acceptable outcome. Let her see how quickly she would be dropped by the woman she believed had her back. How devastatingly alone and cold the world would turn when Agnes walked away as callously from her as she'd walked away from him.

Feeling the bitter and cold fingers of desolation reach for him, he slammed those emotions back where they belonged—in the vault clearly marked *never, ever again*. He'd risen above those first shocking days and weeks of realising he was nothing but a pay cheque to those who should've cared that a twelve-year-old boy had two perfectly healthy parents who still walked the earth but had actively chosen to offload him like a piece of lost luggage just so they could pursue a greater ambition in life.

Hell, he'd even dug deep enough to kill the tears that had threatened after his third or fourth slap across the face when he'd spoken out for himself and other mistreated children under his foster parents' roof. And the scales had long fallen off his eyes when he'd decided he'd be better off alone on the streets than remain in foster care any longer.

Nelios reminded himself how far he'd come. How those tricky few weeks had been the test he'd needed to reforge himself into something unbreakable, untouchable.

These days he surrounded himself with men and women who'd been through similar challenges. Such as Andreas; such as Capaldi. Every single person who held a position of note in his empire knew what it was like to suffer hardship. To go hungry for days. To fight in the darkest pits of hell. To know how to suffer bruise on top of bruise on top of inhumane humiliation and still keep going. They valued life, embraced the comforts of wealth and luxury but never forgot how easily it could all be stripped away, and they worked hard to ensure it never could be.

An apt tenet to live by if there was one.

So why are you revisiting the past?

'Indeed.' He realised he'd said it as much to himself as in response to her. 'You're right. That was what I was thinking. But I'm realising there's no point. You won't be convinced. And this subject has grown boring. You will be put on an aeroplane as soon as a flight is confirmed. I hope, for your sake, we never meet again.'

He knocked back the rest of his drink. This futile endeavour should've ended in Ascension when they'd stopped to refuel. Hell, it should never have started in London in the first place. He'd lowered his guard and allowed intrigue and, yes, his rare fascination with her, overrule his common sense. No more.

He uncrossed his leg and started to rise.

'Wait.'

Nelios wasn't sure why his gut tightened on hearing that husky imploration. Then he remembered when he'd heard it from her last; what she'd said immediately after that: *I'll do anything.* He hadn't yet tested that offer. He had dismissed it out of his mind because, as Andreas had scoffed, it was indeed a rookie mistake to offer such a thing to street-hardened predators such as them.

And yet... Nelios found himself doing as she'd asked: waiting; his senses on full alert and that pool of heat in his groin building, simmering.

She set down her glass and licked a drop of liquid from her bottom lip. 'How do I get you to reconsider what...what you plan to do?'

'It's very simple. You can't. Our association, such as it was, is over. Your hotel will be assessed for its viability and either subsumed as an annex to mine or disposed of.'

She shook her head so emphatically, silk strands slid against her nape. He wanted to touch that too. *Theos*. Was he so hard up? Frowning inwardly, he tried to remember the last time he'd had sex and was taken aback when he couldn't remember. Seriously, had it been that long?

'I refuse to accept that,' she said firmly.

Against his will, amusement trickled through him. Nelios abstractedly noted that she seemed to command varying sensations within him. He wanted to throw her into prison one moment, then wanted to crack a smile in the next. A ping from the phone in his pocket drew yet another emotion: irritation. Three feelings within three minutes. Most likely a record.

Drawing out his phone, he read the message:

Guests list confirmed and attached for the pre-launch party.

Even before he'd returned the phone to his pocket he'd made up his mind. 'You wish to attempt the futile?' he taunted.

Her plump lips pursed. 'I wish to keep talking. You said I had forty-eight hours. You not wanting to hear what I have to say shouldn't change that. I have things to say to you, regardless.'

Again, he felt his mouth curve upward. He killed the motion. 'Your resilience, if nothing else, should prove interesting. The butler will see you out. Be ready to leave first thing in the morning.' He started to walk away, then paused. 'And Vayle?'

Her eyes widened a fraction. 'Hmm...yes?'

'I haven't forgotten that you said, "I'll do anything". And, believe me, I mean to test it.'

'Where are we?' Vayle asked as she wandered onto the widest enclosed terrace she'd ever seen in real life. She was learning 'real life' in Nelios Petralis's world was on a wildly different scale to hers.

She was a little shell-shocked by the dizzying speed of everything that had happened this morning. After a protracted tour of Nelios XV—which had far surpassed everything her imagination had conjured up where tasteful and even obscene luxury were concerned—they'd taken the super-speedy lift to the top of their hotel. There they'd boarded a sleek helicopter with Andreas, Capaldi and a handful of sharp-suited, sharp-eyed, tablet-wielding staff wearing menacing-looking earpieces.

They'd flown north, and upon landing the others had all immediately dispersed with almost robot-like efficiency, leaving her alone with Nelios. Vayle wasn't afraid to admit, she'd been a teensy bit intimidated by it all. But it dimmed beneath the sheer magnificence of their current location.

'A private estate that's been in the owner's family for generations,' Nelios answered. 'They're in dire straits and are thinking of selling. I'm considering adding it to the Nelios Group's portfolio but I haven't decided yet. My short stay here is a test run, of sorts.'

'Well, you should seriously consider it. It's stunning,' she breathed. And, when his gaze pivoted to her, Vayle wasn't even self-conscious about her blatant appreciation of the property. She shrugged and carried on. 'But I don't need to tell you that.'

'No, you don't. But I'm still interested in hearing your theories on how to best position this in a hospitality market,' he said.

'There's no such thing as free advice, Mr Petralis,' she half-joked.

She'd spent the night tossing and turning, swinging between guilt about wondering if Agnes was avoiding her because she bore some culpability, the way her son had accused, and reminding herself of the older woman's unfailing kindness to her over the years. Then, pushing away the unsettling sensation that thought brought, she'd attempted to plot how best to utilise the time she'd bought for herself. Why, given a second opportunity, she hadn't addressed that thinly veiled warning from Nelios about using her words against her. Hell, it was almost as if she wanted him to push her, just to see how far she would let him go...

Which was absurd. *Right?*

His face remained stoical. 'You're still convinced you can change my mind about your hotel's fate?' His voice held a little more bite, altering the atmosphere from taut to downright edgy.

Vayle's belly clenched but she fought to hang onto her composure. 'Maybe this should be less of a professional discourse and more of a personal, human one?'

He approached her slowly. Vayle told herself she remained where she was, and didn't obey her instinct to step back, because firstly it would show weakness—and she *wasn't* afraid of him, despite the wild fluttering in her belly and at her throat—and secondly because Nelios would respect her more if she met him on equal footing.

And, yes, she needed him to respect her. She'd withstood too much from her father and come out on the other side to allow her opinions and needs to be cast aside.

'Personal?' he echoed, his eyes now set to narrow-eyed sizzling as they trailed her from head to toe and back again. 'Is this where the "I'll do anything" is finally unleashed?' he enquired softly. *Lethally.*

'What...unleashed...? What are you talking about?'

Head tilted, his focus never once waned or altered. After another tense moment his mouth twisted and he stepped back. Did she think he intended to ease up on his imposing demands? Not by a long shot. 'You were saying about this place?'

She stared at him for a moment longer before forcing her brain to track with the abrupt change of subject and the peculiar, hollow sensation it'd left behind, almost as if a building anticipation had been dashed. Because it occurred to her now that she'd never quite taken back that ill-advised statement. Never stated categorically that she'd changed her mind and that, no, she wouldn't actually offer to 'do anything'.

So do it now. She inwardly shook her head. Doing it now would be ineffectual—bolting the door after the horse had fled. But when...*if*...it came back up, then she would make her feelings clear on the subject.

Realising he was still waiting for her response, she cleared her throat. 'There's a darling little village in France, barely two thousand acres, that people rent whole for various gatherings. This could be an uber-exclusive version of that. Throw in an excellent ground team, with prime activities and marketing to the super-elite where they're guaranteed they'll have the whole place to themselves, and not have to encounter another snooty billionaire, and you'll have them falling over themselves to jump onto your waiting list. You could be booked out for years.'

The edge had receded from his eyes by the time Vayle was finished, and he almost looked...impressed. Contemplative.

She couldn't stop the little fizz of pride that welled up inside her. At the very least, she could take heart in having distracted him from 'I'll do anything' that still dredged unfathomable feelings inside her.

'Interesting,' he muttered after a minute.

She raised her brows. 'Just...interesting? I challenge you to top that.'

One corner of his sensual lips quirked. 'I will not rise to

the bait, alas. I pay eye-watering sums to far better marketing experts to provide me with innovative ideas.'

The fizz threatened to sputter out but she lifted her chin. 'Go ahead, then. I'll wait with bated breath to see what they come up with.'

For some reason that made his gaze drop to her mouth and made that same mouth tingle so wildly, her breath caught. And, between those two crazy reactions, they were frozen in a charged bubble of intense awareness when Andreas entered. They were still caught in it when he started to speak.

While her head buzzed with whatever the hell was happening to her, Nelios responded to his right-hand man without taking his eyes off her. It took a minute to realise that Andreas had left, and that Nelios was addressing her once again. 'Sorry, what?'

'I said this is also the venue for the pre-launch party for Nelios XV this evening. I'm hosting various ministers and industry people before the hotel officially opens next month. You will be added to the guest list.'

Surprise rifled through her. 'You want me to attend your party?'

He shrugged. 'Or you can stay in your bedroom and let the hours whittle away. Your choice.'

She shrugged. 'But... I don't have anything to wear.' She cringed at the feeble response. 'And I won't know anyone there.'

His gaze trailed over her once more, this time leaving incendiary fireworks where it touched her skin. 'That problem will be taken care of. And you'll be there as my guest. That's all that should matter.'

'I...okay.'

Something glinted in his eyes before they were veiled and he turned away. 'Find Andreas or Capaldi. They'll let you know if you can make yourself useful or where you can remain out of the way if not.'

She went looking for Capaldi because he was the less threatening of the two. So, of course, she immediately found Andreas surrounded by his staff as he fired off instructions. He stopped speaking and fixed her with a censorious stare when she approached. Firming her spine, she relayed Nelios's message.

Flint-grey eyes stared her down for a full minute before he called over a minion and conducted a low conversation. Then, relieving the woman of her tablet, he jerked his head for Vayle to follow to a dank office in the basement that looked like something out of the 1950s and held a desk, phone, a pad and pen.

He slapped down the tablet. 'These are the list of vendors we need to triple-check the supply status for the party. Call, confirm and bring me a list when you're done. And I wouldn't think of sabotaging it, if I were you.' With that statement coldly delivered, he started to walk away.

'I have a fair idea why you think you hate me. But can I ask that you at least give me the benefit of the doubt? I'll be out of your hair soon enough, but do you truly begrudge me fighting for my heritage and my family?'

He reversed direction and stopped six feet away. His whole body vibrated with the strength of his feeling. 'No child should be blamed for the circumstances of their birth. But the adults they grow up to be? Hell, yes, I'll hold them to the highest moral standard. You associating with Agnes Adamis even after learning what she and Apostolis did to Nelios is not painting yourself in glory. Especially since you're requesting the benefit of the doubt but are refusing to accommodate the possibility that the person with first-hand knowledge of what happened is giving you their first-hand experience.'

We share a dislike for wilful blindness. Nelios's words from last night made sense now.

'Do your work, Miss Lancaster,' he stated coldly, then left.

A little shakier than she wanted to admit, it took several minutes of wondering what the history between the two men was, and getting herself under control, before she was composed enough to pick up the phone.

And it took a further ten minutes to discover Andreas had given her 'busy' work, after several vendors expressed mild exasperation that they were being contacted for the umpteenth time. She ploughed through the list regardless, sometimes relying on sketchy Spanish to get her through a conversation. Three long hours later, she left the basement to deliver a list that Andreas promptly passed off to another minion before telling Vayle she was free to go.

Then she was shown into another overwhelmingly beautiful room overlooking acres of manicured garden. She stood at the window for a long minute before a ping from her phone had her dashing across the room.

It was another text from Agnes.

Happy to hear you're safe. But I still worry. Do what you need to do, then come home, agapite. Whatever happens, we'll survive. And while I know my Nelios will have his version of things, please, don't judge me too harshly. For good or ill, I had my reasons.

Just as before, the message triggered mixed emotions. And, just as before, when Vayle called back it went straight to voicemail. She wanted to respect that some issues were too important to discuss over the phone, but she couldn't shake the feeling that Nelios's bitterness might have fertile roots.

But until she knew the full truth...

She walked into the dressing room that dissected the bedroom from the bathroom, then stopped, her eyes widening at the clothes rail sitting next to the shopping bag containing her meagre clothes. Reminded that Nelios had said her party attire would be taken care of, she tentatively approached. The garment bags revealed three stunning party dresses complete with multiple accessories in jade-green, classic black and a blush-pink bohemian dress she never would've imagined choosing for herself. Yet her eye kept returning to the off-shoulder design, the bold cut-out pattern above the hip on the left side reminding her of the charged moment last night when Nelios had helped her with her zip.

Was that why she chose the dress? No. *Absolutely not.* Yet she couldn't suppress the low blanket of heat that suffused her all through the lunch that was delivered and eaten on her terrace as she watched final, feverish preparations for the party. And when she showered, blow-dried and styled her hair, then donned the pink gown, studded Valentino heels and delicate jewellery, before heading downstairs.

Nelios stood with Andreas and Capaldi in the large marble foyer decked out in red carpeting that unfurled outside to the pillared portico to welcome guests.

Fluttering butterflies in her belly turned to ravenous eagles when three sets of eyes turned her way, conversation freezing as she paused three steps from the bottom, her fingers clinging to the banister for dear life. They stared, then Andreas muttered something under his breath that had Nelios spearing him with a narrow-eyed look before, after responding sharply, he strode towards her. Andreas stormed off while Capaldi looked faintly bemused. A second later, he too walked away.

Which left her with Nelios, clean-shaven and impossibly handsome, unyieldingly imposing and mesmerising in a black dinner-jacket and snow-white studded shirt. He stopped before her and, despite her slight height advantage, Vayle didn't even fool herself into thinking she held an advantage.

Because it turned out having Nelios looking up at her held its own alarming thrill. Made her want to do foolish things, such as slide her arms over those muscle-packed shoulders, brush her fingers against the thick hair curling around his nape and press her lips to...

No.

Thorough and ferocious, his gaze trailed over, heightening that simmer in her belly. 'Your choice of wardrobe was adequate?' he enquired, but somehow Vayle believed he was simply making conversation; that his mind, like hers, was wholly preoccupied with the electric insanity seething beneath the surface.

'It was more than adequate. Thank you.'

'It's nothing,' he muttered roughly, eyes the colour of rich coffee lingering at that cut-out at her waist, on her hips.

'It's not nothing,' she parried softly. 'And I really appreciate it.'

That drew his attention to her face. To the pulse leaping at her throat. His nostrils flared for the briefest moment, then he stepped back. 'Then show that appreciation. Come.'

On shaky legs that had nothing to do with the four-inch heels she wore, she stepped down, then walked by his side to the front door...where photographers and reporters waited.

She blinked in surprise at the first flash, then the flurry that followed. It wasn't until Nelios was a few minutes into the interview, while she lingered one step behind him, that it occurred to her she was being used. That, while she'd seemingly blagged her way into having more time to state her case, he intended to take advantage of that time, as he'd openly warned her. Or it was something as simple and retributive as payback for the inconvenience she'd caused him?

Smarting a little at the idea, she started to step away, only to feel his strong arm slide around her waist.

'The most important guest is here. Be so kind as to not cause any disruption now, Vayle,' he rasped silkily without looking her way.

She stilled, her senses leaping with heady abandon when his hand brushed her bare skin.

'Petralis. A pleasure as always.'

Vayle forced herself to focus and gulped. She was face-to-face with Cabral Soares, one of the wealthiest men in the world. As if one billionaire tycoon wasn't overwhelming enough.

'Just between us, I'd been hoping you would build one of your famous hotels in my beloved city. I'm glad you weathered the red-tape storm to bring it to fruition.'

'So am I,' Nelios replied.

Cabral smiled at the stunningly dressed woman on his arm who dripped in diamonds. 'Marika and I are on the maiden Nelios Club Experience. We look forward to being surprised.'

Nelios's smile brimmed with self-assuredness. 'If it falls short in any way, let me know, but I don't think it will.'

'Confident as always.' Cabral turned to Vayle. 'And who is this delightful creature?' He shook her hand, a charming smile curving his lips.

Nelios looked down at her, eyes still charged with wild electricity making the storm brewing inside her rage that little bit wilder. 'This is Vayle Lancaster,' he said simply, with no extras.

And that was how he introduced her to many outrageously influential guests, all eager to pay homage to the powerful Nelios Petralis and the wonder and prestige he'd brought to their city: *Vayle Lancaster*. Letting them draw their own conclusions as to who she truly was or what her presence in his life meant.

And slowly a different kind of storm eddied to life in her chest. A storm fuelled by quiet outrage, three glasses of vintage champagne and, astonishingly, *hurt*. Because she was left in no doubt at all that Nelios had played her like a Stradivarius.

'This wasn't simply a benign invitation, was it?' she asked when, hours later, the last straggling guests had been firmly guided out by Capaldi and his retinue, and she found herself alone with Nelios.

The sight of him loosening his bow-tie to dangle down his chest, and tugging the studs of his shirt apart, threatened to derail her senses, but she rallied like never before.

'Benign?' he echoed without inflexion but his eyes remained watchful, complex with seething emotions held tightly under wraps. 'I can't say I've ever had that label bestowed on me, *glikia mou*.'

He drew to a stop before her and she came face-to-face with the strong column of his throat and his tanned, lightly hair-dusted chest. Her mouth dried. Her body positively vibrated with a need she could scarcely fathom, threatening once again to derail her outrage. She clawed it back with vicious purpose, using the fuel of it to suppress the uninhibited hunger he engendered in her with seemingly very little effort. 'You really don't care who you hurt, do you?'

'Tell me how you believe you've been hurt,' he invited, all loose-limbed sardonicism, a mogul replete after a successful evening of having people hang onto his every word.

'Stop it! You know exactly what you're doing. Those pictures outside, introducing me to the great and powerful without telling them my reason for being here.... Of course, it won't do to publicise the fact that you're in the middle of destroying my family name and the people I hold dear, will it?' She emphasised that last bit to draw a reaction, and predictably his jaw rippled with displeasure, his sensual lips thinning. 'You want Agnes to see, don't you? To open the newspapers in a few hours and see me standing next to you, looking like your...'

'Like my what, Vayle?' he encouraged with a dark rumble.

'Like your conquest!'

'Yes,' he bit out coldly. 'She doesn't deserve to have what she wants—to live happily into her dotage, having achieved her life's work. Not after what she and her husband did to me. You want to save her? I'll double what I'm offering for your hotel. But you will fire her, effective immediately. That's my condition. What you choose to do with your money is up to you. Save her with the proceeds of your hotel, if you wish; that's your prerogative. And, to sweeten the deal, I'll give you the pick of a marketing job in the Nelios hotel of your choosing, anywhere in the world. But you and you alone will work for me. Not her.'

Her eyes widened. As a sweetener, it was right up there in dream-come-true-land. Except she would betray Tolis's memory and hurt Agnes, while losing her inheritance to boot: the very definition of being caught between heaven and hell. 'That's...'

'Cruel?' A macabre twist of emotion turned his face into an abstract painting. 'It's far, far less than she deserves.'

'No, Nelios. My answer is no. I won't throw someone I love under the bus. Not for all the money in the world.'

His face shuttered, his eyes turning obsidian with cold fury and seething recrimination. 'Then there's nothing more to say. Your hotel will be mine, and I'll do with it what I please.' He turned and walked away.

And she stood there, locked in indignation and disbelief. Far too many minutes later, realising she couldn't let him get away with it, she chased after him, past waiting staff who watched her with varying expressions of interest which she blatantly ignored.

He was clearing the first-floor staircase and turning right, presumably towards his suite, when she scrambled up after him. And he was almost at a set of double doors when she shot past him and faced him, perhaps with more bravado than sense, stopping him in his tracks. Every inch of his grim expression warned her not to engage further. Not to attempt to traverse the impassable landscape of his glorious discontent. But chances had come and gone, and been under-utilised. It was finally now or never.

'You do realise this paints you with the same label, don't you? Because what you're suggesting is monstrous.'

A veritable cocktail of emotions swirled across his face before it settled into a rigid, savage mask. 'No, *glykia mou*. This makes me shockingly human, seeking to right a heinous wrong.' A spasm of anger ripped through the mask before he stifled it. 'I might be too late for one, but I will seek accountability for the other who's gone far too long without it.'

'God, you can barely even bring yourself to say her name, can you?'

'Why should I?' he said with a perfectly arctic tone. 'In a right and just world she would be *mama*,' he ground out, his chest rising and falling once, as if that was the only vulnerability he intended to allow himself, when an ocean of emotion seethed just beneath his surface. 'Now? Now she deserves nothing.'

He went to move past her. Where Vayle found the strength to step squarely into his path, she would never know.

'Take heed and stop,' he advised. His voice was even and yet it sounded like a charged echo left behind after a vicious eruption.

'Stop trying to make you feel? To make you see you're only hurting yourself in the long run by doing this? I won't. I can't.'

He tried to step back. She bunched her hand in his shirt,

gripping a handful of expensive cotton-silk blend. His breath hissed out.

'Vayle.'

'Nelios.'

They were captured, lashed together by emotions neither wanted to feel or define. A sound rumbled from him. Vayle heard a softer version slip from between her lips. His gaze dropped to her mouth. They parted as if commanded, her breathing turning sharper, shallower.

He changed direction, pressing into her hold. Her fist unclenched and splayed right over his heart, feeling the heavy *thud, thud, thud*, then feeling the beats gallop faster.

He pressed another inch closer and her fingers danced up past his breastbone, over his collar, sinking into the hair at his nape. They pulled him close, *closer*, held him captive again. Then she surged up on her tiptoes, her silent demand clear.

His mouth swooped onto hers. And what felt like a lifetime in the making was born of fire, of need, of desperate desire. His hands seized her waist and Vayle was only too glad to leap into his arms, wrapping her legs around his hips, delighting in his immediate lunge forward to throw open his suite door, stride inside and kick it shut.

She revelled in his large hands clasping her bottom, dragging her closer still until the imprint of his shaft was unmistakable. The hot groan that rumbled from his chest was smashed between their lips, right before his tongue breached her mouth, seeking entry she was only too giddy to provide.

And then he introduced her to a sensual plane so erotically sublime, she moaned helplessly. Then carried on moaning as he dropped her in the middle of his bed and shrugged off his jacket with jerky, near-desperate movements. 'Is this what you want?'

'Yes,' she breathed, because perhaps on some level she truly believed that it might be a way to reach him. Or, on a purely selfish, needy level, this feeling of having had her world torn from under her would always lead to this: to taking a small triumph from the raging need in his eyes, the escalation of his breathing and, yes, the bold imprint of his cock against his trousers, the culmination of his need for her.

'Yes,' she echoed, stronger, rising to her elbows so as not to miss a second of watching him bare his beautiful body to her.

And then Nelios Petralis was naked, a bronze god who she knew would ignite her every fantasy from now until eternity. But even the thought of him having that supreme power over her didn't matter in this moment. Not when her nipples screamed for attention and her core ached with the need for his possession.

Their eyes connecting, he reached for the side of her dress and, this time, Vayle did not stop her gasp when his fingers deliberately traced the outline of her exposed skin through the cut-out.

'This has been driving me insane all evening,' he said with that dark rumble that stated they might be engaging in a mutually desired connection, but the undercurrents still remained.

'Then do something about it,' she whispered huskily.

Eyes glinting with a feral light that set another raft of shivers dancing over her, Nelios gripped the delicate garment and tore it off her body.

Vayle didn't care. She'd planned to leave these possessions behind when she left tomorrow. When he treated her undergarments to the same vicious, sexy treatment, she gloried in it. And, when he proceeded to explore her with hands, teeth and mouth, drawing not one but two orgasms from her needy body before thrusting hard inside her with a muted shout, she threw herself into the act with an enthusiasm bordering on zealous abandon.

He didn't need to know that this was only her second time having sex; that the reactions he drew from her would be forever sealed in her memory as the transcendent experience it was. Nelios Petralis already had far too much power over her and those she cared about. But she was well aware that she drew equal zeal from him, if not feral desire, in those stolen hours of the night.

And, yes, she intended to hold that tiny win close to her chest, a bolster she suspected she would need in the coming weeks and months. Because, as much as it hurt her to admit it, when it came to salvaging her inheritance from the clutches of the ruthless billionaire, she'd failed.

CHAPTER FIVE

One year later

VAYLE DIDN'T WANT to be reminded of the complexities of human emotion as she stepped out of the lift on the third floor of her apartment building and approached her front door.

And yet, as she pushed the buggy bearing her three-month-old son along the brightly lit corridor, she was assailed by both joy and the overwhelming weight of heartache twisting round memories of the happiest day of her life. Even the tumult and wonder of the days, weeks and months that had preceded the day she'd given birth. Memories of feeling her baby kick for the first time, wondering if she had what it took to be a good enough parent when her father had failed her so badly.

Then, when the very thought of ever giving up on her own child had sent a surge of horror and rejection through her, she'd clung to that bolstering knowledge that she would never allow the trauma she'd suffered to be repeated on her baby. She'd built on that until nothing but pure love existed in her heart for the child she'd never expected to bear but loved beyond all reason even before he'd come into the world.

Her gaze dropped to the swaddled, sleeping occupant and her mouth predictably curved upward, joy superseding every other emotion for a long, heady moment as she basked in the pride and joy of motherhood. Of how her whole world now centred around one tiny human: Evangelos Nelios Petralis. The child she'd created with Nelios in a moment of wild insanity she still couldn't believe she'd been capable of.

The smile stayed in place until she reached her front door, then she took a deep breath. Because beyond it lay the kind of desolation that crept ever closer, like a fog over icy moors. Unbearable. All-encompassing. Unrelenting.

Agnes was deeply miserable. It wasn't until Vayle's return from Buenos Aires that the full scope of Agnes's hope had revealed itself. While Agnes might have tried dissuading her from going in the first place, Vayle had discovered that her surrogate mother had secretly hoped Vayle would succeed in reaching the son who was so determined to remain estranged from his mother. They'd finally spoken as Vayle had made her way back from Buenos Aires the morning after her night with Nelios. And, like a series of evil tumbling dominoes, nothing and no one had been able to halt what came next.

Nelios had succeeded in wresting the hotel from them. They'd been served with an eviction notice mere weeks later, after an unseemly large sum of money had been dumped in Vayle's bank account in payment. Then had come the worst insult. She'd discovered both she and Agnes had been blacklisted from every hospitality job worth having in London and beyond. It was then that Agnes had truly spiralled into despair, her every frantic effort to contact her son hitting a formidable brick wall.

It didn't matter to Vayle that she'd been unable to find another job, or that she resented Nelios every time she was forced to use the money he'd paid her for Vayle Hotel. It didn't even matter that she'd then been secretly relieved that she had that money to fall back on when she'd discovered she was pregnant with Angelos. What wrenched at her heart, and continued to deeply hurt her, was how Agnes was suffering. How nothing Vayle did could coax her out of her anguish.

Vayle stopped for a moment to blink back tears and compose herself, her fingers tightening around the buggy's handle to bolster herself so she could be strong for Agnes.

On Vayle's return from Buenos Aires, Agnes had elaborated a little bit more, although Vayle sensed she'd still held something back from the story—something that made Agnes's eyes dim in deeper despair. She'd confirmed that they'd had to leave Nelios in the care of Tolis's friend to take the much-needed job with George Lancaster because, yes, he had strictly forbidden them to bring a child to the premises of his precious hotel.

She'd accepted Agnes's tearful insistence that the situation had only been meant to be very temporary; that they'd explained that to Nelios, and that she and Tolis had tried their hardest to find their son after he'd run away from his foster home. And, after Vayle's own shocking discovery that she was pregnant in the weeks following her escapade in Buenos Aires, she'd found herself experiencing a sliver of Agnes's anguish.

Because she'd borne Nelios Petralis an heir he'd never bothered to acknowledge...

Quelling emotions that threatened to unravel every time she thought of that night with Nelios, and the pitiless events that had followed the next morning, she re-pinned the smile on her face and entered the flat. Agnes glanced up from the living room sofa, bleary eyed and looking way over her sixty-three years, the ghost of a smile drifting over her face before it fell on Angelos. Then, in a belly-hollowing replication of her son's features, a complex series of emotions drifted over her face: joy; sorrow; anguish; pride.

'I brought you some food from the Greek café you like,' Vayle ventured once she'd shut the door behind her.

She wasn't surprised when the predictable head shake

came, followed by the soft, 'You have it, *glikia mou*. I'm not hungry.'

Vayle heart lurched at the endearment she recalled being uttered in a much deeper voice.

'How is *agapoula mou*?' she asked, cutting through Vayle's impending plea for her to eat something.

'Sleeping like an angel,' she replied with quiet pride. She'd been blessed with a no-fuss baby who knew what he wanted and, as long as he received it, was very content.

'His father was the same.' Agnes's voice caught and Vayle's heart squeezed when tears brimmed the older woman's lashes. Abandoning the carton of moussaka she'd meant to coax Agnes with, she crossed the room and pressed a tissue into her hand. She'd barely swiped at her eyes before they fixed on Vayle.

The vice tightened, as she sensed what was coming. What Agnes had insisted she do with varying degrees of persistence.

'Did you try again?' the older woman asked.

Vayle swallowed a mixture of concern, indignation and frustration. Now she had Angelos, Vayle couldn't fathom how Agnes and Tolis had gone over two decades without tearing the world apart to find their son. But what she did understand, and fully empathised with, was that some things were simply out of one's control. So she took a sustaining breath and exhaled. 'I told you. It's not that simple.' She knew. She'd tried several times to reach Nelios and had met a very formidable wall every time. A wall that had finally threatened dire consequences if she persisted. 'He doesn't want to know,' she added, ignoring the rough squeeze in her chest.

Since Vayle knew first-hand how it felt to slam her head against the brick wall of Nelios Petralis's fortress, she'd recognised quickly that retreat was her best option. Even if it meant withstanding Agnes's palpable sorrow as her gaze shifted to rest on Angelos. Rising, Agnes walked over to the buggy and stared down with fond sadness at her grandson before brushing her fingers down his cheek. When she returned to her seat, her air of despair was so thick, it clogged Vayle's throat.

Eventually, when at Vayle's urging the older woman went to lie down, Vayle snatched up her phone, giving in to the urge to look up Nelios yet again. He wasn't exactly unavoidable, but she'd weaned herself off her near-obsessive cyberstalking the day of her first scan.

And she'd *mostly* succeeded, damn it. So what if his Buenos Aires launch of Nelios XV had been hailed as the most successful in recent history? Or that the hotel had featured in every architectural, hotel and property magazine for months? Or that Nelios himself had graced the covers of *Time*, *People* and *Forbes* as the most influential genius on earth?

Or that every image of him had sent a mini-shockwave through her? Had made her achingly aware of her near-zealous interest when her eyes had burned because she'd stared unblinkingly at him?

She couldn't forget he'd had her unceremoniously thrown out of his mansion the morning after he'd put his seed inside her. Or, worse, what he'd done after *that*...

But for Agnes's sake... Her fingers hovered briefly over her phone before they moved of their own volition, typing his name into the search engine. And there he was—collecting yet another accolade. Her breath caught. *He was right here in London.* Then Vayle's eyes shifted...to the woman on his arm...and her heart lurched, wild and unhinged.

She blinked and shook her head. It was unthinkable—laughable, even. Twin sparks of inexplicable anger and bemusement ignited in her belly. Because the woman...could've been Vayle's sister. The thought that Nelios was dating a

woman who looked like her made her insides jump because...
Had she made that much of an impact on him?

Another choking sensation rose: *jealousy; anger.*

No. Focus. This is about Agnes—only *Agnes.*

But the spikes of turbulent emotion wouldn't dissipate. So, without stopping to think, she scrolled through to the number she'd called a year ago, far too many times before she'd wised up, and pressed the button.

It rang long enough for her insides to churn. For the voice to demand what the hell she was doing.

'Miss Lancaster, I thought we agreed that—'

'I don't care what you think, Andreas. I have a message for Nelios—and, yes, I know you're with him right now. Tell him I thought him many things, but a coward wasn't one of them. Or maybe all that tough posturing was just an act. Tell me, do you feed off each other's trauma to justify the way you treat others, or it is just him?'

He inhaled sharply. 'What did you just say?'

'He really should've got me to sign one of those NDA thingies. But, since he didn't, and he's made damn sure I'm blacklisted anyway, I'm thinking of going on a revenge tour. Who knows? Maybe I'll bring his mother with me and hang out all his dirty laundry for the world to see.' She grimaced, her fingers tightening around the phone as she cringed inside. Was she taking this too far?

'What the hell do you want?'

For him to acknowledge his son! Thankfully, she kept that wish unspoken. She'd tried for Angelos's sake until she'd drawn the line at placing her precious son in the line of fire for rejection.

'I want him to meet with his mother for one hour. Tomorrow.'

Thick, furious silence greeted her demand. Then the line went dead.

Her breath whooshed out and, as she wilted into the sofa, Vayle had the disturbing inkling that she might've done the very thing she'd accused Nelios of—Hulk-smashing when a delicate touch was needed.

Should she call back—apologise? Maybe...

She jumped when a text pinged. Eyes wide, she read the message.

5pm tomorrow. Nelios VIII London. NXL Suite.

For the second time in as many minutes, her breath exploded out of her lungs. She'd poked the beast. And it had finally responded.

Whether it would end up devouring them both was another matter. She tossed her phone away, rose and for the next hour busied herself so she wouldn't dwell on what the following twenty-four hours would entail. Hell, Nelios hadn't even stated whether he wanted her there or if he wanted to see just his mother.

Why would he want you? He's already got your lookalike.

The reminder sent shards of glass through her belly, robbing her of breath and calmness. Because this level of distress made her feel suspiciously as if *she cared*.

And she *absolutely* did not...

The sound of the doorbell brought both relief and mild exasperation, the freedom from her unwanted thoughts warring with not wanting Angelos to be woken up just yet.

Rushing to the door, she opened it. And froze at the sight of the man poised in the doorway, conjured up from recklessness into real life, looking from head to toe like the Greek statue of his homeland.

'Nelios! W-what are you doing here? You said tomorrow!'

Dark-brown eyes fixed on her for an age without responding, then conducted a searing head-to-toe scrutiny, reminding her that she hadn't brushed her hair since morning. That she, in her jeans and simple top, was no match for the designer-gowned woman clinging to his arm in that photo.

Vayle watched him contain every expression that threatened to escape until his face was a rigid mask. After what felt like an aeon later, after every atom in her body was singing a frenzied aria and his eyes were near molten, he glanced into the flat.

'Where is she?'

'She's resting. And you didn't answer me. What are you doing here?'

'Did you not summon me, or were your threats as empty as the lies you're still being spoon-fed?'

'I...yes, okay, I may have laid it on a little thick to Andreas, but I wanted to get your attention.'

His head tilted. 'Well, now you have it,' he said smoothly, low and deadly. 'Do you not know what to do with me now you have me, Vayle?'

She licked her lips, the connotations making her thighs clench, her nipples hard. Crossing her arms to hide his visceral effect on her, she shrugged. 'This isn't about me. It's about your mother. And, if I knew you could be summoned so easily, I would've done it ages ago.'

His gaze swung to her then, almost taken aback by her forced, glib tone. She would've smiled but, far from hoping she would be spared this time from the effect of the electric forcefield Nelios carried with him wherever he went, Vayle discovered she was very much caught in the sizzling static.

'For someone treading on dangerous ground, you don't seem too worried,' he rasped, his eyes still boring daggers into her.

She shrugged. 'I know what it's like to be caught in an emotional wind tunnel, when all around you is a force-five tornado, so no, I'm not worried. I am perfectly fine right now. Happy, even, despite these circumstances,' she tossed out because far be it for him to think she was still fixated on the humiliation of the morning after their night before. 'So, yes, I can be sceptical as to whether anyone on earth has the power to summon you anywhere without a little...incentive.'

'Believe me, you have no idea what I'm feeling right now.'

'Okay, feel free to share it, then,' she invited softly.

He opened his mouth, then seemed to change his mind. He looked around, as if to remind himself of why he'd come. A detached kind of bleakness descended over his face and this time the expression wasn't quickly dispatched.

'You could've waited till tomorrow. Why the rush?' Her heart thumped, hoping. She knew what she wanted, at least where he and Agnes were concerned. Beyond that...no, she wasn't going to think about her son who slept out of sight in his portable cot. It was a waste of time. Nelios hadn't come here for him. 'Because if you've come not to talk to Agnes, but to cause further injury to her, then—'

'Cause injury—?' He cut himself off in near wonder. 'What about the injury *she* caused *me*?' he seethed. But again, it wasn't just fury rolling across his face. It was deep, ingrained anguish, like a wound, buried deep and newly ripped wide open.

'If it's retribution you're looking for, isn't what you've already done enough? You took away your own mother's purpose by blacklisting her. And I won't even start on how you stabbed me in the back as well. What did I ever do to you, Nelios?' Her breath hitched a tiny bit and she hated herself, and him, for it.

His eyes raked her face, once, twice. And, heaven help her hopelessness, but she thought she saw him lose a shade of colour, maybe even experience a flash of remorse, before his expression froze into neutrality again.

'Where is my... Where is she?' he repeated through barely moving lips.

'I told you, she's resting. If you'd bothered to tell me you'd changed the time...'

A shadow crossed his face. 'Andreas responded without my input. I prefer to face some threats head-on, even empty ones.'

Her mouth twisted in a mockery of a smile that seemed to have a direct link to the vice around her heart. 'Some?' she echoed, hating herself for thinking about how he'd left her sleeping in his bed without even the courtesy of a goodbye.

Was it her imagination or had he winced just then? She hoped he had. That he had other emotions over and above the vengeance locked in his heart for the mother who'd brought him into the world. Over and above the wild desire he'd let loose that night in Buenos Aires, followed by the sheer cruelty he'd displayed the morning after.

'Don't test me,' he warned far too coolly.

'Or what? Haven't you already done your worst to me, Nelios?'

He stiffened. And just like that every last emotion was stripped from his face, leaving a cold mask with glinting eyes. 'Don't presume you know what I'm fully capable of, *glikia mou*—'

'Don't call me that,' she snapped before she could stop herself. 'I'm not your sweet anything.'

His nostrils flared but his expression didn't change. '*Ne*, you're right. You're not.' His dismissive gaze landed on the two doors down the short hallway. 'This is the only time I can spare. Or I walk out the door and any more of her incessant attempts to hound me will be treated as harassment.'

Her mouth gaped. 'Agnes is still reaching out to you?' Vayle had believed she'd stopped after Nelios's stony silence.

His eyes turned flint-hard. 'I see she's still keeping things from you.'

She snapped her mouth shut. 'Don't start. Or I'll...'

One eyebrow arched. 'Or you'll what?'

She pursed her lips, knowing there were no further threats to make.

'A word of advice, Vayle. Get your head out of the sand before it's too late. Or you will–'

The small cry interrupted his unwelcome advice. His gaze darted around the room, surprise dousing his face. The cry came again, and his sharp eyes captured hers. 'What is that?'

Her heart leapt into her throat, but she fought the apprehension wrapping around her whole being. '*That* is exactly what it sounds like.'

At some point in the future, Vayle would wonder what would've happened if Angelos hadn't chosen then to wake up. If he'd continued sleeping, blissfully unaware of the tumult unfolding just feet away. But he hadn't. And, now he'd decided it was time to remind the world—and his father—that he existed, nothing was going to stop him. The cry hitched to a stop for a handful of seconds, no doubt to give his mother the chance to do the right thing and shower his presence with endless adoration.

She went into the bedroom she shared with him, just as he decided her time was up. His impatient cry filled the room, quickening her last few steps. She was intensely aware that Nelios had followed close behind her. That she hadn't answered his question and he meant to pry a response from her.

'It's okay, darling. I'm here. Shhh, no need to make such a ruckus,' she crooned lovingly.

Then, the precious bundle in her arms and her heart in her throat, Vayle turned to where a statue-still Nelios stood frozen. Despite not moving, he occupied every square inch of the doorway until she couldn't breathe, couldn't think, couldn't see anything else but him. Or that convoluted parade of emotions which included shock, bewilderment and now, incredibly...*jealousy*?

She didn't understand why his gaze darted towards where her left hand was tangled in the blanket. And, when it searched and apparently didn't discover what he was looking for, recaptured her gaze. 'You're married?'

Why was his voice so hoarse? So *accusatory*?

'You may have turned my life inside out a year ago, but I don't believe I owe you any information now,' she replied tartly.

Angelos whimpered, perhaps sensing the tension in the air. Or perhaps it was simply a demand for milk now he was awake. She shifted him in her arms, and again Nelios's gaze darted to her left hand. She realised he was looking for a ring, and almost laughed.

'It's the twenty-first century, Nelios. A woman isn't doomed to ruin simply because she has a child out of wedlock.' Her inner hysteria threatened to spill over at the very thought of dating another man while pregnant and then going as far as to marry said mystery man—amidst the turbulence of having Nelios proceed with his plans to rip Vayle Hotel from her grasp, leaving them homeless and having to scramble to rearrange their lives. She would've needed to be Wonder Woman herself. And, while she was proud of herself for battling through the trials and tribulations of the past year, she was well-versed in what it felt like to approach breaking point. To teeter over the very edge of the abyss and force herself back just in time.

Another wave of shock travelled through him. 'So the child is yours?' he pressed a little jaggedly.

This time she frowned. 'What are you talking about? Of course he is.'

She didn't think it possible but he seemed to harden further, his breath locked in his towering body. Frantic eyes fell on Angelos, his gaze sharpening into probing drills. Whatever he saw made the great Nelios Petralis positively *stagger* for the first time since she'd known him.

Perhaps it was the brown eyes her baby had inherited from him, or the tiniest hint of a dimple in his chin that would grow as prominent as his father's one day. Or maybe it was an elemental feeling of recognition between father and son she wasn't privy to. Angelos fell silent then beneath his father's scrutiny, his wide eyes taking in the man who looked as though he was fighting a great inner battle. Whether he won or not was questionable because, when he next spoke, his voice remained gravel-rough.

'I am going to ask you a question, Vayle. And I would be extremely appreciative if you didn't play games with me.'

'I don't—'

'How old is this child?' he cut across her, his voice no longer shaken but scalpel-sharp.

Now, Vayle froze. 'What? You know how old he is. He's exactly three months next week. Why would you—?'

'Vayle.' His chest rose, held, fell, eyes turned midnight dark, pinning her in place. 'Is this child… Is he mine?'

The cycle of outrage at the question came and went in split seconds because it occurred to her that she'd missed something—several 'somethings', as it turned out. Nelios Petralis wasn't dim, far from it. He was the most astute man she knew. Yet, every sign pointed to him being in pitch darkness about his son's existence. How was that even possible?

She stared down at her baby, the most precious thing in her life and felt something seismic move through her. A warning? A rallying cry?

Against what? Surely he wouldn't…

Another bedroom door opened behind her, but the brief reprieve she yearned for to parse through what was happening never came because Agnes stepped out and immediately froze at the sight of her son.

'Demetrius.'

'That is no longer my name,' Nelios growled, a mighty predator swinging his mighty paws. 'If you respect nothing else, respect that,' he said through gritted teeth.

She went sheet-white, and stumbled back against the door.

Nelios lunged towards her—so he wasn't entirely unfeeling after all—but Agnes straightened before he reached her and he froze halfway between Vayle and his mother.

And there, caught in some invisible vortex, his head swung from his mother to her. 'It's now clear one of you orchestrated this. So I will ask again—is this child mine?' he breathed.

She might have crafted things into being for Agnes's sake, but Vayle resented the unfounded accusation. Her temper flared anew.

'How dare you come here, all superior and indignant, asking questions you already know the answers to? You claim to despise games, which begs the question—what game are *you* playing? You might have ignored his existence up till now, but don't you dare pretend you didn't know you had a son!'

Nelios had never been in a war zone, beyond the one he'd been thrown into when he'd been too young and ill-equipped to withstand it. He'd never felt bullets whistle about his head though, sure, he knew only too well what the sound of flying fists felt like when they landed.

But in this moment, when emotional landmines exploded across his every sense, he knew what soldiers of war experienced. What it felt like to have one's life flash before one's eyes as devastation unravelled all around. For a long stretch of time, he saw everything he'd imagined the rest of his life would be detonate and turn to ash right before his eyes, leaving him with the most desolate landscape he'd yet endured. But, curiously, even that image didn't linger.

It attempted to morph, take a different shape. He shut it down before it solidified. Because screw fate for attempting to rearrange his destiny without his permission. Screw karma for this...*unacceptable* effort to show him a different landscape from the one he'd meticulously drawn out for himself while enduring those fists and darkness and humiliation.

Ignored his existence up till now...

Know you had a son...

He shook his head, wondering for a moment, but knowing he hadn't misheard her. Vayle Lancaster had many faults but she'd never tossed out words she didn't find a way of expressing one way or another.

Especially the *one particular way* that still had the power to turn his insides out, which he most definitely wasn't going to think about. Even if the consequences of it was right there in his face, in the form of a cherubic angel staring at him with open curiosity an infant this young surely shouldn't possess. Unless that infant was *his* and thus superior in all the ways that counted.

His child.

The ominous sensation that had taken hold of him when he'd first set eyes on the boy built now, seizing every corner of his being. Setting off a pendulum of emotions he only seemed to feel around Vayle Lancaster.

No, that wasn't true. Unbelievably, the woman quietly sobbing behind him also held that power, even after all this time. It was almost laughable that, having sworn never to clasp eyes on these two people again in this lifetime, he now found himself caught in the maelstrom of emotions they both triggered in him.

Well, *three* now. He didn't doubt that, had Apostolis been alive, he too would've merrily riled him. His heart lurched at the thought of the father he'd never seen again after that fateful night. The father who'd thrown him away.

Looking into the child's eyes, something tight, profound and earth-shaking seized his chest, convulsed, jump-started and changed the very fibre of his being.

Glad you didn't have that vasectomy now?

His breath caught, unprepared for that hissing taunt. For the unguarded punch to his solar plexus at the notion that this child, who had the power to trigger such weighty emotions in him, might never have existed.

Which meant what, exactly?

He shook his head again and redoubled his effort to corral his control. And when he succeeded—because he *always* succeeded—he levelled his most fearsome glare at the woman holding the child...*his son*...in her arms.

'I'm willing to accommodate your belief that I knew about my...about this baby's existence.' *Son.* Something inside him veritably *rumbled* at uttering the word he'd stumbled on. He, who *never, ever* stumbled. But Nelios knew, and readily accepted, that the moment he took full possession of the truth a great many things would change, in ways even he wasn't prepared for. So, yes, he was well within his rights to buy himself a little time. 'Just as I hope you will accommodate my need to get to the bottom of it.'

Ne, he sounded more than reasonable. Surprising, considering the tsunami of sensations bombarding him. She must've thought so too, because those alluring blue eyes, eyes he'd watched glaze with pleasure so pure he'd never witnessed the likes of it before, widened a fraction.

'I...could see my way to doing that,' she murmured, then her gaze darted past him. 'What about Agnes?'

His teeth clenched and he forced himself to turn round. To face the woman who'd once held his hand on the way to school before she'd turned into a monster. 'What do you want? Why am I here?'

Agnes's lips quivered for a second. Her gaze lingered on his face before they dropped. 'I wanted to talk to you. Explain what really happened.' Her face twisted. 'And some other things I think you're old enough to know now.'

A different sort of juddering moved through him. 'New information?' he jeered. 'What could possibly explain anything away now?' Nelios unfurled fists he'd bunched without conscious thought. Somewhere at the back of his brain, the hissing voice sounded again, demanding to know who was sticking their head in the sand now. But he refused to heed that vexing question. The simple truth was that he was reaching saturation point—wasn't open to new stimuli.

He cut off the swell of bleakness attempting to drown him and spun round to face Vayle, and the baby, who turned his near-bald head to watch him with... *Thee mou,* was he getting judgement from his own son too?

Impossible.

'We need to talk, Vayle,' he said as evenly as the nonsensical tempest raging inside him would allow him. 'Away from here,' he added, just to be clear.

'But...' Whatever she'd been about to say withered away when her gaze jerked past him to Agnes. Whatever passed between the two of them—and, no, the reaction unfurling in his chest wasn't jealousy—her face softened with a sort of understanding and she nodded. 'Okay, I will spare you an hour. No more, just so we're clear.'

He did well to keep his furious rejection of that limitation to himself. He was experienced in life and business enough to know when to bide his time and bite his tongue until he gained the ground he needed.

And Nelios knew, as he cast one look at Agnes and then at the woman who was settling his son into his push-chair in preparation to wheel it out, that far from coming here to slam shut the book of his horrendous past as he'd believed, a whole new chapter had unexpectedly opened up.

One he intended to have full control over.

No matter what.

'That look between you and Agnes. What was that about?' he asked the moment they stepped into the lift.

She lifted her gaze from the child, withdrew her stroking finger from his cheek and straightened. Then she shot him a glance that was all defiance and fire. 'It was a look that said we're in this thing together, no matter what. And, before you accuse me of soft feelings as if they're flaws I should be ashamed of, I really don't care what you think.'

Since it was exactly what he'd intended to say, he far from appreciated having the rug pulled from beneath his feet.

'Where are you going?' he asked when they reached the ground floor and she turned away from the main entrance.

'To my car. Where else?'

He examined the contraption his son reclined in. 'Is this one of those carriers that converts into a car seat?'

She nodded warily.

'Then we don't need to travel separately. I will have you delivered back here when we're done.'

His driver pulled up the moment they stepped outside. And if the older man was astonished by the novel sight of his boss escorting a woman and child to his car, he hid it skilfully, as he was paid handsomely to do, briskly picking up the skeleton of the buggy Vayle had collapsed while she expertly secured the portable seat in the spacious car.

'No Andreas tagging along?' she asked airily once she'd slid into the seat and secured her seatbelt, but he noted the tight edge framing the enquiry.

'We're not joined at the hip, surprisingly.'

'No? You could've fooled me,' she shot back.

Nelios inspected her expression, something tightening inside him. 'What is that supposed to mean?' His best friend was assertive but he wouldn't overstep in any way that would put their relationship in jeopardy. He knew that as surely as he knew the lines dissecting his palm.

She shook her head. 'Nothing important,' she said, completely undermining her words.

He prudently chose to ignore it—for now. His eyes slid to the car seat. 'What is his name?' he asked, that roughness he couldn't clear away back in his voice.

She held in her response for a few long seconds. 'Evangelos Nelios Petralis. But I call him Angelos.'

Every atom of his being seemed to clench into stillness except his heart, which raced with an unfettered kind of recklessness he'd never felt before. Not even when he'd feared he was close to death in that alley the night his life had taken yet another course.

Theos. 'You named him after me?' A son she'd never meant to tell him about? He wasn't sure whether he should be furious or floored. Or, damn it, both!

'I'm not the kind of woman who believes a child should be punished for who or what their father turns out to be. He's yours. And mine. So I chose his name accordingly.'

The boy turned at his mother's voice, as if he recognised his name even this young. Then he gave a demanding cry.

'He's hungry. I need to feed him. How far away are we from wherever we're going?' she asked, offering the baby one finger to distract him. Which helped—temporarily, he suspected.

'Five minutes. Perhaps less,' he replied, then plunged into the first subject that niggled. 'We used protection.'

She shot him another of those fiery glares. 'Evidently not

even the world's most powerful and influential man is safeguarded from faulty condoms.'

And it really was as irrefutable as that.

They arrived at Nelios VIII, and were whisked to his private residence within minutes. He watched her make a beeline for the living room sofa as soon as they entered, taking not a single interest in her luxurious surroundings.

Realising that she meant to breastfeed his son, Nelios was struck anew by the impending experience. Then by all the ones he'd missed up to now. Trailing behind them, he knew propriety dictated he should look away, give her privacy. But, hell, theirs had never been a remotely proper connection. She had literally dropped at his feet at their second meeting and things had gone increasingly insane from there. Why relabel it something else now? And, since she didn't seem remotely self-conscious about performing a very natural act…

His brain short-circuited when she loosened the belt of her wraparound dress, unclipped her nursing bra and positioned Angelos at her breast. His eager, hungry son wriggled, then latched on the moment he was able. Nelios realised his breath was locked in his throat with wonder, with a prowling kind of possessiveness. Then with a growing certainty that this would be the last time he missed a single thing about this boy. *His son.* So he eased back in his seat and propped his ankle on his knee, patient now that he'd allowed the reforming landscape to unfold. To show him what he already knew in his blood.

'What did you want to talk about?' she asked a little hesitantly, perhaps sensing the change in the air. The change in her very destiny.

'I had intended to talk about a great many things. But I've come to accept that, while what has come before matters, it isn't as vital as what comes next.'

A pulse visibly leapt in her throat then started to race in

earnest. He curled his hand over his ankle when a different need struck: the need to reacquaint himself with the silky skin overlaying that pulse. To drift his tongue over that evidence of her life force and hear that throaty gasp he'd heard far too often in his dreams.

Nelios accepted that, all these months later, a peculiar kind of longing for her still remained. That perhaps he'd left that Buenos Aires bedroom too quickly. That Andreas musing as to Nelios's affinity for dating a certain type of woman since that night who were all poor carbon copies of the one sitting in front of him—women who were inevitably packed off before they even saw the inside of his bedroom—meant something important. Unfinished business that needed dealing with.

'And what exactly is that?'

He looked from mother to child and back again, a primitive claim that defied civility and reason taking full, complete control of him.

'That I want my son. And I will have him. And because you will put up all sorts of a fight—which I will win, by the way—the culmination of it all will be that you will marry me. As soon as possible. And we will raise our son together.'

CHAPTER SIX

SHE REFUSED. OF COURSE she did. And she argued—vigorously. Because...well, she had no choice.

A mere two weeks later, though, Vayle was sipping coffee just before noon on her wedding day, replaying that conversation, as she had so many times, and convincing herself she'd done the right thing for everyone involved.

Well, perhaps not for herself, if she was honest. But for those she cared about: Agnes and Angelos. They were the ones she'd fought for. On whose behalf she'd extracted those conditions from Nelios. Conditions which, in hindsight, it seemed he'd accepted with healthy opposition but surprisingly not as much vigour as she'd imagined. Which had then led her to wonder if she'd missed something in the small print of their agreement that would come back to bite her in the ass when she least expected it.

Taking another sip, she set the cup down on its saucer. As much as she wanted to finish it, she was jittery enough as it was. Hell, she'd been jittery ever since that day when Nelios had stated with unyielding steel while they'd been caught in that sensory force field, 'Make no mistake—I will have full access to my child, Vayle.'

Her hand had wrapped tighter around Angelos, happily oblivious and ensconced in his milk-guzzling. 'I sense a very large "or else" in there.'

Her attempted fierce reply had wobbled a little at the end,

but she'd kept her daring gaze on him. Because, yes, she was a mother bear, and she would fight to the death for her child.

'Or else I will fight you for custody,' he stated evenly. As if he hadn't been threatening to raze her world to the ground just as effectively as he'd snatched her hotel. As if he'd been picking out a colour scheme for one of his stunning hotels.

'Then I'll see you in court,' she'd replied just as coolly and that time, thankfully, her voice had held.

It had been *his* nostrils that flared. *His* ankle that had left his knee to plant on the floor, his long arms dangling between his knees as he'd speared her with his gaze. *His* jaw that had rippled the tiniest bit before he'd loosened it.

'You would put yourself through that?'

She'd stared at him, really stared. Then she'd asked the question throbbing across her brain. 'For the sake of clarity, I didn't lose my faculties during childbirth. So I know I'm not imagining all the times I called you and emailed you and even left a letter with your right-hand man—despite, I might add, you sending him to do your dirty work the morning after we had sex, to dispatch me like some used spare part you no longer needed. So why the hell are you acting as if you're the wronged party here?'

He'd turned to ice. 'Excuse me?'

Hurt, anger and humiliation trawled through her, reawakened by memories she'd desperately not wanted to relive. 'Which part do you want to be excused from, exactly? The part where you took off in your helicopter that morning without bothering to wake me? The part where you sent Andreas to make sure I wasn't around when you returned? Or where you instructed him to tell me never to attempt to grace your presence again because you were done with me?'

A hint of colour washed his cheeks and Vayle would've mistaken it for embarrassment on anyone else. Not on Nelios. Every move he made was with calculated precision and intent. It was why, after several attempts to contact him, she'd accepted that he truly meant to cut her off. That he wasn't interested in knowing the consequences of their night together.

'Andreas was supposed to put you on a plane back to England. Any embellishment made was on his own initiative. And your claim that you tried to contact me—'

'Are you calling me a liar, Nelios?' she butted in, keeping her voice low so Angelos, who stared raptly at her every expression, didn't pick up on her roiling emotions. 'And are you saying, had I decided to stay, you would've been ecstatic to see me on your return?' The fierce blaze, then the immediate shuttering of his gaze told her everything she needed to know. 'Do not attempt to rewrite history. It shames both of us.'

'Watch it, Vayle.'

'Another "or else"? Can we agree that I'm far from impressed by these deep-throated threats? So it's pointless to keep throwing them about. Sure, I know what horrors you're capable of. But I will defend my child until my last breath.'

Perhaps it was a trick of the light, but she thought he lost a shade of colour. 'Defend—from me?' he demanded through thinned lips. And for a moment she was almost convinced she'd wounded him somehow. But, like the great and mythical phoenix, he rose from that almost immediately. Stronger, more powerful, more visually, completely, *unfairly* arresting than ever. And, when he approached, her breath strangled then swiftly abandoned her lungs. He crouched before her, placing his hands on either side of her thighs on the sofa. His eyes lingered on her face for an age, then dropped to Angelos, where they stayed, *stayed* and *stayed*.

'I asked you a question,' he breathed softly without taking his eyes off his son. 'Do you believe I will deliberately harm my own flesh and blood?'

It was a weakening mistake to remember in that moment how he'd helped her when she'd developed her awful cramp.

How he'd fed her on his plane and called off the authorities in Ascension. How he'd bought her a ticket home—certainly to aid her swift exit from his life—when he could easily have dumped her at the end of the street and left her to fend for herself. And today, when he'd reached out for his mother when she'd stumbled.

Nelios was ruthless, intransigent, driven and hell-bent on revenge against those he believed had wronged him. But was he ever unjustifiably wicked or unkind? Her jaw moved, but Vayle couldn't quite find the words to counter. So she settled for a middling, 'Maybe...maybe not.'

Censure filmed his eyes. 'Is that stubbornness or malice holding you back, *glikia mou*? A wish to hurt me the way you think I've hurt you?'

'I don't think it. I've lived it,' she confessed with a drowning rush of memory. He'd gifted her an unforgettable night, then had topped it with humiliation.

His eyelids swept down, veiling his expression as before. 'I am not entirely...convinced I couldn't have handled things differently,' he finally rasped.

Her eyes widened. 'An admission? My,' she said, then wondered why she wasn't appeased. Why part of her yearned to beat his chest for every moment of humiliation she'd felt when Andreas had knocked on the suite door and calmly informed her she had half an hour to vacate the premises, on Nelios's orders—*if* she wanted the ticket for the flight leaving in less than two hours. He'd mocked her when she'd asked to speak to Nelios, informing her that, once the great Nelios Petralis was done with a woman, he never went back.

Especially a woman like her whom he shouldn't have touched in the first place.

Andreas hadn't said those final words, but it'd been vastly evident he meant them from his sneer and the tone of his voice.

Then she wondered if her disgruntlement had something

to do with the woman she'd seen on Nelios's arm last night. She pushed *that* away.

'Do you know what it felt like to do the literal walk of shame?' she asked bitterly. 'What am I talking about? Of course you don't. Men like you think you rule the world and everyone in it, don't you? Well, you don't own me.' She enunciated clearly so there would be no ambiguity.

Of course that temporary ebbing of his haughtiness reversed, his strong jaw jutting until he was staring down the blade of his aquiline nose. 'I don't wish to own you. But even I recognise that you and my son come as a package deal. Hence my offer. Marry me, and there will be no need for unnecessary acrimony.' His lips twisted. 'I'm even open to us parting ways…eventually. With certain conditions in place, of course.'

Ice-cold, a little thrown by that, and caught in warped bemusement, she asked, 'And what would those be?'

'That we remain married until Angelos is of age—eighteen years at the minimum. That under no circumstances are you to disappear from his life unless those circumstances are out of your control or with meticulous advance planning that will not leave him emotionally scarred.' His eyes turned to merciless flint then, the unvarnished evidence of him reliving his own past right there in his eyes. 'Agree to that and I will concede to a demand or two.'

Her brows lifted. Perhaps she should've stopped the words that spilled out but this was…a lot. And no one had said she was barred from reeling or reacting with some sassiness of her own. 'Just *one or two* in return for eighteen years of my life? What a hard bargain you drive. Go on, then, dazzle me with these concessions.'

'Ten million dollars on our wedding day. A further three million for every year we stay married. Plus any marketing position you want in my empire.'

'All out of the goodness of your heart?' she taunted, still

attempting to drive him into betraying an emotion. To scratch beneath his icy facade.

He shrugged. 'Why not? Besides, I don't want the sleazy media accusing me of taking advantage of you.'

'Did you care about how you would be perceived when you took away my livelihood?' she challenged.

'You mean when I left you several hundred thousand pounds richer?' he parried.

She tugged her baby closer. 'Money isn't everything.'

'Neither is clinging to an outdated monstrosity that was worth nothing, certainly nowhere near what I paid for it. Tell me honestly—before I solved your problem for you and paid way over the market price, when was the last time you'd seen a decent profit? And don't trot out the "money isn't everything" excuse. Bursary or not, you didn't go through university and come out with two degrees to manage a failing business whose only appeal was that it bore your name. A business which fell apart at the slightest pressure from competition.'

'Slightest pressure?' she scoffed. 'You're joking, right? You ruthlessly targeted us and didn't let up until we had no choice but to give in.'

His hand slashed through the air. 'And you're well aware of my primary reasons for that. But we're straying from the subject. You can be my opponent in the custody court or my wife. You decide.'

The final, clanging ultimatum.

She sucked in a slow breath. Despite single mothers having been a thing since the dawn of time, she knew first-hand the judgement that could come from society with such a status. People would wonder what she'd done to end up without the support of a man: whether it was a wild and foolish feminist strike for independence or whether she had loose morals or just plain bad luck. Not that being married was any guarantee or insulation from judgement.

Vayle swallowed, every brave and independent reason she wanted to cling to crumbling away, knowing in her heart she could at the very least consider the outcome for Angelos, ensuring her child wouldn't carry even a hint of the stigma that shouldn't exist but still did. That he would at least have his father in his life on whatever basis they could agree on.

Wasn't that the fundamental reason she'd persisted in trying to let Nelios know he'd fathered a child—to give her child options?

And all this option would take would be to submit to a loveless, emotionless union—that or be locked in a legal battle which outcome she could foretell, having just been through a battle with Nelios only a year ago.

Well, she thought a little hysterically, perhaps not entirely emotionless. Because she felt very many things in this moment, including the almost childish urge to scream that life wasn't fair. But, to be fair, she'd landed herself in this situation. She'd chosen to sleep with him. To lose herself in wild, unfettered lust.

But, perhaps childishly, she could blame him for being entirely too handsome, too charismatic and too dynamic with those chiselled good looks, capable hands and sinful lips! He was a sorcerer who'd enchanted her and he deserved some of her ire for it.

'Careful, there, you look as if you're about to claw my face off. Not quite how I imagined you responding to my proposal,' he rasped, eyes backlit with a blaze she couldn't quite interpret. Which made her *feel* some more.

She breathed in and forced her clenched hands to unfurl. 'How did you imagine it, then? Me, prostrate at your feet in abject gratitude?'

His head tilted and, damn him, his eyes glinted in mocking appreciation. 'Hmm. Now there's an idea.'

'Well, dream on. It's not going to happen.' The snap in

her voice drew Angelos's attention. Happily gorged on his meal, he lifted his head, his brown eyes staring raptly before, cracking a milky smile, he turned his attention to Nelios.

Father and son commenced another staring match, which continued even as Nelios lifted his hand and slowly, for the very first time, brushed his fingers over his son's crown. The breath that shuddered out of him—the briefest insight into his raw possessiveness and determination as he cradled his son's head—cemented the reluctant belief that, no, Nelios would never harm their baby. That perhaps, far from that, he would strive to move mountains for his flesh and blood.

Should she choose to stand in his way, she might well be obliterated in the process.

So she chose. *Wisely.*

The stately manor in the Hertfordshire countryside was her choice of wedding venue, because Nelios had wanted to whisk her off to Greece.

That had been Vayle's second demand. Her first had been that Agnes attend their wedding. It had been non-negotiable.

The third demand, that had caused a near-seismic event, had by far been her boldest. Part of her agreement to become Mrs Nelios Petralis for the best part of the next two decades was that Nelios have five-hour-long meetings with his mother, all to take place within the next three months—also non-negotiable.

He'd levelled a withering look at her that she'd withstood while burping his son, then, when the heavens had rewarded her efforts with Angelos's loud burp, she'd enquired whether Nelios wanted to hold his son for the first time.

Ne, he'd said, his voice deep, shaken.

She'd handed him a wide-eyed Angelos. He'd surged to his feet and prowled the living room, all lithe power and grace, his eyes locked on his son. After the third circuit, when he'd dropped the softest, lingering kiss on Angelos's forehead and exhaled long and hard, he'd stopped in front of her, looked down with that primitive, possessive light in his eyes and said huskily, 'You have a deal.'

Lawyers had been summoned and papers drawn up. She'd received an email with a veritable laundry list of what needed to be done by her and by his army of minions before they exchanged vows in a matter of weeks.

And here she was, watching the final touches being put to the transformed grounds which would host the exclusive one-hundred-strong list of Nelios Petralis's honoured guests. Well, ninety-eight to her two: Agnes and Angelos.

She forced down a mouthful of granola and returned to the gorgeous suite decorated with a blushing bride-to-be in mind. Vayle would've snorted under her breath at how far she was from that description if the knot beneath her breastbone didn't rub her the wrong way every time she tried to take a breath. It wasn't heartache, or wishes harboured and discarded. Definitely not. She was going into this thing with her eyes wide open.

Far from not wanting his son, as she had thought, Nelios was in full claiming mode. She still didn't know if he'd known of his existence or not—a fact yet to be established.

She was doing what was best for her son. And her 'surrogate mother'. Agnes breaking down in happy tears on hearing the news had cemented the issue for Vayle. On that, Vayle's heart was at ease. What she was not at ease with was the way her heart behaved around Nelios. And not just her heart. A frisson seized her whole being whenever he was within touching distance, like the echo of a tuning fork.

It was why she'd requested a special clause in their agreement: *no sex*. A demand Nelios had treated with a sliver of sardonicism and a flash of taut rancour before his impressive self-control had reasserted itself, followed by an imperious wave of dismissal, and he'd signed his name with a flourish, sealing their fate.

After checking in on Angelos, judging she had about half an hour before he woke, she stepped into the lavish bathroom and indulged in a luxurious shower, hoping it would dilute some of the jitters swarming her belly.

Predictably, as her hands moved over her body, she was struck by an ominous voice demanding to know if she'd been wise to add that clause to their agreement. Because she had *liked* having sex with Nelios, and eighteen years was a very long time to condemn herself to celibacy.

But, as she braced her hand against the wall and tried to resist taking care of the urgent need pounding between her legs, she accepted that part of why she'd felt so devastated by what had happened the next morning, besides the humiliation, was because their night together had meant something to her besides a physical exchange of desire and pleasure.

There was wisdom to knowing which battles were un-winnable. And, as much as it thrilled her very blood to go toe to toe with Nelios over his domineering manner, she recognised that the subject of sex was one she would do well to stay away from.

Because sex with him had transcended her every reality.

It had sent her to a place where she was at her weakest, where she would've happily handed over more than just her body to him for the chance to experience it again. And, yes, that too was the reason his rejection had hit her all the more viciously. So, sex would have to remain off the table so she could guard more important things, such as her sanity. *Her heart.*

Her son didn't disappoint her and rose like clockwork from his mid-morning nap the moment she stepped out of the shower, demanding a feed. She used it gratefully to occupy her mind as the time ticked down to when the couturier and her small army would descend on her a mere hour later.

By midday, Vayle was fully installed in the ivory Italian

duchesse-satin gown with a pleated corset top and sleeves that sat just off her shoulders. The necklace of round-cut diamonds set in white gold, with a pink teardrop diamond pendant that rested on the pulse point at her throat, had been delivered last night courtesy of Nelios. Matching earrings graced her lobes and a simple bracelet, her right wrist.

The team of attendants had just finished arranging her hair in an elaborate, tasteful chignon when she looked up and saw Agnes standing several feet away, a tearful smile on her face.

She twisted in her seat, her own smile growing tentatively.

'Can we have some privacy, please? Just for a few moments.'

She rose as the attendants relocated to the living room, and approached the older woman, her hands outstretched.

Agnes's lips wobbled a little bit more before she firmed them. 'You look beautiful, *agapita*.'

'So do you,' Vayle murmured.

They exchanged a fond look before the usual wave of anguish washed over Agnes's face. 'I may have lost a son I will never get back, but I gained a daughter despite all my failings. I love you, Vayle. You and Angelos, you mean everything to me. I'm saying it now in case I never get the chance to atone for my...'

'Of course you will have many more chances. I'm not going anywhere and neither is your grandson. Concentrate on working things out with your son.'

Desolation crossed her face. 'What if he never forgives me?'

'You won't know until you try.'

She sucked in a shuddery breath. 'What did I ever do to deserve you?' Her eyes brimmed with tears.

Vayle blinked away threatening tears of her own. 'You saved me. You loved me even though I wasn't yours. Family is originally blood, but often it's also the people we meet and help and love along the way. You didn't turn your back on me when you could have. You made me feel more loved than my own flesh and blood did. I will always love you for that. But you also need to not give up on the other family you do have.'

Wrenching anguish kept hold of Agnes for the longest time. Watching her battle through it brought a heavier lump to Vayle's throat. But the woman who had given Nelios Petralis life, who had had some hand in shaping him despite his insistence that only his trauma had forged him, finally emerged. A steel spine shimmered into being, a little fragile and bendable perhaps, but steel nonetheless. With a firm nod, Agnes grabbed one last tissue and dabbed her damp eyes. 'We've kept him waiting long enough. Let's get our game faces back on and you up the aisle, yes?'

Vayle gulped as the butterflies reawakened. 'Yes.'

Agnes walked her down the aisle—another condition Vayle had insisted upon, especially since Andreas the Ogre was Nelios's best man. In the rush to this wedding, she'd crossed paths with Andreas only twice. She'd sensed he had something to say to her but she'd distanced herself from the interaction, not wanting her already unsettled emotions to be toppled by his caustic opinions. On both occasions she'd been with Nelios, who had also seemed reluctant to leave her alone with his right-hand man.

So, yes, she chalked it up to a win as she proceeded arm-in-arm with Agnes down the aisle.

Of course, all thoughts of winning, losing or otherwise fled the second she clapped eyes on Nelios, in the finest hand-made suit, with his hair combed off his forehead to better display the sheer force of his male beauty. Everything faded to sepia while he blazed in vivid, living colour.

She couldn't even pick one thing that reigned supreme above another: his eyes, his jaw, his unabashed ferocity; the pristine whiteness of his collar against the rich dark-blue of his wedding suit; or the resolute power that snaked out and compelled her to him, her every step seeming to echo his silent, unyielding intonation of *mine, mine, mine...*

She scarcely felt the exquisite bouquet being tugged from her hold, or barely saw Agnes and Andreas retreat to their seats.

She did feel the electric power of his touch when he took her hand and propelled her that last step to his side. Felt every word of the simple yet weighty vows they exchanged. He slid the diamond-and-platinum wedding band onto her finger that perfectly matched the priceless engagement ring, drew her into his arms, fused his lips to hers and rasped, 'It is done.'

Oh yes; Vayle very much felt that too.

He was married.

As he led his new bride across the dance floor, Nelios finally allowed the landscape to settle; allowed himself to open his mind to what he'd negotiated for these past weeks. What he'd vowed when he'd held his son for the first time.

As he'd looked into Angelos's eyes, and sworn to do the polar opposite of what had been done to him, he knew he'd allow very little to stand in his way. Even if it meant having to deal with his mother and hear more lies from her treacherous lips.

To gain his son, he realised he would even withstand that torture, and more. It would only be a few hours of his life, after all, compared to a lifetime of ensuring that his offspring never suffered as he had. As exchanges went, Nelios believed he'd got the better part of the bargain. So why did that chafing still lurk within him? Why did it feel as if this mission wasn't quite complete?

As he guided Vayle back across the dance floor, his gaze connected with his friend's. Andreas still hadn't lost that shadowed tension in his eyes ever since their heated conversation a month ago after he'd delivered Vayle and Angelos back to her apartment.

It took a lot for his only friend to accept blame, because he'd rarely ever stepped out of line. So Nelios had been mildly stunned when Andreas had come to him and immediately offered his sincere apologies for keeping Nelios from Angelos. He'd thought he was doing the right thing by having his friend's back, thinking he was protecting Nelios from a threat they'd both faced before from women who'd made spurious claims of being pregnant by them, with only grasping avarice in mind. In their world, gold-diggers like that were ten a penny. Andreas had thought he was dealing with yet another one in Buenos Aires, so he'd ignored Vayle's calls, had had her emails deleted unread and had discarded her letter.

Nelios truly believed it had been a misunderstanding on his friend's part, and he'd had to accept that he too had dropped the ball, when all was said and done. He'd also had to accept that missing his son's momentous milestones thus far was perhaps his penance. He'd grudgingly let it go.

But clearly Andreas hadn't, if the guilty grimace he slanted Nelio's way was any indication.

'Things not all rosy in friendship land?'

He dropped his gaze to Vayle and, despite the tension lurking in her own features, some of the chafing eased. His own grimace he kept to himself. He hadn't fooled himself into believing this wedding would be an especially happy occasion but, while he didn't really care what his specially selected business and social acquaintances thought, he didn't want to start off his marriage anything but impeccably.

Her eyes held a faint wariness but it was the fire in them that snagged at him. That promised that, whatever lay ahead of them, it would be far from boring.

Nelios found himself anticipating that challenge, even welcoming it. His eyes dropped lower to the diamonds encircling her neck and the hint of cleavage that made other parts of him tighten. 'Have I said how exquisite you look?'

The concoction of ivory satin elevated her glow, and the faint flush to her cheeks and the diamonds only harnessed her stunning beauty. But more than that there was an ephemeral quality to this woman that had enthralled him from the start. That, he was a little disturbed to admit, he'd gone searching for in others, and had failed to find.

'Not going to answer my question?' she replied.

'The issue has been explained and resolved,' he offered.

'Has it? And no one bothered to tell me?' she said sarcastically. 'What is your deal with Andreas anyway?'

His gaze sharpened. 'What?'

She shrugged and his gaze moved over her smooth skin again, hunger slowly prowling its restlessness through him.

'I looked him up like any sane person would when you started your antics. I looked you both up, in fact. There is very little about him on the Internet.'

'Because he is a private man. But our origins crossed at a crucial point which aided the forging of an unbreakable friendship.'

Curiosity sparkled in her eyes and Nelios couldn't drag his gaze away. 'What happened?' She used that same soft, empathetic voice she always used when advocating for Agnes. He shouldn't have fallen for it, yet he felt a certain...*give* in his chest.

Which he immediately suppressed by shaking his head. 'This is neither the time nor the place for confessions, *yineka mou.*'

'What does "*yineka mou*" mean?' she muttered.

He felt that hungry flame burning brighter as he stared down into her eyes. 'It means "my wife". And I would rather talk about us, not Andreas.'

Was it his imagination or did a shiver run through her?

Dropping his gaze, he saw the pulse at her throat speed up and his whole body felt charged, that anticipation building. Which was why he almost growled when a hand tapped his shoulder.

Speak of the devil.

'It's my turn to dance with the bride, I believe,' Andreas murmured.

The right, civil thing to do would be to hand over his wife. But Nelios didn't feel particularly civil.

'No can do. I'm not quite done dancing with my wife. If you're in need of a dance partner, Agnes is free, I believe.'

His friend barely managed to keep his surprise from showing, and after a moment nodded and turned to Vayle.

'In case later isn't good for your husband either,' he said with a hint of a wryness, 'I'd like to take this opportunity to apologise for my actions over the last year. I've been rather… over-zealous in my gatekeeping.'

Vayle watched him and let him stew for a few several seconds before she nodded. 'Apology accepted. As long as you're cordial to Agnes, we won't have a problem.'

The baffled knot in Nelios's gut tightened as his friend walked away to do his wife's bidding.

'You're staring again.'

He bit his tongue against a trite response about her beauty, or something primeval, such as he was allowed to look at her now she was his. Instead he found himself blurting, 'You really do insist on seeing the good in everyone, don't you?'

She stiffened for a moment, then lanced him a challenging glance. 'I'm hardly Mary Poppins, but really, isn't stomping about gathering all the dark clouds around you exhausting for you and everyone else?'

For the wildest, most absurd second, Nelios felt laughter bubbling up in his chest at the image she conjured up. And perhaps she caught a glimpse of it, because her tension eased and her eyes dwelled on his face for much longer than he was strictly comfortable with. But the moment she glanced over his shoulder, her eyes softening at seeing Agnes on Andreas's arm, Nelios wanted her attention back on him.

'I assure you, it's not a chore or burdensome at all,' he drawled, then exhaled steadily when her eyes returned to his. 'Thunderstorms keep everyone on their toes. But they also bring cleansing rain and new starts. In the past, I've had no choice but to forge several of my own.'

Her eyes softened further and Nelios felt the ground beneath him soften along with it, like clouds lifting him, making him feel...buoyant for the first time in a very long time. It was a deceptively addictive feeling. One he knew he needed to resist.

But maybe not just yet.

One song drifted into another as his new wife looked up at him. 'As great as that may be, surely sunshine after all that rain makes things look and feel so much better?'

Again a touch of humour lightened his chest. 'What next, Vayle—a debate about the benefit of rainbows?'

She blinked at him in mock annoyance. 'I love rainbows, and I won't have them disparaged. So why don't I go about sunshining to my heart's content and you thundercloud all you want? And if we happen to clash...' She shrugged smooth shoulders, her body moving under his touch, reminding him what lay beneath the layers of satin.

Just a little while ago he'd speculated that this marriage would be far from boring, but maybe he'd underestimated that sentiment. Maybe there was room for...more. Such as renegotiating the no-sex clause he'd foolishly agreed to...

'Thank you for allowing her to be here.'

Humour and thoughts of sex and rainbows fled as he followed her gaze to Agnes. 'She has my wife to thank for that.' Why did using that term settle something primal inside him?

'I know. But you still could've objected. I know what you're capable of.'

His eyes sharpened on her face. 'Is that supposed to be an accusation?' he asked with a touch of disappointment he sensed was directly connected to losing the pleasant connection they'd shared a minute ago. The dismaying hollow in his belly wanted that warmth back. He was disgruntled to admit that the *exhausting* weight of this bitterness he harboured for Agnes—the constant anger-tinged shadows of grief for not being granted the opportunity to face his father and show him the man he'd become *despite* him—was all so very *exhausting*. *Thee mou*, there was that word again. His wife had planted it in his head, and now it was all he could feel.

She firmed her lips. 'It was truth-stating.'

He barely stopped his teeth from gritting. 'It's our wedding day, Vayle. Let's not ruin it by arguing.'

She nodded. 'Agreed. But you will still talk to your mother, yes? Attempt to put the past behind you?'

The earlier rush of winning, of embracing his new landscape, dimmed a little as he looked into her eyes. What if he failed? What if this would be him two decades from now, gazing at his own son after having failed him?

No. That would never happen. Not as long as he had breath in his body and a memory to keep him firmly on the new path he intended to choose. Snatching his flailing emotions back under control, he refocused on Vayle.

'That's what you negotiated on her behalf. So, yes, I'll stick to it even if I don't hold much hope of being swayed by anything she has to say.' His smile felt mirthless and tight. 'But you'll do well not to push me.'

The end of the music punctuated his statement and he escorted her back to their table, despising that fervent wish to wind the clock back to five minutes ago.

CHAPTER SEVEN

It was the height of pathetic behaviour to wander about like a hapless, jilted lover on his own wedding night. It was even more tragic to lie in bed on a night he should've treated like every other night, considering he'd only married for the sake of his son, and wish for his new wife's warm, delectable body next to his.

He'd left her in that bed in Buenos Aires because he'd tried to convince himself he was done with her. And he'd almost been convinced of that.

Until all the talk of thunderclouds, sunshine and rainbows. To his disarming surprise, he'd found himself dwelling on that conversation for the rest of the wedding reception, wondering if there wasn't some merit to Vayle's argument. Wondering if this woman—who, against all odds, had chosen to keep his child and had striven to let him know he was to become a father because it was *the right thing to do*—wasn't the enemy after all.

Impatient with himself—and, yes, finding it hard to accept he might have read her wrong—Nelios rose and tugged on his dressing gown. He told himself he didn't hope she was losing sleep too; that maybe, if she happened to be awake, there would be a repeat of when she'd charged after him that night in Buenos Aires, slammed those small but firm hands on his chest and demanded he hear her out.

And, no, he didn't hold his breath at all when he pulled open his door... To an empty corridor.

Ne, he was truly pathetic.

Shoving his hands into his pockets, he picked a destination and stalked downstairs towards the ballroom of the manor, his footsteps echoing off the polished parquet floor like mocking taunts. Just hours ago, the room had been brimming with champagne, laughter and the glittering presence of his guests. Now it echoed with silence and the weight of his own frustration.

It was his wedding night, damn it. He should be upstairs with Vayle, tracing the delicate lace of her dress as he peeled it away, kissing down the curve of her neck and watching the firelight flicker over skin he longed to reacquaint himself with. Instead, he'd been banished by his own stupid agreement to what now felt like the dumbest clause ever written into a pre-nup.

No sex...for *years*.

At the time, it had felt like a minor detail—an odd little addendum she'd requested with that careful tone of someone testing boundaries. He'd said yes with barely a pause, more focused on sealing the deal than questioning her motives. He hadn't expected it to feel so vexing. So *immediate*.

Now, hindsight clawed at him like regret soaked in acid. What had he been thinking—that restraint would impress her? Win her over faster so she'd sign the document? He wanted his wife. Perhaps not desperately—he wasn't an untried schoolboy, after all—but the need was there, residing beneath his not-so-calm surface. It was aching, maddening. And she wasn't miles away. She was right there.

He glanced towards the sweeping staircase, half-tempted to storm up there and tear up the clause himself. But what would that prove—that he couldn't honour a promise? That he was just another man ruled by his loins? No.

He clenched his jaw and turned back towards the bar, grabbing a bottle and pouring himself two fingers of scotch with more force than necessary. The amber liquid sloshed in the glass, mocking him.

Years...

Nelios took a slow sip, accepting that, for once in his life, he'd perhaps accepted a challenge he might not win.

He slept like crap, as predicted, dreaming of a house and living room he hadn't seen in over two decades; of a place he'd believed was his sanctuary but had turned out to be false; of three adults deciding his fate, two of whom should never even have considered the abandonment they'd planned.

They'd sacrificed him for *material things*.

Nelios was aware there was a trough of questions still to be answered, but it wasn't as if he hadn't lain awake endless nights, parsing every reason and accepting there was no rationale that could explain such a decision. *Besides greed...*

But he'd promised to hear Agnes out, he recalled as he abandoned his bed at dawn in favour of the study that came with the manor, feeling a lot more like himself as he faced a few hours of satisfying work. When the sound of husky laughter reached him an hour after sunrise, he rose from his desk and padded to the corner of the Edwardian bay windows that overlooked the terrace. Where Vayle was about to have her breakfast with a content-looking Angelos reclining in his rocking cot.

Tossing his tablet onto the desk, he walked out of the study. Her head snapped his way and he braced himself for the unique fizz of tangling with Vayle... Petralis. When no skirmish came his way, he told himself he wasn't disappointed. That cordial relations worked for him. Going over to Angelos, he squatted next to the rocking cot, his insides turning over when soft brown eyes met his. '*Kaliméra*, Angelos.'

His son blinked, then burbled at him.

He turned to his wife. *'Kaliméra.'*

'Good morning,' she murmured.

'Did you sleep well?'

A curious look whispered over her face before she shrugged. 'Not really. Strange beds and all that.'

He was a bastard to hope she'd experienced a sliver of his frustration as he gestured at the breakfast table. 'May I join you?'

She shrugged again. 'It's your manor for the duration. I can hardly stop you, so go ahead.'

Curbing a curious smile at the cute impertinence, he pulled out a chair and sat down. A waiter approached and Nelios discovered he was ravenous. He made his request then sat back, seeing absolutely nothing wrong with letting his eyes wander over his new wife. So what if the label sent a pulse of pure primitive delight through him? In the light of day, his regret about that no-sex clause had receded. He had his son exactly where he wanted him, with a cast-iron assurance that the trauma and torments of the parents would never be visited upon the son. A reality for which he would raze whole worlds to the ground.

So a small but lavish wedding, a ring on his finger and a woman who now bore his name was a fair price to pay.

Are you sure? You're so cocky now, in the light of day. But night will come again, all too soon.

He swatted the question away and fixed his eyes on her, cataloguing her from head to toe so he wouldn't have to dwell on the mocking voice.

The weak summer sun graced her with shafts of light, but as to whether her skin glowed because of it, or it was a leftover from her pregnancy, he didn't wonder about for long. Because, with each second his gaze lingered on her, the higher he felt the need to sit forward and trail his fingers over her cheek, jaw and over the pulse beating steadily at her throat.

He'd tasted her right there. Had made her breath hitch and her lips part with hunger that he'd greedily and decadently taken delight in assuaging.

'You?'

He shifted his gaze to her face. 'Hmm?'

'I asked how you slept.'

He saw no reason to prevaricate, so he didn't. 'Shoddily. For various reasons.'

He waited, for what he wasn't sure. And, when faint colour stained her cheeks and she looked away, he got that urge to smile. He, who never smiled unless it was at an opponent's expense.

'Such as?'

His humour disappeared. Since she was the main reason his sleep had been disturbed, he picked the most pressing reason and offered it to her. 'The fact that it was our wedding night doesn't count?'

Her eyes widened a touch and searched his. 'We agreed on celibacy.'

'*Ne*, but perhaps the question is, why the need to stipulate it in the first place?'

'I'm not rehashing a done deal with you, Nelios,' she said a little hurriedly.

His pulse jumped at his name falling from her lips. 'No? I thought that was right in your wheelhouse.'

'And didn't you insist I should be happy with what I got?'

Hoist by his own petard.

'Have you spoken to Agnes yet?' she blurted.

The douse of ice on his emotions irritated him. 'If you must know, we encountered one another this morning,' he said, recalling the very brief interaction with his mother in the hallway when he'd first come downstairs. He'd forgotten she was an early riser too. Or that perhaps, like him, she'd had a sleepless night, only for different reasons.

'And?'

Nelios wasn't certain which disturbed him more—that he'd agreed to this to please Vayle, or that he hadn't walked away from his mother with as much emotional detachment as he would've wished. Especially when she'd insisted there were supposedly important details she needed to give him. 'I agreed to talk. I didn't agree to giving you a play-by-play.'

Her face fell just before she sent him a disappointed glare. And he absolutely *did not* squirm in his seat... It was the brisk July air, which should've been wonderfully temperate, as it was in Greece, but instead bordered on cold. It reminded him why he disliked the intemperate English weather, and he seized on the other subject on his mind.

'There's no rush, of course, but it would be good for you to get a feel of the Nelios Group before you make a decision about which hotel you wish to work in. I thought we'd start in Greece; introduce Angelos to his other homeland. Then wherever in the world you wish to go next.'

Her glare lessened. 'Really?'

Was it the sun or were her eyes always this luminous, this incredibly breathtaking? *'Ne,'* he confirmed a little gruffly.

She grew contemplative far too quickly. 'I don't want to leave Agnes for endless days.'

He ignored the chafing in his chest. 'Then we'll remain in Europe for the time being,' he assured her. 'Start the tour in southern Italy, then go to Apeiron.'

'I've never heard of that.'

'Very few people have because it's my private island in Greece. We can start from there instead of Italy, if you wish.'

It wasn't his imagination that caught a glitter of pleasure in her eyes because something flipped in his belly. And when the look evaporated he was struck with a fervent need to regain it.

'What does "Apeiron" mean?'

'Several things in Greek, but for my purposes it means "infinite".'

The glitter slowly returned, weaker than before but there. 'Because you believe your mightiness is infinite?'

Was she teasing him? The belly-flip recurred. 'Exactly so.'

He caught the twitch at the corner of her plump lips just before she turned away to shower attention on their son. He told himself he wasn't jealous; that he was perfectly content just to watch their interaction; enjoyed how naturally she doted on him and saw to his every need. How...good she was with him.

But all the while Nelios was stingingly aware of the hunger prowling within him, seeking satiation. Of the voice repeating yet again, asking himself why the hell he'd agreed to that stupid, *stupid* celibacy clause.

Vayle hated herself for missing Nelios even before he had walked away after devouring his breakfast, with a request she be ready to leave by lunchtime. More so for the giddiness that took hold of her entire being, making her feel as if she was permanently plugged into a low-voltage current. Even when Agnes joined them to play with Angelos before the arranged driver took her back home, Vayle could barely concentrate on their conversation.

'You'll love Greece.' The usual sadness tinged her words as Vayle kissed her goodbye.

Vayle finally forced herself to focus. 'Will you be okay?'

Agnes nodded, her gaze drifting over Vayle's shoulder, no doubt looking for the son who was resolutely ignoring her. 'Things aren't going as quickly as I'd like but... I have hope.'

A lump rose in her throat and she embraced Agnes. 'I'll call as soon as I can.'

Agnes shook her head. 'Don't hurry. This is a new beginning for you. And I have a feeling my son needs you more than he's willing to let on. Take your time; treasure this new life you're beginning.'

Vayle shook her head, clenching her belly against the acute yearning that struck her. 'It's not like that, Agnes. You know why we married. It's just for Angelos's sake.' She peered deeper into Agnes's eyes, hoping to see understanding, perhaps even an agreement that it was truly unwise to build hopes on a marriage of convenience.

But Agnes gave a small but confident smile. 'Don't assume a door is locked before you've turned the handle, *agapolou*.'

The words echoed in her head long after they'd boarded a helicopter to the very airport where she'd breached security to stow away on Nelios's jet.

And if the crew, which included Capaldi but was minus Andreas, was stunned to see her board with a baby in tow, they kept it well hidden. In fact, they seemed to forget her existence just as quickly, their attention fully absorbed by Angelos, now learning to smile and collecting hearts in his little fists as he offered one toothless smile after another.

Vayle blinked as Nelios produced a snazzy pair of baby headphones and slotted them over Angelos's head. 'Noise-cancelling to protect his ears,' he muttered, then dropped a kiss on his son's head once the device was in place. 'There's a cot in the back too, for when he needs it.'

That softening threatened again. For some reason, Nelios's demand two weeks ago as to whether he was a monster, and how her instincts had immediately rejected that idea, flared across her senses. She realised she was staring at him, unable to look away as the plane gained speed.

And, no, she didn't trick herself with the lie that it was the steep take-off that took her breath away. It was Nelios Petralis—fearsome, ruthless, towering and larger than life, but with a not so insubstantial vein of humanity buried beneath it all. That was the man who held her in a thrall she feared would overwhelm her if she didn't find a way to break it.

So she was grateful that they had indeed decided to start the tour in southern Italy rather than the luxurious splendour of his Greek island.

Nelios XIV glittered on the shores of the Ionian Sea, a masterpiece of graceful marble arches, sprawling hallways, hidden alcoves and centuries-old charm. The staff displayed the right amount of haughtiness, pride and reverence to their guests.

'Something amusing you?' Nelios drawled beside her as they followed the impeccably dressed manager who personally escorted them to their suite.

'I think you might be coming a lowly second to the adoration of your own creation. They love your hotel more than they love you.'

He shrugged, supremely confident in his appeal even as a spasm of some strange emotion washed over his face. 'It's a lucky thing then that I don't particularly desire to be loved.'

'That's rubbish. Everyone desires to be loved, on some level.' Her vehemence on the subject shocked her a little. As did the rolling quakes that started in her chest and unfurled until they engulfed her whole body. Because it was almost as if his observation...frightened her. As if he had shut a door she very much wanted to remain open.

His sharp look confirmed that, yes, she'd been too fervent. That perhaps he'd even found it objectionable. 'Desires are one thing. Accepting the reality of the hand we're dealt is quite another.'

'You haven't struck me as the type to sit back and let someone else deal your cards, so that argument is hogwash.' Why was she pushing this? Why not just accept his words at face value and save herself the trouble?

Don't assume a door is locked before you've turned the handle...

His footsteps had slowed to match hers, their escort several steps ahead. 'So you believe I should scramble about, petitioning for affection and attention?'

Her gaze dropped to the wide platinum band encircling his ring finger. The band she'd placed there. He followed her gaze, his features tightening again. 'Or I supposed that boat has sailed for me, *ne*?'

She wanted to make a flippant remark about his potential to be supremely eligible again eighteen years from now, when by their agreement she would be free to walk away. When she doubted he would still be anything but jaw-dropping, even as a silver fox. But the words stuck in her throat, the vice around her chest constricting until she was terrified to take a full breath.

Luckily, they'd arrived at their designated suite. And, when the double doors were thrown open and she stepped inside, a different urgency took hold. She barely managed to bite her tongue until the manager had finished his elaborate spiel about the endless amenities available to them—including a makeshift nursery specially set up for Angelos—and left.

'Is there a problem?' Nelios drawled.

'Do I need to point it out? There's only one bed.'

His jaw clenched. 'It's the height of the summer season. I can have the second penthouse guests thrown out, if you wish?'

'No, I don't wish, and don't make me sound like a demanding harridan. We spent our wedding night in separate beds. What makes you think I want that situation to change today?'

His nostrils flared. 'I'm well aware how we spent our wedding night, *yineka mou.*'

Tension swirled as they froze, examining one another as if they were preying cobras waiting for the first sign of weakness to strike.

'Nelios…'

'The neutral venue for our wedding was quite different from my company, where there are eyes and ears everywhere. I didn't think it prudent to crank the rumour mill this soon, especially around employees you might be managing in the near future. Do you?'

Put like that, it made sound sense. If she could only manage to put her sensibilities aside long enough to remember they'd signed an agreement to which they should be able to adhere with minimum fuss regardless of where they slept, since they were adults.

But… As she looked around, she couldn't ignore the distinct sense that the suite had been specially prepared with newlyweds in mind. Such as the console table brimming with an extra-large bouquet of her favourite blush-rose flowers. Or the champagne chilling in an ice-bucket next to the picturesque fireplace. Or the matching 'his and hers' silk dressing gowns and slippers draped enticingly near the bathroom doors.

The room screamed romance.

Her senses screamed for deliverance before she did something foolish. Angelos wriggling his irritation gave her the perfect out. He'd been an angel all through the two-hour flight and transfer from airport to hotel. And she was ready to shower him with praise for it. 'I need to feed Angelos and get him down for his nap.'

Nelios stared at her for a taut moment then, the corner

of his mouth twitching, he ran a hand over his son's head, a gesture he seemed to crave more and more, following it with a kiss. 'Fine. We will do the tour later.'

Watching him turn away, she was struck again by that tightening in her chest. She hated watching Nelios walk away from her. Which was absurd...wasn't it?

When he returned an hour later, it was with Capaldi in tow. Like Andreas at their wedding, he was now less rigid, even bordering on smiling.

'If you're comfortable leaving Angelos to sleep, Capaldi will stay with him,' Nelios said.

At her obvious surprise, Capaldi shrugged. 'I have three young ones of my own. A sleeping baby is a breeze.'

He might have been a near-stranger to her but he wasn't to Nelios. And, after seeing the closeness between Nelios, Andreas and Capaldi, Vayle found herself nodding her agreement. 'Thank you.'

Capaldi's near-smile grew more prominent. Why that made Nelios frown, she didn't get a chance to dwell on as his hand arrived at the small of her back and guided her towards the door. He conducted the tour himself, and it didn't take long to figure out that this particular hotel was run more like a sprawling, eye-wateringly exclusive private villa than the mainstream establishments under the Nelios Group umbrella. And that it was a well-oiled machine.

'I organised a late lunch for us.' He indicated the table for two laid with pristine silverware situated away from the others, with magnificent views of the pool and the glittering sea beyond.

It was gorgeous beyond words but that wasn't what made her heart race. It was the intimacy of it. It was how her entire being came *alive* with yearning at the thought of spending more time with Nelios—the very man she'd never expected to set eyes on again only a month ago. And the alarming thought that part of the reason she'd already decided against working in this hotel was because it wasn't where Nelios would be.

Because she wanted to be around him for Angelos's sake, she added hastily; nothing else.

'Vayle?' he pressed.

She moved towards the table, then paused. 'Is Capaldi...?'

'He'll let us know if we're needed.' His gaze dropped to her chest. 'Unless you wish to return for a different reason?' His voice pulsed with...something. Her cheeks flamed. She hadn't missed the breast pump near the changing table when she'd put Angelos to bed.

'No, I don't.' She cleared her throat and moved to the chair he pulled out for her. 'We haven't even discussed where we will live. Or does that not matter to you?' she asked once they'd sat down. It wasn't an accusation, just a means of gaining insight into this man whose child she'd birthed and whose name she now carried but whom she barely knew, except in the biblical sense. God, why had she thought about that right now?

His eyes lingered for too long on her heated cheeks before meeting hers. 'I'm able to work anywhere in the world, but I primarily base myself in Athens. And, no, England won't be my first choice,' he added with the hint of an edge that said it wasn't just the weather he objected to.

Vayle wanted to pry more into his meeting with Agnes but she held her tongue as the waiter approached and they ordered their food. 'So do you have men like Capaldi and Andreas littered all over the world to aid you in your empire-building?' she started as a means to fill in the watchful silence, but as she said the words she realised she genuinely wanted to know.

He handed the wine list back to the sommelier and fixed his eyes on her after she declined wine in favour of flavoured water. 'Not so many as you might think, but enough that I trust implicitly, yes.'

'And how did they earn your trust?'

His lips tightened and his gaze slanted over her shoulder to rest on the horizon. The tension building told her to leave the subject alone but that urgent throb in her chest said she couldn't. Or perhaps it was the echo of Agnes's words pushing her when she would've withdrawn at any other time.

She sucked in a steadying breath and plunged ahead. 'I know you've given me the broad strokes of what happened the day the foster carer came to your house,' she murmured.

His mouth twisted. 'A truth you thought was a lie, or at best a grand exaggeration, even after feeling a measure of rejection from your own father?' he asked a little bitterly.

Her heart squeezed, for him and for her. 'Will you tell me what happened?' she pushed softly.

His unyielding expression didn't lessen. 'What purpose would it serve?'

She toyed with the crystal glass dampening with condensation from the cold water. 'Beyond wanting a better understanding of the person I'll be parenting my son with? How about so I'm not caught flat-footed and pitied next time I have a conversation with one of your trusted friends? Or are you happy to let everyone wonder why we don't know the bare facts, never mind the most important things, about each other?'

Dark-coffee eyes examined her for a full minute, his upper body relaxed against his chair in a posture of ease she knew was false. 'And all this baring of oneself and risking losing one's appetite for what should be an exceptional meal—is it to be a one-sided thing?' he drawled idly. But the taut skin around his mouth told a different story.

Her insides fluttered with nerves she hadn't felt for a very long time. And, while she knew reliving everything would reawaken a slumbering anguish, bare her failures and vulnerability to his incisive probing, part of her was eager to rise above the wounds of her past rejection, to share this part of herself with him. After all, it wasn't her heart or the strain of fevered yearning she couldn't quite stem. So it was fine…right?

'I hate the dark because part of my father's illness included adverse reaction to bright lights during his manic episodes. Lights out in my house meant things…weren't going well. Even candles bothered him.'

Nelios went statue-still, exhaling harshly as thunder rolled across his face. 'So you were forced to live in the dark when he was unwell? How long were his episodes?'

Yeah, maybe he was right about the indigestion, but even as her stomach roiled she carried on. 'Sometimes hours. Sometimes days.'

His nostrils thinned as his fury grew. 'And you were forced to endure this all on your own?' he seethed.

'After my mother died, yes. Unfortunately, he only got worse with time…until…you know what happened.'

His eyes narrowed but a layer of tension eased out of him. 'So it took the bank to make him seek help?' he asked.

She laughed caustically. 'The hotel was the only thing he cared about after my mother died, so yes, the threat of having it taken away finally got through to him.'

'And then Agnes and Tolis entered the picture,' he concluded.

'Yes.'

'And you think, because they purportedly saved you, you should go around saving everyone else?' he asked, eyebrow raised, and then a hint of regret flashed across his face when she flinched. But he didn't take it back, nor did she want him to, because there was truth rooted in his statement.

She'd nearly fallen off the edge of a cliff of despair from her inability to help her father. To be worthy enough for him to want to seek help. To be worthy of him, full-stop.

She'd failed. But a Greek couple had shown her she wasn't entirely worthless. She'd been saved by the very people her husband despised. It didn't negate her love and gratitude for them, even if she realised they too might have been flawed.

'Maybe. But it may also be because, while we both know that no one can hurt you like family can, family can also heal you, even if that family isn't necessarily your blood.'

His mouth flattened but he didn't say a word. And then their food was brought out, shattering the brittle atmosphere. He examined his plate with clear dispassion that she now felt too.

And, when he sent her speaking look, she grimaced. 'I'm not going to apologise for the timing. You asked. I answered.'

To her surprise he nodded and, rising, he stepped behind her chair. 'I'll have it sent up to our room. Maybe by the time we return, our appetites will have forgiven us.'

She bit her tongue against asking him to reciprocate, since she'd bared her painful past, the helplessness and distress she'd felt.

'I used to think there was something wrong with me. Something that made him reject his own child. Then I wondered if it was a combination of unfortunate circumstances and a mishap in genetics on my father's part that caused all that to happen.'

'No.' His voice was firm from the fury boiling off him. 'Don't excuse his actions as a genetic flaw. You say he loved your mother and yet he picked on everyone else, you included. No one bothered to stand up to him or take steps quickly enough to protect you from him. He wised up when what really mattered to him was threatened—not his child, not your mother. A pile of bricks was what he cared about most. I'd say spare yourself the efforts of forgiving him, but I sense that you already have.'

There was a searching light in his eyes as he stopped in

the hallway and peered down at her, one she couldn't escape. She didn't even need to nod or respond audibly. He knew she'd, if not healed completely, at least come to terms with her father's rejection with help from Nelios's parents.

But the censure she had expected didn't arrive. Instead he continued to search her features, as if looking for answers *he* sought.

And then he placed his hand on the small of her back, triggering a deep pulse of yearning as they neared their suite.

CHAPTER EIGHT

CAPALDI ROSE WHEN they entered, clicking off the phone he had been scrolling through.

'Nothing to report,' he said.

'Efkharisto,' Nelios murmured.

The other man nodded and left after Vayle added her thanks. Nelios followed her to check in on their son. Content to see him resting peacefully, she returned to the living room, just as a knock came on the door. He answered and the same waiter who'd served them wheeled in their lunch.

By mutual agreement they ate in near silence. Then over coffee, he levelled a steady gaze at her. 'I'm sensing this hotel isn't the one?'

She shook her head. 'No.' She gave him her earlier assessment, then carried on with her thought. 'Besides, I don't intend to leave Angelos and go back to work for the better part of a year, so I have time.'

The gleam of approval shouldn't have warmed her the way it did. She didn't need it. And yet, when he lifted his cup to drain it, she followed the movement, then waited for him to speak.

'Then should we reschedule the tour and go to Apeiron tomorrow?'

As far as she could decipher, there was something in his voice close to a...yearning that made her heart leap. That made her readily agree, because she sensed it would give her more insight into this enigmatic man. 'Sure.'

With their meal finished, she rose, but when she walked past him he caught her wrist in a loose grip.

A little startled, both by the gesture and the way her blood rushed that little bit faster through her veins, she stumbled to a halt. 'Is there something...?'

'There was nothing wrong with you. He had a duty of care to you as his child and he failed. The flaws were all his. You know that, *ne*?' he said, a kind of deep insistence in his voice, as if he needed her to believe that.

Or maybe it was in her imagination. Because why would Nelios care what scars she'd been left with? Unless he just... cared about her?

Lightly buoyed by that thought, she bit her inner lip and blurted, 'If I do consider that, would you at least consider that your mother may have had her own flawed reasons, beyond what you believe, and hear her—?'

'Vayle...' His warning was taut. But he didn't release her or freeze her out the way he'd done in the past.

'Just keep an open mind, please?'

A lance of jagged emotion crossed his face, and something else that ludicrously resembled...*jealousy*? 'Why is this so important to you? Actually, don't answer that. I don't think I want to know.'

'Nelios, I...' She paused, wanting to reassure him but not quite knowing how. Or why helping him lift the burden of his past mattered so much to her.

Don't you know—really?

The tangle of shaking her head free of that thought and hoping he would release her culminated in a comical wobbling of her head. Because her yearning for the opposite, for him to pull her closer—preferably into his lap, to touch her, kiss her or do *more*—was chomping like ravenous pack of wolves through her. He accurately read her mind and used the connection to pull her closer until she could count the light flecks in his eyes, the fine hairs that would form his five o'clock shadow soon enough and breathe in his spicy scent. Her breath stalled in her lungs as she took another step closer.

'You done pushing?' he rasped.

'Maybe, maybe not,' she whispered.

She almost took it back when he released her. But when she didn't step away, on account of her feet refusing to move, he held her gaze for a long stretch, adjusted his body then placed his hands on her hips to pull her between his spread legs.

Her hands landed on his shoulders to steady herself. 'W-what are you doing?'

'Preventing you from scurrying off to hide in the darkness.'

'Why…do you care?'

'The elusive harmony we all search for?'

The charged little laugh escaped before she could stop it. 'I don't feel exactly harmonious when you touch me.' Vayle bit her lip as soon as the telling words escaped then, to counter it, rushed on with, 'And isn't sex forbidden in our agreement?'

'I'm doing nothing besides touching my wife. Touching is not forbidden. But let's revisit your other statement about how you feel when I touch you, *yineka mou*,' he drawled with the intense tone that made parts of her body grow heavy with wanting.

'You should forget that immediately,' she tried, knowing she shouldn't have made that unguarded admission.

The smile that curved his lips then—hot, genuine, *devastating*—made the heavy parts even heavier. 'No chance,' he replied.

She watched the brown of his eyes lighten, then heat up until they were a river of melted, dark caramel she wanted to dive headlong into. A rough sound rumbled from him and Vayle realised she was toying with the hair at his nape, and he…he was leaning into her touch.

That tiny evidence of her power was like a drug to her system. She stepped forward, her head falling forward and her breathing fractured to pieces as his grip tightened.

'Do it,' he invited. *Dared*.

And, with that expertly pushed button, Vayle kissed him while the sun dappled around them, the salt-and-flowers-laden air swirled sultrily, and an urgent whisper at the back of her mind demanded to know what the hell she was doing. A voice she actively ignored. Because she remembered this magic, yearned for a repeat.

And, as she'd secretly longed for him to do, when he took control and swept his tongue forcefully between her lips, seeking entry, she gave in with a lustful sigh and let him stoke the fire sweeping between her legs. At some point her fingers curled into his hair and gripped tightly, and she heard him grunt as she moaned her delight, dancing closer to the edge of that cliff spiked with dire warnings.

She was all for ignoring them when a sharp cry ripped them apart. For a stupefying moment, Vayle wondered if it was a wounded animal or a unique bird's cry. Then, eyes widening, she fully registered the sound. She started to step back. His fingers convulsed on her hips, staying her for another moment as he dragged his lips across hers one last time.

'I feel entirely ordinary now, as I believe I'm not the first man to be cock-blocked by his child.'

The wry amusement glinting in his eyes arrested her for several more seconds until Angelos cried out again, his indignation growing.

'I... We should...umm...'

'Go,' he said, adjusting himself with zero self-consciousness, while she writhed in a sea of volcanic need and surging alarm.

They'd been married for less than forty-eight hours of an agreed minimum of eighteen years. And here she was, fighting the strongest urge to have sex that she'd ever felt in her life. A little more than alarmed by her own surging emotions, she hurried away, gladly evolving into mummy mode.

She was just done feeding Angelos and about to change him when Nelios strolled into the nursery, crossing the room to her side.

'I will do it,' he said. He started to reach for the nappy. Then he paused, a twinge of embarrassment crossing his face. 'Show me how.'

Three tiny words. But oh, how powerfully they ploughed through her defences. So much so she could barely speak as she talked him through his first nappy change, with the standard warning about ensuring the correct positioning so he didn't get accidentally doused. And she spotted his supremely triumphant look from the corner of her eye when he deftly completed the task.

She remained a little shaken when she excused herself early evening, leaving Angelos with his father so she could video-call Agnes, relieved when the other woman smiled into the phone camera.

'I thought I might come to Athens soon.'

Vayle's heart leapt but, remembering Nelios's intransigence as recently as lunchtime, she winced. 'Can I suggest you speak to Nelios first before you come?'

'Speak to me about what?' came the query.

She spun round to see him entering the room, Angelos tucked snugly against his chest. The sight of father and son sent another pulse of yearning through her. Which was absurd, because this was exactly what she'd agreed to, so why the further yearning...

Her breath caught as realisation deepened. *She wanted more.*

'Vayle?'

'Agnes wants to come to Athens.'

She watched his gaze shift to the screen and saw myriad expressions flicker over his chiselled features before his eyes swung back to her and stayed for an eternity.

'I would like to spend some time alone with my wife and son. When I'm ready to talk, I'll send my plane for you. Is that agreeable?' he said with very little give.

Agnes's eyes widened before she nodded eagerly. 'Y-yes. *Efkharisto.*'

His gaze was still locked on Vayle. 'I was going to show Angelos the sunset. Join us when you're done.'

She was sure he hadn't meant it as an order, despite it sounding like that. Because they'd just enjoyed a pleasant, non-confrontational few hours, and an invitation to watch the sunset shouldn't be an order. She and Agnes spoke for a few more minutes, then she hung up.

The sun was showing off when she stepped out to join them on the terrace. Deep orange flirted with slashes of yellow and red, but she stopped for a moment to take in the more striking sight of her baby cradled in Nelios's arms.

'Come here or you'll miss it,' he drawled without turning round.

Edging closer, she glanced at his face. Tension from minutes ago remained but, when he looked at her, there was no censure in it. It was almost as if he'd already relegated it to the back of his mind until he needed to deal with it.

'Can I look forward to our time on Apeiron free from pressure about Agnes?' he rasped, his eyes returning to the horizon.

Deciding to take a leaf out of his book, she stepped up to the railing and smiled down at Angelos, who had zero interest in the sunset and raptly stared up at his father instead.

'Yes.'

Nelios nodded and, while he was too formidable to show his relief, she sensed it as he gazed down at his son and the corner of his mouth twitched. 'It seems beauty is lost on him. For now at least.'

'Hmm, maybe not entirely,' she murmured before she could stop herself.

His gaze transferred to her, his eyes glinting.

Then, wrapping his free arm around her to draw her closer, they stopped speaking entirely and simply basked in the moment.

Touching is not forbidden.

As glaring slippery slopes went, this one came with flashing neon lights so bright, they might have been seen from space. But could she push the warning away long enough to rationalise it or remember just why not touching Nelios was the safest option? Because *he* seemed to have zero qualms about touching her after their heated kiss in the hotel room.

He touched her back as he guided her onto the plane bright and early the next morning. And as he offered her a segment of the juicy clementine she'd thought he was peeling for himself right until he held it out to her, his thumb brushing her lower lip when she accepted, heart lurching wildly.

And then there was Angelos's feeding times. Repeatedly Nelios asked if she minded him staying. She always said no, she didn't. She wasn't ashamed of breastfeeding her son in public or wherever his need demanded, so it wasn't what caused the relentless turbulence inside her. It was the possessive hunger in Nelios's eyes, the eagerness to learn everything he could about his son. To record everything, given he'd missed the three months since Angelos was born.

It was as if she'd been given the floor to wax lyrical about her favourite subject on earth to an ardent audience of one. If this was a ploy on his part to gain some sort of leverage in this marriage, then she had to applaud him. He was succeeding hand over fist.

And that was even before the small plane they'd boarded from Italy touched down on a narrow strip of runway on a jewelled island in the middle of the Aegean.

Between what she saw on the internet, her brief jaunt as a stowaway-turned-tourist in Buenos Aires and living in London, one of most cosmopolitan cities on the planet, Vayle thought she couldn't be stunned speechless by anywhere.

She was now. Apeiron was aptly named for its shape that followed an almost perfect infinity sign. The villa followed the outer eastward curve that faced a rolling vista of green bordering white sandy beaches to the pinched middle of the island. The westward curve was much craggier, full of trees, orchards, shallow and steep brown hills and even a tiny church poised on top of a gentle promontory, alongside smaller clusters of villas and a smattering of goats and sheep. It was a place she could see Angelos exploring to his heart's content when he was older.

Altogether, it was less than a kilometre across at its furthest point, but she felt as though it had everything a family needed. A proper family, not one cobbled together by a dozen pieces of paper, signed and witnessed by sharply suited men in a hotel room. That squeeze in her chest signalling the ever-deepening yearning arrived and stayed all through the tour, Nelios escorting them to the fully decked-out nursery that held everything a treasured baby boy would need.

'Is this all right?' Nelios asked, his rapt gaze flicking between his son and her.

Her heart full, Vayle nodded. 'More than. Thank you.' And, if there was the shadow of a crumb of envy that yearned for some of that attention, well, she kept that disgraceful notion to herself.

She spun away to eye the two doors leading off opposite sides of the nursery.

'They're adjoining suites. Mine is through there. And this is yours. We can both check on Angelos when needed.'

Walking forward as he spoke, he threw open the doors leading to her suite...and stunned her all over again. There was a probability that one day she might get blasé about the luxury Nelios seemed to take in his stride. Today wasn't that day.

But you have nearly two decades to get used to it. Her heart didn't jump at the thought. But that squeezing replayed, harder, more insistent than before.

'We share a common terrace,' he went on, watching her with an edgy ferocity, as if it was vitally important to him that he interpret what she felt. Spotting a snazzy baby's rocking chair similar to one they'd used before placed under a large sun umbrella complete with a light blanket, Vayle placed a drowsy Angelos in it and strapped him in. His eyes were drooping even before she turned away and walked to the edge of the terrace where Nelios was staring at the horizon. While the atmosphere was a little charged—and she suspected that, for as long as they were in close proximity, that chemistry they'd both acknowledged would create its own ecosystem—there was a lack of prowling restlessness about it.

It was as if Nelios was at peace here. 'You didn't just name this place for its shape, did you?'

He paused for a second, then sent her a tight smile. 'I had an awakening of sorts here. The previous owner, who was forced to leave for health reasons, didn't want to sell to me at first. Not until I'd given him a vision of what my intentions were for his pride and joy.'

'I'm guessing he didn't want it turned into a hedonistic Club Med destination for the rich?'

His mouth quirked. 'Exactly so. And he wasn't impressed with the prospect of another Nelios hotel, no matter how selective the clientele, or how sympathetic to the environment I intended to be.'

'What was the awakening?'

'That only my life was finite. That what I left behind could be truly infinite.' His gaze drifted to his sleeping son. 'I saw it as leaving a legacy without having actual offspring, but now I'm seeing it's even better with.'

'And that's all it took to sway him?'

He shook his head and a guarded look descended over his face. 'No. I told him that, for every year I owned his island, I would fund a necessary project somewhere in the world.'

Her eyes widened. 'Really?'

'*Ne.*' His gaze paused in the middle distance for an age before he glanced at her. 'That morning after our night in Buenos Aires, I left because I had to oversee one of those projects.' His shoulder twitched. 'Granted, I didn't have to leave that early, but I still would've left.'

She filed away the confession and pushed to satisfy her curiosity. 'What was the project?'

'Five hundred homes for families who need to relocate from the slums. Another five hundred for struggling families with young children who are at risk of being made homeless—or worse.'

Families, children, his possessive claiming of Angelos: she didn't need a crystal ball to show her that, while Nelios was a wildly successful tycoon, there was an equally resolute part of him that was obsessed with righting the wrongs done to him at whatever level he could achieve. He couldn't see that, in obsessing over the past, he was adversely affecting his present...and his future too.

Knowing she risked shattering the relative peace and tranquillity, she licked her lips and pushed ahead anyway. 'You still owe me a re-telling of your story.'

He stiffened and his jaw worked for a few tense seconds.

But the furious rejection never arrived. He remained tense but slowly his jaw unclenched, as did the bunched fists resting on the stone balustrade.

After a minute of his gaze roving the landscape, he finally spoke. 'I told you the foster carer judged me as a problem child on that first day she visited?'

Her nod was jerky, her emotions churning with distress for him. 'Yes.'

He shrugged. 'In the first month alone, I ended up being moved to three different foster homes, each one progressively worse than the last.'

Her heart squeezed tighter when he exhaled harshly.

'In the third month, I was placed with carers who believed the harsher the corporal punishment they doled out, the better.' Naked fury washed over his face and she knew he was reliving the horrendous memory. 'It didn't matter how young or old the children were. They all received the same treatment—a fist or a belt for the smallest infraction.'

'God.'

His head jerked down, his mouth thinning. 'I grew tired of it very quickly. Especially when it became clear they weren't beating us just to be corrective but to merely suppress us because they could. It was base cruelty for the sake of it, because they could get away with and it and be rewarded with a pay cheque at the end of the month. So I decided to do something about it.'

Her eyes widened. 'What did you do?'

'My first instinct was just to leave. I figured the streets would be far better than what I was enduring.' The harsh twist of his mouth suggested he'd discovered differently. 'But I couldn't leave the other children under those conditions, especially the three younger ones.'

Her little finger bumped his and she realised she'd moved closer without conscious thought. He glanced down at where they touched for a long moment before his gaze returned to the horizon.

'By a stroke of fate, luck or whatever you wish to call it, the decision was taken out of my hands. A lit cigarette left untended by a drunk foster mother literally ignited the start I wanted.'

'Your foster home went up in flames?'

He nodded. 'Down to the last cinder. I got the kids out and waited until the fire brigade and ambulance arrived to take care of them. Then I put my plan in place and took my chances on the streets.'

If her chest had been tight before, it barely let her breathe now. Tears stung the back of her eyes. 'That wasn't a breeze, though, was it?' she murmured.

'Far from it. And especially not when I discovered I wasn't alone.'

She blinked. 'What?'

His mouth twitched. 'Turns out another kid had the same idea.'

'Andreas?' she guessed.

He shook his head. 'Capaldi. He'd followed me. So I was a thirteen-year-old in charge of a ten-year-old on the streets of Athens.'

Her heart leapt into her throat. She glanced back at her peacefully sleeping son, dying inside at the horror of imagining him ten years from now suffering what Capaldi had. And when her hand moved to cover his it was a conscious effort of empathy and encouragement. 'How did you manage to...survive?'

'By the skin of our teeth,' he rasped. 'And sometimes with borrowed fortitude.'

'Is that...when you met Andreas?'

He jerked out a nod. 'On the very night when I believed my luck had run out. We were cornered in an alley with a gang who believed we were trespassing on their territory. Andreas happened to be hiding in the same alley. And he, it turned out, had more experience with gang warfare than I did.' He didn't elaborate and she didn't ask. He'd previously told her that Andreas's story was his to tell if he wished, but she got the awful gist of it.

They remained in sombre silence for several minutes until she drew in a shaky breath. 'What you said to me before, about my father's flaws not being mine... You know that applies to you too, right?'

The corners of his mouth turned down but he remained in stoic, rigid silence. It felt essential that she try to get through to him. To break through the fortress of bitterness he'd built around himself.

'Look around you, Nelios. See how far you've come. You've risen above the worst things thrown at you and triumphed. Don't you think it's time to let that little boy go?'

His smile was humourless. He didn't follow her gaze, didn't take in the evidence of all he'd achieved. If anything his face grew more sombre, more resolute. 'That's where you're wrong. I don't intend to ever let that little boy go. He's the motivation that fuels me to remember what human beings are really capable of. How utterly despicable they can be.'

'But keeping such a tight grip on the past means you can't reach for a better future. Don't you see?' Again, the sense of urgency throbbing within her said she was pushing not just for him but for herself and Angelos too.

He glanced down at her, the blind fury in his eyes telling her he didn't hear; that he was locked in that very same past. Several seconds passed before he controlled it. 'Do you know, I kept track of those last foster parents? And, the second they found themselves a new hovel, they tried to round up the kids they'd endangered again. I made sure they never fostered again.'

'How?'

His smile was filled with satisfied vengeance. 'Turns out if you bombard a certain helpline with stories of abuse, even the laziest social worker eventually gets off their ass to do something.'

'This just proves my point. You've done so much for others. Don't you owe it to yourself to take that next step and put your past to rest?'

His jaw clenched tight in resolute mutiny.

She sighed. 'Then you'll never leave that alley. Never truly find peace. Is that what you really want?'

He snapped his gaze from hers and returned it to the glittering sea. 'What I want is answers. And so I guess I should thank you for facilitating that.'

'Once Agnes gives you all the answers you need? Then what?'

Another macabre smile etched his face for a single moment before it was gone. 'Then I'll use it as fuel to ensure I'm by far a better parent than they ever were. Then I will be vindicated for cutting them out of my life. I moved on a long time ago, Vayle. This will just confirm I was right to do so. But moving on doesn't mean the broken parts of me will eventually be fixed. It's too late for that. Sorry to burst your little bubble, but that's never going to happen.'

Shock rocked through her, keeping her rooted to the spot as he turned and walked away. Far from believing she was breaking through to him, it seemed Nelios didn't intend to budge an iota, despite his clear pain. So, while her every instinct screamed at her to follow him, to keep battering at the fortress, her head overruled it. Nelios was deeply entrenched in his ways and beliefs. One conversation wasn't going to overcome that.

If she had the time and patience, and it seemed she had eighteen years of it, then what was the hurry?

She turned from the blissful view and padded over to pick up her son. Hugging him close, smelling his baby scent, she told herself that, no, there was no hurry, even if that clock inside her whispered that time might not be the tool she needed in this endeavour.

That she might need...something else.

Something *riskier*.

If Nelios had expected an unhappy wife at the dinner table when he walked into his dining room after hours of steaming away in his study with an unhealthy amount of righteous indignation, he was mistaken. Pleasantly mistaken—perhaps that even unsettled him.

There was no hint in her manner that him walking away from her, after practically criticising her for bothering to find the silver lining in the cloud of his past trauma, had upset her. He knew his intractability hadn't sat well with her if the dull light in her eyes had been any indication.

He nearly tripped over his own feet when she looked up... and smiled. Not the blindingly fake one some women used to express their rabid glee to be in his presence. Not the batting-eyelashes one that said a request for a favour lurked just beneath the surface. It was heart stopping, groin stirring—not that he needed help for that to happen. Not when she looked more breathtaking each time he saw her.

And with that smile... He sucked in a slow, control-restoring breath, which failed miserably.

She wore a white halter-neck dress threaded with gold that seemed to reflect off her smooth skin. Her hair was down in gorgeous waves around her shoulders and those hoop earrings that had driven him insane in Buenos Aires were on show once more. Her perfume, floral and exquisite, called to him and it felt positively sinful not to bend and place a kiss on her cheek. Or on that gentle slope of her shoulder. So that was exactly what he did.

'If it's not against your infernal rules, can I say how beautiful you look?' he said when he lifted his head.

Her smile remained in place but a breathless quality to her breathing surged pleasure through him, increasing the pressure in his groin.

Her teeth toyed with her lower lip and she tucked a strand of hair over her ear before shrugging. 'I'll allow it.'

It was absurd that something eased inside him then, as if he'd been on tenterhooks, when he was his own man and had earned the right not to need to placate anyone. *Especially* when he was in the right. *'Efkharisto,'* he drawled as he sat down and shook out his napkin.

Equally disturbing—and the reason he'd spent hours staring into space when he was supposed to have been working—was that the decades-old weight he'd carried seemed somehow…lighter. A realisation that logic insisted had something to do with unburdening himself to Vayle.

But, now they were back on an even keel, he didn't need to think about it any more. They were done with the quid pro quo of trauma-sharing. Now they could move onto better things.

She asked about his other humanitarian projects and he gladly told her about the one-thousand-strong children's charity in Panama, the bird sanctuary in Lithuania and the children's education funds in a dozen countries. And, dearest to his heart, the camps for orphans and street kids right here in Greece, ably managed by Capaldi's wife.

'I'm not sure why I'm so stunned he's married with kids. He seems so…' Vayle's voice trailed off.

'Fearsome?' he offered with a hint of a smile—another thing he was doing more and more around her. 'It's a prerequisite for working for me.'

She rolled her eyes as she smiled and, *thee mou*, he wanted to kiss that mouth more than he wanted his next breath.

Which made the words that came out of his mouth as they were enjoying coffee and dessert quite absurd. Because even he knew he was skirting the volcanic rim of temptation. 'We'll take the boat out tomorrow—explore the island some more, *ne*?'

She nodded, and her hair slid over her skin in a silken curtain he wanted to run through his fingers so badly, he had to curl them around his coffee cup to stall the impulse.

'Sounds good.'

And so their surprisingly delightful evening went, followed by a nightcap in the salon and half an hour of television, until a wide yawn from her had him surging to his feet, his hand held out.

She blinked, a little warily, perhaps also fighting off the charged mood that hovered far too close. But she rose, put her hand in his and let him walk her to their suite door.

Together they checked on their son then, in tones echoing the unnerving yearning he didn't want to voice, he wished her *kalinikta*. He watched her blink again before nodding, then she disappeared behind her own doors.

Leaving him standing there—a little shaken, a lot stunned. Because it seemed, in just under seventy-two hours, his wife had slid so effectively under his skin, and he would be so very hard pressed ever to remove her.

And he wasn't entirely sure he wanted to.

CHAPTER NINE

'I THINK YOU either need a dictionary or a pair of prescription glasses. Because that is definitely not a boat.'

Vayle looked from the massive vessel growing bigger as they neared it to the mildly amused man sitting at the helm of the tender. Nelios shrugged. The heart that'd expanded then wedged itself hard against her ribcage when he'd knocked on her door after breakfast in a pair of designer shorts and a white T-shirt raced harder as her gaze moved over him.

Surprisingly, she'd gone to bed with a smile on her face and had slept sounder than she had in years, rising to feed Angelos before topping off her sleep and waking up delightfully refreshed.

'It's a floating device that suits our purposes for the day.'

She snorted. 'A floating device is a dinghy. This is a...a...' She shook her head, unable to locate an accurate descriptive for the immense super-yacht in front of them.

It was gorgeous, granted, as was everything Nelios owned. And it resembled a small floating city. As they rounded it, she caught glimpses of jet skis, swimming pools, sun-lounging decks and even a helipad—all the bells and whistles a billionaire could want.

'Are you finally rendered speechless, *yineka mou*?'

My wife. This particular endearment secretly thrilled her. As did the careful way he lifted Angelos's portable cradle, then turned to hold his hand out to her to help her off the launch. It didn't matter that half a dozen staff and crew waited to assist them. It made Vayle feel special. Which made the yearning deepen into a wish for...more.

She bit her lip as she followed him on board the super-yacht, then up a flight of stairs onto the first of many sun-splashed decks. They had a long day ahead of them. And the little scheme she'd concocted bubbled all sorts of warnings at the back of her head as the hours passed.

Nelios slanted her increasingly frequent looks as they swam, lunched and played with Angelos, telling her she wasn't hiding her nerves very well.

'What's going on in that mind of yours?' he drawled after returning from putting Angelos down for his afternoon nap. 'You've been jumpier than a hot bean in the last hour.'

He handed her a fresh glass of fruit punch and helped himself to mineral water. When he raised the sunscreen bottle, she swallowed and nodded, watching him walk in a loose-limbed, drop-dead hot prowl towards where she stood against the railing.

They were anchored just off their private beach, on the widest deck of the super-yacht, surrounded by loungers, a bar and a pool for when it got too hot and they wanted a dip. They'd circled Apeiron earlier and he'd pointed out the various places for diving, snorkelling and which beach was the best for all-day sun.

She bit her lip, wondering how best to phrase her crazy idea. In the end, it came tumbling out. 'I want to amend our rule. Not break it entirely, just...tweak it a little.'

He stilled behind her, the hand with which he'd been about to apply the lotion hovering an inch from her shoulder. Staring up at him, Vayle couldn't tell how he felt about that, his face a carefully neutral mask.

'In what way, specifically?' he intoned then, low and deep. His voice had taken on that timbre ever since she'd dropped her white beach kaftan to reveal the burnished orange bikini she wore underneath. The pre-wedding spa pampering her wedding coordinator had insisted on, and the pockets of sunshine she'd enjoyed since Italy, had added a warm glow to her skin. And her secret thrill had increased after seeing Nelios couldn't take his eyes off her.

When both hands slid down the slopes of her neck to circle lotion into her shoulders, it made it easier for her to say a little more vehemently than she'd intended, 'I don't want to completely change the "no sex" part.' An assertion that didn't go unnoticed when his eyes narrowed and the hands gliding down her spine paused just above her bottom before reversing their journey up her spine.

'Are you attempting to convince me you didn't enjoy sex with me?' he asked silkily, with more than a hint of mocking disbelief laced in there.

'Not at all,' she hurried to say, the effect of his hands on her making her voice husky and many parts of her body tingle and unfurl and dampen. 'On the contrary, I enjoyed it a little too much. Which is why I'm still advocating abstaining, but with a small amendment.'

'That doesn't make any sense, *agapiméni*,' he stated indolently.

'Does it not? I'm told liquid morphine and sky-diving are some of the best highs ever to grace this earth. But do you see me hankering after either of them?'

His breath seemed to stall. Then he caught her elbow and turned her round so he could start on her arms. Those done, he dropped to a crouch in front of her and began on her legs.

And once he had one foot propped on his knee, applying sunscreen in slow, spine-melting strokes, he glanced up at her with hooded eyes. 'Are you saying you fear an addiction to me, *glikia mou*?'

Well...she'd stepped right into that one, hadn't she? She

tried to shrug her way out of it. 'An addiction to the act—not you. There's a difference.'

His nostrils flared. 'I fail to see how there is. And you should think carefully before you suggest sex with another man will be the same as with me. Because, for one thing, you will never get the chance to find out.'

Since the very thought of it made her skin crawl, and she didn't see the point in aggravating him any more, she waved him away. 'My point is, you should be pleased I'm troubleshooting this problem before it gets us both in trouble.'

'Speak for yourself. I'm extremely adept at self-control.'

That he took vast pleasure in informing her of that, riled her. It made her immediately want to put that titanium control to the test, even if it was to teach him a lesson.

Before she could talk herself out of it, she was unhooking the clasp of her bikini top. Letting it loosen, she pulled it off and tossed it away.

He stiffened, his nostrils flaring wide before pinching in a sharply drawn breath. 'Vayle, what the hell are you doing?' His voice was oiled gravel, grinding desire into her bloodstream.

'What does it look like? I'm testing your famous control, of course.' Last night she'd convinced herself making Nelios snap was the best way to kick down if not all of his guard, at least some of it. Enough so she could push through to him, make him see past what he thought was broken to consider a different perspective. One that included him...*them*...having a semblance of a pain-free life. One in which she wouldn't be so terrified to admit what her heart was telling her—that she felt more for him than was anywhere near wise, even if she wasn't going to back away from that revelation. Yet—unless she knew all hope was gone.

She'd taken a chance once and opened her heart to affection when she could've remained mired in bitterness from her father's rejection. And she'd found a family who'd cared for her. Maybe lightning would strike twice. If she was brave enough to let it?

His head whipped about, even though his staff knew better than to interrupt them. When he was satisfied there were no prying eyes, his scorching gaze returned to her. His laziness evaporated as he slowly surged from his crouch, his eyes fixed squarely on her chest as he tossed the sunscreen lotion aside and braced his hands on either side of her, caging her in.

'And how do you mean to do that?' he rasped.

Good question. Now she was half-naked and burning with the inferno in his eyes, she seriously questioned what she was doing. But the thought of backing down, of scooping up her top and retreating, rubbed her the wrong way.

So she did the opposite. She stepped forward, cocked her hip and revelled in the rapt zeal in his eyes when he followed the movement. 'To see which one of us breaks first, without the final act.'

Oh, God. Really? Was she insane?

'Are you insane?' he echoed.

She thought she must be, because his query only spurred her on. 'If you don't want this, just call uncle.'

'Absolutely not.'

She licked her lips, stifling a moan when his dark eyes hungrily followed her tongue. 'Well, then…'

'Are there rules to this dangerous game you're playing or are you making it up on the fly?'

Her eyes dropped to the T-shirt stretching across his chiselled chest. 'You're allowed to take one item of clothing off too.'

The words were barely out of his mouth before he ripped the shirt over his head and tossed it away, leaving her with a view that rivalled what lay beyond the yacht. A view that made her nipples bud painfully; made his sensual lips curve with pure vainglory.

'What next, *yineka mou*?' Gravel had turned to a silken web he was using to entice and enthral. And when he sprawled back to his original position, supremely confident he had regained the upper hand, she fought not to grit her teeth. Or call uncle herself.

'One kiss—no hands. Who breaks or retreats first loses.'

An unholy light gleamed in his eyes for a distressing stretch, during which she questioned her judgement once again and almost prayed he would say *hell, no* and back out.

But, damn it, on top of this insanity cake she'd baked for herself now sat the exquisite promise of the cherry of kissing Nelios once more. An act she hadn't quite allowed herself to admit she'd missed desperately until this second.

So when he slowly walked back without taking his eyes off her, sat down on the nearest sofa and patted his thighs with two hard slaps of invitation, she stopped herself from the visibly vulnerable act of swallowing. She hastened to close the distance, dropped a knee on either side of his thighs, then grasped the top of the seat. The small win of seeing him swallow instead didn't last very long when he leaned forward immediately and brought his mouth *dangerously* close to hers, leaving it right there...tantalisingly just out of reach.

'If you want me, come and get me,' he taunted, rough and undaunted.

She withstood the bait...barely. But she countered by arching her back, dragging her naked chest over his and letting him feel the warm peaks of her nipples.

His hands clenched at his side. 'Fuck,' he muttered under his breath.

She continued the figure-eight roll, almost losing her rhythm when she felt the power of his arousal between her legs—a little salty, a little musky but all rampant, raw man.

She nibbled along his jaw to his ear, then caught his lobe between her teeth, smiling when a shudder coursed through him. But then the fine hairs on his chest whispered across her nipples and she was shuddering and jerking in his lap. Vayle felt her core dampen and prayed he would mistake it for being the result of her dip in the ocean.

But then he inhaled greedily. 'You smell incredible, *eros mou*,' he praised gutturally.

She squeezed her eyes shut, just to gather her fraying composure. 'Thank you.'

Then she sealed her mouth to his, letting free the moan trapped inside her for an eternity. She'd barely tasted him before he took control, swiping her mouth open with his tongue and diving in to tangle and conquer hers. Need drove her to gyrate on top of him, dragging her nipples across his chest to alleviate their ache. But all it did was build and build the tension and scream at her to quench her thirst. Their kiss turned increasingly frenzied, Nelios biting, laving, coaxing then cursing when it didn't feel like enough; when every second poured further fuel on the fire.

The urge to throw in the towel arrived like a lightning strike. Before she could act on it, firm hands grasped her waist and Nelios set her aside with jerky movements. He shot to his feet, his fingers ploughing through his hair. When his hands dropped, they clenched and unclenched, then he stalked over to the drinks cabinet and poured a shot of cognac as she hurriedly tugged on her bikini top.

After he downed the drink, he spun round. 'Enough. We will call it a draw. This time.'

Vayle shook her head, face flaming and trembling with unsatisfied need. 'There won't be a next time. I...shouldn't have done that. It was reckless.'

His eyes darkened. 'Or it simply proved that you shouldn't have implemented that no-sex clause and I certainly shouldn't have accepted it. Not when our chemistry is this volatile. It'll only lead to other incidents like this, inevitably.'

Hot denial rose, then died on the tip of her tongue. Because even now the brutal withdrawal her body was going through went beyond shaming her. It laid bare the truth he'd stated. They were weak when it came to one another. Games, challenges and denials would get them nowhere. Looking to shatter his control and meeting resistance while laying herself bare would only lead to turmoil.

He exhaled harshly and her gaze latched onto him, a slave to her need. The imprint of his erection made her stifle a moan.

'Nelios...'

'I don't know about you, but I need a cold shower—right now. The ball remains in your court. But know that, if you find your way to my bed, this time I will not be setting you free any time soon.'

With that mike drop, he walked off, his long strides carrying him away before she'd drawn the shuddering breath which did zip to calm her.

She managed, barely, to throttle her need until it was a manageable bubble lodged deep inside her for the rest of the day.

Whether Nelios's control was back in place, she couldn't quite tell. She felt his heated gaze often, but every time she glanced his way his expression was either shuttered or fixed on their son. Conversation flowed calmly during dinner and on their return home, but when they said goodnight she wondered, *feared*, if she'd only made things worse.

It was a relief to be awakened by Angelos for his nighttime feed. But she'd only just placed him on her breast when the door to Nelios's bedroom opened and he walked out.

'Oh, you're up. There's no need for you to be... I mean, I'm okay with...' She stumbled to a halt, hiding a grimace.

He smiled a crooked smile, then slotted the snazzy little baby monitor into his pocket. The act pulled down his silk pyjama bottoms a little, displaying the chiselled line of muscle that framed his pelvis so gloriously.

Feeling that bubble expand, Vayle dragged her gaze away, concentrating on Angelos, who was already being lulled back into a milk coma. When they'd first arrived here and she'd seen his nursery, she'd wondered why there were two arm chairs. Watching Nelios sink into one with every intention of sticking around, she got it.

He shrugged one bare, deliciously muscled shoulder. 'You have to be up, for obvious reasons. But there's no reason to do it alone.'

There was a time when she'd called this man a monster. No longer. With each considerate act, he was burrowing into her vulnerable places.

And she felt inclined to...let him. Especially when he continued to watch her with that hungry fascination she suspected he wasn't fully aware was on display.

He stayed until Angelos had fallen asleep again. Stayed at her side as she placed him in his cot and drew his blanket over him. Stayed to drop a kiss on his son's head. Then, with a heavy-lidded look, he bade her goodnight and retreated as silently as he'd arrived.

Leaving her staring at his closed door, her heart racing madly.

She felt inclined to...let him.

It might have been seconds, or an hour. But, with a compulsion she couldn't deny, Vayle found herself standing before his door, her hand shaking as she reached for the handle that might not be locked against her after all. She squeezed her eyes shut for a second, then opened them. She turned the handle and nudged open the door open.

He wasn't asleep but sitting up in bed, as she'd half-suspected he would be. His gaze founds hers immediately, as if he'd been waiting for her.

'Come to test my peace of mind once more, to drive me out of it, or is it something else?'

She couldn't speak past her overpowering need so she shook her head.

'You'll need to speak the words, Vayle. So there's no equivocation or misunderstanding.'

Her mouth dried. She couldn't very well say she wanted to reach his heart through sex; that would be too exposing. And being here, right now, felt exposing enough. 'I...' She paused, her heart hammering loud enough to fill her ears with a thunderous roar. 'I need you.' That would have to be enough, she adjudged.

And if that was a glint of disappointment in his eyes, he hid it well by veiling them with his long lashes, tossing back his sheets and ordering her to, 'Come here, *yineka mou*.'

She went. Hell, she *stumbled*. He caught her easily, expertly, and before she could draw another breath flipped her beneath him, pinning her to the bed with his powerful body. Staring down at her with a predatory gaze.

'You agree that attempting to drive us both to the brink of insanity, only to withdraw, was an exercise that was always going to fail, yes?'

Her nails bit into his shoulders in protest and in irritation that, yet again, he'd been right. 'Yes! Fine, it was a ridiculous thing to do. Are you happy now?'

'Not yet. But I'm getting there. Now, spread your legs for your husband. Let me taste you, *omorfi mou*.'

He devoured her with a confidence-stroking hunger that bordered on frightening, it was so heady. And she let her delight show freely, vocalising, touching and stroking with abandon.

'Thee mou,' he muttered. 'You really throw yourself into your passions, don't you?'

'Are you complaining?'

'Absolutely not.' He took her hand and dragged it to his groin, his eyes blazing into hers as he wrapped both sets of their fingers around his sizeable girth. 'Does this feel like a complaint to you, *eros mou*?'

'N-no.'

He smiled, looking a little pained, infinitely hot. Until she stroked him. Then a different look etched his face. 'Fuck!'

'Yes. Please. I want you.'

Her fervent whisper transformed him. Transported him to a higher plane. Between one heartbeat and the next, he'd tugged on a condom and her flimsy lace and silk was a useless tangle on the floor.

'I will take it slow next time. Worship you as you deserve. But you will admit you've driven me to the brink, wife?'

'Yes, worship later. Need you…now.'

Her grasping hands reached for him, and she loved it when he leaned down over her, then moved her onto her side. Slotting in behind her, he pulled her hip into his, holding her steady with one hand.

With the other speared into her hair, eyes as rich and dark as the cosmos at night, Nelios surged into her. His groan synced with her scream, a private, decadent symphony of lust and pleasure never before experienced by her. And, from the words that fell from his lips, she would wager a great deal that it was unique for him too.

'Vayle… Vayle… You feel…so good.'

'Don't stop. Please don't stop,' she begged hoarsely, her fingers scrambling back to clutch him any way she could, ensnare him in this divine space with her.

'Impossible,' he growled, his voice barely coherent.

When the hand on her hip moved to circle her waist to trap

her harder against him, she felt her throat clog, tears springing to sting her eyes. She was thankful for the former, because it prevented her from pleading for him never to let her go. To want her beyond what a piece of paper decreed. Even beyond what this insane chemistry had thrust upon them.

Instead, she squeezed her eyes shut and surrendered to the majesty of making love with Nelios. She didn't even care when he wrecked her by keeping her poised on the edge of climax for an eternity before, with a guttural command to, 'Open your eyes for me, *eros mou*. Show me your desire,' he kept her waiting for another sublime minute before diving with her off the cliff into a sea of pleasure so pure, she knew in her soul it was changing her for ever.

Realigning her very existence in ways she might never recover from.

The days that followed blurred into a golden haze, each moment so exquisitely saturated with bliss it bordered on the surreal. Their impromptu honeymoon unfolded like a fantasy spun from silk and starlight, each hour with Nelios a heady mix of seduction and serenity that lodged itself deep beneath her skin.

He made her laugh—deep, unguarded laughter that burst free before she could stop it—then kissed her until the world fell away, until fear and caution melted like sugar on her tongue. Until she couldn't remember what she'd ever needed protecting from.

He was present at each feed of Angelos. And in the mornings, she woke tangled in heat, scent and masculine strength, his arm heavy across her waist, his breath a whisper against her nape. His touch—possessive even in sleep—anchoring her in a reality that felt too good to be true.

And that was the danger, wasn't it? Because, in those precious moments between night and day, when dreams lingered and reality hadn't yet sharpened its claws, she let herself imagine that this was real. That this wasn't just chemistry or obligation dressed in silk sheets and sun-drenched kisses. That maybe—just maybe—he felt it too.

But always, without fail, reality slid in on quiet feet. In the way his gaze sometimes drifted, shadowed and unreadable. In the way his silences occasionally stretched too long, heavy with words he refused to say, more often than not after her conversations with Agnes. But she told herself that, as much as it hurt to watch him retreat to that fortress with no drawbridge, she wasn't about to neglect her contact with Agnes to please him.

Unfortunately, the tension was what kept her heart in limbo. The clause they'd so spectacularly broken had been her last defence, the final line between falling and freefall. And she'd leapt, willingly, into his arms.

Yet, as the blissful weeks turned into a month, then closer to two, it was less a soaring through ecstasy and more like plummeting straight towards heartbreak.

Because, as soul-searing as it was, this had never just been about sex—not for her. It was *him*. The man who held her at night as if she was the only thing tethering him to the earth. The man whose past stood between them like the Great Wall.

So, even as they danced barefoot on moon-washed sands, she held part of herself back. She clung to hope desperately, even as it slipped through her fingers.

Because fairy tales weren't meant to last.

Were they?

CHAPTER TEN

NELIOS SAT ON the beach, arms resting on his knees, watching the sun rise and the waves crash from the sea he'd just swum in.

For a man neck-deep in the most pleasurable weeks of his life, his gut churned far too agitatedly for his liking. It was what had driven him from his bed when he should be wrapped around his wife.

But... The feeling of time running out wouldn't leave him.

In all the years he'd thought of the parents who'd abandoned him, he'd never been this riled up *emotionally*. Sure, there'd been much fury and bitterness, as was his right. But it'd been ruthlessly overlaid with icy, implacable resolve. And, once he'd divorced himself from the past and got down to the very real business of surviving, he'd locked any superfluous emotions away.

Yes, they'd been ruffled when he'd come face-to-face with his mother and tangled with Vayle and her last year. But control had soon reasserted itself, as it so often did, when he'd won and then triumphantly walked away.

He didn't feel so much in control now. The growing emotions he didn't really want to label as nerves and...*panic*... but couldn't see any other way to describe them, tunnelled a different path through him.

The past weeks had been blissful—another term that greatly alarmed him, but admittedly in a good way. Vayle had come to him and they'd obliterated that terrible clause that would've made them both suffer unnecessarily. And, boy, had they taken advantage of it since then.

He'd enjoyed his wife anywhere and everywhere all over Apeiron, delighting in showing her different sexual experiences that left a deep flush on her cheeks and stars in her eyes.

As for him... Having been intent on eradicating any emotional fallout from the women he'd tangled with in the past, he'd never slept with the same woman for this long before. It was...novel, pleasurable. Satisfying, even.

He knew enough to know he didn't want to upset that particular apple cart. He didn't want Vayle upset. But also enough to know a giant spanner was heading into what had become a smooth operation.

You know the root cause of this situation—how to fix it.

He shifted and rolled onto his feet, impatient with the persistent voice. Then with the far too beautiful view that taunted him with its perfection, highlighting that his life was far from perfect.

Vayle's admonishments about the consequences of living in the past rang in his ears. His thoughts were so busy crowding each other, he didn't realise he'd walked all the way to his suite until she turned from viewing the sunrise on their terrace.

'Hey, you were gone when I woke up. Are you okay?' she murmured softly, examining his face in that way she had that made him think she could see his every bitter—perhaps irredeemable—thought. That all this examining and hedging was if not now, then soon to be the very thing that wrote him off in her eyes.

'No need to worry about me, *glikia mou*.'

There was a defensive bite in there that made him shift again, annoyed when he saw his glib remark hadn't quite done the trick of reassuring her. Silence stretched just a little too long. He knew her well enough by now to recognize the slight tightening of her shoulders, the way she absently traced the lip of the coffee cup in her hand.

She was winding up to tell him something. He didn't look at her. He didn't have to.

'Agnes called again,' she said, voice low.

A muscle flexed in his jaw. He froze. Not visibly, not enough for anyone else to notice—but she would. She always did.

'She left a message,' she continued, careful now. 'She's in Athens. She wants to see you.'

He finally turned his head and met her gaze.

'You should call her back,' she pushed.

'No.' The word cracked out of him, too sharply, too desperately. The slipping sensation intensified.

She inhaled slowly, and he could feel her fighting to keep the peace. To keep this moment from detonating. 'Nelios... we had an agreement.'

'And I believe I said I would talk to her, but in my own time.'

She was quiet for a beat. 'If not now, then when?'

Her words curled around something deep inside him, something old, scarred and better left buried. Only it wasn't. She was raking it raw.

'Why does this matter to you so much?' he seethed.

'Because I see what it's doing to you,' she said. There was no accusation, no pleading—just truth; soft, dangerous truth. 'The way you lock parts of yourself away. The way you flinch from your past like it might still reach for you. She's your mother, Nelios.'

His laugh felt acid-sharp. 'She hasn't been. Not for a very long time.'

'Then ask her why. Because if you don't...'

Something sliced deeper, sharper than a scalpel. The panic spurted, then gushed. He clenched his belly tight. 'Be very careful what you say next, *glikia mou*.'

Her gaze lingered on the horizon for a beat, then two, then returned to his. 'Maybe today is a day to be completely reckless.' She folded her arms around herself—a shield. 'I'm not trying to fix you, Nelios. I just want you to stop pretending you're happy dwelling in the past when you're not. You're still bleeding somewhere beneath the surface, and at some point it'll be too late.'

He rose, an instinctual move. He hated looking up at her when he was cornered like this. Hated even more the flicker of guilt in her eyes—because it mirrored the feeling inside him.

'Have at it, if you insist. But you'll be participating on your own,' he said tightly. Then he turned, striding away from her.

'Nelios!'

He didn't stop. But each step dragged something heavy behind it. And, even though he didn't look back, he felt the precise moment his time dwindled to zero in the silence he left behind.

She stood there long after he left.

The terrace felt colder now, as if the sea breeze had turned on her too. A single tear slipped down her cheek—not dramatic, not even bitter, just inevitable.

She lowered herself back into the chair, arms wrapped around her ribs, as if she could hold the crack in her chest closed with sheer will.

He'd walked away from her.

After the past weeks, despite knowing that harsh reality was waiting to pounce, that hurt more than anything else ever could. It was time to accept that Nelios would keep guarding his pain as if it was the only thing that made him who he was. She'd seen the shadows in his eyes when he thought she wasn't looking. Felt the tension in his body when her fingers brushed too close to his heart. Too close to the fortress he'd spent decades building and lovingly tending.

But love—real love—couldn't survive in the dark.

And definitely not the love she now accepted that she felt for him. The kind that wanted to dance in the sunlight all day, every day. The kind that came with rainbows shortly after cleansing rain.

If he insisted on keeping that door locked, then maybe it was time to stop knocking.

Unfortunately, putting thought into action wasn't as easy.

For the next week she withstood the frosty silence and heavy censure, broken in the dead of night in bed when Nelios almost unconsciously dragged her into his arms and they fell on each other with almost desperate abandon.

Despite the hollowness of it, she attempted to convince herself that maybe sex was the stepping stone to this marriage of convenience, based on a piece of paper she didn't want. Vayle suspected it was that abiding demonstration of care and affection for his son that made her own yearning so acute. That made her wish for more, *damn it.*

She wanted Nelios Petralis to throw off the pain from his past so he could decalcify his heart. *So he could love her.* Because, unless things changed, she was dooming herself to decades of one-sided longing and heartache. Or, she desperately feared, an even quicker exit.

Then a whole new facet to their journey struck.

Her heart swung like a pendulum, one side elation, the other desolation, as she stared down at the test stick in her hand. Despite the care they'd taken, and the fact that she hadn't had her period since Angelos's birth, it seemed somewhere along the line, probably after one of those frantic, middle of the night, half-asleep couplings, nature had taken its course. And lightning had struck twice.

She was pregnant with Nelios's child.

Again.

And, with the bombshell she'd just discovered ticking away furiously beneath her skin, she went in search of Nelios.

To find him packing a bag. 'Wh-where are you going?'

His face was set in forbidding lines she'd hoped never to see again after those hours on his jet that first time. 'To Athens. I have an urgent issue that's arisen there.'

'Were you planning on telling me? Or just sending another of your minions to tell me?'

Was that a wince or was she deluding herself, as she had been about everything?

'I guess we haven't come as far as I thought if common courtesy can fall away so quickly,' she muttered.

'Did you want something, Vayle?'

'Of course. I always want something.' The smile that accompanied her flippant words missed by a mile. 'But alas it seems I'm destined to just want and not get.' She glanced at his case, her heart lurching. 'And I thought you could work from anywhere on earth?' she demanded, her fingers closing around the stick in her pocket.

He stiffened. 'Some meetings are better had in person.'

She frowned, the sense that he wasn't telling the full truth gripping her.

'Nelios—'

'Enough, Vayle. You say you're not trying to fix me, but we both know that's not true, don't we? Because you keep eyeing that can of worms, itching to open it, *ne*? Even though I cannot give you what you want.'

'And what is it that you think I want?'

He looked almost impatient, pained. As if he'd expected her simply to accept that and cower back into her corner. 'What every woman with a ring on her finger seems to want.'

'Security? A roof over her head? Health and happiness for those she cares about? I'm confident I have all of that, thanks to your billions. Or am I missing something?'

He shot her another impatient look. 'You know very well what I'm talking about.'

'And what—you can't bring yourself to say the word? It terrifies you that much?'

His chin jerked as if she'd slapped him. And, while she hoped something had jarred loose, his shuttered expression said he didn't much care for that verbal slap, nor did he intend to alter his thinking. 'You will not taunt me into this.'

'Into what? Into admitting that you're scared to utter the word "love" because you believe it's the Holy Grail destined to be forever denied you? Well, here's a newsflash, Nelios: it's already found you. You mother, our son: they love you. They don't believe it's a flaw to hide from.'

His gaze searched hers with sizzling fervour, searching for something, and for a moment she considered tossing herself onto that pile too, risking it all. But the fear that it might be too harrowing if he rejected her held her tongue.

Already he was retreating. And, as much as she believed she would be strong enough to carry on, eventually, if Nelios Petralis broke her heart, she wouldn't be able to bring herself to walk through that fire.

His jaw gritted. 'Even if that's true, I also believe they're still better off without my brand of...whatever it is that's inside me. The thing that pushed me to take over your hotel, content to make you collateral damage in a war that wasn't even yours to wage.'

She sucked in a shaky breath, then set it free. 'I'll consider forgiving you. You didn't know better. There, that's that taken care of. What next?'

His fingers bunched into fists, so he couldn't reach for things he couldn't have. 'Nothing has changed. Nothing *can* change. I can't risk the freedom of feeling.'

The finality behind the words as he started to walk out shattered her heart. But she couldn't let him have the last word. 'You're so focused on holding onto the prison bars in front of you, you can't see that the doors opened behind you a long time ago. Run, then, if you insist. But I can't promise we'll still be here when you come to your senses.'

Nelios froze, chasing the cycle of emotions on Vayle's face. From hurt to wariness to anger, each one drilled further holes in him.

He wasn't a fool. He could see she wanted more from him. He dragged his gaze from hers, the imploration in her eyes too much to bear. Everything was too damn much. And the more he absorbed the bigger his misfitting parts chafed. He was a broken puzzle, destined always to remain tossed aside in a dusty box. The sooner he accepted that, the better.

Yes, he was better off without that...*love*...anvil-heavy emotion that left a person wide open to the vulnerabilities great and small. When a smile or a frown had the power to turn one's world upside down. It was the sort of weighty responsibility he'd sworn never to fall prey to, even if he could summon such an emotion. Which he couldn't.

As his wife had warned, and Nelios had feared, it was probably already too late. That time on the streets had changed him. And he hadn't exaggerated when he'd told Vayle something was broken inside him. Something that would never let him be free of that frightened little boy who had learned in the most vicious way possible that love was a meaningless construct. A myth tossed about to justify all the anguish and bitterness it had wrought.

But you're not feeling much bitterness any more. And that anguish isn't as terrifying as it used to be, so why don't you—?

He jerked his case off the bed. 'I'm not sure when I'll be back. Maybe a few days. Perhaps a week.'

She shrugged. 'Like I said, take all the time you need.

We might be here when you come back, or we might not,' she flung at him.

His insides shredded. Protesting words rose to his lips and one by one they died. He told himself the first lie—that it was better this way.

It wasn't. And the different kind of anguish that filled him was clear evidence of that.

He wasn't even sure why he'd withheld the truth from Vayle—that he was in Athens to speak to his mother.

No. *He knew why.* He'd been...afraid to tell her in case it made no difference, couldn't fix him.

As he entered his suite in his flagship hotel in Athens, Nelios was struck by a new discovery. The room was cold. Not in temperature—no, the marble gleamed with sunlight and fresh lilies spilled fragrance from crystal vases—but cold in the way only a room teeming with bitterness and acrimony could be.

Thee mou, if he could sense this in the air, did he even want to know what was happening inside him? What Vayle saw each time she looked at him, took him into her body?

Agnes sat ramrod-straight on the edge of a silk-covered chaise, a cup of untouched tea in her hand. She wore her apprehension like a shroud, but she managed to summon a smile. 'Nelios. It's good to see you.'

He stood opposite her, back to the unlit fireplace, arms crossed, jaw tight.

Her keen gaze rested on him, searching. *For what?* he wanted to snap. Signs that he was broken, past the point of no return? He bit his tongue.

'You have a beautiful place,' she continued. 'It looks even better in reality than it did from the pictures.'

She was making conversation to cover the awkwardness. Against his will, something softened inside him. 'A tour will be arranged if you wish.'

Not by him, though. A handful of months ago, he would've jumped at the opportunity to further demonstrate how far he'd come without a single helping hand. But he'd only been away from Apeiron a matter of hours and he was already at breaking point.

The voice screaming inside that he'd made a mistake leaving Vayle and Angelos clamoured louder. What if she carried through with her threat to leave? Could he even blame her if she did?

'Maybe later, thank you.'

He imagined Vayle's wide, relieved smile at discovering he was here with Agnes and patted himself on the back. Brownie points with his wife were important.

Why, when it might not be enough to…to…?

His muscles tensed as the churning intensified. Damn it. The last time he'd walked a rope this tight was in that alley. But he'd come through that. He would come through this too. Put his past to bed, as Vayle had so passionately advocated. Maybe then he could finally seek greater pleasures.

Satisfied with that direction, he pinned his gaze on the woman who'd given him life then treated it so carelessly. And for a moment, he saw her—not the woman who'd disappeared from his life without a fight, but his mother. She was haunted and human. Flawed, as Vayle had insisted.

'You've been avoiding me.'

'I had practice,' he replied. 'You avoided me for half my childhood.'

Her breath hitched. 'I deserve that.'

He didn't deny it. He just let the silence stretch until it crackled.

'So,' he said, voice like glass, 'Let's get on with this. You've asked to see me often enough. Let's talk.'

She swallowed, nodded. 'Since the sin was mine, I guess I'll start?'

It should've appeased him that she was finally taking the blame, but all Nelios felt was a deepening of that hollow in his soul. It took several moments of prying open that rage-filled emptiness, forcing himself to look into the chasm to recognise what he felt. Fury, yes. Pain, definitely. But...sorrow too, for all the wasted years.

'Was it worth it?' he asked, his voice weary. Another question he'd buried deep, pulling it out only when the demons won and he couldn't fight the vault of pain.

Her mouth quivered. 'In hindsight? No.' Her voice was barely above a whisper. Then she shook her head. 'That's not quite true. This path I took, it brought me Vayle.'

His heart shredded. 'A fair trade, I suppose. How lucky for you to be able to toss one child away and pick up—'

'Stop saying that! I never tossed you away. We always planned to come back for you. At least, I did. Always.' Her voice brimmed with the kind of certainty that battered his fury.

'There were so many ways you could've ensured what happened to me didn't happen. Even at twelve, I could've told you that. And, you forget, I overheard everything you and Apostolis discussed. There was never a second, third or fourth option. You chose foster care, without doing your due diligence or even caring where I landed.'

He stopped, collected himself. 'I want to know why,' he said at last, low and controlled. The kind of quietness that masked years of rage. 'Why you left me. Why you, my mother, chose to trust a complete stranger with your son's wellbeing. Then you got on a plane and forgot all about him.'

Agnes flinched—actually flinched. 'It wasn't that simple.'

'No?' He stepped closer, gaze hard. 'Because from where I stood—alone, confused, in a stranger's care—it looked very simple.'

Her hands trembled around her tea cup. 'You were never supposed to stay in foster care. The woman was recommended by Apostolis's friend. He owned a care company. And it was only meant to be temporary, just a few months, while things settled.'

He laughed then, sharp and humourless. '"While things settled". You mean until your pockets were fat enough? Did you even bother to call to check on me?'

'Yes. I called the foster carer once a week, every week.' Her face crumbled. 'I was told it was best not to speak to you myself and unsettle you, as you were already making friends...'

'Of course, you believed her. You wanted your conscience appeased.'

Her lips trembled and she didn't even need to confirm that. He saw it written all over her face.

'I thought you were happy, and the situation at the hotel was extremely challenging. I expect Vayle has told you about her father?'

'Another monster who shouldn't have been allowed to sire children.'

'*Parakaló*, don't say that,' she begged.

Aware his emotions were near to imploding, he reined himself in. Settling back, he stared at her. 'Fine. Go on, then.'

'I came back for you—six months later. When I realised I was being put off. Discouraged from asking questions.'

Shock rushed to fill the hollows inside him, then he shook his head. 'That's a lie! You never came back.'

She sent him a sad smile. 'I came, but no one knew what had happened to you. I eventually traced you to a home that had burned down.' She wept silently, shaking her head in despair. 'I was so terrified...' She stumbled to a stop.

Nelios was reeling from the revelation that she'd returned to find him herself. And from a niggling he couldn't quite pinpoint.

'So you came for me. And left again. Then what?'

'Every moment I could spare, I came back to Athens. But you...you seemed to have vanished off the face of the earth.'

His lips pursed. 'Between the authorities, who were very keen to lock me away in another home and throw away the key, and unsavoury characters who preyed on children my age, I was forced to become a master at hiding on the streets.'

She flinched. Her hand darted out, beseeching. He clenched his gut because his feelings were in danger of softening, her pain feeding into his. And he couldn't afford that.

Then the niggling congealed into a tangible question. 'You keep saying "I". Where was Apostolis?' he demanded.

Tears filled her eyes, and a different hollow opened inside him.

'Forgive me, Nelios. We... I was always going to tell you when you were older...'

'Tell me what?' His voice as sharp as a scalpel digging straight into his heart. Because that heart *knew* what was coming.

Her eyes closed. 'Apostolis was not your father.'

That stopped him, numbed him from head to heel.

'What?'

Agnes's hand twisted in her lap. 'You were conceived before I met him. I was young, naïve. Your biological father left before you were born. Apostolis had always wanted me and he married me to save my reputation. To give you a name.'

Nelios stared at her. The floor had shifted under him, but still he didn't move. 'And he hated me for it.'

'Not at first, but...' Her voice cracked. 'Eventually, he resented how much I loved you. He saw you as a barrier to me loving him. And he...he gave me an ultimatum.'

He swallowed. 'Say it.'

'He said it was him or you.'

Silence.

Nelios stepped back as though she'd struck him. 'And you chose him,' he whispered.

'I thought I could fix his relationship with you. That if I

kept the marriage intact, he would relent and I could bring you back. But time passed and—he made it impossible. Every time I tried, he reminded me of what I owed him. And I couldn't stand against him.'

'Yes,' he said, voice low and lethal. 'You were a coward.'

She didn't argue. 'Yes, I was.'

The truth settled between them, finally out in the open.

'You were my mother,' he said, softer now, but somehow more brutal. 'You were supposed to fight for me.'

'I know.' More tears slid down her cheek, catching the light like glass. 'And I'll never forgive myself. But you must know—I loved you, Nelios. I loved you so much. And that's why he came to hate you. Because you were always mine.

'A year—that was all I planned to be away from you, regardless of what Lancaster or Tolis wanted. Not...'

Two decades.

His throat burned and his fists clenched, but the dam didn't break. Not yet.

He turned away, facing the tall windows. The sun outside was too bright, too cruel. But he let it burn him.

'I don't know if I can forgive you,' he said after a long pause. 'Not yet.'

Agnes nodded. 'Then I'll wait. For as long as it takes.'

He didn't answer. Just stood there in the wreckage of his life, knowing it was indeed too late. He had nothing to offer Vayle, after all.

Nothing at all.

Agnes continued to speak. 'I also hired a private detective to look for you.'

Another bolt of shock lanced his middle. 'You hired a detective?' he echoed woodenly.

'*Ne.* But that went nowhere.'

He knew why. He, Andreas and Capaldi had paid a fisherman to smuggle them into Sicily on his boat so they could find menial work on a vineyard. He'd scrimped and saved for the better part of two and a half years. He'd returned to Athens and bought his first hotel for pennies, courtesy of the failing economy. He'd put in the papers to change his name the same day and never looked back.

Her soft sobbing refocused his attention on her. 'The investigator said it was likely you were...' She stopped, unable to form the words.

He spoke them for her. 'You were led to believe I was dead.' And here, now, was the *exodus* he'd always wished for. But, rather than experience the satisfaction of a well-earned denouement, his own personal Greek tragedy appeared entirely formed of acts of poor judgement and mistimed endeavours.

'Until Vayle and I heard from your lawyer wanting her hotel.' She rose, approached and caught his hand in hers, gripping it tightly. 'Forgive me. *Parakalo*. There wasn't a single day when I didn't think about you. Regret what I did.'

Nelios didn't pull away.

But, even as he allowed himself to absorb the series of unfortunate circumstances that had brought him to this point, something whispered to him that he'd been irreparably altered.

In a way neither he nor anyone else might be able to fix.

Vayle opened the French doors and started walking, just as she'd done yesterday after putting Angelos down for his nap. Nelios had been gone just under twenty-four hours. It felt like years.

She walked past the middle point of the island, through the olive and orange groves, skirting the craggy beach and climbing the cliff till she reached the highest point. There she sat, watching the waves crash relentlessly against the rocks below. Salt spray mixed with tears she didn't want to dash away as an hour passed, maybe two.

It was good to get it all out so she could be strong for Angelos...for the new life she carried. With a hiccup, she slid her hand over her belly, heavier emotions clogging her throat. She hadn't even had time to absorb this miraculous news until now. Now she had, an untouched piece of her heart filled with love her for the baby growing inside her. 'I will love you too, through thick and thin. I promise you.'

'Vayle.'

She shook her head, believing the deep echo of her name was a trick of the wind.

'*Agapita*, please come away from the edge.'

Startled, she glanced over her shoulder in time to catch Nelios's deep flinch and paling face. She didn't want to hope and couldn't bear another bout of rejection, so she faced the turbulent view once more. 'Why should I?'

'Because watching you tumble off this cliff will be the tragic melodrama that finally kills me; I'm sure of it.'

She shrugged and kept facing forward. 'I'm feeling melodramatic. I thought I'd come and see the literal expression of my feelings.'

'It would please me greatly if you stepped back a little more.'

Perhaps it was cruel to relish the strain in his voice. To know the thought of losing her shook *some* part of him. Anger bubbled up. She'd put everything on the line, and for what?

Her fingers tightened around the white plastic stick in her pocket, resenting the jolt of unjustified guilt she felt. She managed, *barely*, to kick herself out of that mindset. She'd done nothing wrong. They'd done this with their eyes wide open.

'I'm not in the mood to please you, Nelios. What are you

doing here, anyway? Weren't you going to be in Athens for several days?'

'At the risk of more melodrama, I couldn't stay away.'

'It's a good thing then that this island is big enough. Until I leave, we can stay out of each other's way.'

A rough sound escaped him. 'So you're leaving?'

Misery filled her but she forced a nod. 'I don't see that I have a choice,' she said. Then waited...and waited.

When the tiny seeds of hope died, she snatched the plastic stick from her pocket. 'I don't know what you're doing back here so soon when you seemed hellbent on leaving, but I've already kept this from you when I should've told you yesterday.' She held the pregnancy test out to him.

For endless seconds he looked poleaxed. Then he lunged forward and snatched it from her, staring at it before his eyes met hers, then dropped to her belly. 'You're...'

'Pregnant with our second child? Yes. As fate would have it.'

His gaze dropped back to the test and this time she read his emotions accurately: shock; pride; *elation*. But those emotions were locked away far too quickly, leaving behind a landscape that grew increasingly grey...inhospitable.

'I will be a good father to this child too, you have my word. But...' He paused, his chest heaving far too dramatically, rivalling the heaving in her soul. The certain knowledge he was about to knock her world to smithereens. 'I'm terrified that's all I can give, Vayle. After what I discovered...' He stopped, inhaled, then blew out his breath. 'If you're open to a fifty-fifty custody arrangement, I'll be in your debt for ever.'

Her heart squeezed, but she shook her head to clear it. 'What do you mean, what you discovered?'

A wave of guilt swept over his face. 'I met with Ag...my mother. She told me...' He shook his head. 'Forgive me for not listening to you, Vayle.'

'Not until you tell me everything. I have a right to know, I think.'

'Ne,' he agreed.

She listened as he retold his conversation with the woman who'd birthed him. Relief shuddered through her, over and over. Her every hope for him, for the woman she'd believed in who'd been like a mother to her, had been realised.

'So they came looking for you. They didn't abandon you,' she affirmed softly.

'*She* didn't, no.'

His emphasis made her stiffen. But she still couldn't bring herself to look at him. She waited, because there was more.

'Tolis wasn't my father.'

Her head snapped up. 'What?'

'I think, deep down, I always knew. We were never close. And when he died the only regret I felt was never getting the chance to tell him what a poor parent he was.'

As he finished his story, her heart bled for him for a minute. Before she reined it in. Because she had a baby, *two* babies, to think of. And heartache to manage.

'Vayle, I feel... I can't... You did this for me. All of it. And I've been nothing but monstrous to you. How can I ever make it up to you?'

Nelios ventured closer, his every sinew straining to grab her, to anchor her to him, to snatch her back from the terrifying edge of loss. But he didn't. Couldn't—not yet. Instead, he crouched lower than her, heart in his throat, remorse bleeding from every pore. He'd spent so long protecting his pride, his pain, that he'd forgotten how to reach for what truly mattered. Only then might he avert the very exodus he'd foolishly claimed to crave—on his knees. Perhaps he deserved no less.

The weight of the small plastic stick still in his hand felt almost too sacred for his touch. A miracle, another undeserved gift from the woman whose love he'd abused with silence and distance. His fingers curled around it like a lifeline.

She didn't look at him. Her spine was stiff, her body drawn tight with grief she hadn't allowed to show until now. 'Take a tranquiliser,' she said, her voice sharp. 'Go lie down. You'll feel like yourself in no time, I'm sure.'

His lips twisted into a ghost of a smile, one that didn't feel as monstrous. That she could throw such cutting remarks even now... She was glorious. Far more than he'd ever had the right to dream of. But the smile died quickly. The agony of being parted from her returned to crush his chest like a vice.

'Drugs won't help, I fear,' he said, voice rough. 'Only gaining back the very thing I've spent my life throwing away might save me.'

She didn't move. But he saw it—the small hitch in her breath. The tiniest tremble in her fingers.

It was enough to let the floodgates open. 'You were right, *agapi mou*. About everything.' His voice cracked. 'I was a coward. I've been running all my life. Hiding behind righteousness and pain because it made it easier to believe I didn't need love. That I didn't *deserve* love.'

He shook his head, shame slicing through his soul. 'Watching you give it so freely, so wholeheartedly... I made myself believe it was weakness to want you. That what you were offering couldn't possibly be real. So, yes, I fought it—you, us. I fought the very thing I now know was my salvation.'

Still no response. But he didn't stop. He couldn't.

'I convinced myself I was incapable of love. That I was too damaged, broken. That I'd been discarded once, so I should protect myself.' He swallowed. 'It was easier than facing the truth—that loving you scared me more than anything in this world.'

She turned then, slowly. Her eyes were fire, storm and

heartbreak. 'You're not broken,' she said, her voice sharp with pain. 'Stop saying that. Stop *believing* that.'

His heart crumpled at the raw conviction in her words. 'Maybe I'm not, not any more, because you saw something in me when I saw nothing. Because you gave. And gave. I witnessed a warm, generous, loving woman who would go to the ends of the earth for the lucky ones who called her theirs. And I—I rejected you, every time, like a fool.'

'So you came to tell me you've seen the light. Now what?'

He edged closer, pulse thundering in his ears and true terror gripping his insides. Because that agony he heard in her voice—he'd caused it.

'I came back thinking I'd lost you. That I'd finally succeeded in destroying the only good thing in my life. And the truth is—I don't want to live without you, Vayle. I can't. I couldn't even breathe on that plane on the way home. It felt like I was being flayed open, cell by cell.'

A sound escaped her—choked, disbelieving.

He pressed a fist to his chest. 'This? This pain? I recognise it now. It's love. It's *you*. And, if you give me a second chance, I swear I'll spend the rest of my life earning every breath you give me. Every smile. Every piece of your trust I've shattered.'

He dared to touch her—just a fingertip to her wrist. She didn't pull away. She said nothing for an eternity. But her eyes...*thee mou*, her breathtaking eyes created his every vision of heaven.

'I should make you wait. Make you suffer. But I just don't have it in me, *agapu*,' she murmured.

His heart tumbled over. He ventured another inch closer and touched her back. Felt her sway towards him. '*S'agapo*, Vayle. You are my air, my gravity, my home. Forgive me. I'm a fool for waiting this long to grasp the gift you were giving me. I love you. Please forgive me.'

For a moment, the sky itself seemed to hold its breath. Then, with a soft, broken cry, she twisted and launched herself into his arms. He caught her like a drowning man clutching his final hope, this treasure he'd come so close to losing. She fitted against him as she always had—effortlessly, like destiny.

'I love you too, Nelios!'

His heart soared, so high and free he wondered if his feet would ever touch the ground. God, he hoped not. He held her tighter and crushed her close, his own tears hot against her skin.

'Thank you. Thank you for still having space in your heart for me.'

She pulled back just far enough to cup his face. 'It was always yours, even when it hurt. Even when you walked away.'

'My love, can I coax you away from the edge now, please?' he breathed reverently, trembling. 'My heart really can't take it and I very much need to kiss you.'

Her laugh was husky and tear-tinged as she nodded.

He stood and scooped her into his arms, cradling her tenderly. Slowly, carefully, he brought her away from the cliff, from the precipice of everything they'd nearly lost.

Then, right there beneath the sky, in his favourite place on earth, and in the arms of the purest love he didn't deserve but fully intended to keep, he kissed Vayle. It was long, slow and deep until every chasm filled and overflowed.

She was flushed and her eyes glittered beautifully when he lifted his head. 'Can we go home now? We have a contract to rip up and forever to plan, I believe.'

He brushed his thumb over her cheek. 'We do. I should never have left you, my heart, even for a day. Now I'm back, I'll spend every moment proving I'm worthy of you.'

When she burrowed into his neck, Nelios held her tighter.

He wasn't falling any more. He was home.

EPILOGUE

SOFIA AGNES PETRALIS was born at home on Apeiron to a mildly terrified father who then broke into reams of smiles, showering kisses the second he held his daughter.

And for the next three nights he straight refused to leave the nursery, completely in love and in awe as he experienced every small gesture his baby girl made.

Vayle had yearned to see what a besotted Nelios would look like in those testing weeks before they'd confessed their love. Now it was almost overwhelming.

Not that she took it for granted. They'd been through fire and anguish to get to where they were today. Seeing Nelios and Agnes finally at peace with one another was heart-warming. *Healing.*

'It's time, *agapita*.'

She turned at the low, sexy rumble and smiled when Nelios strode towards her. Her heart flipped at the sight of their daughter cradled in his big hands, the bib thrown over his shoulder as he carefully propped Sofia up and held out his hand to Vayle.

Slotting the hoop into her ear, she checked that her cream-and-yellow sundress was in place and crossed the room.

'I'm ready. Guess I can't be fashionably late to my own baby's christening, huh?'

He smiled, his heated eyes trailing appreciatively over her body before lingering on her mouth. 'We have time for me to steal a kiss then, *ne*, we must go. Andreas is vocalising his unhappiness at being kept waiting to hold his goddaughter. Capaldi is aiding that rebellion.'

She rolled her eyes but smiled.

She'd agreed wholeheartedly when Nelios had asked his two trusted friends to be godfathers to their children. Now that she knew what they'd been through, she was certain both men would move heaven and earth to protect them if needed.

Nelios caught her in a one-armed hold, pulled her close and sealed his mouth onto hers, kissing her until they had to come up for air. His forehead touched hers and they breathed each other in, just for another moment. 'My heart is full. You've made me so happy, *eros mou*. I love you, so much.'

Vayle blinked back tears, reaching up to wipe the traces of lipstick from his mouth. 'If it's half as much as I love you, then I'm so glad I stowed away on your plane.'

He laughed as he caught her hand and led her out of their bedroom. 'Indeed. And I'm thrilled I let you.'

As his senses compelled him to do these days, Nelios sought out his son as soon as they stepped onto the terrace.

Angelos, now a boisterous sixteen-month-old, could barely sit still on his grandmother's knee. It became an impossibility the second he spotted his parents and sister. He bolted towards them, and his wife caught him up and perched him on her hips.

Nelios, attempting to look stern but failing, walked with his family to the aisle of the tiny chapel, then tried to keep himself together as his daughter was baptised.

And failed. Not a single soul dared to call him on it, though. So he presumed some of his monstrous reputation remained unsullied.

Later, he was celebrating his many bounties when his friends joined him beneath the largest orange tree in his grove as the sun went down. For a moment, all three men observed the festivities, Vayle charming their guests and spreading her infectious joy all around.

'Never thought I'd see the day,' Andreas muttered after swallowing a mouthful of beer.

'Me neither,' Capaldi agreed.

Nelios shrugged. 'What can I say? I'm a changed man and it feels fucking great.'

They slapped his shoulder, laughed and drank some more.

Until a ping from Andreas's phone distracted his friend. Nelios's eyes narrowed at Andreas's dark expression. 'Everything okay?'

'It will be. But I need to go.'

'To Athens or Sicily?' he asked, hoping it wasn't the latter—for his friend's sake and the family ties to the mafia Andreas had been trying to escape all his life—but fearing it was.

His jaw clenched. 'Sicily.'

It was Nelios's turn to slap his friend's shoulder. 'Go, my friend. But if you need me, I'll be there.'

'Me too,' Capaldi echoed.

They watched him leave, then Capaldi was distracted by his wife and kids.

And, even before he walked away, Nelios strode towards his own, a compulsion he fully surrendered to drawing him to the love of his life.

'Everything okay?' Vayle murmured, sliding her arms around him.

Nelios watched his wife kiss his daughter then hug their son, pure adoration on her face.

He wrapped his arms around his wife and kissed her. Then dropped his forehead to hers.

'With you here in my arms and an abundance of love around me? Absolutely.'

* * * * *

Were you captivated by Keeping a Greek Secret? *Then why not explore these other steamy stories from Maya Blake?*

Greek Pregnancy Clause
Enemy's Game of Revenge
Crowned for His Son
Out of Office Nights
Snowbound and Royally Forbidden

Available now!

BLACKMAIL TO WHITE VEIL

CLARE CONNELLY

MILLS & BOON

To the Love Shack Ladies.
It's often said that writing is a solitary endeavour, but with friends like you, it definitely doesn't feel like it! What a joy it is to be able to share this wonderful, exhilarating and at times frustrating journey with you.

PROLOGUE

THE HUNGER IN his belly was not a new sensation. He'd known it, on and off, for almost every one of his thirteen years. It was the kind of hunger that gnawed at a person from the inside out, so extreme one couldn't even faint from it, because the agony of being so utterly empty and depleted refused to allow any reprieve.

From where Theo sat, back pressed to the wall of an Athens street, he watched some of Europe's wealthiest and most elite pass him by, none so much as glancing at the grimy, skin-and-bones boy huddled on the ground—as though he were invisible. His clothes were tattered, his skin covered in soot and his eyes were sunken.

But oh, those dark grey eyes. They could still see. And his mind, though malnourished, could understand.

The inequities of this world. The imbalance. The unfairness.

He watched Europe's elite, as they moved like a relentless tide, undulating in and out of the revolving glass doors of one of Athens's most exclusive hotels, and inwardly, he cursed them all. How could there be such wealth in the world, when he had to live like this?

Still, it was better, in Theodoros Leonidas's opinion, than the alternative. He'd known many temporary homes, and had hated each and every one. It wasn't always the fault of the foster parents with whom he was placed. Theo appreciated that he was difficult—he'd been told it often enough, but he recognised the truth of it. He was angry and defensive, and given the choice between being thrown into the home of a stranger, or living on the streets with his own wits, he would always choose the latter.

Even when it meant a hunger such as this.

He closed his eyes. Not to sleep—his hunger wouldn't allow it—but to wait, and blot the world from his mind. As night fell, he would move, driven to take what no one would give him. Just a little food, to keep him going. Just a little food, for a young teenager with no one else to get it for him.

CHAPTER ONE

THE MAN ANNIE LANGLEY had known five years earlier wouldn't have been seen dead in a place like this, yet there he sat, in a booth on the other side of the exclusive Sydney bar—a regular haunt for him, apparently, while he was overseeing his Australian business interests. Once upon a time, Theo had *hated* this sort of place, had despised restaurants of its ilk, too. Back then, when they'd been young and purportedly 'in love', his idea of a good time had been sharing take-out at his apartment. Annie had known her over-protective parents wouldn't want her to get involved with someone like Theo—older, and more experienced, who'd lived rough. Keeping things low-key meant they weren't ever photographed, or spotted by high-society friends, and their relationship could remain a secret, so avoiding this sort of place had suited her, too.

A lot had changed in five years, though.

A familiar tide of grief surged through Annie, at what she'd lost and how she changed, but she forced herself to remain numb to it. Not to think about her mother's death, her father's slide into depression and grief and Annie's inability to hold it all together, no matter how hard she tried. Those might be the reasons for her having flown halfway around the world, from her home in Athens, to Australia, to come face-to-face with the man she'd once imagined spending the rest of her life with.

The man she'd broken up with, and refused to speak to ever again.

Annie stood just inside the door, concealed by the plush burgundy curtains at the entry and the dozens of well-moneyed guests who stood between them, needing a moment—a lifetime?—to catch her breath and rebuild her courage.

This was a last resort—and it was a moment for last resorts, after all. Without help, her family's company would have to declare bankruptcy, and everything her parents had worked towards their whole lives would be destroyed. On Annie's watch.

Her throat thickened with the threat of tears, but she swallowed the. It was a time for strength and determination: not grief. Not fear. Not sadness—even when there was so very much to be sad about.

Digging her fingernails into her palms, Annie tried to focus on the Theo she'd fallen in love with. Not the Theo she'd crushed on from afar, when he'd first moved in next door. Then, she'd been just a girl of eleven, and the first time she'd spied him getting into his foster parents' car, across the expansive front lawns their properties shared, her heart had gone into total meltdown. From that point on, she'd achieved almost stalker-level obsession, the kind of adoration teenagers almost held a patent on.

She'd watched from afar, equal parts craving and fearing interactions, because having to talk to him left her tongue-tied. For the first time in her life, she'd cared about something and someone other than her parents and being the perfect daughter for them. Theo had started to take up a huge portion of her waking thoughts and sleeping dreams.

That seemed like ancient history now, though. Because

eventually, he'd noticed her, too. When she was much, much older, on the night of her twenty-first birthday, and she'd begged him to kiss her, to make her teenage wishes come true... It had been the start of a whirlwind year, in which she'd sworn her heart had become so full it was at risk of bursting. For the first time in Annie's life, she felt seen for who she was, not what she was meant to represent, and it was all because of Theo.

That Theo had promised Annie he'd always be there for her, that if she ever needed anything, he would be her helpline. Her port in the storm.

That was the Theo she was appealing to for help, tonight. Not the Theo who'd been so coldly angry with her when she'd ended their relationship. Not the Theo who'd said such awful things, tearing her apart, piece by piece, and with such ease, until she was shaking and frozen to the core.

She couldn't think about that morning without wanting to slip into a crack in the earth's mantle and disappear for ever.

With knees that knocked together, she began to walk, slowly, carefully, through the crowd, wiping a trembling hand over the silky material of her champagne-coloured dress.

She'd grown up in this world, and had always been a part of it. Her parents' wealth had opened many doors for her, and the fact she'd gone to a prestigious international school meant her friendships had all been with children of similar financial backgrounds. Yet she'd never really felt at home in this sort of environment; it was like play-acting. Being the woman everyone expected her to be.

Except with Theo, a little voice reminded her, and out of nowhere, she was bombarded by memories of them together. Her in jeans and shirts, or better—his shirts, lounging around together like they had no money and no cares in the world. Watching silly action movies, ordering fast food, just being together. More than that, he'd let her be herself. Unlike her parents, who had seemed to exist purely to keep her alive at all costs. He'd loved taking her out on adventurous dates, like jetskiing or hiking or riding on his motorbike. Her parents would have had a conniption if they'd found out.

Palms moist with sweat, she was almost at his table when his eyes, slowly scanning the room, landed on her, and the whole entire world seemed to grind, loudly and tangibly, to a halt. The earth stood still, the dust from the tectonic plates' arresting flooding her throat and making everything dry. Legs that weren't quite steady were far better than this: legs that refused to cooperate. All she could do, was stand still too.

She stared at him through the veils of time, the man she'd just been thinking about—the man he'd been five years earlier—morphing into this version of him. Not visibly older, but somehow, so much harder. His face, which she supposed had always had a tightness to it, now radiated tension and cynicism. His eyes, which once upon a time she might have described as a dark grey, seemed almost black tonight, and as she looked at him, one corner of his lips lifted in a gesture that was far more mockery than smile.

With effort, she forced her legs to move, one after the other, carrying her the rest of the way across the room, until she was at the edge of his booth, hips pressed lightly to the table's edge for support. He had been wearing a suit, but the jacket was now discarded on the plush velvet seat to his side, and if there'd been a tie as well, it wasn't in evidence. Instead, his button-down shirt was undone at the collar to reveal the thick column of his tanned throat, and a hint of his chest; the sleeves were pushed up to just beneath his elbows, reminding her of how strong and leanly muscled his whole body was.

She glanced away quickly, drawing in a quick breath.

'My, my, if it isn't Annie Langley,' he drawled, that accent so familiar it panged in her belly. If he was surprised to see her, there was no evidence of it on his handsome symmetrical features. 'And here I thought I was rid of you for ever.'

It was like a knife being plunged into her heart anew. Their breakup had been...awful. Actually, that word was completely insufficient, but in the moment, Annie couldn't think of an alternative. The bleakest and most necessary decision of her life had led to an argument that still shook her insides if she thought of it.

'Nice to see you, too, Theo,' she managed to croak, her voice barely audible above the fashionable electronic music pulsing through the bar.

'I did not say it was nice,' he corrected, eyes on hers, probing her, so she squared her shoulders, refusing to let him see that she was intimidated or afraid.

'True. Do you have a minute?'

His lips flattened and for a moment, she thought he was going to say no. She hadn't let herself imagine that possibility, even when she'd known it was there. She hadn't wanted to contemplate what she'd do if he turned her away without giving her a chance to present her case to him.

'I'm meeting someone,' he said, glancing at his gold wristwatch.

'Okay, well, until they get here,' Annie said, desperately, and because she really couldn't take no for an answer, she slid into the booth opposite, immediately regretting it when their knees brushed beneath the table, and her pulse went into dangerous territory. Suddenly, she was twenty-one again, the young woman who'd loved and wanted with every fibre of her awakening body, and never had the chance to have.

His lips quirked in something like a mocking half smile, as he lifted a hand and immediately drew the attention of a waitress in a silky white blouse and fitted black pants.

'I'll have another.' He nodded towards his scotch. 'And something for the lady.' Even the way he said 'lady' was inflected with the kind of disdain that made her heart hurt.

'Of course, sir. What would you like, ma'am?'

Annie was about to refuse, but suddenly, the offer of some Dutch courage was infinitely tempting. 'Um, a white wine, please.'

'A sav?'

'Sure.' She nodded quickly, frankly not caring.

Theo said the name of a wine bottle, and the waitress beamed a megawatt smile his way. 'Oh, excellent choice.'

Annie resisted the impulse to roll her eyes. She needed Theo's help and she sure as heck wasn't going to get it by antagonising him. Out of nervous habit, she pulled her long, silky dark hair over one shoulder, the curls she'd carefully wrapped into it bouncing against her pale skin as she then toyed with her fingers in her lap, oblivious to the way his eyes were resting on her face, making their own inventory of changes.

'So, Annie,' he prompted, his voice a dry drawl. 'Is it a coincidence that you are here?'

'No,' she said. She had no intention of lying to him. 'I've been trying to contact you. Have you been getting my messages?'

Another twist of those lips that had once driven her wild with pleasure and promises. 'Yes, I've gotten them.'

Her heart trembled and the betrayal of that admission thudded against the walls of her gut. 'Oh, right.'

'You might remember, I asked you never to contact me again?'

'I remember,' she whispered, then cleared her throat. 'But I also remember you saying you'd always be there for me.'

For the briefest, tiniest moment, she thought his eyes showed something. A softening. Interest, remorse, concern? But it was gone so quickly, she realised she was layering her own wishful thinking over his expressions.

'That was a long time ago.'

'Not so long,' she said, as the waitress returned with a tray and two drinks. She cleared Theo's glass before replacing it, then slid Annie's wine to her. Annie wrapped her fingers around the stem gratefully, without lifting it to her lips.

'A lifetime.'

'Six years. Not even.'

He arched a single brow. 'Did you come here to discuss the past?'

Her lips parted on a quick sigh. 'No,' she said, dropping her gaze. There was no point. They'd said everything there was to say. She'd dumped him because her parents had insisted on it. He'd been angry at her reasoning, had fought for her to try to make it work, had fought for their relationship, and she'd shut him down. Again and again. It had not been an amicable split.

She took a quick sip of her drink, barely noticing the world-class wine as it spread across her palate.

'Then what is it? As I said, I'm waiting for someone, and it would be better if you weren't here when she arrives.'

She.

Annie ignored the rolling in her gut.

She knew he'd dated since they broke up. *Everyone* knew he'd dated. One of the richest men in the world, responsible for several tech innovations, as well as world-famous property developments, from Sydney to Dubai to Shanghai and Paris, Theodoros Leonidas had taken his foster parents' not-insignificant wealth and somehow turned it into a global powerhouse.

No, not somehow. She knew how he'd done it.

Because as often as there were pictures of him printed in the papers with beautiful women on his arm, there were stories written about him in the financial broadsheets: his ruthless, dog-eat-dog, take no prisoners negotiation style credited with his ability to make some of the toughest deals, and to walk away from anything that didn't serve him.

So what if he was waiting for a woman? That had nothing to do with Annie. She wasn't here for personal reasons, but rather, for business.

'I have a proposition for you,' she said, a little unevenly, glugging back some more wine.

'I see,' he murmured, though his voice was now as cynical as his half smile had been earlier. 'How fascinating. And here I thought I had nothing to offer you.'

She flinched. 'It's better if we leave the past in the past.'

He dipped his head once, in what she took to be an agreement to that.

She took one more sip for courage. 'I'm here with an investment opportunity,' she said, faltering slightly.

His expression was sheer mockery now. 'Because you think I need help in that department?'

He could not make it any clearer how he felt about her if he grabbed a permanent marker and scrawled across the table, 'Annie Langley is Scum'.

Did she deserve that? Maybe. Every accusation he'd levelled at her in their break-up argument had been fair, and she understood the things he hadn't said. She'd chosen her parents over him, and to someone like Theo, that had been a betrayal. One he couldn't forgive. But he'd also misunderstood her reasoning. He'd thought it was because she was a snob, that her parents were snobs. He'd thought it was because he had grown up poor, that he didn't belong in their world. While that might have been true for some of Annie's friends, money had nothing to do with her parents' reactions. Not really. At its heart had just been their overarching need to keep her safe, and alive. Like they'd failed to do, from their perspective, for her older sister, Mary.

'And I'm here because you're the only person I know who can help.'

'Which is it, Annie? Charity or opportunity?'

She'd at least hoped he'd express a little concern when she told him it was about help, but there was that same icy tone in his voice.

'Both, I suppose.'

'Fascinating. Why don't you start at the beginning? You have precisely as long as it takes for my date to arrive so if I were you, I would not sit there fumbling with your hands longer than is necessary.'

She felt like the gauche teenager lusting after him that she'd once been. She swallowed, glancing away, his cruelty cutting her in a way she hadn't expected. Her eyes came to land on the wall just behind his shoulder.

'I'm looking for someone to buy a forty-five per cent stake in my parents' company,' she said.

She wasn't looking at him, so did not see the way he reacted to that, the tension that tautened his whole expression, the way his eyes darkened to almost black. Annie couldn't bring herself to see what she thought might be triumph in his face as she admitted, 'It's not in good shape, but there is so much scope for improvement and growth. You'd be getting a relative bargain and we'd...' *be able to keep going.*

The infusion of cash was just what she needed. And the addition of someone like Theo, to reassure their staff? They had been hemorrhaging leadership positions. The company was in an untenable position.

'I do not buy partial shares of companies,' he said, reaching for his scotch and taking a drink before replacing it on the tabletop. Her eyes slid to his and her heart twisted inside her chest.

'I know.' She swallowed. 'But I thought, in this instance—'

'That I would make an exception? And why, exactly would you think that, Annie?' He leaned forward a little way, bracing his elbows on the table, and she bit into her cheek, as she was reminded of just how big he was, how much larger than her. She'd always felt so safe, pressed to his side, or wrapped in his arms, like he was some kind of gladiator who could protect her from everything.

'Let me guess. Because, once upon a time, a long time ago, we went out, you think I owe you some kind of favour?'

She flinched again, visibly recoiling against his crude characterization of their relationship. 'We—did more than go out.'

His lip curled in that derisive way she'd seen several times already tonight. 'If you insist.'

She opened her mouth to argue, but then wondered if he was laying a trap for her. Getting her to go down memory lane and rehash their failed relationship, rather than stay on track and discuss her reason for being here.

'I've got all the financials for you,' she said, pulling a USB from her handbag and pressing it across the table. 'It's password-coded with your birthday.' Her voice hitched a little as she admitted the detail, but she'd wanted to protect the documents in case anything happened to the USB, and hadn't wanted to use her own birthday, in case he didn't remember it, and had to admit that to her.

'Fascinating, but I told you, I do not buy partial stakes. That's not how I do business.'

'I'm aware of that. Did you think I'd come here tonight without doing my research?'

'Then you've wasted your time.'

'If you look at the details, you'll see it's still a good deal for you. What we can do in the market—'

'My date is here,' he said, moving from the booth, his jacket in one hand, his legs brushing hers beneath the table, so sparks flooded her bloodstream. He stood, unfolding to his full six and a half feet, his lap at her eye height, so she had to quickly wrench her gaze to his face. 'Excuse me, Annie. I'd say it was nice seeing you again, but we both know that would be a lie.'

He began to move away, to greet a woman who'd just walked in, wearing a denim mini skirt so short it almost showed her bottom, and a camisole top with lace trim. Her hair was blond and glossy, and hung halfway down her back.

Annie watched as Theo's demeanour changed, his smile easy as he drew the woman into his arms and then kissed her on the lips. It was only brief, just a few seconds, but

Annie acknowledged she could have lived her whole life quite happily without ever having to see that. It was bad enough that she'd seen photos of him with women clinging to his side like limpets, but those had been still photographs—a world of difference between that, and this.

Still, she'd come this far. She reached for the USB and curled it into her palm, crossing the bar and almost knocking a waitress off her feet in her haste to reach Theo and his date. They had already stepped outside by the time she caught up to them, and Annie, on autopilot, extended a hand to curve around his arm, to get his attention.

Theo glanced back at her, frowning, looking at her like he barely knew her now.

Hurt spread through Annie, but she refused to feel it. Later, when she was back in the hotel room, she'd wallow in the shame and degradation of this whole experience, but for now, she needed to make some headway.

'Just look at the financials,' was all she felt capable of saying, given the other woman was now staring at Annie, too. 'My phone number is in the document. I'm in Sydney for another two days. Take a look, and then call me.' She cleared her throat. 'Please, Theo.'

For a moment, his eyes narrowed, and then, without nodding, or uttering a word of reassurance, he took the USB from her and slid it into his pocket.

'Goodbye, Annie.'

She watched him walk away with no idea if she'd ever hear from him again.

CHAPTER TWO

THEO COULD HAVE gone a very long time without ever hearing the name Langley again. Annie had been one of the biggest miscalculations of his existence—and Theo didn't generally make mistakes, particularly not with people, and certainly not with trust.

Yet, he *had* trusted her. She'd worked her way through his carefully maintained defenses, wearing him down with persistence, and her insistence that she wasn't what he thought. So he'd let her in, bit by bit.

When Annie had turned eighteen, she'd drunk too much champagne with her snobby friends and begged him to kiss her. It had been a dare, he'd later found out, from the redhead she was always with—Bianca someone or other. They'd thought it was funny, how much Annie moped about after him with her oversized crush—given that he was just a street kid who'd moved into a mansion next door and never really belonged. He was certainly not someone anyone in that clique thought good enough for Annie Langley.

He'd refused to touch her.

She was barely more than a kid, and he hadn't been interested in providing entertainment for her entitled social circle.

But at twenty-one, it had been different. She was older,

more experienced, completely sober, and as far as he knew, begging him to kiss her was all her own idea. Her friends were nowhere to be seen. And by then, he was the heir apparent to the Georgiades's fortune—his foster parents, having no children of their own, and having been blown away by Theo's business aptitude, had signed everything over to him. He was his own man, making his way in the world.

So, he'd kissed her.

That should have been the end of it. Except, even then, there'd been something addictive about Annie Langley. Something dangerous, too, because she seemed like the kind of person who could make him want what he'd never wanted before: to be needed. Loved. To want to stick around.

Theo had more than an average amount of experience with women; only Annie hadn't been anything like the women he usually slept with. She was so innocent and artless in her reactions, so responsive and hungry for him. It was a miracle they hadn't slept together that night—even more so that they hadn't slept together at all. Waiting had seemed right, with Annie.

At first, he'd done everything in his power to control their relationship. He'd wanted to keep Annie boxed into a single partition of his life. He enjoyed spending time with her, but he wouldn't let her shift his focus. Already, he'd made sweeping changes to his foster parents' business model, revolutionising their core values, increasing their wealth. He owed it to the child he'd once been to continue working towards his business success.

Yet night by night, in ways he still didn't understand, she pushed at the walls of the partition he tried to keep her contained in, so that while it still existed, it morphed into something so much larger than he'd ever intended. She became the first thing he thought of when he woke up, the person he went to call when he had a success.

And then, she'd ended it, because her parents had told her he wasn't good enough for Annie. The worst part of it was that he knew her parents thought that, because her father had told him. Had tried to buy him off to end the relationship; had told Theo that he was the kind of man Annie needed to steer clear of. Didn't Theo understand that Annie was aristocracy? She was destined for greatness, and Theo was certainly not that.

He could never forget that conversation. As a street kid, he'd been called a lot of things, but somehow, hearing them from Elliot Langley had cut him to the quick. Because deep down, he'd wanted the other man's acceptance. The more he came to care for Annie, the more he knew it would be essential to earn her parents' approval to keep her in his life.

'Do you think I would ever allow my daughter to become serious with a man like you?' He'd jabbed a finger in Theo's direction. 'You are scum, from the darkest slums of the street. The Georgiadeses might have been fooled by your business acumen, but what do I care for that? My daughter can trace her lineage back to William the Conqueror, and who the hell are you? Do you even know, boy? How dare you so much as look at her, much less touch her. Much less think you have any right to get serious about her. If you ever speak to Annie again, you'll be sorry.'

It had gone on, and on, in that vein, but Theo had blocked most of it out by then. He'd focused on assuming a mask of non-concern, sneering with half of his lip—and his insolence only angered Elliot further, so in the end, he was all but threatening to call the police for the very fact that Theo had once upon a time lived rough.

Theo hadn't taken the threat seriously. What could Elliot Langley do to him, after all? By then, Theo had been worth an absolute fortune, and in dating Annie, he wasn't breaking any laws. It wasn't the threat that shocked him, so much as the tone of his voice. The entitlement of the man had chilled Theo's blood, reminding him of how often he'd felt ashamed of his life on the streets, when he would walk past those incredible hotels and have wealthy couples turn up their noses at the sight of him. He remembered one such person making a cruel remark about the way he smelled. Another threw a half-eaten sandwich at him, where he sat on the footpath. And everything Elliot Langley said, in that conversation, brought it all back, and made Theo realise: the Langleys were just as bad as those people had been.

But it was Annie's betrayal that had stung, worst of all. Annie's betrayal that had made him feel foolish and stupid for ever having believed she was different to the rest of those moneyed bastards. When the next morning she arrived and told him it was over—coldly determined—he'd known instantly what her reasoning was. She was dumping him because her father had found out about them and insisted upon it. And Annie hadn't had the strength of character to stand up for their relationship. Whatever promises she'd made, whatever he'd thought they'd shared, had just been a construct of his mind. Annie wasn't what he'd believed: she was just as superficial and snobby as her parents.

He swore that was the last he'd ever see of her, no matter what, and he'd stuck firm to that. He'd sold the Georgiades's house, having no interest in returning there, lest he happen to run into Annie again—or her father. He'd put her from his mind, focusing everything on business, his success, and yes, on other women. Yet now, after a brief ten-minute conversation in an overcrowded bar, she was suddenly back, bursting through the partitions of his brain just as quickly as before, taking over his thoughts in a way he bitterly resented.

He glared at the sweeping views of Sydney Harbour afforded by his penthouse suite, before finally giving up on resisting. He stalked across to his laptop and stabbed in the USB drive. He had fully intended to throw it out, but whenever his hand curved around the plastic to do just that, he saw the anguish in her eyes, heard the plea in her voice, and he shoved it back into his pocket.

Fine.

So he'd take a look.

What harm was there in seeing what her family's business was about? Even when he knew one thing for absolute certain: he would never, in a billion years, for all the money in the world, get in bed with the enemy. And that's what the Langleys were, and always would be, to him.

Annie really hadn't expected to hear from him again. His face had been the definition of immutable, his eyes chilling, his jaw locked in an expression that might as well have been a verbalised rejection.

Yet the next afternoon, his assistant had reached out to arrange a meeting. Annie could well have been knocked over with a feather, but she'd kept her voice as steady as possible as she'd agreed to the details.

Not in an office, as she'd expected, but in the penthouse apartment Theo was based out of while overseeing the crucial phase of development approvals and design for a high-rise in the CBD.

A keycard had been left for her at the front desk, so that she could access his private level of the hotel, and as the elevator whooshed Annie upwards, she barely had twelve seconds to contemplate what this meeting would involve, and to quell her nerves.

She kept her focus on the necessity of this though, and on the hope that his agreeing to meet was a positive sign. She doubted he'd have arranged a meeting just to hand back the USB.

Yet, with Theo, and the way he'd been the other night, the animosity that had sparked from him to her, she couldn't rightly say what she was expecting when the elevator opened to reveal a huge tiled foyer with only a single door in it. She moved towards it a little hesitantly, cleared her throat then lifted her hand to knock, before realising there was a doorbell. She pressed it once, then stepped back and waited, hands fidgeting at her sides.

She was just about to ring the doorbell again when the door was pulled inwards and Theo was revealed on the other side, dressed almost the same as the other night—in a suit that had been dressed down. This time he wore no shoes, as well.

She was glad she'd opted to buy herself a suit—she felt better seeing him again dressed like this: for business. The navy pants were wide-legged, teamed with spike heels, and she'd tucked a cream-coloured blouse into them before adding the tailored blazer. Her hair she'd pulled into a neat pony tail, to remove the temptation to toy with it as much as possible.

'Annie,' he said, with a slight nod. It was a slightly better greeting than the night before. He gestured with his hand for her to enter the penthouse and she hesitated for only a millisecond before forcing herself to move through the door, ignoring the hint of his masculine fragrance she caught as she passed him.

Inside, she was immediately hit by the stunning view of the harbour, first, with the world-famous opera house right in front of her, and then, inside the apartment, the luxury of the furnishings. Not a cent had been spared in creating the kind of home away from home that only the world's wealthiest could possibly afford.

'Not bad,' she said, lips pulling to the side, trying to remember the Theo she'd known who'd been so averse to obvious signs of wealth, who'd virtually equated extravagance with the gutter. She turned to face him, and her stomach twisted viscerally. 'I was surprised to hear from you.'

His features shifted, ever so slightly, in a sort of acknowledgement of that.

'I take it you looked at the financials?'

'I looked at them, yes.' He crossed the room, so he was standing toe to toe with her, his nostrils flaring as he looked into her face. 'The company is in a mess.'

She winced. 'I know.'

'What happened?'

She let out an uneven breath as she tried to work out how to explain it all—how her father had barely been able to function after his wife—Annie's mother's—death, and so Annie had done her best to step into the breach. She'd also been grieving though—she'd barely recovered from the blow of losing Theo, and then her mother had died. So she'd hired a temporary business manager to work with her, but it had all gone pear-shaped.

'It's my fault,' she said, slowly, heavily, the admission hurting to say. 'I thought I could handle it, but I messed up, and if I don't fix it, if I can't fix it…'

He didn't say anything, but she felt the force of his gaze on her face. She refused to cry in front of him, but she did sniff a little, to stave off the emotions that were rioting through her.

'Why did you think I would be interested in this?'

She made herself meet his eyes. 'Because you used to care for me, and I thought there might be some part of you that still does.'

A muscle jerked in the base of his jaw. 'You were mistaken.'

It felt like a blade was slicing through her midsection. She nodded slowly, but now, anger was usurping grief. 'Is that why you organised this meeting? To see my reaction when you told me that to my face? I never had you pegged as a sadist, Theo.' She waited a moment, to see if he would explain, apologise, say *anything* that would lessen her anger, but he just stared her down, face neutral. Annie made a sound of disapproval, then began to stalk towards the door, but Theo was right behind her, his hand curving around her wrist, bringing her to a stop.

'I did not arrange this meeting to insult you,' he said, crisp and calm. 'I was genuinely curious about your reasoning for seeking me out. After all, you have many friends who could help you with this.'

Annie's heart hurt. The truth was, she'd seen what her friends were really like in that god-awful year of intense grief, when Theo was gone, and her mother had died. There wasn't a single one of them she'd turn to in a crisis. Not after that. When Annie was no longer a source of lighthearted fun, she'd ceased to be someone they thought of at all.

If anything, the last five years had turned her into a recluse.

'You made the most sense.'

'No, that can't be it. I drive hard bargains. I'm renowned

for it—I was, even back then. You must know that having seen your financials, I would offer you only what the actual value of the company is—and such an amount would be an insult to your father.'

She noted the fact he referred only to her father, confirming that he knew her mother had died. And hadn't reached out.

She'd been dead to him, like he'd said she would be.

And oh, how she'd needed him then. How she'd wanted him to kiss her and make her tattered heart better.

'I had hoped—' but it had been a stupid hope.

'I'm not a charity.'

She flinched. 'The company is in bad shape—I'm the first to admit it. But the potential—'

'Yes, there is potential,' he admitted. 'To be frank, there is potential that I doubt it has even occurred to your father to think about harnessing, but I can see it. And if the company were mine, I have no doubt I could reverse its course in eighteen months.'

She drew in a shallow breath. 'Aren't you tempted, to see what you can do? When was the last time you had a challenge like this?'

His lips quirked in an expression of wry amusement. 'Every investment I make is a challenge. I seek that out.'

'So seek this out,' she half begged.

'I told you, when I acquire an asset, it is in its entirety. That's just how I do business.'

'I can't do that,' she whispered. 'I know I need help, to turn things around, but this is my father's pride and joy. He's lost so much, Theo, please, I can't ask him to lose this, too.'

For a moment, Theo's eyes flexed with a dark tumble

of feelings, so Annie felt like the floor had fundamentally shifted beneath her feet.

'How badly do you want my help, Annie?'

She blinked, something like hope flickering, albeit briefly, in her chest. 'I—need it,' she admitted, aware she was putting all her cards on the table. 'I'm begging you, in fact.'

'Excellent. Now that we've established my preferred bargaining position, let me explain what would make this deal worthwhile, and we can see just how desperate you are, hmm?'

The hope flickering in her chest extinguished as wariness stole through her instead.

'I hate your father, Annie. I want to be clear about that, from the start. Your goal is to help him, my goal is to hurt him. However, through this merger, we can both achieve our ends. You should be aware, though, what my intentions are, going in.'

Her lips parted in shock at the darkness of that admission. 'How can you say that?' she whispered.

'Your father is an elitist snob, the kind of man who sees suffering and turns up his nose to face the other way. He is a judgemental bastard I would happily never think of again, for my entire life.'

Annie's heart felt as though a mountain had been dropped on it. She blinked now, unable to step the moistness gathering behind her eyes. 'How can you say that?' she repeated.

'We both know how—and why—I feel as I do. What you are perhaps not aware of is the amount your father offered me to leave you alone, nor the conversation we had that night. Unlike you, I told him precisely where he could take his interference. Unlike you, I chose to stand by our relationship.'

Annie's lips parted on a rush of shock. 'What?'

'If I hate your father, it is because of the things he said to me that night, the way he acted. I have no doubt he has said similar things to you about me, often enough, to spare us both the need for a rehashing of the conversation. Suffice it to say, he is not someone I would be interested in helping, were it not also a means to achieving my own ends.'

Annie could have been blown over by a light breeze. She could hardly think straight. She'd had no idea her father had gone to Theo, no idea he'd offered to pay him off, to get him out of Annie's life. Though she shouldn't have been surprised: her parents would stop at nothing to control every aspect of Annie's life, but she hadn't thought them capable of that. What had her father said to Theo? The idea of Elliot Langley offering Theo money made her skin feel all clammy—like she was some kind of commodity—but she couldn't focus on that now. She'd come here with a single purpose, and she didn't intend to leave empty-handed. 'What exactly are your "ends"?' she asked, steeling herself for whatever his response would be.

Annie hadn't realised he was still holding her wrist, until he started to stroke his thumb over the soft skin there. She glanced down, surprised by the familiar sight of his hand on her flesh, and how much it made her insides glow with warmth.

'Your father made it abundantly clear that the last thing he wants is for his precious princess of a daughter to be with someone like me. So we are going to present him with that reality, Annie.'

She gasped.

'You and I will get married. It will be fast, it will be public, and it will be completely in his face. *I* will be in his face, and you, my dear Annie, if you want my help, will love me slavishly and devotedly in front of your father, lavishing me with affection, attention, until he almost can't stand it.'

The world seemed to be cracking apart, splintering into a thousand pieces. It was too cruel, too impossible to contemplate.

'I can't believe you,' she ground out. 'How can you even suggest—'

He dropped her hand then and the ice that seemed to flood her veins was a deluge of frigidity.

'This is non-negotiable. Those are the only terms that will allow me to contemplate breaking my usual practices and buying less than half of a stake of a company.'

She shook her head, lifting a hand to her lips.

'And I will not just buy it, Annie. I will make it a point of pride to turn your father's company into a jewel of my crown. It will be ten times more valuable than he's ever dreamed of. I can make that happen—but only if you marry me.'

'You are such a bastard. How can I have ever thought otherwise?'

His smile was laced with cruel amusement. 'I'm not sure. Everyone else seemed to have my measure.'

She looked beyond him, towards the white leather sofa, then crossed the room and sank down into it. He was right. Everyone had warned her that he was dark, and tortured, that he'd been through too much for her to ever really be compatible with him. They'd all said he was unpredictable, that he'd hurt her. But she hadn't believed it. She hadn't, for one second, thought he was capable of behaving like this.

'They were right about you,' she said, squeezing her eyes shut on a surge of nausea. For years, she'd felt guilty and remorseful for having ended it with Theo, for having ignored her own affection for him, her own instincts, in favour of her parents' wishes. And now she saw they'd been right. Her friends who'd warned her had been right.

Theo was the devil, and here she was, trying to make a deal with him.

'By the way,' he said, moving into the kitchen, his tone now careless. 'In case you are wondering, this marriage will be real, in every way.'

When she looked up, it was to find his eyes latched to hers.

'Yes, by that I mean we'll share a bed. If I'm going to go along with this, there has to be some inducement.'

Her heart stammered; her pulse trembled. Did he have any idea what he was suggesting? Innocent Annie, who'd never been with a man before, was being propositioned into a loveless marriage that was to include sex.

Her voice wobbled as she said, quickly, 'You're the one who suggested marriage.'

'As I said, an inducement.'

She flinched, hating him for speaking to her like that. When they'd dated, he'd been so patient, so careful with her. He hadn't wanted to rush her, to pressure her; even when she'd been desperate to sleep with him, he'd said there was no rush. She shuddered now, at the ease with which he was trying to pressure her into a marriage that would include casual sex. 'You are horrible.'

'Apparently.'

'I can't—'

'That is your prerogative. I also have a business Realtor I can put you in touch with, if you'd prefer to find a buyer on the open market. I will warn you, though, you are likely to struggle to find someone who'll consider the company in its current state. Bankruptcy is more likely.

And if you're thinking I wouldn't enjoy that prospect, then you really are clinging to some romantic notion of the man you thought I was.'

The grief devouring her was overwhelming. How had she been so stupid and wrong about him? How had she misread him so completely?

Besides, she knew a business Realtor wouldn't get her anywhere. She'd consulted with one six months ago, when she'd realised how badly things had been mishandled. He'd advised her just as Theo had—though he'd chosen his words with a little more compassion than the man opposite.

'Why on earth would you want to marry me?'

'I told you.'

'Just to hurt my father?'

He dipped his head in silent recognition of that.

'I can't believe it.'

'Nonetheless, those are the facts. And one more thing, Annie.'

She hadn't thought he was capable of anything else, but then he surprised her. 'Every single cent of my profits will go to a charity of my choosing, that supports children like I used to be. Every cent. Your father will see the company he loves so much flowing to the hands of impoverished street kids.'

Annie's jaw parted. Well, that wasn't something she had any problems with. After all, she'd still own a controlling stake, and the profits from that would be used to support her father.

'As for the percentage,' Theo continued, pulling the rug out from under her once more, 'only a fool would agree to allow you to continue to hold the lion's share. I will buy a fifty-five per cent stake, but,' he held up a finger to silence her. 'On the day we divorce, I shall return the whole thing to you. One hundred per cent.'

Annie's brain hurt too much to fully understand what he was saying. She shook her head. 'What?'

'I am not interested in owning your company long-term. I will take it over, fix it up, make your father rich again, then walk away. But he will have to know two things,' Theo said, his nostrils flaring with the force of his emotions. 'It is because of me,' he tilted his jaw. 'And that you were mine, for as long as it suited me, and then I left you, on my own terms. If you can live with that, then you have a deal. Otherwise, I wish you well.'

CHAPTER THREE

HE HADN'T BEEN surprised she'd told him to go to hell and stormed out of the penthouse. He'd been deliberately harsh in his offer, hoping she'd refuse. It was his standard operating procedure: only offer what he'd be happy to have accepted. Those were the only terms under which he operated. He'd intentionally presented the deal in such a way that made it almost impossible for a woman like Annie to acquiesce to.

Almost.

But then again, she'd loved her parents so much she'd given Theo up without a second thought. She'd lived her whole life in their shadow, had been theirs to control and dictate to. So it was little surprise that his doorbell rang a few hours later, and a fierce-looking Annie stood on the other side, her eyes sparking with sheer, unadulterated hatred and distaste, reminding him, for a moment, of her father, who'd regarded him with just such a look of scathing contempt, several years earlier.

Back then, Theo had still been just softened enough by Annie and her influence on him to have started to hope that the older man might one day look at Theo like a son. He'd still had a hope, somewhere deep inside, that he had a value beyond what he could bring to a company. He'd had a hope that he was worth loving.

How stupid he'd been.

Still a damaged child, hurt and seeking to be repaired, instead of just accepting that some people couldn't be fixed, and that was okay.

'Twice in one day, how fortunate,' he drawled, stepping back in silent invitation, but Annie shook her head.

'I don't need to come in. This won't take long.' If her expression had been a mask of contempt, then her voice was utterly dripping with it.

He had to admire her. When she'd left this place a few hours earlier, she'd been obviously furious, but also, clearly reeling. Her petite, slender frame had been shaking like a kitten, her skin whiter than snow. Now she was all fire and flame, spitting fury at him. He much preferred that—he felt more comfortable staring down anger than he did looking at pain, and knowing himself to be the cause.

'I'll go along with your proposal, but I have a counter proposal to offer.'

His admiration increased, but he didn't convey so much as a hint of that. 'Perhaps you're misunderstanding your bargaining position, Annie. I hold all the cards. You need something from me, and I need nothing from you.'

'I understand my position just fine, and I also understand you now. You're lying when you say you don't need anything from me—you revealed your hand this afternoon.'

Something crept inside his gut, a feeling like surprise. No one had stood up to him for a very long time—and the fact that challenge was now coming from Annie was strangely appealing. Strangely attractive too, if he was honest. 'Oh, did I?'

'You want revenge. You want to hurt my father. Hell, I'm pretty sure you want to hurt me.' She tilted her chin with courage, though, holding his gaze, even when her eyes were burning with rage and disgust. 'And that's fine. If that's the means to the end I need here, I'll go along with your sick plan. It will be worth it.'

In the back of his mind, he was aware of how empty his response was to her agreement. Usually, a victory elicited a rare moment of joy for Theo, a feeling that he was completing his purpose, that he was fulfilling the one thing he was good at. But Annie's acceptance left him strangely hollowed out, almost as if he really had wanted her to walk away.

'However, I need more.'

'More—' his skepticism sounded totally relaxed '—than the small fortune it will take to acquire your father's business?'

'I want a guarantee of a settlement in our divorce.'

His gaze narrowed. 'I already told you, you'll get the company.'

'Yes, but it occurs to me that you could gleefully destroy the company—whilst being married to me, your apparently fawning wife—thus utterly destroying my father for good. Only a fool would take that risk with a man like you.'

Her words cut through him like acid might a flimsy piece of fabric. That she could think him capable of such a betrayal was no surprise—not after the way he'd spoken to her this afternoon. But if there was one thing Theodoros Leonidas lived and died by, it was his code of honour. 'My word is my bond,' he said darkly.

'Yes, well, it's not enough to bond me to you. I want an ironclad prenup, with a divorce settlement that will make this whole charade worthwhile, regardless of what happens with the company.'

'So you will walk away with the company and what? A multimillion-dollar settlement?'

'No,' her smile was saccharine. 'If you are able to rebuild the company to an agreed-upon commercial value within eighteen months—and I will not be married to you for a day longer than that, you understand?—I'll forego the divorce settlement. It's one or the other. Believe me, I don't want a cent of yours if I can avoid it. But if we're going to do this to my father, I need to know he'll at least be financially looked after for the rest of his life.'

It was an *excellent* suggestion by her. He had absolutely no intention of going back on the promise he'd made her that afternoon, nor on reneging on the terms of their agreement, but her precaution was protective and wise, and very, very canny. He was so focused on her negotiating abilities, he didn't notice that she made no reference to her own comfort, and the rest of her own life—it was all about her father.

'And you agree that from the moment we put this in motion, our relationship will become public. Very, very public?'

Her cheeks flashed with a hint of colour—infinitely preferable to the paleness he'd seen that afternoon. 'That's part of the deal, yes.'

'Fine.' He nodded curtly. 'I'll have the wedding contract drawn up. Now, would you like to shake hands, or is there another way we can seal the deal?'

She glared at him, then took a step forward, her eyes overflowing with challenge as she spoke coldly and with barely contained rage. 'Let's be clear about something. I hate and despise you with every fibre of my being. I am marrying you for one reason, and one reason only: to save this company. I will do whatever you ask, I will be whatever you want, but know this, Theo—you have ruined, forever, anything good I ever thought of you. Any warmth I ever felt for you, any idea I ever held of you as some wonderful, perfect man. You destroyed that. *You.* I came to you at my lowest ebb, needing your friendship, and instead, you blackmailed me into a deal for the sole purpose of hurting my father. You are the lowest of the low, and I have never been gladder that I listened to sense and walked away from you back then.'

Each word was delivered like a slap to his skin, spiked and laced with intent, so it took all of his strength to simply stand there and absorb her words with a mask of impassivity, like she wasn't shredding a part of him to pieces he hadn't even known still existed.

'My lawyers will be in touch tomorrow,' he said, simply, so she nodded, and walked back towards the lift.

He'd thought that was it, but once she'd stepped inside, and was staring at him fearlessly, she said, 'I'd say I'm looking forward to it, but we'd both know that would be a lie.'

Annie knew Theo's intention was to hurt her father, and he probably wanted to do that by somehow getting their photos in the papers, and surprising the older man with the relationship. Over Annie's dead body. Having been contacted by Theo's intimidating team of lawyers that morning and gone over the prenuptial agreement, and had her own lawyer then peruse the documents and approve them before signing, she now faced the reality of what she'd agreed to. But it would all be worth it.

Since her mother's death, she'd done everything she could to hold her father and his company together, but it had been too much. Too much loss and grief for one man to bear, and Annie hadn't really been in the right headspace either, to do what was necessary.

Well, that was an error she intended to fix, right now, starting with this marriage. But it would be her way, her terms. Theo would live to rue the day he thought he could bully her into marriage and not pay the price. A smile tickled the corner of her lips as she reached for her phone—she was almost looking forward to making his life a misery.

Gone was the compliant, adoring girl who'd worshipped at his feet like a puppy dog. Now she was a modern-day Boadicea, without the titian-red hair and with a few more clothes. He wanted revenge? Yeah, well, he wasn't the only one.

She pressed her father's name in her phone and waited for it to connect. When he answered, she felt a pang in the centre of her chest. He was only in his early sixties—still a young man—but life had knocked the wind from his sails, and he sounded at least twenty years older than his age when his voice, thin and frail, came down the phone line.

'Annie, darling? Is everything okay?'

She swallowed past the lump in her throat, hating that he always worried about her. 'Yes, Daddy, everything's fine.' She slipped into the childhood name out of habit. Though she'd been raised in Greece—her parents had fled there in grief, after Mary's death, needing a fresh start and a place where nothing reminded them of their late daughter—she was English, like her parents, and so were her habits and mannerisms. 'I'm calling with good news,' she said, infusing her voice with a happiness she didn't feel.

'Oh?' She could tell he was trying to rally himself, to remember what it was like to be happy for someone. 'Yes?'

'I'm getting married.'

Silence. She could just imagine his lined face growing even more creased with concern.

'It's okay, Daddy. This is a good thing.'

A sound of surprise. She pictured him sinking into the sofa, staring out at the view of Athens he had always loved from their palatial lounge room.

'I didn't know—I've been so—busy—I didn't even realise you were dating.'

'It's all happened very quickly,' she murmured. 'In fact, it's someone from my past. Someone you once knew, too.'

'Oh? Not that nice Beauchamp boy?' Her father named one of the many young men her parents had set her up with over the years. All nice, all handsome, all left her utterly desolate and cold. Disinterested and bored.

'No, not Harry Beauchamp. You know we're just friends.'

A sound of disappointment. 'Randall Chesterton?'

'No, Dad. It's...' She hesitated a moment, aware that her father would *not* be at all pleased but knowing she had to get this over with, like ripping off a plaster. 'It's Theo Leonidas. Remember, from next door?' she said, as though they hadn't had a screaming match over her parents' insistence that she break up with him. As though that awful, awful night wasn't etched in both their hearts.

'Leonidas?' he said, his voice no longer just weary, but worried, too. 'No, Annie. I told you, that boy is—'

'He's not a boy, Dad. He's a man, and he's the man I've chosen to marry. I need you to accept that, and be happy for me.' Her voice cracked a little, as a tear slid down her cheek, thudding against the carpet.

'I can't do that. He's wrong for you, all wrong.'

Her heart splintered. If only she could be honest with him—but that would hurt him more. She had to convince her father that she was happy and safe. Which was ironic, because that was also part of what Theo had insisted on. They were to fool her father into believing the marriage was real, and joyous. For Theo's part, he hoped that would wound Elliot Langley, and Annie knew it would. But there was still a part of her that hoped her father might find it within himself to have a normal parental reaction: happiness for the choice of his child. After all, she had been through enough in her life to know that she was making the right decision, given the cards she'd been dealt.

'You don't know him.'

'I know him,' her father contradicted swiftly. 'He is the last person your mother or I want in your life. Please, don't do this.'

She closed her eyes on a wave of frustration.

'We dealt with this,' her father pushed. 'You broke up. You've dated other nice men. Men who are far more suitable for you.'

Yes, she'd broken up with Theo, but not without a fight. She had argued with them, she had fought for them to understand, to give him a chance, but then, her mother had suffered the first of a series of heart attacks, and what choice had Annie had?

But now the circumstances were different. She was fighting for their financial standing, and for the family company her father cherished—one of the few things he had left from the tatters of their family.

'We're going to get married quickly, Daddy. I was thinking a garden wedding, at home, something simple,' she said, then realised Theo had said it needed to be public. 'Though we've also talked about a hotel, in the city. The details don't matter. But we want to be together, for the rest of our lives.' The words stuck in her throat a little, because of how desperately she'd felt them, six years earlier. 'And we want that to start right away.'

'Oh, Annie. I cannot support this.'

'Whether you support it or not, it's happening.'

'But, Annie. Who is this man? You know nothing about his family, and you are—'

'I know, I know. You've told me how you feel about him, but that doesn't change anything.'

'I can't accept this.'

'I'm sorry to hurt you,' she whispered, with honesty. 'But it's just how it has to be.'

'Are you sure?'

Annie almost laughed in despair. Was she sure? Sure that this could backfire spectacularly, yes. Sure about anything else…debatable.

'I'm getting married, and I want you to be happy for me.'

'I will never be able to give you that,' was all he said, in reply, before disconnecting the call.

She'd extended her stay by a couple of nights in accordance with a handwritten note that had been dropped off with the prenuptial agreement, stating that Theo would pick her up for dinner the following night at eight o'clock. On the afternoon of their appointed 'date', or rather, the beginning of her 'sentence', as she'd started to think of it, a bag from a designer boutique was brought up by the hotel concierge, with another note in Theo's darkly confident handwriting.

'For tonight.'

She'd pulled the dress from the bag once back in her hotel room, and marvelled at the elegant simplicity of it. She had bought and worn enough expensive dresses in her life to know the brand was one of the most exclusive in the world. She couldn't resist trying it on, and the moment she glanced at her reflection in the mirror, she was very, very tempted to wear it. It transformed her into a sophisticated, elegant heiress—just the kind of woman everyone expected her to be. Everyone except Theo, she might have said, if this wasn't evidence to the contrary.

She slipped the dress off again before she could weaken, stuffing it back in the bag before choosing something far simpler from her wardrobe—a black cocktail dress that fell to just above her knees and hugged her body like a second skin. She styled her hair in a braid that ran like a crown around her head, and kept her make-up minimalistic. For jewelry, she chose only her mother's earrings—pearls, which reminded her so much of Elizabeth Langley it couldn't help but bring Annie a shot of strength to wear them.

Her door buzzed at eight o'clock—on the dot—and Annie's stomach suddenly burst to life with butterflies and a dragon's fiery flames. She was hot and cold as she crossed the far more modest hotel room to the door, and wrenched it inwards to find Theo on the other side, in yet another suit, though this time with the sleeves down, jacket on, and custom shoes, no doubt, firmly in place.

He took one look at her and flattened his lips in a line of disapproval. Hardly a compliment, yet she dipped her head to hide a grin.

'You didn't like the dress?'

'I didn't need the dress,' she corrected, glancing up at him when she was confident her face once again bore a mask of casual non-concern.

'May I come in?' he said, though it was less of a question than a demand.

'I thought we were going out.'

'In good time.'

Her heart began to race faster at the thought of being alone with him in *her* hotel room, which, though elegant, was far more like an ordinary room in proportions. With one big king-sized bed in the middle.

He strode in and took a look around, frowning with bemusement to see she didn't have a suite.

'I only intended to stay here two nights,' she found herself saying defensively, as she shut the door. 'And I don't need more space than this.'

She'd taken two steps away from the door when the buzzer sounded and she paced back to it, opening it with a half smile in place. A waiter stood there with a room service trolley adorned with an ice bucket, French champagne, two flutes and chocolate-dipped strawberries.

'Ma'am,' he said politely. 'Would you like me to place this inside?'

Annie was too flummoxed to respond, but Theo's voice came down the narrow corridor. 'Leave the trolley, thank you.'

'Very good,' the waiter said, brandishing a small clipboard for Annie to sign.

She reached for it, but Theo was there, signing his own name with a flourish after adding a generous tip to the line on the bottom. The waiter disappeared down the corridor, leaving Theo to roll the trolley into a room that already felt far too small for them.

His eyes rested sardonically on Annie as he removed the champagne bottle and unfurled the foil top, then with a bang removed the cork.

'Are we celebrating?' she asked, one brow arched.

'I believe it's tradition to toast an engagement with champagne.'

'But ours is not a normal engagement. Behind closed doors, we don't need to pretend.'

'We can still toast to fresh starts.'

'Are you forgetting what I said the other day?' she demanded, nonetheless taking the glass he held out, hating the way her traitorous body responded to the feeling as her fingertips brushed his.

'Definitely not.'

'Good.'

'Are you afraid that you might forget, Annie?'

She almost spluttered at such a preposterous idea, and took a big drink just to wash away the angry response she was tempted to deliver. 'I'm confident I won't,' she managed, a moment later.

One corner of his mouth shifted in a half grin.

'To the future,' he said.

'To us both getting what we want and never seeing each other again.'

'Eighteen months is a long time to wait for that.'

'It'll be worth it.'

He sipped his drink, eyes resting on her face. 'You love your father a great deal.'

'What kind of statement is that? He's my father—of course I love him.'

Theo's eyes flashed with something, and his response was unnerving. 'Do you think it's mutual?'

'I know it is,' she said, shuddering a little, because her parents' love had been overwhelming—to the point of stultifying. She'd only really acknowledged that after her mother passed away, and to Annie's shame, mixed in with her grief had been a sense of...freedom. Because her father had been so wrapped up in his own immense sadness, and Annie had, for the first time in her life, been able to make choices for herself, without her parents constantly worrying and watching.

Theo, though, was silent, and that bothered her. 'What

would you know about love, anyway?' she muttered, sipping her drink.

'Not a thing,' he responded without hesitation, yet the answer left her cold. It reminded her of the conversational no-go zone that his childhood had always been.

She knew the basics. He'd been bounced between foster homes, had run away multiple times, and finally ended up with the Georgiadeses next door. But how he'd come to be with the childless older couple, had always been a mystery. Though Annie and Theo dated for a year, he had been carefully guarded with biographical details, always brushing her off with a half answer, or occasionally giving just enough information to satisfy her without really telling her anything. Yet something in the way he answered so readily now made a flick of sympathy stir in the pit of her belly.

The Georgiadeses loved him, she knew that, but she hoped that before them, there'd been at least someone. Everyone—even Theo—deserved love.

The silence in the room was like a form of static electricity, buzzing and humming, creating a sense of cotton wool filling her ears. Finally she spoke, just to cut through the tension. 'I spoke to my father this afternoon. I told him about us.'

Theo's eyes landed on hers. 'And?'

'Would you like me to tell you he bawled his eyes out? Begged me not to marry you?'

Theo's brow lifted. 'Did he?'

'I wouldn't say he's jumping over the moon about it, but he accepts it's happening. I think.'

His eyes gave nothing away. 'And the contracts?'

'With the lawyers.'

'I presume your father has to sign for the company?'

'The company passed to me legally on my twenty-fifth birthday. That was always their plan.'

Theo frowned. 'Yet you still refer to it as "your father's".'

'It's always been his. I never wanted it, truth be told.'

He nodded. 'No, you were going to own an art gallery, if I remember.'

She ignored the warmth that spread through her at his recollection of that small fact. She'd gone on and on about her dreams back then, and he wasn't stupid. Naturally he remembered.

'Just a childish fantasy.' She waved it away like it was meaningless.

'It didn't have to be. You could have opened the gallery at any point.'

'No, I couldn't.'

'Why not? You had money, time…'

She sipped her champagne and turned away from him, walking towards the bed and sinking down onto the edge of it, staring at the small kitchenette opposite rather than looking at Theo. She didn't want to explain any of this to him. To tell him what her life had been like after he'd left and she'd been all alone. And then, with her mother's death, the new reality that had faced her. It had been such a difficult time, made all the harder for how much she wanted the one thing she couldn't have: Theo.

'I gave up on childish dreams,' she said, instead, her voice heavy even to her own ears.

'Good.' He walked towards Annie then, standing right in front of her, before pressing a finger lightly to her chin and tilting her face upwards to meet his gaze. 'Realism is a better outlook, Annie. There's less room for disappointment.'

She could almost believe the advice came from a place of kindness, but then, Theo wasn't kind, and he certainly wasn't kind to her. She flinched her face away from his touch, grinding her teeth, and was rewarded by a mocking smile.

A moment later, he reached into his pocket and removed a black velvet box. 'This is for you.'

He handed the box over with no fanfare, no romance, nothing. Not that she'd have expected anything from Theo along those lines *now*, but the Theo she'd once loved, or thought she'd loved—oh, how she'd fantasised about this moment a thousand times back then. She cracked the velvet lid open and pulled a face at the monstrosity inside.

This was a ring that screamed 'look at me', and it was the very last thing Annie would ever have chosen.

'And here I thought you hated elitism,' she murmured, pulling the giant diamond solitaire ring from its home and squinting at the brightness as the brilliant cut speared thousands of little light prisms across the room. 'I mean, I'm going to stun someone with this thing.'

'I thought it would be what you'd like,' he said, shrugging. 'Certainly what your father would want—an ostentatious show of "love", the kind of thing a "suitable" aristocratic fiancé might gift you.'

'Tacky and garish? How well you know me,' she said, sliding it onto her finger and trying to guess whether it was fifteen or twenty carats.

'At least no one will miss it,' he said, and she glanced up at him again.

'You're enjoying this.'

'Yes.' He didn't attempt to deny it, nor to hide his pleasure. 'But there are other things I'm going to enjoy far more about marrying you, Annie.'

And despite everything she knew she should feel, a slick of moist heat, of delicious, desperate warmth, flooded her body, and a pulse began to throb between her legs, so she glanced away sharply and then quickly stood up, almost bumping straight into him.

Damn him for still being able to do this to her. Damn him for being the only man she'd ever felt anything like this for. How she hated him for that! Hate was good, though. Hatred and rage were excellent protective mechanisms, though Annie didn't stop to wonder why she should think she needed to protect herself. Once bitten, twice shy was her mantra—no way would she let Theo in again. Not now she knew what he was capable of.

CHAPTER FOUR

FOUR WEEKS PASSED in the blink of an eye, and before Annie knew it, the wedding day arrived. She hadn't seen her fiancé since their dinner date in Sydney. She hadn't needed to. Photos of them had gone up online even as they'd been eating a meal, pretending to have a wonderful time, thus meeting his requirement that their engagement be public and known. No doubt, Theo had had someone tip off the paparazzi. It just made Annie glad that she'd forewarned her father. Having lost her mother to a bad heart, she worried about the same with her father, despite the fact he was in excellent health.

Although Theo's remarks had hinted at him being attracted to Annie, he'd dropped her at her hotel without so much as a suggestion of joining her. And she'd been glad for that, too. Not that she would have minded rejecting him.

Annie had left all of the wedding planning to Theo—or someone he hired. Had it been a real wedding, she would undoubtedly have wanted to weigh in on every single decision, but given that he had blackmailed her into this, she figured he could take on the stress of planning.

The only thing she'd done for herself was select the wedding gown and bridesmaid dresses. For the latter, she'd chosen a pale yellow prom style, and for the former, an elegant off-white silk slip with a dropped back. She wore three fine gold chains that dangled at different heights down her spine. She looked like she was going to a fancy party, rather than a wedding, and though she had conceded to the wearing of her mother's veil, she refused to let it cover her face like a bridal innocent—she was going into this with her eyes wide open. No need to pretend otherwise. Her glossy dark hair had been styled into voluminous curls that hung around her face, and her fingers were painted a simple nude. On her feet, she wore black stilettos—a striking contrast to the dress—and her lips were painted a deep red. She revelled in bucking the traditional bride model. This wasn't a traditional wedding.

Perhaps on some level it was because she wanted to save the real bridal gown and look for one day, if and when she were to marry for real. After all, in eighteen months or less she'd be free of Theo, and one day, surely, she'd meet someone special. Someone she might love, who would love her back, like she'd once upon a time thought Theo did.

She'd chosen two school friends to act as bridesmaids, though she hadn't felt close to them for a long time. Theo had organised a large wedding, so what choice did she have? She hadn't asked who he was having as groomsmen; she hadn't wanted to show interest in his life.

'Are you ready, my love?' her father, misty-eyed, asked as he poked his head around the door to her room in the luxurious Athens hotel suite Theo had booked out for the bridal party.

Annie stared at her reflection, drawing in a deep breath. Was she ready?

Not really.

And yet, at the same time, she just wanted to get this over with. The sooner they were married, the sooner Theo's money would flow into the company, and they could start focusing on how to rebuild it. Instead of a honeymoon, they'd have a corporate merger. Relief twisted inside Annie, even as butterflies overtook every part of her body.

'Darling?'

She blinked her gaze sideways to where her father stood, a hint of concern on his handsome face.

'Yes.' She forced a bright smile. 'I'm ready. Let's go.'

'Annie.' Her father hesitated, though. 'If you have any doubts, you can back out.'

Annie's heart thumped.

'You say you're happy, that this is what you want, but you look as though you're on the way to the executioner.'

Damn it. She had been brooding. She forced a bright smile. 'I'm nervous—isn't that normal for a wedding?'

'Not my wedding,' her father said, shaking his head. 'Marrying your mother was the happiest day of my life. I would do it a thousand times over if I could.'

Emotions threatened to topple Annie's determination. She ran her fingers over her veil, thinking of her mother, drawing strength from her even when she wasn't there. This was necessary, and marrying Theo would be the answer to all their problems; she had to do it. 'I'm getting married.'

'But today, and to him? Why not wait awhile. Meet some other men. You've barely dated—'

'No, Dad. No. It's Theo, or no one.' That was true, though not for the reasons her father might have supposed.

'Your mother would have hated this,' he said, and with such sadness and disapproval in his tone that Annie's heart splintered apart. She didn't want to disappoint her father, but this was the only way she could save the business. She dropped her hand from the veil, hoping he was wrong, hoping that Elizabeth Langley would have understood.

'I hope not,' Annie said.

Her father just grunted, shook his head, so Annie said, 'Are you going to be able to walk me down the aisle? Because I'll go alone, if I need to.'

She could see her father was actually contemplating that, which gave a good insight into how much he was against the wedding.

'Come on, Dad,' she cajoled. 'It's just a quick ceremony, and then it will be all over.' Or just beginning, for Annie. But to her relief, her father put his hand on her forearm to lead her deeper into the suite.

When they stepped into the main room of the suite, Angela and Maria stopped talking and came to Annie, hugging her. It all felt so performative, though. Annie would never have chosen this for her real wedding day, but that didn't matter because this was just a performance.

It was part of what Theo required, and she'd go along with it, purely to get what she wanted: help with the business.

The wedding itself was to take place in the hotel ballroom. They rode down the lift as a group, and then walked through the corridor to a large set of double doors. Several staff members stood there in suits, and a woman with an earpiece and clipboard nodded her approval when Annie appeared.

'Right on time, excellent. Are you ready?'

Annie nodded.

'Good. Bridesmaids, here, and here.' She pointed to the carpet near the door, then turned back to Annie. 'I'll tell you when to go.'

Annie turned to her father, then slid her hand into the crook of his arm. He looked grey beneath his tan and a pang of remorse filtered through her. She'd do anything to spare him this pain, only it was the lesser of two evils. Allowing the company to become bankrupt would utterly destroy him. She couldn't do it.

The doors opened and there was a huge amount of noise as the assembled guests—goodness, there must have been four hundred people, at least—stood as one, like a tide rising, and turned to face the door. A familiar classical song filtered through to them, and then, Angela and Maria began to walk down the aisle. They obstructed Annie's view of Theo, so it wasn't until they were almost at the front of the assembled guests that she saw him, flanked on one side by two men in dark suits. But she barely looked at them, except to see if they were familiar—they weren't. Her eyes were trapped by Theo, locked to him in a way that made her whole body tingle.

He wore a jet black tuxedo, with his dark hair brushed back from his brow, and his face was hawk-like—studying her, perhaps wondering if she was going to bolt. Not likely.

She straightened her spine, squeezed her dad's hand, and then, began to walk, slowly, as though she were enjoying it, down the aisle, even managing to shape her bright red lips into a curve, as though she were genuinely jubilant to be there. Wasn't that the point? To sell this as a love match?

But the closer they got to Theo, the more her heart started to ram against her ribs, the more her knees felt trembly and her pulse weak, so that by the time they came to him, she was barely aware of the way her father's body had grown tense and rigid.

'Elliot,' Theo said, voice gruff, eyes glinting with something that Annie knew to be triumph. He reached out and took Annie's hand from her father's, a symbol of his removing an object deeply valued, so she wanted to shake his touch off her—but she didn't. She was playing a role.

She did, however, turn to her dad and kiss his cheek, and say, 'I love you, Daddy,' smiling at him encouragingly.

The older man's eyes slid to Theo's, and for a second, Annie wondered if he was going to say something. As far as she knew, this was the first time they'd come face-to-face since the conversation Theo had only recently enlightened her to having taken place, three or so years earlier. He didn't, though. A moment later, Elliot Langley turned and walked to his seat at the front of the audience.

Annie moved closer to Theo, and then, staring at him, her heart almost gave out, because this felt so close to what she'd fantasised about, so often, she couldn't believe it was happening—and like this.

He leaned closer to her, and murmured in her ear, 'You look beautiful.'

It was the last thing she'd expected him to say. Kind and flattering—she hadn't thought him capable any longer.

'Thank you,' she whispered.

He pulled his head back, turned to the celebrant, and nodded.

'Dearly beloved...' Annie tried not to think about the wedding beyond being a scripted event. She didn't want to think about what would come next, about the night ahead, about the next eighteen months. She repeated the lines as required, smiled, and almost went into a form of stasis. But when Theo lifted her hand to slide the wedding ring in place, his touch was electric, shocking her out of the almost sedated state she'd fallen into.

And then, of course, came the kiss.

That part she'd prepared for, braced herself for. They'd kissed hundreds of times, so she knew what kissing him felt like.

At least, she thought she did.

But when this Theo swept her into his arms, holding her body tight against his, and dropped his head, the whole world began to spin way too fast. He smelled so good and felt so strong, his presence was overwhelming, right down to a cellular level. She simply parted her lips and then he was kissing her, his mouth not gentle, not brief, but rather, possessive and dominating, his lips parting her mouth wider, his tongue clashing with hers, his body shifting her slightly to shield them from the view of the audience, for the most part. It was not a long kiss—perhaps five seconds at most, but it was earth-shattering, regardless. When he lifted his head, she stared up at him, dazed, in a fog of need that he'd stirred so easily.

It was such a different kiss to before. Almost as though back then he'd treated her like she was young and innocent. As though he hadn't wanted to break her, when now, Annie realised, she wanted that. She wanted rough and hard and flooded with passion—it felt appropriate, in their vitriolic new relationship.

'If there were not five hundred people staring at us, you would be naked by now,' he muttered, eyes dragging from hers to her mouth, to her breasts, which had peaked nipples and were flooded with tingling awareness.

'That's a little presumptuous, isn't it?' she said huskily.

His laugh was hoarse and mocking. 'No. Nice try, though.'

He shifted them so they were once more in full view of the assembled guests, and that was it. They were married.

After the wedding came the party, and though it was filled with loud revellers and good wishes, Annie knew barely anyone and found she didn't want to speak to many people. It surprised her that Theo had invited such a large number of guests. Then again, his business interests were enormous—he employed tens of thousands of people around the globe, so within those ranks, presumably he had large executive teams. No doubt they'd all received an invitation.

From what she could tell, none of the guests were particularly close friends with Theo. She watched him work the room though, the way he spoke to almost everyone, from what she could tell, his body language relaxed, his manner charming. She'd never seen this side of him before: she was surprised he possessed it. So debonair and sophisticated, you could easily imagine he'd been born to this sort of wealth and privilege. Perhaps that was the point.

She knew he guarded the truth of his upbringing with care; he probably preferred to interact with people who simply presumed he was every bit as entitled as they were.

At almost midnight, he circled back to Annie, who'd been having a mind-numbing conversation about childcare with two of her high school friends who were married with small children. They were debating the merits of their nannies, comparing the duties each performed, and Annie had to keep biting back a yawn.

'You look exhausted,' Theo murmured in her ear from behind, surprising her with his approach.

She startled, as his warm breath caressed her cheek. 'Thank you so much. That's just what every bride wants to hear on her wedding day.'

He shrugged insolently. 'It is a point of fact.' His eyes raked her face. 'Shall we?'

'Shall we what?'

'Leave.'

She looked around. 'Can we do that?'

'Yes, Annie. It's time.' And from the way his eyes held hers, she guessed there was a double meaning to his statement. Her stomach twisted in knots as he reached down and laced their fingers together, guiding her from the wedding ballroom, and out into the night.

'Honeymoon?' Annie repeated drowsily, as his car pulled up—not, as she'd expected, to his Athens home—but rather at a small private airport. She'd fallen asleep almost as soon as they'd left the hotel, and it was only Theo's words, 'it's time for our honeymoon', that had wakened her. 'But why?'

'Is it not what usually follows a wedding?'

'Yes, but this isn't a real wedding,' she said, as though she were talking to someone very dimwitted.

'Tsk, tsk,' he murmured, reaching over and unbuckling her seatbelt, then leaving his hand to hover on her hip a moment. 'Remember that we agreed it would be real, in every way?'

A shiver of anticipation brushed through her. 'Yes, but...'

'This is not up for negotiation. The arrangements have been made.' He pulled back and opened his car door, leaving her staring, frowning, at the black leather seat across from her. He then opened her car door, and stared down at her. 'I will carry you, Annie, if you do not walk yourself.'

She stared at him, half tempted to act belligerently and remain in the car, just to feel his big strong arms wrap around her again. But what kind of stupid was that? Where was the dignity?

She clamped her lips together and glared at him as she stepped out, shivering for a different reason now. Despite the warmth of the day, the night had turned cool, and her slip of a dress was hardly adequate protection.

Theo immediately slipped out of his tuxedo jacket and

wrapped it around her shoulders. If she hadn't known for herself how unfeeling he was, she might have experienced a sense of warmth at his thoughtfulness.

'I'm fine,' she said dismissively, starting to shake out of it.

But his strong hands pressed to her shoulders, keeping the jacket in place. 'Wear it, Annie. It's not going to kill you.'

She made a noise of skepticism, but chose not to fight with him.

A private jet was just across from them, and going by the 'Leonidas' on the tail, it clearly belonged to Theo. It was not a small jet, either, but rather the size of a commercial airliner. Curiosity propelled her forward, then up the stairs, and when she reached the top and stepped inside her eyes almost popped out of her head. For there she was confronted with the most incredible space she'd ever seen. It was more six-star hotel than plane, from the plush lounge suite at the front, to a full dining table, an enormous flat screen TV on the back wall. She presumed there would be a bedroom and bathroom beyond that, and who knew what else?

'Jeez, Theo, this is...' She waved a hand in the air, searching for the right word.

He glanced from her to the plane, waiting without speaking.

'This is a lot.'

'Yes.'

She ran her hand over the back of one of the leather lounge chairs, moving deeper into the plane. 'Did you have this when we dated?'

'No.'

She nodded, wondering why he'd bought it, and when.

She moved past the dining table, which she supposed he might use for boardroom meetings, and past more comfortable chairs that were angled to face the cinema screen. A partition with a timber-looking door was beyond the screen. She turned to face Theo, only to find he was almost on top of her, so when she stopped walking, his chest brushed against hers, and warmth licked her every cell.

'Can I keep going?'

His eyes flared again, in that way he had. A brief flicker of flame, of passion, before he could control it. Fascinating.

He dipped his head in acknowledgement, and Annie turned away again, glad for the reprieve of looking right at him. She opened the door, and stepped right into an enormous bedroom. It took up almost the whole back of the plane, with its king-sized bed, sofa and another huge screen.

Just looking at the bed made her mouth go dry. She twisted the enormous engagement ring on her finger, the huge diamond something she'd strangely gotten used to over the preceding four weeks despite her initial disdain for it. To distract herself from the bed, she pointed to two other doors. 'What's through there?'

'The gym,' he murmured, close enough that she could feel his breath on the top of her head. 'And the bathroom. There's time to freshen up and change before take-off, if you'd like.'

Her heart twisted at the simple courtesy. It had been a long day, and the thought of a hot shower and fresh clothes was suddenly instantly appealing.

'My bag?' she asked.

'Stowed, but there are clothes in there for you.'

'Oh.'

He really had thought of everything. Then again, it probably wasn't the first time he'd 'entertained' on his luxury plane. The thought drained the warmth from her body, leaving her ice-cold.

'I won't be long,' she said, turning from him easily now, and wrenching open the door to the en suite. As she might have come to expect, given the rest of the plane's fit-out, it was also the kind of room that would be more at home in a mansion than a plane, with white tiles, gold fittings and a shower that was big enough for two.

Yes, definitely a flying bachelor pad, she thought with distaste, as she slid the dress from her body, then her silky white briefs. The water came out warm and with good pressure, so she stepped under it and just stood there for several minutes, before reaching for the body wash and lathering herself all over, ignoring the way even her own touch sent sparks of need through her over-sensitised nervous system.

She hated that he could so easily do this to her, and yet...anticipation was a flickering flame in the pit of her stomach.

This marriage was a necessary evil, so far as Annie was concerned, except in one way. There was no denying their physical connection, and even though Annie barely recognised the man he'd become—so filled with hate and rage—she knew better than to lie to herself.

She wanted him, just as much as she always had. It was a need that defied logic and explanation—it was simply a part of her.

Ten minutes later, she had dried herself off with a towel, and dressed in one of the outfits that had been left hanging in the wardrobe—a simple pair of shorts and a comfortable T-shirt. It hardly screamed seduction, but maybe that was a good defense to what they were inevitably hurtling towards.

She fidgeted her fingers and counted to ten before opening the door to the bedroom and scanning it for Theo, only he wasn't there. She frowned, padding through the plane in the towelling slippers she'd found, back into the main living area. Disappointment was a heavy stone in her gut.

She'd expected him to be in the bedroom. She'd wanted him to be there, waiting for her, and she couldn't believe that. What kind of fool did that make her? A lamb, willingly led to slaughter, that's what.

His eyes glanced up from the newspaper he was reading when she entered, and perhaps he saw the vestiges of disappointment on her features, because his smile was one of mocking indolence.

'Something the matter?'

'Of course not,' she snapped, taking the seat across the aisle from him. 'Where are we going, anyway?'

'My island.'

'Your *island*?' she repeated. 'Since when?'

'I've had it a long time, in fact.'

She frowned. 'You've never mentioned it before.'

'It never came up.'

She looked across the corridor towards him. 'That's weird, because it feels like something you probably should have mentioned.'

'Why, Annie? Do you think knowing I had an island might have convinced your friends and your parents that I was good enough for you, after all?'

She flinched at that anger in his voice, the barely concealed disgust.

'No, I just think it's something that's not super common, and as such, wouldn't have killed you to tell me.'

'It never occurred to me to mention it. I bought it as an investment.'

She pulled a face. 'You bought an island as an investment?'

'The former owner got into financial difficulties, and needed to sell it quickly and quietly. I had the cash, so I bought it.'

'In cash.'

'Annie, you grew up surrounded by wealth, yet you seem totally baffled by the fact I have these things, like an island, and a private jet,' he said, gesturing to the plane. Before she could answer, a flight attendant in a smart grey suit strolled down the aisle, a tray balanced skillfully on one hand. She removed a flute of champagne, only half filled, and a mineral water, giving the latter to Theo and the former to Annie, before placing a tray of cheese and crackers in front of Annie.

'We'll be taking off shortly, sir,' she directed to Theo, then smiled at Annie before retreating. If she thought it strange that the newlyweds were sitting separated by an aisle, so what? Annie was tired of playing the part of the loving wife—it had been a long day and night, and she wanted to let the mask drop, just for a little while.

'You always hated status symbols,' she said, when they were alone again.

'This is not a status symbol, it's a practical necessity. I have operations all over the world. I travel frequently, often on short notice. I choose to do so in comfort and privacy.'

'And the island?'

'Is worth triple what I paid for it,' he said nonchalantly.

She shook her head, something still not adding up for Annie. Then again, how well had she really known Theo? Back then, she would have said she knew him better than she knew even herself, but it turned out, he was nothing like she thought.

'Do you go there often?'

'No.'

'So you have a private island—where exactly?'

'Off the coast of Italy.'

'Right, okay. So you have a private Mediterranean island, but you don't even use it?'

'What's your point?'

She couldn't say, exactly, only it sounded both sad and wasteful. 'Why don't you go there?'

'I don't have the time.'

She knitted her brows together. 'Because you work so much?'

'You sound skeptical.'

'No, I'm not, I always knew your work was important to you.' It was true. He'd acted like he had a monkey on his back, and building himself the biggest and best business empire in the world was the only way he'd ever shake it off.

His eyes glowed when they met hers, and she felt the fierce determination that was like iron in his veins.

'You have an active social life, though,' she said, as the engines began to roar to life and the plane accelerated along the tarmac.

His smile was laced with knowing cynicism. 'Social life, or sex life?'

Her stomach seemed to flood with acid. She glanced away, her finger running up and down the slender stem of her champagne flute. 'I guess sex life, if you have to be crude about it.'

'And how would you know that, Annie?'

She jerked her gaze back to him, hating that he sounded so triumphant, like he'd caught her out in admitting she was basically his stalker.

'It's not hard to know it,' she snapped. 'You have a habit

of going to high-profile bars and restaurants and you're incredibly rich, successful and handsome, so guess what? Your photo gets on all the social media gossip sites and in the tabloids. I can't so much as scroll Insta without seeing you and some vampy-looking woman on my feed. Tell me, Theo, is that what does it for you these days?'

'What, exactly?'

'Skirts that barely cover cheeks, boobs pretty much out on display. Is that your thing now?'

'How do you know it wasn't always my thing?'

That stung. Annie had simply worked on the assumption that *she* had been his ideal woman when they'd dated, but for all she knew, he'd been coveting something else all along. Wishing she was more sophisticated, that she'd dress like all her friends did.

'I really, really hate you,' she said, glancing towards the window and staring out, as the plane lifted up and Athens turned into a delicate blanket of lights, far beneath them.

'Be that as it may, you're married to me for the next eighteen months, and I find that's all I really care about.' She heard the snapping of his seatbelt. 'I'll be in the bedroom. If you feel like joining me, you're more than welcome.'

CHAPTER FIVE

THE FEELING OF satisfaction he'd been hoping for never came. Ever since she'd agreed to marry him, he'd expected that the wedding would ease the strange heaviness in his chest, but if anything, seeing her dressed like a bride had tugged at something deep in his gut. A memory he'd refused to examine since they'd parted ways.

There had been a time when he'd fantasised about this future with Annie, for real. A time when he'd not only imagined but simply accepted as fate a future life with her constantly by his side.

For someone like Theo, who'd been let down by everyone he'd ever known, who'd learned from a very young age that he was the only person he could rely on, the way she'd slipped into his life without his realising it, becoming a part of him without his consent, had been shocking.

Accepting their breakup had been a little like leaping off a tall building—he'd had to scrape himself up and rebuild himself, piece by piece, *without* her at the centre of his being.

And, he had done it. He had excised her from his thoughts with sheer strength of will, had cut her from his mind, and from his heart, where he had begun to understand she'd taken up the most shocking residence.

With time and perspective, he'd realised that caring

for Annie had weakened him, and made him vulnerable, in a way he never intended to be again. Whereas life on the streets, his whole damned childhood, had made Theo tough, carved him like granite, something about Annie had eroded that. Or threatened to. He hadn't liked it—not once she'd ended things, and he'd realised how much of an impact she was having on him. He'd been relieved they were done, so he could go back to his solitary, diamond-tough existence.

And yet, he still did care. Not *for* her, in the same way he once idiotically had, but about her. Despite every shred of anger he felt for her snobby parents, and for the fact she'd so easily fallen into their plans, he hadn't enjoyed seeing her today. When she wouldn't notice, he had watched her. He had seen the tension in her features, the worry in her eyes as she'd sought out her father, to reassure herself he was okay.

This, though, had been a promise he'd made himself, that very morning they'd broken up.

Part of rebuilding himself had been knowing he would one day get his own revenge.

He had thought it would come just from his success. Her parents hadn't believed he was good enough for Annie? Then he would become the most successful, lusted-after man on earth, the kind of man ambitious parents would give their left arms to have their daughters marry. He'd spend a lifetime with women like Annie's friends between his sheets, and he'd make sure everyone saw that.

He would wave his success—and his womanising—in their faces. Yes, Annie's, too. He'd relished the thought of her seeing those photos. Every woman he went out with, and paparazzi snapped images of, he imagined her seeing and regretting the decision she'd made.

It had been a childish, stupid anger—totally beneath him—but there it was.

It would never have gone beyond making himself *this*, the very image of unquantifiable wealth and success, but for the fact Annie had turned up in his life and handed him revenge on a silver platter. How could he say no?

He'd acted on instincts, but now that they were actually legally married, he couldn't help wondering if he'd made a rare mistake. He'd acted on the assumption that he could easily control his feelings for Annie this time around—and that included the powerful desire that flared between them. But just a few minutes in her company had left his insides zinging—with physical need, yes, but with something else, too. A confusing array of uncertainty, and a lack of clarity when it came to his plan.

With frustration zipping through him, and a need to refocus on his goals here, he changed into shorts and a shirt and made his way into the gym. A run would help—or at least burn off some of the energy that had a stranglehold on his body and wouldn't let go.

Annie wanted, with all of herself, to go to the bedroom and get this over with. Not because she wasn't looking forward to it, but because she *was*. She wanted him so badly it almost hurt, and the thought of making love to Theo filled her with adrenalin. She hated that it was so, but there was no sense pretending otherwise, at least to herself.

The first time would be strange, though, because everything was so different to back then, when she'd thought they were in love and going to spend the rest of their lives together. Then, she'd been desperate to sleep with him, to know the pleasure of his body, the togetherness of making love. It had been as much about their emotional connection as anything else, whereas now, it was sheer chemistry.

Just like their kiss at the wedding, when a different kind of passion had hummed between them. Something far more adult and overwhelming. Exhilarating, and exciting...she couldn't stop thinking about what it would be like to be with him now.

Yet, she stayed in her seat, stubbornly refusing to go back to the bedroom, even when he'd issued a lukewarm invitation for her to join him. Pride died a slow death, and Annie knew she would need to hold on to hers, in this marriage, which meant the only way they'd end up in bed together was if he pursued her.

She wasn't going to show him how much she wanted that, even when it was something she'd tacitly agreed to on the day he'd suggested this arrangement.

He didn't come back out to her until the plane was beginning its descent—and for Annie, that was a hair-raising enough experience as to leave her distracted by the perils of landing on an island in the middle of the sea to barely give him so much as a passing glance.

It was late at night, and the island was indistinguishable from the ocean—just a big patch of black that the plane was steadily careening towards. As they drew closer, however, she saw the runway lights guiding the pilots in to land, and in the distance, a gold glow which she presumed to be his house.

Curiosity then had her leaning forward in her seat to get a better view from the portal window, but she couldn't make out anything besides what looked to be a thickly lush amount of greenery on either side of the airstrip.

The plane touched down with a bump and she startled,

glancing at Theo to see if he'd noticed, but he was once more absorbed in his newspaper.

She smothered a wry smile. So much for a honeymoon.

The house was definitely not what she'd expected. Oh, it was huge and modern and clearly very expensive, perched as it was right on the edge of the beach, with three walls being made almost solidly of glass. But it was the open plan nature of it that she hadn't expected. As in, no walls, except for the bathroom.

Despite being more than large enough to accommodate dozens of actual rooms, there were no partitioning walls. There was a massive kitchen and living area, with a grand piano and a flat screen TV the size of a cinema screen, several sitting areas, all plush and fashionably chic, and then, there was a bed. Just *one* bed. It was towards the back of the large room, but it was *right there* staring back at her, inviting her, demanding to be lain in and used for making love.

Heat flushed her cheeks as she dragged her gaze away to the blackness beyond the windows. In the morning, she would see the ocean in all its daytime glory, but for now, there was just a hint of silver foam, frothing atop the waves that rolled towards them, the cacophony of their crashing to the sandy shore rhythmic yet not at all reassuring. If anything, it formed a drumbeat of need, echoing the thundering of her pulse, making her want more than she wished to.

'This is it?' Her voice emerged squeaky and high-pitched. She swallowed, trying to tamp it down.

'Do you have a problem with it?' he asked, in a way that was almost completely blanked of emotion, and yet she heard it anyway—because she knew him too well to miss it. Smugness. He *wanted* to unsettle her. To make her uncomfortable.

She turned to face him, her eyes wide, but she shrugged, like it was no big deal. 'It'll do,' she said, moving through the room, running a hand over the shiny top of the grand piano, then pressing a few keys. 'Do you play?'

'No.'

She sat down on the stool and held her fingers to the keys, closing her eyes a moment before she began to move her fingers, to play Pachelbel's Canon in D, the song that she'd walked down the aisle to.

'I forgot you learned,' he said, his voice close by, so she opened her eyes to find him standing just in front of her, to the side of the piano, watching her with an intensity that made her blood fire. She ignored the insult buried in those words—the fact he'd forgotten she'd learned, when she couldn't forget anything about him.

Bastard.

'All my life,' she said. 'Well, until I was nineteen, anyway.'

'Why did you stop?'

'I guess I'd learned enough.'

'Do you still play for pleasure?'

Her lips twisted to the side. She hadn't played since her mother had died. In the six months between her first and last heart attacks, she'd played for her often. Her mother had loved to hear Annie's music—it had reminded her of Mary. Mary, who'd been a brilliant pianist, who'd taught herself by the time she was three to play Mozart. Mary, who'd been a legitimate prodigy, and left Annie to follow after her, never as good, of course, no matter how much she practiced. That didn't matter, though. By the time she was proficient enough to play Mozart, her parents could close their eyes and pretend, for a little while.

'No,' she said, simply, when it was anything but.

'You are very good.'

She let the praise fall into a little black hole in her chest—a place that could never be filled, no matter what was said. She was competent, but she was not gifted, and her competence was really just a byproduct of how much she'd cared, how much she'd wanted to gift her parents her piano playing, as a token of love to Mary, and of their love for the daughter they'd lost.

'Why do you have the piano if you don't play?'

'It came with the house.'

'Ah.' She dropped her hands into her lap and looked around, then pulled her silky dark hair over one shoulder, toying with the ends distractedly as she considered the room. 'Was it all like this when you bought it?'

'Mostly.'

She bit into her lip—now washed clean of the burgundy lip stain and returned to their natural dusky pink. 'You didn't think about walls? Extra bedrooms?'

His eyes probed hers, and she felt the spark of heat travel between them, felt it bloom in her belly then incinerate her whole soul.

'What for?'

'I don't know. Entertaining?'

'There are twelve bunks downstairs, for staff,' he said. 'If you're bothered by sharing a bed with your husband, you are welcome to use one of them.'

'Staff?' She clung to that. 'So, we're not completely alone here?'

His smirk showed that she'd given away too much of how she was feeling. Though it was very likely he'd mistaken her hesitation for a lack of willingness, when if anything, the opposite was true.

'The staff are for when I'm *not* here, which is most of the time. If I come to the island, it is to be alone. They leave me, then.'

'Just like that?' she pondered. 'You click your fingers and they simply disappear?'

'Believe it or not, they have lives and families off island that they're happy to return to.'

He was so confident within himself, so much a man now. Then again, he was when they were dating, too. His reputation in the boardroom had been forged from the time he turned eighteen and started stepping into his foster father's shoes, taking an already successful business and turning it into an empire. Seven years later, when they had started dating, he'd already made an enormous mark in the business world.

But with Annie, he'd just been… Theo. She'd always seen beyond his success, his achievements, to the man he was.

'I don't suppose you'd consider sleeping in a bunk downstairs?' she asked, mainly because she felt like she *ought* to ask it. 'It would be the gentlemanly thing to do.'

He came to stand right in front of her then, pressing a finger to her chin and tilting her face to his, just like he had when he'd given her the engagement ring. 'We both know I'm not a gentleman though, don't we?'

Her heart turned over in her chest and it took every ounce of her willpower to deny that. A long time ago, she'd thought him the epitome of character and yes, gentlemanliness.

She swallowed past a bitterness in her throat as their eyes locked together in a battle of the wills. In a silent exchange, from which Annie had no idea if she, or he, emerged the victor. Eventually, he dropped his hand away, though remained close enough that if she shifted ever so slightly, her hand would be brushing against his leg.

'Are you afraid of me, Annie?'

The question surprised her, so too the delivery: deep and gruff.

She stared up at him, her eyes round, her pulse racing. She could tell him that of course she was—having seen the darkness in him, how could she not be? But the truth was, for some reason, she wasn't afraid. Not of Theo; she couldn't be. For as much as he clearly hated her father, and Annie, for what had happened five years ago, she still knew he'd never truly hurt her. Certainly not physically.

'No,' she answered, simply.

'Yet you're shaking all over.'

'Am I?' She hadn't noticed.

'Or is there another reason for you to be trembling from head to toe?' he asked, and then his finger landed on her shoulder and stayed there a moment, hovering against the fabric of her T-shirt.

She shook her head, knowing why she was shaking, knowing he knew it, too. She hated her inexperience. Hated that he could stir her to this sort of fever pitch with just a look. If only she'd been with someone, then perhaps he wouldn't have this effect on her.

'That's a shame,' he murmured, letting his finger trail lower, to the upper part of her arm, and then flicking the shirt sleeve a little, so he could connect with her bare flesh. She had to bite back a groan.

'What is?' She couldn't think properly.

'That you're not willing to admit what you want.'

Her lips parted on a husky breath. 'Does it matter what I want?' she asked, trying to regain the upper hand. 'We both know what's going to happen. I'm as good as bought and paid for.'

His smile was laced with mockery. 'True,' he said, slowly. 'But I'm not interested in having sex with you on those terms.'

Her heart stammered. Something slipped inside of her. Doubts fired in her blood.

His finger tracked sideways, to the curve of her breast, and the nipple that was straining against the soft cotton of the shirt. He flicked it with his forefinger, his lips twisting at her obvious reaction—a gasp and then a soft, husky whimper.

'Are you saying—you don't want—' She couldn't finish the sentence. Not when he was now cupping her breast with possessive need.

'Oh, I want,' he ground out. 'Make no mistake about it, I *need*. But what I wish for, most of all, is for you to beg for me,' he said. 'I want to hear you cry my name, as though you are driven almost mad with need for me.' He leaned closer, so his mouth was right by her ear. 'Only then will we both get the release we're craving.'

She whimpered, but before she could say anything else, his lips crashed to hers, just like in the wedding ceremony, hard and fast, possessive and desperate, and all semblance of thought fled from her mind, leaving only this. The immediacy and passion of their kiss, the white-hot desire that was exploding through her body. Her hands reached for him, even as his were tucking beneath her arms and lifting her, then pushing her back to sit on the keys, which clunked beneath her bottom. She pressed the ball of one foot to the piano stool as Theo stood between her legs, his lips expertly moving over hers, a masterclass in persuasion and temptation.

And though thought had deserted her, somewhere deep in the recesses of her brain was a strand of pride, whispering not to beg for him, not to give in to him. Not yet. Not so easily.

'You taste the same,' he said, into her mouth, and the words were discordant, initially making no sense. But after a moment, she realised he was talking about when they'd used to kiss, all those years ago.

'You're different,' she said, honestly, because he was. This Theo was all hard edges: in his behavior, his attitudes, his body, and his kiss. Everything was rough and harsh. Back then, he'd kissed her like he might break her. Now it was as though he was daring her to break him.

She scrunched her hand into the fabric of his shirt, her heart racing so hard she thought it might pound right out of her chest. The word *please* flooded her brain, screeching through her, but she buried it in their kiss, refusing to speak it, refusing to ask for him. Refusing to give him that satisfaction.

As if he could hear her determination, he pulled away from her, dark eyes glittering when they met hers. 'What do you want, Annie?'

Her pulse washed through her ears so loudly it was like a hurricane had come and whipped up the sea outside. She bit into her lip, refusing to say it, even when her body made a liar of her silence.

A single dark brow of Theo's lifted, and his expression was so calmly cynical that it was hard to know how *he* felt and what *he* wanted.

'Is this some kind of game to you?' she asked, after a beat.

He lifted a finger to her cheek, and stared at it, as if mesmerised. 'Everything is a game, in a way.'

'You don't seem like someone who's having much fun.'
'Don't I?'
She shivered. 'You're enjoying this?'
His eyes moved to hers and for a moment, she saw a glimpse of the man she'd once known, but it was gone again, immediately. 'I play to win,' he said, but it was too cryptic to understand. He straightened, his touch gone, her lips aching for his kiss, her body liquid with need. 'It's late. Go to sleep, Princess.' She flinched at his use of that name. He'd never called her that before, but her father did, and Theo knew it. She heard the disdain in his voice and a small, fragile part of her seemed to wither up and die.

CHAPTER SIX

ANNIE HAD FALLEN asleep in a state of utterly mixed and spent emotions. On the one hand, she'd been dreading Theo coming to bed, hating the thought of being so close and not touching him, hating the thought of wanting to reach for him, fearing that she might do so on autopilot. And yet, in the end, she'd been so utterly exhausted that she woke to the sound of crashing waves the next morning, in the exact same position she'd fallen asleep in—hugged right to the side of the bed.

Her eyes flared wide as she lay perfectly still and listened intently to see if she could hear Theo breathing beside her. Silence. Perhaps he had been a gentleman after all and slept on one of the huge couches?

She moved softly, flipping onto her back then turning her head to the pillow beside her. An indent showed he had lain there at some point, but when she brushed her hand over the sheets, they were cool to the touch.

With a small frown, she sat up, and took in the settings anew. The view now, in broad daylight, was beyond stunning. The glass windows showed a striking vista out over the ocean in one direction, unimpeded by anything, just beautiful sand and sea. It was the other windows though that displayed the landscape of the island like some kind of artwork—on one side, rugged, mountainous terrain, covered in lush greenery, and on the other, an expansive lawn, then colourful shrubs and trees, that made Annie itch to go out and explore.

The open-plan layout of the house meant that she could quickly ascertain that Theo wasn't here. Telling herself the fluttering in her stomach was relief, she pushed out of bed, the sunlight catching the enormous diamond on her ring finger as she moved the sheet aside, and paced towards the kitchen. She reached for a coffee pod, but stilled as she hooked a mug beneath the spout, her eyes arrested by something moving in the water.

Her mouth went dry as Theo drew his arms over his head, swimming in a horizontal line with the shore, each stroke powerful and contained, drawing him through the ancient waters as though it were butter and he a knife.

She struggled to properly inflate her lungs as she watched him swim, mesmerised both by his power, and the power of her memories. The first time they'd really kissed, in a way that had hinted at so much more, had been in his pool. Water lapping around them, his hands on her body, gentle but also promising, so she'd moved onto his lap where he sat on the pool step, straddling him, her own body answering that promise with one of her own. She'd felt him grow hard against her sex and a sharp throb of need had almost taken her breath away.

'Not now, Annie,' he'd murmured. 'Not yet.' Even when he'd wanted her, he had made sure she knew nothing would happen until she was ready. That she hadn't felt pressured or rushed.

She glanced away, tears filming her eyes unexpectedly, as the sweetness of that memory hit her for the discordancy with the situation they were in now—for the contrast between that Theo, to this. A man who told her she must beg for him before he'd give her what she wanted. Who wanted to belittle her, because five years ago, she'd had the hide to leave him.

She blinked quickly to clear the unwelcome tears, and finished making her coffee. Yet she stayed in the kitchen, eyes gravitating towards the sea, as he reached the far edge of the cove formed by the natural indentation of the island's shore, and turned around, to swim back the other way. His head lifted, just a sleek, dark shape in the bobbing ocean, but she took a step backwards, anyway, hiding from him, even when there was no way he'd be able to see her so quickly, and from so far away.

When he'd reached a space in the ocean that was in line with the house, he stopped swimming and stood, and her fingers went completely numb, so the coffee cup she'd been cradling slipped from her hands and smashed against the tiled floor. Her jaw dropped, and her eyes stayed glued to the visage of Theo emerging from the ocean, like some kind of ancient god, gloriously naked and absolutely masculine. They'd dated a long time, but she'd never seen him like this.

The closest she'd gotten had been when they'd swum together. This was a revelation and an awakening that sent her pulse skittering wildly.

She couldn't look away.

He was so bronzed and well-built, so muscled and strong, so lean and taut. Every step from the ocean was intentional and controlled, the rolling tide no match for this man. When he reached the water's edge, he paused, looking left and right, completely relaxed in his nudity, totally at one with the earth, the water, with himself. He continued to walk then, long, easy strides carrying him across the sand and closer to the house, so she swore, belatedly realising that he'd soon be there, with her. Naked? Her heart pounded as she galvanised herself into action, looking down at the black puddle of spilled coffee, and the shards of broken ceramic.

She stepped over it gingerly, towards the sink, opening the doors and finding paper towels. She was crouched down, mopping up the spill when the front door sounded.

She couldn't look.

She *couldn't*. Her cheeks flamed as she concentrated very, very hard on focusing on the job at hand and *not* thinking about the naked state she'd just observed.

'You're up,' he drawled, from close by, so she really had no option but to be brave and glance in his direction. She looked his way slowly though, as if steeling herself for what she might see.

Somehow, this was even harder than if he'd been naked. That she'd been prepared for. But a towel wrapped loosely around his hips, concealing his anatomy from her, but making her want to peel the towel away and take another peek, was all too confusing. She jerked her head back to the coffee cup quickly, but not so quickly she missed the quirk of his lips—a knowing smirk, as if he'd taken one look at her bright pink face and the spilled cup and worked out what was going on.

'Enjoy the view?'

Yes, that confirmed it, she thought ruefully. 'I've seen better,' she heard herself respond, the words curt—and untrue.

A hiss from between his teeth confirmed she'd hit her mark. Well, good. His arrogance and the way he lorded her attraction to him over her was wearing thin. So what if she'd lusted after him from the minute she'd first laid eyes on him? That had been a schoolgirl crush, and it had prevented her from seeing him as he really was. It was only this last month in which the scales had fallen properly from her eyes.

'Are you trying to provoke me, Annie?'

'Why would I want to do that?'

'Perhaps you're trying to goad me into kissing you again.'

'Believe me, kissing you is the last thing I want to be doing,' she muttered, aware it was a dishonest statement to make.

He let out a sound of amusement, but then, to her chagrin, he was reaching down and pulling her to standing. They were so close, she could see the flecks of grey in his eyes, in amongst the dark, almost black. 'You are a liar,' he said, but it was with a hint of amusement.

'I'm not—'

He pressed a finger to her lips. 'We both know I could prove it, just by touching you.'

Embarrassment curdled in her gut, and she wished then, more than anything, that she'd at least slept with *someone*. It wasn't like she hadn't had opportunities. She'd been on dates, set up by her parents, and then later, after her mother had passed away, by her father. She knew she'd dated men who'd been attracted to her. But Annie had never felt a spark of interest in anyone besides this man, and back when they'd been an item, he'd been painfully determined not to rush her into bed.

'What's your point?' she asked, after a beat.

He dropped his finger lower, to her shoulder, his eyes shifting a little, before spearing her once more with the intensity of his gaze. 'I believe in calling a spade a spade. That's a quality I think we both share. You do not need to goad me into kissing you, Annie. I've already told you, ask for what you want, and I'll give it willingly.'

She swallowed past the lump in her throat. 'I can't work out if you want to demean me, by making me ask.'

His eyes flared wide.

'Is that it? Are you still so angry with me for daring to dump you, that your ego needs to be stroked by me now? Do you need to hear me say it was a mistake? That I wish we hadn't broken up?'

He swore then, a quiet yet guttural sound ripped from the depths of his belly.

'It was not a mistake,' he said, slowly, clearly. 'We both know that.'

The ground seemed to tilt beneath her feet. It was the last thing she'd expected him to say. 'Yes,' she said, valiantly, refusing to let him see that she was reeling. 'It was the right decision.' It had been. She couldn't have ever done anything to put her parents through more pain and grief. Even now, marrying Theo, whilst hurtful to her father, was simply the lesser of two evils.

'For a while, I thought I wanted something different with my life.' He was talking to her, but almost talking through her, as though he was back in the past, remembering the way he'd been then. 'But it was an illusion. *You* were an illusion.'

'I could say the same about you,' she muttered. 'The man I thought I was spending time with clearly doesn't exist.'

'That is also true. See how good we are at this honesty thing?'

'You want more honesty?' she asked.

'You've already told me you hate me,' he reminded her.

'I suppose it doesn't hurt to repeat it, though.'

'Nothing you say has the power to hurt me,' he said, simply. 'But you are welcome to keep trying.' He leaned closer, so his lips were just a hair's breadth from hers. 'I like fighting with you, Annie. I think we both know that if you keep it up, we'll end up in bed together, so by all means, do your worst.'

Her jaw dropped and her brain went blank. He was so casual about sex, about referring to going to bed together. Would he be the same if he knew she was a virgin?

Annie frowned, the idea not one she'd really contemplated. But somehow, she suspected even this version of Theo might balk at the idea of being her first lover under these circumstances. She was a twenty-seven-year-old innocent. Not really by choice or design, but because of circumstances. Almost her entire life, it had been about Theo. After their break-up, and her mother's death, she had come to the conclusion she didn't have a sexual bone in her body. She simply wasn't interested in dating, or exploring that side of herself.

'You have a one-track mind,' she muttered, and then he laughed, a deep, throaty sound.

'I take it back. Honesty is difficult for you.'

'Why do you say that?'

'If I were to touch you right now, you'd burst into flames. You are so hungry for me, you are practically drooling. Which is not to say I do not feel the same for you—but if I do have a one-track mind, it is something we share.'

Her tongue darted out, licking her lower lip. 'But we're not animals,' she said, her voice soft, though, most definitely lacking conviction.

'Actually, we are. And the desire we feel is the very definition of animalistic passion.'

Her cheeks flashed with warmth and her body felt unimaginably heavy. 'Well, you'd know more about that than I would.'

'Meaning?'

'That you're no stranger to casual sex, whereas I—'

'Only sleep with men your father approves of?' he supplied, a hint of anger in the words. She opened her mouth to dispute that, to throw her virginity in his face, but the words died in her throat.

She didn't want him to know. She didn't want to risk that it would change things between them.

'How does that work, Princess? Does he give you a list? Pre-screen your dates? Ask for proof of their aristocratic lineage before you're allowed to drop your pants?'

She closed her eyes, his questions stinging.

'I'd rather not talk about my father, particularly not with you, and definitely not now.'

'Why not now, *agape*?' He put his hands on her hips then, pulling her towards him, away from the spilled coffee and broken cup, and against the knot of his towel, beneath which she knew his dick was barely contained by the fabric.

Her tongue was thick in her mouth, and refusing to cooperate. She could barely think of words, much less say them. She felt backed into a corner, so all she could do was shake her head and feign exasperation. 'This is ridiculous,' she finally managed to squeeze out.

'Why?'

'Because I'm never going to beg you to make love to me. You're the one who said you wanted this to be a real marriage, you're the one who insisted on that. So if *you* want us to have sex, then fine. But don't expect me to take the first step.'

Another laugh, this one short and sharp, before he

dropped his head so his lips were just an inch from hers and her pulse was a throbbing, twisty mess.

'Okay, I'll take the first step,' he said. 'Would you like me to kiss you?'

She rolled her eyes. 'You're still asking me to ask you.'

'I'm asking you to tell me,' he said. 'Tell me it's okay to kiss you.'

Her eyes widened, because it was a nuanced difference. He was asking for consent, for permission. She could say no, and he'd respect it. This was her line to draw. But a kiss was just a kiss. In fact, a kiss was a good way of showing him they could feel the stirrings of physical need and ignore them.

'I married you, didn't I?'

'That's not an answer.'

And despite having said she wouldn't take the first step, it was Annie who was lifting up onto the tips of her toes and seeking out his mouth with hers, Annie who was kissing Theo, Annie whose need was so strong she momentarily forgot everything they'd been, said, and were, and existed simply in the moment for *this*.

Annie kissed Theo, but she only had control for a few seconds before he was deepening the kiss and taking over, dominating her as he had at the piano, and earlier, at the wedding. It was Theo whose hands roamed her body, her back, her sides, before curving around her buttocks and pushing her forward, hard against him, against his arousal, his bare chest, Theo who ground his hips so she could feel *all* of him, so she moaned hungrily. Theo who made stars flood her eyes when he dragged his lips from her mouth to her jaw, flicking the pulse point there, before tracking upwards to the flesh just beneath her earlobe and sucking on it, the combination of his warm, moist mouth and his breath make her whimper and cry his name. Theo who lifted her and carried her to the bench, sitting her down and standing between her legs, kissing her until she was crying out. His name, a curse, but somehow, even in that moment, she was able to stop herself from begging for him, even when the word *please* ran around and around her mind like lightning in a bottle.

Last night, he'd cupped her breasts through her shirt but this morning, he had no patience for that, as he pushed the fabric up her stomach and over her head, removing the T-shirt carelessly, throwing it on the ground. She tilted her head backwards and his mouth dragged from her throat to her collarbone and then lower, his stubble rough against her soft skin, leaving pink marks in his wake, as he found a nipple and took it in his mouth, his hand squeezing her other nipple until the heat between her legs was a form of mind-altering madness, like some kind of hallucinogenic drug.

'Theo,' she groaned, and wiggled forward on the edge of the bench, needing to be closer to him, needing him. She wouldn't use her words to beg, but with her body, she pleaded, needing his touch, his possession, his everything.

'I want to hold your breasts when we make love,' he said, pulling up to look into her eyes. 'I want to take you from behind, and watch in the mirror as you fall apart.'

She shivered at the imagery, the heat of it, the promise, but she bit into her lip to stop herself from saying that she too wanted that. That she wanted everything he wanted. That she was utterly and completely in his hands.

'All that time, I stopped us from having sex,' he muttered, his hands now shifting to her thighs, one creeping higher, beneath the loose fabric of her shorts, all the way to where her leg met her body and resting there, before his fingers began to draw invisible circles, making her shiver. 'I didn't want to rush you, to pressure you. Yet now, all I can think about is the fact other men have had you, have worshipped you, and I have not. Do you have any idea how that feels?'

Intellectually she knew it was a gross double standard, given he'd lived whatever the opposite of celibacy was, but that didn't stop it from touching something deep inside of her. His jealousy. His possessiveness. Would he feel that if, on some level, he didn't care about her? Or was it all just about ego and ownership?

Before she could answer that, his hand had crept down a little, his finger finding her underpants and pushing them aside, then pressing against the heat of her sex.

His eyes latched to hers, a question in their depth, and he moved slowly. So slowly, as though he was giving her every opportunity to object, to tell him to stop. But she didn't. While she wasn't ever going to beg him—pride was on the line, after all—nor would she put a stop to *anything* they were doing, because it all felt too damned good.

It was Theo who moaned as he pushed a finger into her wet, warm core, brushing against the muscular wall so that Annie bucked her hips in pleasure.

'You are so wet,' he ground out, shaking his head a little. 'And still you refuse to ask me to take you?'

She bit into her lip, speech beyond her.

'It is a shame, Annie, because I would love my cock to be here, instead,' he pushed his finger in harder, faster and she cried out at the sharp sense of invasion—the welcome feeling of having any part of him inside her. She wanted to tell him she wanted that too, but whenever she opened her mouth to say it, she held back. They were playing a dangerous game, and if Annie were to concede so early, to give away her power, she knew she'd live to regret it. He was trying to break her. He was trying to get her to admit that no matter what he said or did, she would fall in with his plans, that she would be his again, and she instinctively knew she had to fight that.

'Since when do you need a handwritten invitation?' she muttered. 'Are you telling me you make every woman you sleep with beg for you?'

'Oh, no, Annie, this is just about you,' he said, confirming her thoughts. 'I want *you* to beg for me. I want you to admit that you still want me. I want the woman who acted like I meant *nothing* to prove herself wrong...'

'I've told you,' she moaned, as he moved his finger faster, and tilted her head back, eyes clinging to the ceiling as a wave of pleasure spread through her body. 'I—can't—'

'You can't what?'

Pleasure built, intense, fast, hard. 'Beg me, Annie,' he said, pulling his finger out, so she whipped her head forward, staring at him, heart racing. 'All you have to do is ask me to take you, and I will make you feel better than you've ever known possible.'

The throb in her gut demanded that of her. She needed him; what was the harm in admitting it? *Please.* Such a simple word and yet when she opened her mouth, it wouldn't come out. He stared at her, his own cheeks slashed with colour, so she knew he wasn't unaffected by this, that it was taking a degree of willpower all of his own.

'Please,' she said, and then, added quickly, 'stop. Stop now.'

His eyes widened with surprise and his lips clamped together to form a grim line, but he did what she'd said, every part of him growing still, and then Annie's heart sank as he pulled his hands away from her, his chest moving though with the force of his breathing.

'Is this really what you want?' she asked sadly, her heart heavy. 'Do you need to demean me, by hearing me beg, because five years ago I had the nerve to break up with you?'

'I don't give a shit that you dumped me, Annie. That's always been your prerogative.'

She tilted her chin, ignoring the way pain seemed to slice through her.

'It's your reason for ending it that I think pathetic. To leave someone, when you are grown woman, because your mummy and daddy don't think he's good enough? It's my own fault, but I did think better of you.'

She flinched.

'I was wrong. You're just as superficial as them. What is that expression about apples and trees?'

She glanced sideways, trying to catch her breath. It was a body blow, even though he'd used a few short words.

'You don't know what you're talking about.'

'I know that you were a coward then, by not standing up to your parents, and you're a coward now, for not admitting how much you want me. You live your life with your head in the sand—I'm disappointed in you, Annie.'

She ground her teeth, trying not to react, but she could feel her emotions spiralling out of control. Given the choice between anger, and showing how hurt she was, she firmly chose the former. 'Seriously, Theo, just go to hell.'

He leaned closer then, his eyes locked to hers, somber and intense. 'Are we not both already there, Annie Leonidas?'

CHAPTER SEVEN

A WEEK AFTER arriving on the island and Annie was in the worst mood of her life—and it didn't take a genius to work out why.

Ever since that passionate encounter in the kitchen, on the morning of the broken coffee cup, Theo hadn't touched her. He'd been cold, reasonably polite when necessary, but also distant. Despite that, Annie couldn't stop. She couldn't stop *wanting* him. What had started in that kitchen had ended in dramatic fashion, and she'd tried so hard to hold on to her anger. It was still there, stirring around in her belly, but more and more there was just a static electricity sort of awareness of every single movement Theo made.

Sleeping in the same bed and diligently not touching was its own form of torture. She'd barely let herself drift off because she was so worried her subconscious would take over and drive her towards him in the middle of the night.

Theo, meanwhile, either knew how distracted she was, or had no clue and didn't care. Either way, he swam naked each morning, so it had become her guilty pleasure to get up as soon as she heard the front door click shut, creep into the kitchen and watch him walk, glorious and raw, towards the ocean, to disappear into it, all beautiful manhood and masculinity.

If he knew she watched, he didn't say. He left her mostly to herself, and Annie therefore set about reading her way through the small collection of books she'd found on a shelf, and pretending not to notice him, even when she was focused on him with a laser-like intensity.

There were a million things she wanted to ask him. To learn about his life since they'd parted, to understand him better, but she had barely any opportunities to ask those questions—even if she'd thought he'd be receptive.

They didn't eat together—the fridge was well stocked, so she simply grabbed what she wanted when she was hungry and out of an abiding sense of pride, tried to pretend her husband didn't exist.

But a sense of needing him, aching for him, craving him, was driving her almost mad.

So finally, on the eighth day of their 'honeymoon', she snapped. Maybe it was that same sense of pride, or maybe it was just lust. She knew only that he thought he could call all the shots, and she was sick of it. He wanted her to beg for him? Well, maybe she wanted that, too. Maybe she wanted him to admit that he was as powerless in the face of their attraction as she was. Or maybe she just wanted to pull apart his defenses, to strip him to his most animalistic self, to see the real man, not this edifice he was presenting her with.

Watching from the kitchen window as he carelessly strode towards the ocean, all stunning naked masculinity, she ground her teeth together, as a plan born purely of instincts formed.

Moving before she could properly think it through, and certainly before she could second-guess herself, Annie stripped out of the T-shirt she'd slept in and then, before she could hesitate, the shorts as well, but she stopped short of removing her underpants. She wanted to give him his just desserts, to subject him to the same temptation he'd been throwing at her all week, but she wasn't quite as daring as him.

Still, dressed in just a skimpy pair of briefs, with her dark hair pulled over one shoulder, she stepped out of the front door and on autopilot, looked left and right, before grimacing at her silliness—because there was no one else there. It was a totally private island. She picked her way over the stones that were inlaid between the lawn, and then, to the sandy grass that gave way completely to the shoreline. He was swimming away from her, powerful strokes taking him in the opposite direction.

Good.

Let him swim, she thought, refusing to listen to common sense and turn tail back into the house.

The truth was, she was almost being driven mad by the way he was ignoring her. Infuriated and yes, hurt. Her ego was smarting by the way he appeared to have simply turned off any awareness of her, while she'd been drowning in the distraction of wanting.

So today, she'd see.

He saw her head, at first, though initially he didn't realise it was a person, just something in the ocean, not too far in front of him. But he slowed and took a second look, switched his stroke so he could keep his head above water, and then, he saw her face, too, in profile, her lips parted, her eyes closed, as she breathed in deeply. And then, she stood up, which brought her body just a little above the water's surface. Just enough to suggest that she too was naked, the top of her breasts revealed to him, so he cursed and stopped swimming, his first instinct being to turn right around again.

But perhaps with his subtle change in movement, something drew her attention, because she turned her head, towards him, her intelligent, clear eyes landing on his face, her soft, pink lips parted as though she were silently begging him after all.

Awareness was like a lightning bolt right to his cock.

When they'd been dating, he'd been so determined to respect her boundaries. Theo had never had any issues falling right into bed with a woman before, but Annie had been different. She'd been different from the first, but then, on her eighteenth birthday, when she'd begged him to kiss her, he'd known she was vulnerable and sweet, and that he'd do anything to protect her. It was the first time he'd felt like that in a long time—the first time he'd *ever* felt like it for someone in his new life. These people were all rich and spoiled, but Annie...not Annie.

He'd wished her a happy birthday, then kept an eye on her for the rest of the night—from a distance. Making sure she didn't ask anyone less scrupulous, and get taken advantage of.

Her twenty-first birthday had been different.

On her eighteenth, he'd known it was a dare. A silly game to seduce the man who'd once been the boy from the wrong side of the tracks. But it hadn't mattered. At eighteen, she'd been too young and innocent anyway. By twenty-one, when she'd asked again, it hadn't been a dare. She'd wanted him, and he'd presumed her to have the experience to know that she was playing with fire—and to welcome the consequences. So he'd kissed her, and tasted her, and he'd been hooked from that moment on.

Yet he hadn't slept with her. Even when they'd gone beyond that night, and started dating—secretly, because she hadn't wanted her parents to know—he'd somehow just understood that he wanted to silo what they were off from his other short-term relationships.

She was different, and he'd treated her as such.

But now, she was his wife. His goddamned wife, and she was staring at him like that, across the ocean. A wave bobbed past her, above her breasts, and then the ocean sucked out a little, so the water fell, and he saw her nipples, dusky pink, like her lips, peaked in the middle of her small, rounded breasts.

Slowly, he swam towards her, trying to bring his body back under control, to fight the surging heat of desire pounding him from the inside out. But what was the point? Hadn't she come here to tempt him? To do exactly this to him?

When he was close to her, just a foot or so away, he stopped swimming and stood, his eyes probing hers, studying her, his hands aching to reach out and touch. He waited for her to say something, but she was breathing hard, as though she'd just run a marathon.

As though she was nervous.

Or something.

'Did you feel like a swim?' he prompted.

She bit into her lower lip.

'Or something else?'

Her eyes lifted to his, her expression uncertain.

For God's sake, why was she tormenting him like this? All she had to do was ask him to make love to her, and he would, all day and all night, until this damned beast of need was finally slayed, satiated. It was the only way to end this.

'Damn it, Annie, why are you here, naked?'

'I'm not naked,' she said, her voice a husk, in the early morning. 'And I thought it was just what we did here.'

He arched a brow. 'Does it offend you?'

He gestured to his chest, inviting her to look. She did. Her gaze dropped lower, her tongue darting out and licking her lower lip, so his cock jerked and his gut tightened.

Slowly, she shook her head, and then lifted a trembling hand, slowly, pressing it to his chest. 'I guess I just got sick of looking.'

He sucked in a sharp breath. Her touch was so tentative, so innocent, and yet it was also the most erotic thing he'd ever known.

'How exactly are you not naked?' he asked, the words bitten out, gruff and deep.

Her hand dropped from his chest, to lace with his fingers, which she pulled towards her hip, so he felt the elastic of her thong and bit back another curse.

'That seems tokenistic, at best.'

Her lips flicked in a small smile—a genuine smile, so for a second, he was back in the past, and she was just Annie. His Annie.

Until she wasn't. Until she was taken away from him— until she walked away from him, rather than standing up to her rich, entitled parents. She was nothing like he'd thought, because the Annie he'd held up on a pedestal was not the kind of woman to end it with a guy just because her parents told her to.

The memory was a timely reminder of who she was— and why this had to happen on his terms. He wouldn't let himself feel anything for her again. He wouldn't let her get under his defenses.

'Why did you come out here?' he said again.

'I told you—'

'No, Annie.' He pulled his hand back, glad for the shift in his feelings, glad for the way the past had reared its head at just the right moment, to reinforce why he had to keep his cool. 'You cannot get out of it that easily. If you want to touch, touch. But if you want me to fuck you, you're going to have to ask.'

She gasped, the hurt on her features something he wished he didn't see, and didn't care about, but the past was a complex beast, and tangled up in his anger and disappointment with her was the warmth he'd once held, too. The understanding of her—more of an understanding than he'd probably ever allowed himself to feel for another person.

'Why are you like this?' she asked, her features still pinched.

'Why do you think?'

'Your upbringing? Did someone hurt you? I don't know, Theo. You were always a closed book about your past—'

'My past? Annie, don't be obtuse. If you're wondering why I'm like this, then look in a goddamned mirror.'

Another gasp, this time, with her hand lifting to cover her lips. 'Don't say that.'

'I thought we agreed to be honest.'

She flinched.

'You were the first person in my life I ever really cared about,' he said, almost conversationally, aware that the words had washed through him so often they'd lost their power to cut him now.

'What about the Georgiadeses?'

'I liked and respected them, and that was mutual. I did not care for them like I did you. And you discarded me without a backwards glance, because your parents asked you to.'

She shook her head. 'I didn't, it wasn't—'

'You did, and it was,' he contradicted fiercely. 'But don't worry—I'm glad. You showed me who you really are. What you really value. And you also reminded me of something I already knew but somehow, had let myself forget.'

She stared up at him, blinking quickly.

'I don't like people,' he said, and then, he reached out and put his hands on her hips, pulling her to him, so his cock nestled against the fabric of her pants, but his chest was hard to her soft, rounded breasts. 'I particularly don't like rich people.' His lip lifted in a cynical smile, as he saw the way her eyes shifted, the inner battle she was waging between her mind's indignation and her body's needs.

'You're rich,' she pointed out, voice trembly.

'No, I have money. It's not the same thing. You were born rich, and you have the prejudices to prove it.'

'I hate you,' she whispered, and in that moment, he knew she really did mean it.

'Yes, but you still want me.'

She looked away from him, her breath held, her chin angled in a pose of pure defiance, before she glared up at him, her eyes practically fulminating with rage. 'Yes,' she said, finally. 'I do.'

It was hardly the plea he'd been hoping for and yet, it was enough. It was more than enough. It was still a concession for her, that no matter what she might think of him, desire was ravaging her as it was him. He could only wish he wasn't stuck in the same metaphorical boat.

'But you want me, too,' she said, with a hint of angry resentment.

He stared down at her, admiration shifting in his chest. 'Do you need to hear me say it, Annie?'

She bit into her lip, a lip he was desperate to taste for himself, and nodded once, but her eyes were awash with uncertainty.

'I have no problem admitting that I want you.' He leaned closer, his voice brushing her ear. 'I am not a coward.'

'Do you really think that?' she asked, lifting one of her small hands and pressing it to his shoulder, like she was trying to physically shake him.

'I did, Annie. But coming to me for help was brave. Marrying me was braver still.'

Her eyes flicked to his, and she opened her mouth to say something, but he forestalled it.

'Then again, we both know there's no limit to what you'd do to keep your daddy happy.'

Her eyes shut as his words hit their mark—and he wished, almost more than he'd ever wished for anything, that he could take them back.

'Just shut up and fuck me,' she whispered then, blinking her gaze open and letting it land on his. And then, the word he thought he'd wanted and quickly came to despise, fell from her mouth: 'Please.'

He blotted out the horrible feeling spreading through him, ignoring anything but this. Later, he'd work out why he felt like a part of him was being torn to shreds. For now, he just wanted to experience this woman—this pleasure he'd denied himself, the whole time they'd dated.

'Good, Annie,' he murmured, lifting her higher in the water, and he kissed her as he wrapped her legs around his waist, supporting her weight, his hard body seeking her, needing her, so he broke the kiss only long enough to say, 'Are you on the pill?'

She nodded quickly, her cheeks flushed, her lips parted. 'Yes.'

'Thank Christ,' he groaned, nudging aside her briefs and then saying, for good measure, 'I'm clean. I presume—'

'Of course,' she said, and then, she hesitated, so he waited, though it was an agony not to plunge into her. He still waited, for her to say whatever she was thinking. She stared down at him and then, on a sob, repeated those awful words, 'Please, Theo, please.'

He drove into her with all the desperate, angry, years-old need that had been tormenting him right to his core. It was not gentle, and it was not soft, it was the act of a man driven by passion, who felt that answering need from his would-be lover.

But the second he thrust into her and she cried out, not in pleasure, but from pain and discomfort, and her face contorted, he connected her tightness with the cause of it and swore, staring at her face, his body buried too deep in her to move, to take it back. Anger though was firing through him, along with a sense of confusion.

'What the hell?'

She glared at him.

'You were—are you a virgin?'

'Well, not now,' she snapped with an impressively withering tone, given the situation, and digging her heels into his back and shifting a little, moving on his length so he had to reach for her hips to hold her still, because the pleasure was too good, and he needed to damn well think.

'You're telling me you were a virgin until a minute ago?'

'So what?'

'So what?' He stared at her, disbelief a whip, slashing through him. 'How the hell—'

'Can we possibly talk about this later?' she asked, her cheeks flushed, lips parted, as she moved again, and this time, he let her. Hell, he couldn't take it back, even if he wanted to.

'Damn it, Annie, we are going to talk about it,' he muttered, but he began to move, this time, more gently, slowly, careful to give her time to adjust to the fullness, to the feeling of being with a man for the first time.

He was still reeling from that, when she dug her nails into his shoulder and snapped, 'No, Theo, not like this. Don't treat me like you might break me. I want you to take me. I want you to treat me like you would if I was any of the woman you usually sleep with.'

He ground his teeth together, knowing instinctively he could never do that, because even now, Annie was different.

Not just because she was his wife, but because she was Annie; it would always be more complicated between them.

'Please,' she whispered, and he grimaced at the sound of surrender in her voice, at the knowledge that he'd taken something that should have been born of mutual passion—begging one person to pleasure them, and be pleasured in return—and turned it into a power play that she resented.

He felt the world spinning, out of his control, the decisions and instincts he always listened to now suddenly seeming questionable.

'Theo,' she said, sharply, so he gave up on thinking, questioning, analysing and wondering and just lost himself in her, and this, until she tipped over the edge and he held her shaking, trembling body against his own, murmuring reassurances in Greek, until her breathing returned to normal and he could trust himself to speak again.

Then, he pulled out of her, still rock hard and aching for his own release, and eased her down, so she could stand on the ocean's floor. The water was much deeper for her than him, so he kept his hands on her hips, in case a wave came that she needed to be lifted over.

But Annie could hardly meet his eyes. He ignored the pang of something rolling through him, hardening himself to anything like pity or doubt.

Nonetheless, he heard himself ask, albeit grimly, 'Are you hurt?'

She shook her head. 'I told you, I don't want you to treat me like—'

'It was your first time,' he said, swallowing back another curse as the reality of that landed like a thud against his chest. He didn't want to wonder why. He didn't want to question any of the suppositions he'd made about her lifestyle and choices in the years since they'd dated. Instead, he focused on his anger with her, at having been caught out like this. 'It should not have happened here, like this. It should not have happened with me.'

She closed her eyes, so her lashes were two dark crescents against her cheek. 'Why not?'

'Because it is a beach... It is—'

'Why not with you?'

He dragged a hand over his jaw. 'Because you hate me, for one,' he reminded her crisply.

'Yes, but you're also my husband.'

'Do you think I would have married you if I'd known?'

'Yes,' she said, grimacing. 'But I don't think you would have slept with me.'

A blinding light of clarity exploded before his eyes. 'You did this on purpose.'

Her eyes lifted to his and clung there a moment.

'You chose not to tell me.'

'Would you have slept with me, if you'd known?'

'Of course not. I have no interest in virgins.'

She frowned. 'Is that why you wouldn't sleep with me, back then?'

He thought back to that time, to how much he'd wanted her, yet had resisted, and he couldn't say why, except it had felt somehow important to wait. To show her that she was different to the many women he'd slept with before her.

But he was quiet too long, and apparently Annie drew her own conclusions from his silence. 'Well, I'm sorry to disappoint you, but if you thought I'd gone and gathered a heap of experience in the last five years, you were wrong.'

'You are twenty-seven,' he said, shaking his head.

'I'm aware of that.'

'I'm just trying to understand—'

'Well, maybe you shouldn't,' she said, but her voice wobbled a bit, belying the anger she was trying to infuse into her words. 'Maybe you should just stick to what you're good at and keep being an arrogant bastard.' She sniffed, and he had a sinking feeling that she was about to cry.

Hardly how he would have wanted her first time—or any woman's—to go. Guilt tore through his gut, along with a very familiar sensation from his childhood. A sense of not being able to keep precious things and people safe, of not being able to do the right thing by anyone. Of being not good enough.

'Excuse me, but I've had enough swimming for one day.' He didn't look back over his shoulder to see if she was following him; he told himself he didn't care, either way.

CHAPTER EIGHT

'WE'RE LEAVING FOR Athens in an hour,' he said, later that morning, interrupting a long stretch of silence that had been seriously grating on Annie's last nerve. Yet she hadn't dared be the first one to break it. Not after the beach.

Sex with Theo had been paradigm shifting. Wonderful, physically. Fulfilling and perfect and achingly good. But it had also been complicated and awful, because of how it had been afterwards. The accusation in his voice, the anger. She'd felt like a total inconvenience, and it was all she could do to remember the moment he'd pulled out of her, clearly without experiencing his own climax, and started tearing strips off her.

Except, he hadn't been mad, he'd been confused and judgemental, and she'd felt like a child who'd been caught doing the wrong thing.

'Annie, did you hear me?'

She glanced up at him slowly, then nodded.

'The silent treatment?' he said, the same scathing tone in his voice that made her feel like a misbehaving teenager.

'Fine.' She pasted a saccharine smile on her face. 'Thank you for consulting me, by the way.'

He stared at her, obviously pissed. 'Well, Annie, would *you* like to stay on this island another night, after what just happened?'

'What just happened?' He dragged a hand through his hair. 'We had sex—isn't that what you wanted?'

'It's what we both wanted.'

'I'm not saying otherwise. But what about my virginity changes the fact we both knew what we were doing?'

'*I* didn't. You took away my ability to know and act accordingly.'

'It's just sex,' she spat out.

'Your first time is different.'

'I never had you pegged for such a romantic.'

'It's not romance, it's—' But he faltered, and she knew she'd caught him out. 'Just how it is.'

'Oh, really? Was your first time some big, special, candlelit affair?'

He made a noise of dark amusement. 'Hardly.'

'So, what's the problem? Why the double standards?'

'Because you deserved better,' he shouted, silencing her, so she blinked up at him, and he frowned, shaking his head, like he wanted to take the words back.

And was it little wonder? He was still so angry with her, angry enough to blackmail her into this marriage, and yet there he stood, admitting that she deserved better? 'That's why I didn't sleep with you back then, Annie. I wanted your first time to be special. I wanted you to understand that *you* were special. I wanted you to know that I saw it, and would wait for you, that nothing mattered more to me than taking care of you. And even though that was many years ago, and I feel very, very differently now, apparently, there is still a part of me that cares. That wants to know you have what I believed you deserved in life, even when I have no interest in being the one to provide it.'

The words took her breath away. They sucked the life

from her. The very oxygen she needed to exist seemed to evaporate like dew on a leaf.

'It was special,' she whispered, because it had been. Somehow, making love to Theo in the elemental, passionate ocean, the ancient, time-worn water washing over them, was like a baptism of sorts. A cleaning of the slate—a new start. She stood up, a little uncertain, but also, driven by his honesty to be honest with him.

'I cared about you, too, Theo. I know you don't believe that, because of how—and why—everything with us ended. You asked why I'm a virgin?'

His jaw shifted as though he were grinding his teeth, but he nodded.

'It's because of you,' she said, pressing a hand to his chest. 'When I was eleven and you came to live next door, I thought you were the most beautiful person I'd ever seen. When I was thirteen, I thought I was in love with you. I have a whole notebook somewhere in my room with Annie Leonidas scrawled all over it.' Her smile was rueful, but Theo stood still, completely frozen to the spot. 'When I was sixteen, I couldn't get you out of my mind. By the time I turned eighteen, I was yours for a song. Do you know how long it took me to work up the courage to ask you to kiss me?'

'You were drunk.'

'Yes. I thought it would give me courage, and it did.'

He stared down at her.

'After that, I dated other guys. My parents set me up with the sons of some of their friends,' she said, aware of the way his body tightened.

'Suitable men,' he said grimly.

She nodded, because that was exactly how they'd described the men to her. Men who came from families like theirs. Old families, aristocratic and wealthy, with proud names and coats of arms. Annie had known for as long as she'd been alive that the expectation was to marry just such a man. 'But I couldn't get you out of my head. So, by twenty-one, you were the sum total of fantasies and crushes, the only man I'd ever wanted. And when you kissed me, I just knew.'

'What did you know?' His voice had a hard quality to it, despite the way she was opening her heart to him.

'That I wanted you to be my first.'

'You aren't saying you've been waiting for me.'

'No.' Her lips twisted in a grimace. 'After things with us ended, and…everything with my mum… I just wasn't interested in dating. I've become quite reclusive,' she admitted.

'You should have told me.'

She bit into her lip. 'I didn't know how.'

He nodded, slowly, but when he reached out and pressed a finger to her chin, his touch was so gentle that his words, when he spoke, seemed totally jarring. 'It doesn't change anything, Annie. Sex is just sex to me, and you will always be who you became the morning you left. I can't forgive it. I don't want to.' He padded his thumb over her lower lip, evidently with no idea how hard she was finding it to breathe, much less remain upright.

'You know why I left,' she said, unevenly.

He dropped his hand away. 'Yes.' The word was laced with anger. 'I understand your reasoning.'

'You're still so angry.'

A muscle jerked in his jaw. 'I'm angry at myself, not you.'

'Why?'

'Because I should have known better than to let it go so

far. I have always been able to walk away—from anyone and anything. And then you...'

'What?' she asked, quickly.

'You made me forget, for a while, that's all.'

She wished she understood, but he'd always been so reluctant to speak freely, so cryptic in his answers. 'Don't you think we should talk about this?' she asked.

His eyes ran over her face, and for a second she thought he might relent, but then, he shook his head, just once, but it was a death knell to any hopes she might have had of his opening up to her in a meaningful way. 'There is no time. The plane will be here soon, and I have things to take care of before we leave. Pack your bag, Annie. Real life is calling.'

He was silent as the plane took off, and it did nothing to ease the stretching of her nerves. Annie felt like she was at sixes and sevens, with no idea which way was up. She knew only that she hadn't wanted to leave the island.

She had a feeling she couldn't shake that Theo was running away.

But why?

If it really was a case of 'sex being just sex', as he'd claimed, why should it be such a big deal? Did he realise the contradictions in what he said? One minute it was an easy, physical thing, the next, she deserved her first time to be 'special'. And what did that even mean? Did he think that having careful, slow sex in a bed with some other man would have been *more* special than what they'd done?

Irritation built inside of her, stretching like a rubber band, and yet she'd presumed it would stretch and then snap, eventually. She'd presumed that at some point, he'd look at her and say something, or reach for her, or they'd share a moment and things would return to a more normal footing.

But the flight was almost completely silent, as was the drive to his mansion, on the other side of town. At some point during their honeymoon, all of Annie's belongings had been relocated from her father's to Theo's, and she tried not to think about how that must have pained her dad. And how Theo had probably enjoyed that knowledge. Had probably organised it for that reason.

His hatred of her father—and late mother—was like a constant niggle in the back of her mind; so too her betrayal for being able to ignore it, and fall into the way of craving him, despite that.

When they'd made love, she'd thought the ocean was like a wiping clean of their past, a rebirth of sorts, but she'd been wrong. There was far too much water under the bridge for that.

He said she'd made him what he was. That her rejection was the reason he was so cold now, so famously ruthless. And for Annie? Theo had hurt her, too. Why hadn't he understood that she'd had no choice? Why hadn't he seen that her parents were acting out of love?

His resentment had scored marks deep in her heart.

Maybe it just wasn't possible for either of them to move past that.

Maybe she was stupid to even hope.

But why would she hope? This was a temporary arrangement, the purpose of which was to rebuild her family's company. Why did she need to heal their past? Was it just a case of wanting to know that Theo was alive, and no longer angry with her? Or was there something more at the heart of it?

From the minute they got back to Athens, Theo launched

himself into work, leaving the house before seven each morning and often not returning until close to midnight. She knew he worked long hours—he was renowned for it—but she'd become so used to him on their honeymoon. Even when they were pretending not to notice one another, he'd always *been* there, in that enormous, open-plan beach house. She'd been able to glance up and see him, to hear him, to breathe in and taste him in the air if he happened to walk close enough. Now she had to put up with just seeing little signs of him—like his toothbrush and his coffee cup.

It was pathetic. The whole thing.

She was no wallflower, waiting to be acknowledged by her husband, on his terms. She refused to be that woman.

A week and a half after returning to the city, she gave up on sitting around waiting for things to change, and began to formulate a plan. He was a workaholic, which made it easy to know where to find him, at least. She dressed with care in a black mini dress, styled her hair in big loose waves, applied a minimum of make-up that included her dark red lipstick, and added a pair of killer heels before stepping out of his mansion and hailing a cab—though she supposed she could have taken her own car, she didn't want the hassle of parking.

He owned the entire building in which his office was located, and when the cab pulled to a stop at the bottom of it, she took a second to glance up, right to the top, where she knew Theo would be, and took a beat. She could go home again. She didn't have to do this.

But then what? Eighteen months was a very long time of living with someone whose very presence had the ability to set your nerve endings alight, and who also seemed determined to pretend to ignore you.

The security for the building was tight. She had to give

her name, so she knew he'd be expecting her, which wasn't exactly as she'd planned it, but so what?

She caught the elevator to the top floor, where an elegant woman in a pale-coloured suit was waiting with a polite smile.

'Mrs Leonidas,' she greeted deferentially. 'Mr Leonidas is expecting you.'

Half of Annie's lip twisted in an amused smile at that. He hadn't been, until about two minutes ago?

'Thank you,' she said, falling into step beside the other woman to a set of double doors that led to the Theo's office. The assistant knocked once, and Theo was there, drawing the door inwards.

'Thank you, Helen,' he murmured, barely glancing at her.

He only had eyes for Annie, and it was a very necessary shot in the arm.

She strode into his office, heels clicking against the large pale tiles. When she was in the middle, she put a hand on her hip and turned to face him. But the way he was looking at her was so smouldering that she completely lost her train of thought.

'Did you wear that out in public?'

She glanced down at her admittedly very short dress, and shrugged, her eyes daring him to complain. Daring him to pick this fight.

'Is there something wrong with it?'

A muscle throbbed at the base of his jaw, but he wisely stayed quiet. 'What can I do for you?'

'I'd like to discuss the terms of our marriage.'

He crossed his arms over his chest. 'The terms of our marriage have already been agreed to. I have the contract to prove it.'

'I'd like to vary them.'

'That's not generally how contracts work.'

'What's the matter, Theo? Are you scared of what I'm going to suggest?'

'What do you want?' he asked, but stayed where he was, so for a second, she thought maybe she was right: that he *was* scared.

'Well, definitely not this.'

He arched a single brow. 'You knew what you were getting into when you agreed to marry me.'

'No, I don't think I did.'

'What precisely is the problem?'

'You're ignoring me.'

He frowned. 'Am I?'

She rolled her eyes. 'Don't gaslight me. We both know you're staying out of the house so you don't have to see me. What happened to a "public marriage"?'

He moved to his desk then, pressing his fingers into the edge of it, his expression thoughtful. 'You'd like to go on more dates?'

'I'd like to not feel like I'm either walking on eggshells or being completely ignored.'

'You are the one who asked me to turn your father's company around.'

'I know that.'

'Did you think I would just snap my fingers? It takes work, *agape*. Long, hard work.'

Chastened, she bit into her lip. She'd barely thought about the company since he'd agreed to take it over and help her.

'I know.'

'Is this about dinner dates, Annie, or something else?'

Her heart began to race so loudly, it was all she could hear.

'It's about spending time together.'

He walked towards her then, his gait predatory, like a cougar, prowling, intent on his catch. 'I told you, sex wouldn't change anything.'

'And I told you, I get that.' She angled her chin belligerently. 'Why can't you take me at my word and accept that I can walk and chew gum at the same time.'

'What does that mean?'

'I can sleep with you, talk to you, and be fake married to you, without any part of this changing. In eighteen months, I will be demanding that divorce we've discussed, no matter what happens between us now. All I'm saying is: Why can't we just make the most of this, in the meantime?'

He stared down at her, as though she'd started speaking a totally foreign language.

'I'd never had sex before that day,' she said seriously, honestly, staring up at him. 'And now, you hardly seem to want to touch me. Did I do something wrong?'

Theo didn't move, so Annie's heart sank.

'I mean, I wasn't sure...'

'No.' His voice was rough. 'You did nothing wrong. It was fine.'

'Fine?' she squeaked, mortified.

'Great, okay? It was great.'

'Because you didn't—'

'No, I didn't,' he said. 'But that was not because you erred in any way.'

'It's just—I liked it. And I want—I would like—'

'More,' he said, moving a hand to her hip and placing it there, fingers splayed.

She nodded mesmerized. 'Yes.' It was a whisper. And an admission. It was also terrifying, because she felt so exposed to him, so raw and vulnerable. 'Yes, I want more. I want you.'

'Oh, Annie,' he groaned, dropping his head forward, like he was trying to blank her out. 'This has the potential to be very complicated.'

'Why? What's changed since that day in Sydney? You were fine with sex, then. What's different now?'

'You know what's changed. I presumed you were—if not exactly like me, at least experienced.'

'Get over it. My inexperience doesn't mean anything to me, it shouldn't to you. It's just...happenstance.'

He made a grunt, which could have been agreement or disagreement.

'If you don't want to sleep with me, okay, but I don't want to be married to someone who won't even talk to me.'

A muscle ticked at the base of his jaw as his eyes held hers for a long time. 'You know why we got married. So far as I remember, talking to one another was not a factor.'

She stared at him, hating how much his words hurt, hating that she couldn't properly conceal it. The fact he wasn't going to compromise was blatantly obvious, so she'd have to work out a way to get what she wanted. Which was to know her husband. To have him get to know her again, too. 'Fine. Then I want to stick to the original deal—a public marriage, like you suggested. I want to go for lunch with you.'

His expression was practically a scowl. 'Lunch?'

'You've heard of the concept, I presume?'

'Today?'

'It is lunchtime, isn't it?'

'Wearing that?'

'What's wrong with this dress? I've seen photos of the women you usually date—I know what you like.'

He looked her up and down, shaking his head once. 'That's not— Annie—'

'If you don't want to eat with me, just say. I'll go somewhere on my own.'

She could see his cogs turning, and knew enough now about Theo to recognise that jealousy was shifting through him. 'No,' he said, sharp and decisive. 'I'll take you to lunch. It's fine.'

It sounded anything but fine, yet Annie didn't focus on that—she chose to take this for the victory it was. Theo was going to stop ignoring her, right now. Because Annie had a feeling there was so much more about him she didn't understand, so much she didn't know. Back then, she hadn't had a single clue how to scratch beneath the surface. He'd so easily been able to shut down her lines of enquiry, by just changing the subject or diverting her attention. Annie was older and wiser now, and she wasn't going to let him get away with it this time.

Operation Get To Know Her Husband was about to get underway.

CHAPTER NINE

THE ROOFTOP BAR of the fashionable boutique hotel boasted an exclusive clientele and stunning views of the Acropolis. The menu was unapologetically Greek, and their table private, set on the corner of the terrace, with a concrete planter filled with spiky green plants separating them a little from the other diners. In the background, there was a low hum of conversation and the soft strains of jazz music, the husky acoustic singing ringing with emotion.

She could imagine this place would be packed at night, filled with Athens's elite, here to see and be seen. On one level, it surprised her that Theo had brought her to a place like this. Then again, a lot had changed in five years. She didn't really know that much about the man she'd married, which was the whole point of this lunch.

'Your usual, sir?'

Annie blinked across at Theo, surprised by the waiter's question. Evidently, Theo came here often enough to have a 'usual'. With a date?

Of course with a date. She knew he'd hardly been a monk since they parted ways.

'Would you like a cocktail?' Theo asked Annie.

She glanced at the waiter, and nodded. 'An Aperol, thanks.'

The waiter nodded once then left.

'You come here often?'

'It is close to the office.'

She frowned. 'So you come for...work lunches?'

His smile was tight. 'Something like that.'

Annie suppressed a sigh. That hardly told her anything. Five years ago, Theo had been reluctant to share anything too personal, but he had at least made conversation. Now it was like getting blood from a stone. But she'd expected that. She just had to warm him up a little.

'How are things going with the company?'

His frown was reflexive. 'It's a mess.'

Her brows shot up. 'That bad, huh?'

'I'm still trying to work out if it's a case of incompetence or—'

'Or?' she asked when he broke off mid-sentence.

The waiter returned with a tray and two drinks, placing them down. Both Theo and Annie waited until they were alone again.

'Or something more serious.'

'You're talking embezzlement?'

'Possibly. Fraud. I'm not sure. I have a team of forensic accountants going through your books now.'

Annie squeezed her eyes shut on a wave of nausea. 'Oh, God.'

'You didn't suspect?'

'I didn't know how everything got so bad, so quickly, but my involvement is peripheral at best—I hired someone who came very highly recommended to run the company. By the time I realised we were over-leveraged, it was too late.'

'What about your father?' he asked with obvious contempt.

Annie bit into her lip, hating how much Theo despised

the older man, even when she understood his reasoning. 'He hasn't been the same, since Mum…'

Theo's eyes rested on Annie's face a long time, before he glanced towards the view. 'That was a long time ago.'

'There's no statute of limitations on grief, apparently.'

Theo turned back to Annie. 'And you, Annie?'

'What about me?'

'I imagine you were also grieving.'

A constriction formed in her throat, making it hard to swallow. She nodded quickly, then took a sip of her drink. It was sweet and sparkly. 'She'd been sick for six months, though. I hoped she'd get better, but at the same time, I was prepared that she wouldn't. She wasn't the same after the first heart attack.'

Theo's eyes narrowed. He knew the timing of it. Annie had told him, the morning she'd ended things. She'd explained that her mother was so devastated by the idea of their being together she'd had an actual heart attack.

'You understand that it was not your fault?' Theo asked, echoing something he'd said at the time. Only back then, he'd grabbed her arms and pulled her to his chest, his face lined with passion, with a need to make her understand. Now he was the opposite, cool and calm, asking almost like he didn't care one way or the other.

'We'd argued,' she whispered, pressing her fingertips to her temple, reliving that awful night. 'They'd insisted we break up, I was blindsided. I mean, I knew you weren't who they expected me to be with, but they'd never been so overt in telling me what to do.' She shook her head, oblivious to the way his eyes narrowed, and his lips formed a compressed line of disapproval. 'I was surprised and I probably overreacted.'

He made a sound of disapproval. 'You were twenty-two years old.'

'But you know, the situation with Mary,' she whispered. 'Ever since she died, they spent every ounce of energy protecting me, carving out the life they thought I should lead, to keep safe.'

'What point is life if you do not actually live it?'

She'd lived it with Theo. For that one perfect year, Annie had felt as though she were brimming with vitality. As though she had a purpose beyond standing in for Mary, was seen as someone other than a poor replacement.

'They had my best interests at heart.'

'How can you say that, even now?'

'It's true. I know it must seem over-the-top to you, Theo—'

'To anyone with eyes or a brain.'

'Thank you for that.'

He leaned forward, surprising her by putting a hand on hers. 'You were right to stand up to them. If only you'd had the courage to see it through.'

She bit on her lip, looking across at him, her heart racing wildly. She ignored the condemnation in the way he'd accused her of lacking courage—like he had any idea how strong she'd had to be, all her life—and focused instead on his implication. 'And what would have happened, if I had?' she asked, toying with her napkin.

She sensed his withdrawal, even before he removed his hand and returned it to his glass. 'I don't deal in hypotheticals.'

'Indulge me,' she rebuffed.

'For what reason? We'll never know what our future might have been had they not interfered. Had you felt that our relationship was important enough to fight for.'

She looked across at the Acropolis, but for once took no solace in the ancient, familiar stones.

'You have no idea what my life was like,' she said, unevenly, toying with her napkin.

'I knew you.'

'No, I'm starting to think that's not true.' Her brain was shifting from one spark to another, connecting dots, so when she looked at Theo now, it was with a dawning comprehension. 'You hid yourself from me, you know. Anytime I asked about your childhood, your life before you came to live next door, you would change the subject.'

His nostrils flared.

'But maybe I did the same thing,' she pondered, lips pulled to the side. 'I mean, I told you Mary died, but I didn't tell you what that did to me. What it did to my parents, and how they treated me. I didn't explain to you that I spent my entire life knowing that they wished our places had been reversed. Or that my intrinsic value wasn't in me, personally, but in being their last surviving daughter. My mother would say to me, every night, that she couldn't handle it if anything ever happened to me. That I had to stay safe and stay alive, just for her. Do you have any idea how terrified I was to even cross the street, Theo? The pressure of it, their expectations—that's been my *entire* life.'

He was watching her with an expression that gave nothing away, but Annie wasn't really seeing him, anyway. 'I love them, so much, but I also...it's hard to forgive them, for how they were with me. And how they were with you,' she admitted.

'And yet you still do his bidding.'

'With the company, you mean?'

'You were so desperate to save it, for your father's sake, that you agreed to marry a man you profess to hate.'

'The company is all he has left.'

'He has you.'

'I don't know if he really even sees me, anymore,' she whispered. 'Since Mum, it's just been…'

She searched for the right words and drew a blank. The truth was, it had been hollow. Empty. 'Anyway…' She trailed off into nothing, grateful for the reappearance of the waiter to take their food orders. Though she hadn't even looked at the menu and instead appealed to Theo to choose for her.

He ordered a selection of things, and by the time they were alone again, Annie had resolutely pushed the grief of her own life aside. She hadn't come here to unburden herself to Theo, but rather to find out more about him.

'That's my sad story,' she said, tilting her head to the side and considering him. 'Now it's your turn.'

'Is that how this works?'

'Yes, usually. You know, conversation ebbs and flows.'

His smile was tight. 'I'm familiar with the concept.'

'But not particularly skilled with the execution.'

His next smile was more of a grimace. 'We can't all have your charm.'

She flinched, because it didn't come across as a compliment at all. He expelled an angry breath, then surprised her by saying, 'I'm sorry. I didn't mean that as it sounded.'

'Like you resent my "charm"?'

'In fact, I admire it,' he said, slowly, as though the words were dragged from him against his better judgement.

'Coming from the man who can walk into any room, say one word and have everyone fall silent to hear you speak?'

He let out a gruff laugh. 'Is that how you view me?'

'It's how everyone views you.'

'That's because I have money.'

'No, it's not that.'

'Believe me, it's a factor.'

'I grew up with money,' she demurred. 'Surrounded by it, in fact. Your charisma is regardless of your bank balance.'

'Are you saying if I'd still been living on the streets, you'd have looked at me twice?' he pushed, his voice dark with resentment, so she felt a hum in her brain telling her she was close to a source of pain for him. And it wasn't that she wanted to cause him distress, but rather, to get to the heart of his life's experience, so she could better understand him.

'I don't deal in hypotheticals,' she volleyed back, with a small smile. He rewarded her with a flicker of his own lips, and her heart stammered. But she wouldn't be misdirected by a simple smile. 'How long were you on the streets for, Theo?'

She sensed it again; that immediate withdrawing, like he was physically erecting a structure between them. 'Long enough.'

'A year? Two years? Four?'

'Does it matter?'

'Yes. I think it matters a great deal to you, and it matters to me, too.'

'Why?'

'Because it's a part of who you are.'

'I left that boy behind a long time ago.'

'Did you?' she pushed, pressing her elbows to the table and lacing her fingers together beneath her chin. 'Are you sure?'

His eyes bore into hers. 'What are you suggesting?'

'In the same way my life to this point has shaped me, so too has yours. It's incredibly naive to suggest that you can just shirk the bits of yourself you no longer want.'

'It's amazing what willpower can achieve.'

'Don't be glib.'

His nostrils flared. 'Did we come to lunch to examine my biography in detail?'

'Partly, yes,' she said honestly.

'Damn it, Annie, this isn't our deal.'

'It's not expressly prohibited by our contract,' she pointed out, then tried a different tack. 'What are you afraid of?'

'Nothing,' he denied.

'Then why not answer my questions?'

She'd laid a trap and he'd stepped right into it. She could see him weighing that up, considering it and she just hoped and prayed the waiter wouldn't come and interrupt, giving Theo an easy excuse to change the subject to something banal like the quality of the olive oil.

'I was in foster care from when I was three until I was seven, when I ran away for the first time. After that, I was mostly on the streets, except for a few occasions when I was arrested and returned to care. It never lasted long. By then, my manners were not particularly conducive to being looked after,' he said.

'What does that mean?'

'That I was very difficult. Aggressive, defensive, untrusting, angry. On the street, those qualities served me well, but in someone's home, it didn't tend to go over too well.'

'Oh, Theo,' she said, her heart breaking for the little boy he'd once been. 'Why did you run away, when you were only seven years old?'

For the briefest moment, she could have sworn he looked afraid. Desperate to end the conversation. And she was tempted to take pity on him and let it go. But this was all so crucial to understanding him, to understanding the decisions he made, even now, that she held her ground.

'Why do you think?'

'I couldn't say.'

'It's better to leave it.'

'Why?'

'There's no advantage to reliving that time.'

'Were you hurt, Theo?'

His eyes stayed locked to hers. 'It was not the first time I was hit, but it was by far the worst.'

She gasped, tears filling her eyes.

'See, Annie? Sometimes the truth is not really what you want.'

That was accurate. She didn't want this truth for him, but the fact it had happened made her ache to comfort him. She pushed up out of her chair, going around to him, uncaring that they were in a restaurant. She needed to be close to him, and perhaps he felt that too, because she wouldn't have been able to sit in his lap without Theo pushing back from the table a little.

Her heart was splintering apart for that boy. Seven years old. 'I'm so sorry,' she whispered, catching his face in both hands, staring into his eyes. 'You should never have known that pain.'

'No,' he agreed. 'Nobody should.'

She dropped her head forward and pressed her lips to his forehead.

'I can't imagine what it was like,' she said, after a beat. 'Living on the streets…'

'For a start, that's a very sanitary euphemism for what it was like. Every day was a baptism by fire.'

She pulled away so she could look into his eyes. 'In what way?'

It was abundantly clear that Theo didn't want to have this conversation, but to his credit, he didn't hold back. 'The first month was the hardest. I was large for my age, but still just a boy. Skin and bone, and scared of the dark,' he admitted, lips twisting in a self-deprecating grimace. 'I begged, but one night, was mugged for what little I had, including my only pair of shoes,' he said. Annie's heart cracked apart. 'But a few weeks later, I met a man—little more than a teenager, actually—called Simon. He took me under his wing, along with a few other kids. He showed us where the good corners were to beg, how to steal from shops without getting caught.' Theo's Adam's apple bobbed as he swallowed. 'I hated stealing. Even then, I knew it was wrong, but I was so hungry. And Simon—while he cared for us, he also had the potential to lose his temper—spectacularly—if we didn't bring enough food or money back to him. After a few years, he and I fell out. We fought. I had to leave.'

'Leave?'

'I went to the other side of town. It was darker. Poorer. Rougher, but by then, I was at least able to take care of myself. I heard that Simon died a few months after I left,' he added, clearing his throat, so Annie knew, without him having to say it, that he somehow blamed himself. 'He got in a fight with someone bigger. He always had more bark than was wise, for someone his size. But I used to be there, to help. To defend him,' Theo admitted.

'But you were so much younger.'

'I was a quick learner. You have to be on the streets. I knew how to fight, to the death, if necessary.'

She gasped. 'Was it ever necessary?'

'Are you asking me if I have ever killed another person, Annie?'

She blinked, the thought one that had never occurred to

her. She nodded slowly, but held her breath, and only let it out when he shook his head to indicate no.

'But back then, I would have, if I'd needed to. Maybe if I'd been with Simon, that afternoon, I would have, to save his life. I don't know. It was a different time, and I was a different person. Hunger, poverty, desperation—they change you.'

'I don't know,' she said, lifting a hand and curving it around his cheek. 'I don't think you're capable of it.'

'Don't you?'

She shook her head. 'Of defending someone, absolutely. But you're not violent, Theo.'

Their eyes held for a long time, and the longer they looked at one another, the more Annie felt a sense of conviction deep in her gut. She knew the real Theo. She always had done. She saw beneath whatever he projected and saw what was in his heart.

At least, she thought she had.

'I have never spoken about Simon,' he said, slowly, as if only coming to that realization himself.

Warmth spread through her. 'I'm glad you told me.'

'I have felt a sense of responsibility for a long time. I walked away from him, and I shouldn't have. I should have stayed. I knew what his temper was like. But by then, I had my own feelings and thoughts...'

'You couldn't have been with him twenty-four-seven.'

'No,' Theo agreed, but quietly, as though he wasn't convinced.

'You cared for him,' Annie prompted, remembering Theo's assertion, the day they'd left the island, that she, Annie, was the only person who'd ever inspired that emotion in him. Maybe that hadn't been entirely accurate.

'We were part of a team,' he said, with a small shake

of his head. 'It's different. For all I felt it my obligation to defend him, to protect him, I expected nothing in return. I did not rely on Simon, I did not need him to need me. But I would have given my life to spare his, if I could have.'

Annie shuddered at the very thought of Theo having died as a teenager. 'What happened next?' she asked. 'Did you find another...team?'

'No, Annie. After that, I was resolutely alone. Until I met the Georgiadeses, and then, until I met you.'

Silence fell, heavy with the weight of their past, their difficulties, the hurt that each brought to this. And yet there was also a strange sense of peace flooding Annie, because for the first time, they were really connecting honestly and openly, about something of substance. He wasn't trying to shield her from the brutal reality of his childhood, and in hearing this truth, she felt like she would crack other parts of him open, too.

Annie stayed there, on his lap, as close to him as they could be in a public space, even when the waiter brought their food. She wasn't ready to relinquish this, and she was relieved—and delighted—that he evidently felt the same way.

But the longer she sat on his lap, the more her feelings morphed, from sympathy and concern to something far more grown up, her awareness of him, as a man, flooding her body. She dropped one of her hands to his chest, and pressed it there, feeling his warmth and strength, the hard beating of his heart.

'Why don't you not work late tonight?' she murmured, her eyes dropping to his lips. 'In fact, why don't you take the afternoon off?'

One side of his mouth lifted in a mocking half smile. 'Would you like to go shopping? Or perhaps to see a movie?'

She pulled a face. 'Neither of those things holds much appeal.'

'Then what were you thinking, Mrs Leonidas?'

Her heart turned over in her chest to hear him call her that. 'I was thinking we could go home,' she said, letting her hand drift a little lower.

'Are there some more books you wish to read?'

She laughed. 'You're enjoying this.'

'Having my wife demand I take time off work to make love to her? Yes. I think I actually am.'

'Is that a "yes"?'

He looked at her long and hard, and she held her breath, wondering if he might be going to turn her down, despite the way the air was sparking with a mutual and consuming awareness.

'I have to work,' he said, gently easing her from his lap. At least she could hide the disappointment that was all over her face. 'But I will see you tonight, Annie.'

He had been so terrifyingly tempted to turn his ordered life on its head and go home with his wife. Not after lunch, either, but then and there. To toss a few hundred euros down on the table, throw her over one shoulder and storm his way to the waiting car. Hell, he wasn't even sure if they'd have made it home. Once in the confines of the back seat, he'd have probably wanted to sink right into her.

If he was honest with himself, he'd thought of little else since that morning on the beach, which was why he'd spent almost every waking minute hiding out in his office, avoiding her. Because if he couldn't see her, he couldn't reach for her, and beg her to come to bed with him.

It was just the same as always. Annie had a power over Theo that he refused to allow to take hold. Not again. Not even when she'd revealed such heartbreaking details about her life, explaining something he'd never quite understood: why her parents had such a hold over her. Why she'd simply agreed to break up with him, and let that be the end of it.

Then, talking about his past had only served to stir up the feelings that were the root cause of his approach to life. Every day had been loaded with danger and risk, uncertainty and insecurity. He hadn't known if he would find food, be in a fight, end up in jail—it had been a constant gamble. He'd needed to use all his wits to stay alive, and as much as he'd worked as part of a team led by Simon, he'd still retained his independence and autonomy, refusing to grow close to the other children, refusing to be comforted by their presence.

It really was only Annie who'd ever made him weak there, who'd drawn him in, made him think—for a brief year—that maybe life could be different after all.

And yes, he wanted her physically—and he would have her again, he accepted—but it wouldn't be because she asked and he came running. It would be on his terms. It had to be—it was the only way he'd make it out of this marriage unscathed. He had to call the shots, to know that he was part of their strange, transactional 'team', but that he was just as autonomous and independent as he ever had been. And most importantly, he could never forget who she was, who her father was, and how they viewed him. Nothing there would ever change.

CHAPTER TEN

ANNIE HAD NO idea what to expect. Theo had politely turned down her invitation, and she'd been smarting ever since, though she'd done her best to hide that for the rest of their lunch. The spirit of closeness was broken, though. They'd stuck to small talk, inconsequential and bland, and Annie had come home *alone*. Frustrated and alone.

So much for her little black dress working some kind of magic.

She'd done a workout in Theo's gym, gone for a swim, contemplated cooking something special for dinner but decided that was pointless when she'd probably end up eating alone, again. At some time around five, her father's housekeeper had texted to remind her that Elliot's birthday party was the following weekend. Annie might have been offended by the insinuation that she could forget, except it had actually completely slipped her mind, in the hubbub of her marriage.

She'd texted back that she'd be there, but when the housekeeper had asked about Theo, she'd immediately written back in the negative.

Theo hated her father—no way would she bring him to a birthday party in his honour. There was no need to poke that particular bear.

She was just contemplating another swim, when she

heard the front door open, and every single cell in her body began to reverberate with anticipation. She moved on autopilot towards the lobby, so she saw the moment Theo stepped through the door, his eyes immediately landing on her.

Annie's lips were parted with surprise, her eyes widened, because after his rejection that afternoon, she'd presumed he'd stick to his usual routine of working until almost midnight.

'Does the offer still stand?' he asked, cutting out any need for small talk, any pretense that they both didn't know why he'd come home.

Her mouth went dry but she nodded quickly, then swallowed. 'Take me to bed, Theo. Please.'

His lips curled in something like genuine amusement and her heart slammed into her ribs. 'Princess, you are going to be begging me at the top of your lungs in a few minutes.'

'We'll see,' she replied impishly, so Theo surprised her by laughing, and stalked the rest of the way between them, before scooping Annie up in his arms and carrying her towards their bedroom, shouldering in the door then placing her on her feet.

'I'm disappointed you're not still wearing that goddamn dress,' he muttered.

She bit into her lip. 'I have to say, disappointment is not the response I was aiming for.'

He grinned. 'Wrong choice of word. I should have said, I haven't been able to stop thinking about how hot you looked in that thing.'

Pleasure spun through her. 'I can put it on again.'

'No. Don't do that.' His eyes were hooded when they met hers. 'I'm much more interested in what was under the dress, anyway.'

'Ah.' She smiled knowingly. 'Well, I think you'll find the same thing is under this as that.'

'I'd better make sure,' he said.

'Probably a good idea.'

His hands caught the hem of her T-shirt, but as he lifted it, he paused, a frown shifting his lips. 'Annie, remember what I said, after last time?'

Sex is just sex. She nodded. She'd remember forever.

'Good.' He kissed her forehead, so her heart went all mushy even when she tried to shield it as quickly as she could. 'I don't want there to be any miscommunication.'

'There won't be,' she assured him. She'd gotten the message loud and clear, and it was one she agreed with.

He pushed the shirt the rest of the way, over her body, his hands tracing its progress, roaming her breasts, her back, curving over her arse, as he lifted her and held her body to his. She couldn't simply stand there and be undressed, though. She also wanted to touch and feel, to know the perfection of his nearness. She pushed at the buttons of his shirt then slid it off his body, before leaning forward and kissing his shoulder. His skin was warm and smooth; she ran her lips over him, flicking his nipples with her tongue, before letting her hands find his belt and unfastening it.

He made a guttural noise from deep in his throat and an ancient, feminine pride trilled in her veins as he stepped out of his trousers and boxers so he was completely naked. She glanced down, her cheeks flushing at this now familiar sight of him—those early morning swims on the island had indelibly imprinted his form into her mind's eye.

'I don't know what to do,' she admitted softly, yet without fear. She trusted Theo, she realised. At least in this way. She knew he wouldn't judge her inexperience, that he'd help awaken this side of her.

'You must have some idea of what you'd like,' he said, as his hands roamed her body, touching, flicking, teasing, before he pushed at her shorts, so they ran down her legs, and she too was naked. She shivered then, simply because it was so intimate, so laced with promise.

'Show me?' she invited, her eyes hooked to his, so she saw the way his irises darkened and his lips parted on a hiss of breath.

'Yes, Annie,' he agreed. 'I'll show you,' and then he kissed her, his lips meshing with hers, their tongues duelling, as he lifted her easily and wrapped her legs around his waist, just as he had in the ocean. She rolled her hips, silently inviting him to take her again—how she'd loved that feeling—but Theo wasn't to be commanded. This was his show; he was as in control here as in the boardroom.

He moved to the bed, placing her in the middle of it. 'Lie down.' He stared at her, dragging his eyes over her body with a possessive heat that made her feel as though she was burning up. 'Good girl,' he murmured, when she lay on her back, and his praise made her skin lift with goose bumps. 'Now, let's try something,' he said, bringing his weight over her, so his nakedness was tantalisingly close.

'What?' she asked, lifting her hips again so that he shook his head and tsked.

'I want you to be completely silent,' he said, his grin showing his skepticism. 'Not a sound.'

'I thought you wanted to hear me scream your name?'

'That will come later,' he said, and she shivered in anticipation. 'Are you ready?'

She nodded, already submitting to his request for silence.

His eyes held a challenge, but then, his lips were on her collarbone, before dragging lower, to her breasts, his tongue flicking and rolling her nipples so that she arched her back and bit into her lip so hard she almost drew blood. A curse filled her mind, but she held it back—just.

'Good,' he murmured his approval against her stomach, as he dragged his mouth lower, until he was beneath her belly button. She pushed up onto her elbows, her jaw dropping when his hands gripped her thighs and spread them wide, so her most intimate self was revealed to his hungry gaze. 'So beautiful,' he said, his eyes slipping to hers almost accusingly, before his head dipped down and his tongue was running over her. She let out a heavy breath—not a noise, exactly, yet it was a sound of utter churning pleasure, and her fingers gripped his hair, simply because without holding on, she thought she might tumble all the way over the edge of the earth.

'Not a sound,' he reminded her, glancing up at her, before his mouth began to move again, sucking, tasting, discovering which buttons he could push, before moving one of his hands there so he could press two fingers inside of her.

'So wet,' he murmured. 'Do you want me?' he asked, as she pulsed around him.

She nodded, without speaking.

'How much?'

She glared at him, as the world began to shake, and pleasure was a radiant force.

'Say it,' he invited. 'I want to hear you now.'

'God, please,' she groaned, tilting her head back with relief. 'Don't stop. I want—I need—I need everything.'

'Yes,' he agreed. 'And I'm going to give it to you.' And he did. First, with his fingers, which sent her over the edge, so that she was trembling all over, before he brought his body over hers, his head level with hers, and his knee nudged her legs wide again, so he could press his cock to her sex.

'Ready?' he asked, stroking her head gently so that her

heart trembled for a different reason. She nodded, dragging her nails down his back and digging them into his buttocks.

As he drove into her, he kissed the flesh just beneath her earlobe, and the sensations were almost too much to bear. He moved as though he'd been given the key to understanding exactly what she needed. Every time he shifted, he brushed new nerve endings, so she was almost exploding with the power of her pleasure, coming apart at every seam she possessed.

'Theo, Theo,' she said, over and over, forgetting that she'd once been determined never to give him that, never to show him how much she wanted him. 'Please,' she cried into the bedroom, not even caring that she'd probably see a look of triumph in his face, that he'd revel in her weakness.

When he dragged his mouth to her breast and took a nipple into his mouth, sucking on it until she saw stars, Annie was gripped by a fierce orgasm, her whole body writhing from the force of her pleasure.

'You are so beautiful,' he muttered and then pulled out of her, moving to stand at the edge of the bed, staring down at her, so for a second, she feared history was repeating itself, and he wasn't going to experience his own pleasure. And she wanted him to. She wanted to know that he'd been as driven wild as she had been.

But then, he crooked a finger, indicating for her to stand up. Heart in her throat, she did so, going toe to toe with him. His hands on her hips were strong, commanding, as he turned her over, to face the bed, then pushed at her shoulders, guiding her so she was bent at the hips, her elbows braced on the bed.

'Remember what I said,' he asked, and before she could answer, he'd pushed into her again, this time, harder, faster, more like that first time, in the ocean, and his hands came around her body, one massaging her breast until she was crying out with the sensations he could so easily stir, and the other moving to her clit, brushing it as he took her from behind and made the whole world stop making sense. How could anything be the same once she'd known pleasure like this? How could *she* ever be the same?

She tried to remember what he'd said—sex was sex—but the truth was, this was mind-altering, personality-changing sex, and she would never be the same afterwards.

'Theo,' she cried out, but this time, her voice was drowned out by his own gruff, rasping cry into the air. After that, there was only the sound of their rapid breathing.

'Can I ask you something?' Annie murmured, her breath warm against his chest. His hand, stroking her back, stilled, but then, he began to trail his fingers once more over her soft, smooth skin.

Her voice was soft, and yet, something inside of him braced for her question. He'd shared more with her over lunch than he'd intended. She had an ability to reach inside of him and draw out whatever she wanted to know. 'Yes,' he said, though, after a beat.

'How did you come to live with the Georgiadeses?'

His hand began to draw invisible circles in the small of her back, as he replayed that time in his life. It felt like a lifetime ago.

'I was fifteen,' he said.

She propped her chin on his chest, her eyes resting on his face. 'I remember.' A quick glance at her showed a knowing smile, one he felt tugging at his own lips.

'You were eleven.'

'And totally smitten.'

His laugh surprised him.

'Anyway, that doesn't answer my question.'

'No.' He nodded once. It wasn't something he, or the Georgiadeses, had ever really discussed, but that didn't mean it was a secret. There was no reason not to tell Annie. 'Paul saw me shoplifting—just an apple and a bag of crisps. I stuffed them under my shirt. He followed me out of the store. I was going to run. I thought he'd drag me to the cops or something. Instead, he just asked me if I had somewhere to sleep.'

'Were you scared?'

He shook his head. 'You remember Paul. He had kind eyes and a gentle, patient voice.'

'Yes,' she agreed softly.

'He was older, too—in his seventies by then. He couldn't have hurt me, even if he'd wanted to.'

'He could have called the police, like you said.'

'I would have outrun him easily.'

'But you didn't.'

'No,' he frowned. 'And he surprised me, by asking if I wanted to come and stay at his house for the weekend. He pointed across the street, to a café, where his wife was sitting at a table on the footpath. She waved at me, and smiled. It was very strange, *agape*, but I almost felt as though I knew them. As though I had known them before.'

'Had you met them, do you think?'

'No, how could I have? We moved in very different circles,' he said, with a wry grimace.

'So you just went home with them?'

'I said "no". I wasn't stupid. Why would I trust them? But Paul was insistent. He asked if I wanted to just come and have dinner. I didn't have to go into their house, I could eat on the driveway, but they would feel better knowing I'd had a proper meal.'

'That's very kind of them.'

'They were kind.'

'Yes.'

'And that's it? You went for dinner and, what? Just stayed?'

'It wasn't that easy. I went for dinner, and ate on the driveway. They invited me in, I refused. They asked me to come back the next night, and I did.'

'Why do you think they went to the trouble?'

'I asked him that, once. You know they could never have children of their own? And yet, they didn't adopt, they didn't foster. But he said that when he saw me, so skinny and hungry, he just felt like he'd been put on earth to take care of me.' His voice was gruff as the memory of that permeated his chest. 'They never pushed me. I never felt like they wanted anything in return for their generosity, except my safety. After about a month of dinners, I trusted them enough to stay. It was supposed to be for a weekend, but then Paul began to talk to me about his work, and it was like a fuse had been lit in my belly. For the first time, I felt all these neurons in my brain connecting, lighting up like a Christmas tree. I was obsessed with everything he said: the business, the opportunities. He saw it, and gave me a chance to work with him, on the basis that I went back to school. And so, there you have it. For the next three years, I went to school, worked with Paul, and ate Stephanie's food. I grew healthy again, nourished, and though they never asked me to say that I loved them, or to pay them back in any way, for the first time in my life, I had a bed, and I didn't fear that it would be taken away. They gave me the greatest gift I could have known. Security.'

He didn't realise she was crying until a tear thudded

onto his chest. He brushed his thumb over her cheek, wiping her tears away.

'I didn't even cry, when they died,' he muttered, staring up at the ceiling, remembering the bleakness of that day. 'But it was like an anchor point in my life had been ripped away. I had briefly known what it was like to belong to a family, of sorts, and just like that, it disappeared.'

'Oh, Theo,' she murmured, pulling up higher so she could press a kiss to his lips, before resting her head on his shoulder. 'I'm so glad you met them, that they took you in.'

'As am I,' he agreed. It had been a perfect relationship for him—and for them. Neither had wanted something that the other wouldn't give. He knew that if they'd pushed him for more, he'd have run a mile, but they hadn't.

'I just remember you appearing, and yes, you were skinny,' she murmured. 'But you were also so vital, so...'

He tilted his face to look at her, and despite the seriousness of their conversation, a smile lifted his lips at the memory of the crush she'd had on him.

'Yes?'

She rolled her eyes. 'I'm not here to make your head any bigger.'

He grinned, his fingers drawing invisible patterns on her back. But they slowed, as his mind went back to that time, those first few years with the Georgiadeses. 'You were such a quiet kid,' he murmured. 'So withdrawn.'

'You made me nervous.'

He shook his head, though. 'It wasn't just around me. I saw you with your friends, your parents. You were always watching.'

She bit into her full lower lip, in a way that made his cock react instantly.

'I was always watching,' she admitted, several moments

later, so he'd wondered if she was going to answer him at all. 'Or maybe it would be more accurate to say I was always anticipating.'

'Anticipating what?'

She sighed. 'Trigger points for my parents.'

'What does that mean?'

'Like, little things that people say, or do, that would tip them over the edge. Make them think of Mary when they weren't prepared.' She cleared her throat.

'You managed their grief.'

'Yes,' she admitted, huskily.

'Annie, you know it's not your job, don't you?'

She nodded, but frustration whipped his insides.

'Because you seem to still be caught up in this—in turning your life into an act of service. What else explains why you came to Sydney? Why you agreed to marry me?'

Her cheeks flushed and he let his hand drop to the mattress. Her eyes lifted to his, and he felt the weight of things she wasn't saying then, in a way that made him pull back. Because this was the kind of conversation he knew they were better avoiding. He didn't want to feel sorry for his wife; he didn't want to feel anything for her. And so he pulled his arm away from her and stepped out of bed, uncaring for his nakedness, just knowing he wanted to get away.

Despite what he'd said, sleeping together changed everything. Without discussing it, they no longer tried to keep one another at a physical distance. The moment he walked in the door, they reached for each other, coming together hard and fast, and then taking hours each night to explore and feel, to pleasure and be pleased by. Working late was a thing of the past. Theo did his level best to stick out a full day, but by the early afternoon, all he could think about was getting home to his wife and sinking into her. The only reason he accepted this shift in their dynamic was the certainty he held that it was purely physical. There would be no more deep and meaningful conversations in bed, no more letting her get under his skin. This time, the partition for Annie would remain firmly locked in place—she would not take over his thoughts again, as she had five years ago, no matter what happened between them physically.

They made love in the pool, the spa, the shower, on the kitchen table, against walls, on the floor, in the car—wherever they were was no barrier. It was as though the floodgates had been unlocked and there was no going back. Or maybe it was because they knew they had a finite time for this, and they didn't want to waste it.

Without discussing it, they spent every minute they could in each other's arms, so when the night of her father's birthday rolled around, Annie found it almost impossible to think of going out without him. But what choice did she have? She particularly didn't want to risk things changing between her and Theo, going back to what they'd been like before. While they were hardly sharing each other's deepest, darkest secrets, there was an inherent intimacy to what they were doing, and the thought of losing that made her body feel weak with despair. In the back of her mind, she knew that wasn't without risk.

She knew that at some point, she'd have to walk away. The terms of their divorce were already agreed upon, after all, and she couldn't lose sight of that fact, no matter how good it felt to just be with him again. But for now, she wanted *this*.

'You look stunning,' he murmured, when she walked into the kitchen wearing a red dress with a low-cut neckline. 'If a little overdressed.' He indicated his own attire—just a pair of shorts.

Anxiety trembled inside of her—aware that she was on the brink of upsetting the apple cart and desperately wanting not to—but she pushed it aside. They'd come so far; she could be honest with him, without ruining the good thing they had going on. 'Actually, I'm going out,' she said. 'I have a dinner.'

His expression was immediately closed off to her—familiar, though she hadn't seen him react like that in a week and a half. 'I see.'

She could practically hear the questions forming inside his mind—questions she didn't want him to ask, because she didn't want to lie. 'I won't be late,' she said, hoping it would assuage whatever he was going to say, and strolling around to put a hand on his chest. 'Wait up for me?'

His eyes raked her face, a frown touching the corners of his lips, as he nodded once: a crisp, curt acknowledgement.

She let out a soft breath of relief then kissed him, her body immediately stirring to life. He pulled away though, his eyes distant. 'Have fun.'

Her chest hurt as though a bag of cement had been pressed against it. She turned away quickly, wishing, more than anything that she could stay here with him instead.

Her hand was on the door, when he caught up with her. 'You're not going to say where you're going?'

She closed her eyes against that, before turning to face him, lifting a hand to play with the diamond necklace she wore. 'A birthday party,' she said, after a beat.

He nodded thoughtfully. 'For a friend?'

Her eyes were hooked to his. She wished he hadn't asked. She shook her head, slowly.

'I see. Someone I know?'

'Theo—'

'You weren't going to tell me?'

'It's—'

'Your father's birthday.'

She pressed a hand to her brow, trying to think. 'How did you know?'

'Is it a secret?'

She bit into her lip. 'No, but—'

'I remember the date, Annie—it is a week before my foster mother's birthday,' he said, reminding her of that fact.

She swallowed past a constricted throat. 'I have to go—you don't.'

'He's my father-in-law,' Theo pointed out.

'Yes, but we both know how you feel about him.'

Silence sparked between them, the weight of what they were both feeling making it hard to wade through.

'Are you forgetting why I suggested this marriage, *agape*?' he asked, almost conversationally. 'The whole point was to show your father, at every opportunity, that he lost, and I won. That he was wrong about me—about us.'

She felt like her heart was undergoing a series of electric shocks as she shook her head. It was the truth, and yet she wanted to argue against it, to deny it. That couldn't really be at the heart of why he'd suggested this. Not after the last week and a half. Not after how everything had changed between them. Surely, that same angry hate didn't still consume him?

'It's his birthday,' she said, weakly, as her mind tried to keep up with this development.

'And?'

She pressed a hand to his chest, eyes imploring. 'Don't do this, Theo.'

But his eyes were glittering with dark determination, and she barely recognised the man he'd become. 'I will be ready soon. Knowing your father, I presume it's black tie?'

She closed her eyes on a wave of despair. 'Please,' she said. 'Don't pick this fight.'

But when she blinked up at him, Theo was gone.

A stone seemed to drop, right through her body, landing hard in her gut.

She pressed her back against a wall, sucking in a deep breath that hardly seemed to touch her lungs.

All Theo could do was stick to the plan. It was, as he'd pointed out to Annie, the reason he'd proposed this marriage. The thought of throwing their relationship in the face of the man who'd once told Theo that he was *'pure scum and always would be'*, was something he'd relished the thought of.

As for Annie, she'd just have to cope with that.

And yet, glancing across at her, as the car slid through the streets of Athens towards her family home, something gnawed at the edges of his gut, as awful as the pervasive hunger he'd known as a child. Tension radiated from every line of her slim body. It was evident in the way she clasped her hands in her lap, the way she refused to look at him. He ached to do something to stir feelings in her, so she'd appear more like the wild, passionate, beautiful woman he'd been lusting after nonstop.

But sex—no matter how good—was just sex, and Annie was a woman he'd married as a means to an end. He owed himself this. Nothing could trump that—not even their chemistry.

So he sat in stony silence beside her, not reaching for her, not even to hold her hand.

There was no comfort he could give anyway, and he wouldn't pretend otherwise. For as long as his plan was to hurt her father, to make him eat crow, using Annie as a tool for that, he could hardly expect Annie not to mind.

As the car pulled to a halt in the busy driveway of their mansion, he did reach for her though, putting a hand on her knee and drawing her churning gaze to his face.

'I want you to remember two things, Annie,' he said, his voice heavy with loathing for the words he was about to speak. Hating himself then, even when he didn't dare question his commitment to this plan.

She was almost unrecognizable, with her pretty face so pale and pinched. 'Yes?' Her voice was barely a whisper.

He clenched his jaw, hesitating a moment, to draw strength.

'At the end of this marriage, your father will be a very rich man again. That's all you care about, remember? That's why you came to me. You're getting what you wanted. What you agreed to.'

She fidgeted with her fingers so violently he had to fight an urge to reach out and clamp his hand over them.

'And the second?'

'We have a deal. You play your part, just like we agreed, or the arrangement's off.'

Her lips parted in surprise and whatever had been gnawing at his gut burst it apart completely. He put a hand on his door, opening it before he could take the words back, or at least apologise for what he was about to put her through.

Theodoros Leonidas didn't do regret, or uncertainty or compassion. He was stronger than steel, determined and ruthless. Those things had stood him in good stead—he wouldn't change now, not even for Annie.

CHAPTER ELEVEN

From the moment they walked into the party, Annie could feel the whispers. The speculation. And yes, the jealousy, from all the women who looked at Theo, saw his beauty and his wealth and wanted a piece of it, wondering how she, Annie Langley, had secured the hottest bachelor in Athens. Though their wedding had been widely publicized, and was well-known in these circles, this was only their second time out and about, in public together, and she fully expected her family's 'friends' to descend like hawks.

As for Theo, the change in his behaviour gave her whiplash. In the car, he'd been so calculated and businesslike, inflicting pain on her without appearing to care, so it had taken a monumental effort not to give in to the tears that she'd felt stinging behind her eyes.

Now, in the throng of the party, he was a study in attentive husbandry, one hand on the small of her back the whole time, his fingers stroking the base of her spine, his body so close to hers she could feel his warmth—even though it did little to thaw the ice in her heart.

'Darling,' her father's greeting, when they arrived, encompassed her alone. He pressed a kiss to her cheek, then said, 'Thank you for coming.'

'We wouldn't have missed it for the world,' Theo responded, drawing Annie even closer to his side, and moving the hand from her back to her hip, possessively holding her to him. 'Would we, *erota mou*?' My passion.

The term of endearment was not one he'd used before, and though she might otherwise have liked it, the knowledge that he'd employed it purely to sting her father took any pleasure out of his huskily spoken words. As did the kiss he planted on the top of her head.

Elliot Langley did then look at Theo, and with such undisguised contempt Annie shivered. 'I wasn't aware you were coming.'

'My wife and I are inseparable,' Theo said, dropping any pretense of warmth. The words were, if anything, an arctic challenge. 'A wise man would know better than to try it.'

Annie glanced up at Theo, and opened her mouth to warn him, to scold him, anything, but the look he threw her held a warning, and she remembered what he'd said in the car. Any diversion from the role she was supposed to play, and the wedding would be off.

'A wiser man would know trying is unnecessary,' her dad surprised her by saying, but his own voice was just as frigid and unyielding as Theo's had been. 'You two have unfinished business, I can see that. But sooner or later, my daughter will realise that she can do so much better than this—Annie has a lot of potential to reach for, and a street kid from Athens isn't it.'

'Please, Daddy,' Annie said, her heart dropping to her toes, hating the words he was saying, hating the scene they were going to create if they didn't take care. 'Not now, not here.'

Elliot's lips were grim. 'You shouldn't have brought him.'

'Annie would not have come without me. Not knowing that I was unwelcome,' he said, and guilt flicked through her, because that's how she should have felt. Wasn't it? Knowing that her father had invited her, and not Theo. That he'd organised a big party and tried to exclude her husband. At the time, she'd been glad: she didn't want her father's birthday to ruin the status quo she and Theo had established. Except...

She looked up at Theo and now her heart sank for a different reason. She'd betrayed him, five years ago, by breaking up with him because her parents had insisted, but had tonight been another betrayal? Another failure to stand up for him, and do what was right? When had Theo ever had anyone in his corner?

If theirs had been a real marriage, she would have done just what he said. Come hell or high water, she would have stuck by him *this time*. But knowing that his sole objective was to pain her father, she'd been trying to do the right thing by everyone.

'Theo,' she said, softly, her words weakened by confusion. 'Let's go and get a drink. I'm parched.'

'The bar is by the pool,' Elliot muttered. 'Try not to fall in.' The last rejoinder was for Theo alone.

When they were at the bar, she looked up at her husband and said, 'I'd apologise for his behaviour, but I suspect you're delighted to have been able to goad him like that.'

Theo looked anything but delighted though, which only made her feel worse. His dark eyes glinted with disapproval when they locked to hers. 'I'm starting to remember why I hate these people so much.'

'You're the darling of these people. I swear half of these women, at least, are staring daggers at me.'

'I will never be a darling to these people,' he contradicted swiftly, turning away from her to order their drinks—a scotch for himself and a champagne for Annie. 'They know as well as your father does—I don't belong.'

'I don't know why you have such a chip on your shoulder.'

He sent her a look that spoke volumes. 'Just as well. You do not need to know. You just need to act the part.' And to cement that, he dropped his mouth and claimed hers, in full view of anyone who cared to look their way. Pleasure ripped through her, but it was a heavy weight of intensity, too, a sadness and grief at the way he'd relegated anything she might feel, putting the focus purely on the physical. She didn't need to know anything too deep about him: it wasn't relevant. All he cared about was this newlywed act.

Knowing the kiss was for show, feeling the hurt of that lash through her, didn't change the effect it had on Annie. It didn't change the way her pulse went haywire and her whole body seemed to catch fire, so that she very quickly forgot where they were and fell against him, her whole self surrendered to him, and the pleasure he could dole out, whenever he wanted to.

He pulled back, looking down at her with a smile that didn't reach his eyes. 'You're an excellent actress, Annie. Perhaps you missed your true calling.'

And her heart, battered and splintered as it already was, exploded into a billion tiny shards that would be, so far as she knew, impossible to stitch back together.

'Keep it up and I might have to think of a way to give you a bonus.'

'Go to hell,' she said, pasting a smile to her face even when she felt like sobbing. 'You really are a complete bastard.'

His eyes glinted and she could have sworn she saw relief on his face. 'Yes, I am. Don't forget it again.'

***

He knew the futility of hatred, yet he couldn't stem it. Or perhaps it was just that he was seeking refuge in it. Like the more time he spent with Annie, and the closer she got to pushing out of her little box again, the more Theo leaned into his anger. Anger was familiar. Anger was useful to him. Anger had never betrayed Theo.

Elliot Langley had torn shreds off Theo five years ago, unconsciously reviving every single stroke of pain Theo had been handed in his life, making him feel worthless, useless, as though he were a complete waste of skin. He'd hated the older man for a long time, but until Elliot took to the stage to thank his guests for coming, Theo hadn't fully grasped the extent of his hatred.

The thank-you speech started with an acknowledgement of how many people had shown up—and Theo had silently, cynically mused on the likelihood that the full guest list probably had something to do with the exceptional quality of the open bar, and the fact several journalists were circulating, taking photographs for tomorrow's papers. But then the speech had moved on, to pay tribute to those who couldn't be with him: his wife, and his daughter, Mary. He spoke for at least twenty minutes about the older sibling, and all the while, Annie stood at Theo's side, still like a statue, a polite smile frozen on her face. He listened to descriptions of Mary's prodigal piano playing, her kindness, how she'd brought such meaning to their lives, and he waited, and waited for anything of a similar ilk to be said about Annie.

Finally, at the end, he finished with, 'But at least, I still have Annie. My Annie.' Except, when his eyes had slid sideways to Theo, Elliot's lips had tightened in a dismissive line, and any further adoration he might have deigned to offer had been swallowed up by obvious disgust. 'Enjoy your night,' Elliot had concluded, to a round of polite applause.

Theo had turned to Annie, wanting to say something to placate her, to offer sympathy, or at least show that he understood, but Annie simply turned that ghoulish smile on him and said, 'I'm not in the mood, okay?'

'Annie—'

'Am I allowed to go to the bathroom on my own, or will you take that as some kind of failure in my playacting?'

Now he knew what was twisting at his gut. Shame. It seemed to take over his whole body, and he hated the feeling. He didn't want to overthink it, to analyse why he felt like he'd followed a road he thought would lead to salvation and now instead suspected might pave the way to hell. He tightened his shoulders, tamping down on his self-doubt and said, voice calm, 'I'll be here.'

'And I'll be right back—' and then, for good measure, she added, with obvious disgust '—*erota mou.*'

Theo swallowed back whatever he'd been about to say in response, and the knowledge that he'd done something tonight he would never be able to undo, even if he wanted to.

He watched her walk through the guests, head held high, with the sense that once upon a time, practically another lifetime ago, he'd held something very, very precious in his hands, and he just hadn't known how to keep a hold of it. All this time he'd blamed her for breaking it off, for being weak under her parents' snobbish pressure, perhaps even for feeling as they did about him, but maybe the problem had been Theo all along.

Maybe he hadn't really understood her life.

Her pressures.

Her aching need to fix everything for everyone.

Maybe he'd been the one to let her down, by walking away without a backwards glance, too proud to push her to reconsider, refusing to beg and be rejected again. He'd gleaned how her parents had molded her, trying to turn Annie into Mary, trying to stem their grief with a perfect replacement, and he'd known how much of a toll that had taken on her. But until tonight, he hadn't really understood just how programmed she'd been—all her life—to do whatever her parents asked of her. To be the perfect daughter, even at the expense of her own happiness, and what a futile, unrewarding duty that was.

She'd tried to tell him when they'd shared lunch at the restaurant near the Acropolis, but even then, he'd let the conversation go rather than pushing her to expand. Because he hadn't wanted to know the truth? Because he'd been afraid of what it might mean for him if he started to see how hard Annie had had it, all her life? Had he avoided asking questions because he didn't want to be forced to question his actions in pushing her into this marriage? The realization that he was not so dissimilar to her parents, in expecting Annie to play a part for his benefit, sat in his gut like a stone.

But what good was there in raking over the embers of their past? He'd done what he'd done, as had she. They'd both made their choices, and now they had a marriage bed to lie in together. The past could not be changed—it was better to accept that owing to the past, they had no future. Even if he could get past what had happened all those years ago, Annie would never be able to forgive him for the way he'd blackmailed her into this. And after starting to understand her life better, he wasn't sure he'd be able to forgive himself, either.

***

She stared at her reflection for a long time, trying to pick out the familiarity of her features, to anchor herself to the core of who she was. What she believed. What she knew.

But it had been such a long time since Annie Langley had really thought about who *she* was and what *she* wanted. All her life, she'd been a daughter. A dutiful fill-in, needed to make their family somewhat full again.

From the moment Mary had died, Annie's purpose on earth had changed. She'd been content to live in Mary's shadow before, aware that her sister was a rare diamond, shining brighter than most other people. But after Mary had died, Annie had been rubbed and rubbed and rubbed by parents who were desperate to try to make her shine in all the same ways Mary had, never mind that Annie might have had her own ways of shining, if only she'd been allowed.

Distant memories of having, once upon a time, loved drawing and art—which had led to her wanting to own her own art gallery—flared to life in her chest. Her parents had shown no interest in her artistic talents, for that was not something Mary had shared. She remembered that she'd loved poetry, too, and had read all the romantics before her tenth birthday. But over the years, she'd morphed into a strange half human, exhibiting a performative role in the family, acting as she thought Mary might have. Then, when her mother died, Annie had taken on those roles in the house, too: organising social events, keeping in touch with their friends, overseeing the family business. She had tried to be everything to everyone to the extent she no longer recognised any part of her true self.

But back then, all those years ago, she'd felt like Theo

understood and saw her. Even without talking deeply about her life, about any of this, he'd looked at Annie and seen *her*. She'd fallen in love with him, but she'd also fallen in love with the woman she'd been when he was around—because she could just be herself. For the first time in her life, she'd been with someone who didn't want anything of Annie except *her*. Her happiness, her thoughts, her pleasure.

But that version of Theo seemed a thousand light-years away from this reality. Which would hurt a lot less if she didn't feel so much for him. If she didn't look at him and experience a yawning ache to go back to what they were. And yet, even then, what they were now was somehow more real, more honest, warts and all. Was it better to be in a flawed relationship than a seemingly perfect one that didn't have depth—because he kept her at arm's length?

Or was it possible that she was blinded by feelings that she really wished she didn't have. She'd gone into this swearing that she hated him, because of how he'd maneuvered her into this marriage, but when she glanced into her heart, it wasn't hate she saw. It was so much more complicated than that. But swirling at the depths of all her regret over the past was this one, shining kernel of truth—almost as bright as her enormous engagement ring—she loved him. She was in love with the husband who'd married her for revenge. And what kind of fool did that make her?

No matter how Annie felt, if he was determined to constantly bring them back to how this had started—in hatred and revenge—then there was no hope for them. Maybe she needed to take a page out of his book, and focus purely on protecting herself. Give Theo what he wanted: a public marriage, and nothing else behind closed doors.

She sniffed, pinching her cheeks to bring some colour back to them.

She hated it. She hated it so much, but what could Annie do? She'd agreed to this, and there was nothing left but to see it through. In the end, her father would have his company, but Annie might, at that point, hang up her acting shoes for good. It was time to find herself—away from the pressures of anyone else. It was time to stand on her own two feet. Or at least, it would be, when this marriage was over.

'I've made reservations for the Asteri tonight,' Annie murmured without looking up from her book the following morning. For his part, Theo was trying not to think about the fact they'd barely spoken since coming home from her father's party the night before, and for the first time in a long time, had also not touched.

He'd spent a deeply unsatisfying night staring up at the ceiling of his room, aware of his wife's soft rhythmic breathing, replaying every glance of hers, every word, every look that had indicated her hurt and sense of betrayal.

She'd played her part to perfection, of course. After coming back from the bathroom, she was impeccably attentive, standing at his side, making polite conversation, sipping champagne and acting as though she had not a care in the world. But it had been so fake, her act so brittle he felt as though one word from him might cause her to snap.

In the end, he'd ushered them out of there as quickly as possible, rather than subjecting her—or himself—to another moment of the tense estrangement.

'The Asteri?' he frowned, though he was familiar with the venue. It was one of *the* hotspots of Athens.

'You want our marriage to be public, right? Where better than somewhere like that,' she said, her voice blanked of emotion. Frustration zipped through him, but he couldn't name why. After all, she was right, but after last night, he wanted to make everything *less* public. He wanted to batten down the hatches here at home, keep her here, in his bed, until the Annie he'd glimpsed over the last week came back to him.

Except, the whole point of this was to rub their marriage in her father's face—to make him realise that the exact thing he'd forbidden from happening five years ago was now a reality. All Theo had to do was think back to that conversation, to the things the old man had said, and his resolution firmed. He just hadn't realised how much he'd hate making Annie collateral damage.

When he'd made this deal, he'd presumed he'd almost enjoy putting her through this, but for whatever reason, he had to admit to himself now that the opposite was true. She was hurting, and he wasn't enjoying that. He was hating it.

'Great,' he said, adopting the same, nonchalant tone, despite the turmoil of his thoughts. 'What time?'

'Nine o'clock.'

He nodded once, trying to think of something to say to fill the silence. An explanation or apology, but both died on his lips.

She glanced at him, though somehow he felt more as though she was looking through him. 'I'm going out—shopping. I'll be back before nine.'

He watched her leave, and told himself he was relieved. This version of Annie was like a knife being dragged over his flesh; she made him feel things he didn't want to face. Better to spend time apart than face that guilt front on, even if that made him a coward.

Five nights and five very public dates later, Theo had to admit—to himself at least—that he was at his wit's end. Annie had played the part of doting wife to perfection, but only for as long as they were in public. The minute they were collected by his driver, and nestled in the privacy of his car, the mask dropped, and she was back to icing him out, almost like she wished he didn't exist.

Except she didn't do anything quite so overt. She was still polite to him, speaking if he asked questions, offering cool smiles, and she still slept in their bed, albeit huddled to one side of it. But she'd pulled a shield over herself, and no matter what he said or did, he couldn't crack through it.

Worse than having her break up with him because her parents had demanded it was this: living alongside her quiet, brutal contempt. Knowing that she was choosing to ice him out, not because her parents didn't see any value in him, but because *she* didn't. He was in freefall, and all of his usual anchor points were insufficient to stop it. Just looking at her made the whole world lose its shape.

The following night, when Annie announced yet another public engagement—this time, the opening of a restaurant followed by drinks at the pier—he'd almost snapped at her that he was sick of being dragged around town for the sake of photographers before remembering that it had been *his* requirement, not hers. She was simply living up to it.

When she appeared in the living room in yet another stunning dress that showed way too much skin, he ground his teeth together and tried to ignore how much he wished they were just staying home.

They'd made their point. Their photograph had been splashed over the tabloids. Everyone knew about their marriage.

'Can you be bothered going out again?'

'I wasn't aware I had a choice.'

His gut felt like it had been washed in acid. 'Don't say that.'

She tilted her chin, glaring at him. 'I'm doing what you asked of me. If you've changed your mind, fine. I'm just as happy to stay in.'

But she wasn't happy. Annie was anything but, and it was all because of him. He ignored the pain in his chest, the feeling of something beautiful being tarnished forever. 'No, you've made the reservation. We'll go out.' At least when they were out, she pretended to like him. Here, at home, he couldn't escape her silent judgement, and it was eating him alive.

'Great,' she smiled, over-bright and clearly false. 'I'm ready when you are.'

The restaurant was in an industrial part of the city that had gradually become a haven for exclusive bars and clubs, though Theo couldn't for the life of him say why. He presumed it had started as some kind of ironic joke, but now some of the most exclusive haunts in the city were in between abattoirs and box factories.

He couldn't fault the decor of the restaurant though, nor the menu. He sat opposite his wife and made the obligatory small talk, admiring the way she volleyed it back, as though she wasn't hating him the whole time. They were interrupted often, by people he knew, or she knew, or sometimes, people who knew them both, and for Theo's part, he was as equally glad for the interruption as he was resentful of it.

It gave him a momentary reprieve, while also allowing him to watch her at work. To watch the way she assumed a role so easily—not because he'd asked her to, this time, but because he suspected she'd been doing it all her life. Being who she was expected to be. Playing a part. Being Mary. Then her mother. Being whatever was needed of her, always putting other people first, always being what was needed, not what she wanted.

Had that been true of her then, too? Had she been that way with him—playing the role of what she believed he wanted?

He'd thought not. He would have sworn the Annie he'd spent time with was true to herself, to the woman she wanted to be, but how could he know? She'd been so perfect for him, their time together so—right—but maybe that was down to her acting skills?

As Annie spoke to the two women who'd approached their table, Theo looked at her without really seeing. No, he was back in time, in the water at the island, making love to his wife in a way that was totally real, without pretense, without make-believe. That had been an act of total honesty—his need, her need, raw desperation and hunger, bringing them together, bonding them in a way he'd resented at the time, because it had been her first sexual experience. Now he felt so differently about that.

Everything felt flipped on its head, and he hated it. He wanted to see the real Annie again, to strip her back to the essence of who she was, before this play-acting had come into the equation.

The waiter appeared to clear their plates, and the women dispersed with a manicured wave in Annie's direction, which Theo barely noticed.

'Let's go back to the island.' And until he heard himself say it, he hadn't even been aware he was going to suggest it.

For a second—barely even a second, in fact—her mask slipped, and she looked at him like he'd sprouted two heads.

'Why?'

Great question. But now that he'd made the suggestion, he found himself wanting to see it through. He leaned forward, an intensity in his gaze, as if he could make her understand if he just looked hard enough. 'To get away from this.'

Annie compressed her lips in a gesture he was intimately familiar with: contemplation. She was trying to make sense of his statement. '*This* is what you wanted.'

And she was right. This had indeed been what he'd originally envisaged, back in Sydney, when she'd come to him for help. And he'd responded by blackmailing her. His chest seemed to compress, as though a cement truck had dropped its entire load on him. So much had changed since then, not least of all his certainty that this revenge plan was wise. 'Now I want the island.'

Her lips pressed together again, harder, so her mouth was white-rimmed, and her eyes showed something a lot like panic. 'I don't think it's a good idea.'

'Are you saying no?'

'Am I allowed to say no?'

That cut right through him, and he felt almost as though he couldn't breathe, as though he were drowning. The last thing he wanted was for her to feel trapped. 'Annie...' He leaned forward. 'No one forced you into this. No one is forcing you to stay.'

Desperation contorted her features. 'Really? If I asked to leave, wouldn't you just point out that we have an agreement?'

He hated that she was right. He hated that she evidently felt trapped. But most of all, he hated the fact that if he were to invoke their agreement to get her to stay, he knew now that it had less to do with the terms they'd reached and more to do with him just wanting her in his life a bit longer. Acknowledging that to himself was like leaping off the edge of a building. It was a warning, and in an instant, his whole mindset shifted. They couldn't go back to the island. They couldn't do anything that would strip away their barriers, and draw them closer together. He refused to weaken where Annie was concerned. Never again.

'Are you saying you want to leave?' His voice was grim, and already he was preparing for the reality of that. She'd walked away from him once, and he'd known she'd do it again. Was he really surprised?

'Please, let's not do this here.' She smiled tightly, for the sake of the audience, but he couldn't wipe the stern insistence from his own features. 'We still have the bar to go to,' she reminded him. 'I don't want to fight.'

'I'm not fighting.'

'Nor am I.'

'You're implying that you don't have any autonomy in this marriage. That's not true.' He had to hear her deny it. He had to hear her agree that she'd walked into this with her eyes open.

She pulled a face. 'I told you, not now.'

And the fact she couldn't give him the reassurance he suddenly needed was like a storm cloud breaking over his world. Everything seemed different, seen through that lens. 'Then let's go home. I'm not in the mood to preen around in some bar so we can get our photo taken.'

She flinched. 'I thought that's exactly what you wanted.'

'No. All of Athens knows we're married, including your father. Job done. Let's go.' He scraped his chair back abruptly, dropping some money onto the table and holding out a hand to her. She stared at it for a long time and his heart dropped at what he felt to be yet another rejection: not touching him.

'Annie.' His voice was meant to be a plea, but he supposed it could also have sounded vaguely like a warning, if she was intent on seeing him as some kind of monster—and why wouldn't she? Her fingers trembled when she put them in his palm. He closed his own around them, in an effort to bring stillness, and when she got to her feet, he pulled her close to his body. 'We need to talk.'

He didn't know what he'd say, but with every single fibre of his intuition, he knew this was no way to live—even for eighteen months. He was not going to subject her to it, not for all the revenge, or all the money, in the world. Even when he desperately wanted her to stay, it wouldn't be like this. It couldn't be.

CHAPTER TWELVE

ANNIE'S NERVES WERE stretched almost to the breaking point. She'd spent the last week acting her little ass off, hoping to provoke him into a reaction. Hoping to provoke him into saying or doing *something* that showed he *felt* anything. Anything other than a soul-destroying need for vengeance, at least. Anything other than hatred for her father.

And tonight, she'd seen that, but she had no idea what he was feeling, and the not knowing was making her stomach twist into billions of tangly knots. They drove home in silence, like the calm before the storm, she'd presumed. But even once they walked inside his luxurious mansion, he was still lost in thought.

So much for talking.

She went to their room and took a long shower, scrubbing her body with a loofah, hoping to bring about a sense of calm. Or if not calm, at least familiarity. But everything was all twisty and knotty and so by the time she stepped out of the shower and wrapped a towel around herself, and walked into the bedroom to find Theo just unfastening the top button of his shirt, something inside of her snapped.

'I thought you wanted to talk,' she said, uncaring of the fact she was all but naked.

He turned to face her slowly, a look on his face she'd

never seen before. 'We need to,' he agreed, but his tone was grim, and she had a feeling a lead balloon had been dropped right on top of her.

Or an executioner's axe was about to fall.

She stared at him, waiting, her heart thudding against her ribs.

'This isn't working.'

'Really?' Her voice came out strangled. 'Because if you wanted to upset my father, I'd say you've done an excellent job.'

His eyes narrowed a little and his lips flattened. 'That is what I wanted. I thought it was what I wanted more than anything, but it turns out, the price was too high.'

'Price?'

'I can't do this.' He cleared his throat. 'I won't do this. To you, Annie. I won't do this to you.'

Her heart stammered now, fast and irregular. What was he saying? 'It's already done. We're married. We have a contract.'

'That doesn't mean anything.'

Her jaw dropped. 'I don't understand.'

'We can change the contract.'

She felt weak enough to pass out. She'd wanted to goad him into a response, but she'd never thought it would be this. 'Is that what you want?'

His eyes closed, and when he spoke, his voice was low and gruff, loaded with accusation. 'What I want is to have never met you.'

'How can you say that?' she whispered, staring at him across the room, body trembling. It hurt so badly, she had to lift a hand and press it to her chest, to stop her heart from splintering through her skin. 'What have I ever done to you, Theo? What have I ever done to deserve that?'

A muscle jerked in his jaw, but she was too angry now, too angry to even think about what she was saying. The words just tumbled out of her, drawn by emotion. 'All I have ever done, from the moment we met, is love you,' she shouted. 'I have loved you since I was eleven years old. I loved you when I was thirteen, fifteen, eighteen and begged you to kiss me—'

'On a dare,' he interrupted.

'Yes, they dared me to do it, but that's not why I asked. I wanted you to kiss me. I wanted you. Just like when I was twenty-one and begged you again. I have loved you always—'

'You walked away from me.'

'But I never stopped loving you,' she roared, shaking all over. 'I loved you even when I came to you in Sydney. When you suggested this marriage, I knew, deep down, that for me, it was something I actually wanted, because of how I felt about you. I couldn't admit it to myself, not when you were so angry with my father, but every single day, I have come to understand my heart, and now, I see it. I love you. And yet you stand there and tell me I am the bane of your life?' Tears ran down her cheeks but she refused to wipe them away, to say anything to him.

'I never asked you to love me,' he responded, his voice the opposite of hers—cold and calm.

'You didn't have to ask. That's not how it works.'

'I never *wanted* you to love me,' he said instead.

'Then what the hell were we doing back then, Theo? I fought with my parents over you, I fought for you. My mother had a heart attack in the middle of one of those fights. But I fought with them because I thought... I thought you loved me, too.'

He turned his back on her, his shoulders moving with the force of his breath.

'You told me I was special.'

He whirled back to face her. 'You are special. That has nothing to do with whether or not I love you, or want to be loved by you. We never had a future.'

Her jaw dropped and her knees felt impossibly weak. She moved to the edge of the bed and sat down, her knees no longer able to support her.

'I thought you understood,' he said, darkly. 'And I thought we could play this game without either of us getting hurt. But I am hurting you, every day of this marriage, and knowing that is cutting me to pieces. I do not want to live like this.'

She blinked across at him, her heart shifting in her chest. 'Cutting you to pieces?'

'I'm not a total bastard, Annie. I don't want you to suffer. Not because of me.' He frowned. 'Not because of anyone. I want you to be happy—I've always wanted that. Don't you get it? That's why I wish I'd never met you— I'm ashamed of what I've become. Ashamed of who I am to you.'

'Are you hearing yourself?' she demanded, standing up again and pacing across to him. 'You hate seeing me upset, you want me to be happy. Yet you think you don't feel something for me? You think you don't love me?'

His eyes swept shut.

'Do you really think you suggested this marriage just to get back at my dad? Or is it that deep down, it's what you really want, too, but don't want to admit to yourself?'

His jaw shifted as he ground his teeth. 'I've never wanted marriage.'

'You haven't let yourself want it,' she corrected. 'You

were bounced from pillar to post as a child. Nobody loved you. You never knew security until you came to live with the Georgiadeses, then they died, too. And even now, a grown man of thirty-one, you're terrified to let yourself reach for happiness, in case it goes away again.' She bit back a sob. 'I understand that, Theo. I don't think anyone who's lived through what you have would feel differently. But at least take a second to think about what's in here.' She pressed a hand to his chest. 'Think about why it hurts you so much to see me hurting. Think about why you have been so angry at my father, for such a long time. Think about how it feels when we're together, why your first thought when I came to you for help was to lock me into this marriage, and ask yourself if that's really something you want to let go.'

'How it feels when we are together is like I'm holding a stick of dynamite, likely to go off at any moment, without warning.'

She frowned, not understanding the analogy.

'I don't know when this is going to end, but I know it will. All things do. Whether because you leave me, or your father makes you leave me, or because one of us dies, nothing lasts forever. I would rather control that, and I think it's best for you, too.'

'Don't you dare be such a paternalistic jackass. I don't need you deciding what's best for me. If you want me to move out, I will, but you should know that's *your* decision, not mine.'

'What do you want, then, Annie? Do you want to stay here, living with me, like this, for another seventeen months of this godawful marriage?'

She flinched. 'No. I want to stay living with you forever, in a wonderful, happy marriage, where we stop fighting everything we feel and accept that when I was eleven and you were fifteen, we met the loves of our lives, and our fate was sealed. I want you to accept that sex with us is never—and could never be—just sex. That every time we're together it's meaningful and beautiful, and special. I want you to know that I will always be here for you, that you can relax with me—'

'How can I after what happened last time?'

'Are you hearing yourself? You're making no sense. Two minutes ago, you told me that you never thought we were going to last. So why did it matter that I left you?'

'It's *why* you left me.'

'Because I love my parents?' she demanded. 'Because I have spent a lifetime playing the part of a stabilizer to them, and I didn't know how to stop? You think you're the only one who learned from that experience? I love my father, and I want him to be happy, but it's time for me to live my life, regardless of what he thinks and wants. And I choose you. I want you.'

A muscle jerked in his jaw. 'This isn't what I want.'

'Well, I don't believe you,' she said, moving to the wardrobe and removing her nightgown. She dressed quickly, staring at him the whole time, hating that even in that moment, she could feel heat and need building inside of her.

'This was a mistake.'

'How we got married, yes. But not that we are.' She put a hand on her hip. 'I'm not leaving you, Theo. If you really want me out of your life, you have to leave me. Divorce me. Announce it in the papers. Do whatever you have to do, but it needs to come from you. I'm not going to walk away from you again.'

'There's nothing to walk away from,' he muttered. 'This isn't a relationship.'

She rolled her eyes. 'You are completely delusional.'

'Annie.' He raised his voice. 'Listen to me. Our marriage is over. I don't want this. I don't want you. I made a mistake, and now I'm fixing it.'

Each word landed against her with a heavy thud. She shook her head, needing to clear those words, needing not to hear them, but he just stared at her, no hint of doubt on his face.

'I'll go to a hotel for a few days, while I find somewhere else to live. You stay here. I will uphold everything I agreed to in our deal, naturally. I'll fix your father's company, and then return it to you. I'm sorry I used you like this. I will always regret it.'

'Used me,' she whispered, shaking her head. 'Is that really what this was to you? Was I honestly just a means to an end?'

He closed his eyes at the accusation in her voice, but then, he was stuffing things into a bag and Annie was staring at him with the realization that he was actually about to walk out of his own home.

'Don't,' she shouted, eyes filling with tears. 'Don't you dare pack that bag. If either of us is leaving, it will be me. This is your home. I'm not staying in it without you.'

'You can leave, if you want, but either way, I'm going.'

'Does it mean nothing to you to hear that I love you?'

'It means I was even more careless than I thought. All I can hope is that you are mistaken.'

'I'm not,' she said. 'I love you. You need to look at me, and accept that. Accept that you are walking away from someone who has given you their heart, for always and ever. And Theo? That means something.'

He was silent.

'Coward. You're running away from me because you're

terrified to love, knowing there's a risk that you'll lose me. So what? Aren't I worth taking that risk for? Don't we deserve a chance?'

His response was to walk out the door.

Theo went to the island, rather than a hotel, and that was a mistake, because memories of Annie chased him there. Even in the ocean, there was no solace. Whatever their first time had been about, it had imprinted on him in a way he couldn't shake. She was in the wind, the sand, the sky, the very air he breathed.

He stayed for a week, each day, hoping to wake up and feel something like his normal self, but without success.

On the eighth day, he returned to Athens with a heaviness in his gut he couldn't shift.

He thought about going home, but he couldn't. He didn't want to see Annie. He wished this whole thing had never happened. He'd been so focused on the chance for revenge against her father, he hadn't stopped to think about what that revenge might do to Annie. He hadn't stopped to think about the fact he was making her collateral damage, nor the fact that he really, really cared about that.

And even though he knew he couldn't be with her, he also knew he couldn't be responsible for ruining her life—and her relationship with her father.

She'd called him a coward? Maybe she was right. But he was going to stand up and fix at least one part of this debacle, starting with her father.

Nine days after walking away from Annie, he arrived at her father's house, grim-faced but determined, and pressed the doorbell.

A maid answered after a few moments.

'Is Elliot Langley in?'

'May I take your name?'

Theo compressed his jaw. 'His son-in-law.'

Even then, when'd come to relieve himself of the burdens of guilt and hate, he found it hard to step back from what he was feeling.

'Very good, sir. Please, come in. Mr Langley is in his study.'

Theo nodded once, but having only come to the house on the occasion of Elliot's recent birthday, he had no idea where that was. That must have shown on his features, because the maid said, 'Please, follow me.'

Theo strode behind her, noting the lack of photographs of Annie on the walls, whereas everywhere he looked there were pictures of his late daughter, Mary.

He knew what the dynamic had been, because Annie had told him, back then, but that didn't make it any harder to see. To imagine how it had been for Annie, growing up here, amongst this museum—a tribute to the little girl they'd lost. A little girl she could never replace, no matter how much her parents wanted her to.

Something cavernous opened up in his chest as Annie's spirit flooded through him. Annie, who'd never really been loved, either. Who'd only been wanted to stem the tide of grief, and hadn't been enough for that. Annie who had learned her role in life was to give up everything to please her parents, including her own independence, her own desires. Including him, even when he was what she'd wanted most.

Annie who'd come to him for help, and received instead the weight of Theo's bitter resentment and anger, who'd been destroyed by him when she'd most needed compassion.

The gnawing, cavernous hollow in the middle of his

being expanded out. Regret was a third footfall, right behind him, chasing him relentlessly.

'Leonidas.' Elliot pushed back his chair, staring across his office at Theo, as though he'd seen a ghost. 'What the hell are you doing here?'

'We need to talk,' he said, striving to infuse his voice with a hint of cordiality, and failing.

'What the hell for? I thought I made it clear the other night—you're not welcome in my house.'

'Even as your son-in-law?' he asked, his lips sneering, before remembering he'd come here to be honest, to at least fix things, as much as he could, for Annie.

'The fact she was stupid enough to marry you doesn't change a thing about how I feel. She'll wake up and see the light one day.'

'And if she doesn't?'

'It's inevitable. You're not right for her. How could you ever hope to be? Someone like you...'

Theo crossed to the window and stared out at the familiar view of Athens. His own outlook, from his bedroom in the Georgiadeses' house next door, had been in this direction.

'It's good to see your elitist streak hasn't mellowed with age.'

'Is it elitist to speak the truth?'

'Your truth is exactly that—yours. Not mine, not Annie's. Never Annie's.'

'You were a mistake. You were always a mistake. She'll see that eventually.'

'Yes.' Theo dropped his head forward, the words piercing his soul. 'Our marriage was a mistake, you're right. My mistake, not hers.' The weight on his chest grew heavier. 'Annie married for love. I married for revenge.' He turned then, dark eyes glittering with ruthless anger, and saw the way Elliot had to brace himself against the desk. 'She married out of a love for you, and, I believe now, a love for me. Perhaps she hoped she could love us both enough to get beyond how much hatred you and I share for one another. One thing has become very clear to me, though. Our marriage will destroy her. Loving me will destroy her. You were right about that.'

'What do you mean, you married for revenge?'

Theo hesitated for the briefest moment, before forcing himself to admit what he'd come here to say. 'Annie needed my help with a professional matter. I gave it on the condition of this marriage.'

Elliot cursed loudly. 'You blackmailed my daughter?'

'Yes.' What was the sense in hiding it?

'For what possible reason?'

Theo compressed his lips.

'To get back at me,' Elliot groaned. 'Because I made her leave you back then. Are you really so petty and broken, that you cannot let bygones be bygones? Are you so damaged that you couldn't see Annie would be the one you hurt with this? Annie, who stood up for you until she was blue in the face. Annie would probably have walked out of her home for good that night, rather than lose you, if it hadn't been for her mother.'

Theo absorbed those charges with no small measure of hurt.

But Elliot was not finished. Face puce with anger, he shouted, 'Good Lord, what in God's name have you done?'

'Done?' Theo ground his jaw. 'I've let her go, Elliot. Just like you wanted me to. She's free. Annie and I will be getting divorced. It turns out, you win, after all.'

Elliot sat down in the chair behind his desk, staring at the wall opposite. 'You really are a fool, Leonidas.'

Theo made a scoffing noise of surprise.

'I never thought much of you, but at least you showed yourself to have good judgement. Are you telling me you've ended things with my daughter? *You've* broken up with *her*?'

A muscle jerked in his jaw as he heard the older man's shock. Hell, he could even understand the reasoning for it. What man in his right mind would walk away from Annie without a gun to his head? Even then...

'If you've hurt her—' Elliot said, the words ringing through the room.

Theo paced to the desk and pressed his fingertips against the inlaid leather surface. 'Isn't that a little like the pot calling the kettle black?'

'What the devil does that mean?'

'Annie came to me hurt. She came to me broken. Because of you. Because of how you treated her—because of how you pushed her, her whole life, into Mary's shadow.'

The older man paled immediately, his lined face showing surprise and indignation, as well as something else. Something like guilt. 'You don't know what you're talking about.'

'I know that woman deserved better than to feel like a substitute for someone you loved more.'

'*I* love my daughter.'

'Perhaps. But loving someone doesn't always go hand in hand with treating them well.' The words fell like stones against him, thudding into the emptiness of his chest cavity in a way that he knew would leave permanent scars.

'I have always protected her, and tried to do what was right for her—'

'You've done what was right for you. You've spent your life trying to turn Annie into the person you thought she should become, rather than appreciate the woman she is.'

'This is none of your business.'

Theo opened his mouth to dispute that, to say that anything that concerned Annie would always concern him, but that would have been a lie, wouldn't it? Annie was not his wife in anything but name, and even that would soon be dissolved.

'If you've hurt her, Theo, so help me God—'

He narrowed his gaze, his gut rolling with acid waves. 'I would *never* hurt her.'

'Then where is she?' Elliot asked, eyes narrowed. 'I haven't heard from her since my birthday party. I could tell she was annoyed with me, but she would usually have called me by now.' The older man stood, then. 'Where is my daughter? Where is my Annie?'

Theo flinched then, because the sound in Elliot's voice was unmistakably worry, and yes, love. It might have been a love that was warped and shaped by his grief, but that didn't make it any less valid or sincere. Even though he hadn't been able to be the kind of father Annie wanted or deserved, that didn't mean he wasn't feeling concern for her now. He was a lot like Theo in that regard. They were married, and yet, Theo had been far from the kind of husband Annie had wanted or deserved. She'd loved him, and he hadn't been able to love her back. He hadn't been brave enough to let himself.

Ironically, he'd called her a coward at the beginning of their relationship, but if he forced himself to regard their relationship with honesty, wasn't it *he* who was afraid? He who was running? Heat flushed his skin.

'She's at my house,' he said, his chest cleaving apart to

imagine her there. 'I told her she could live there as long as she wants, and I meant it.'

'Take me to her,' Elliot said, standing up. 'I want her home, here, with me.' He strode towards Theo then, his eyes laced with fury. 'You never were good enough to even breathe the same air as her, much less touch her. But then, you came back, and married her, and a part of me actually thought maybe you understood how special she is? Maybe you saw it? But you don't even love her, do you? You just did this to get back at me. And yet you can stand there, telling me I don't value my daughter for who she really is. You're a hypocrite, Theo.'

Theo wanted to say something to contradict that, to explain the complexity of his thoughts, to point out that many things could be true at once, but the words were strangled in his throat. All he could do was stare at the other man, his face an unknowing study in tortured contemplation.

Elliot, though, apparently didn't notice the turbulent ruminations going on inside Theo. 'How dare you? How bloody dare you? Take me to my daughter and then get the hell out of our lives, once and for all. She needs to get over you, you bastard.'

On that score, at least, they were in agreement.

Theo collapsed on the sofa, staring between his feet, his heart thudding heavily in his chest. There was no way of knowing when the note had been left, but a quick perusal of his security system showed that Annie had left the house an hour after him, the night they'd fought. The night he'd told her he didn't love her.

The night he told her their marriage was over.

He'd watched the grainy night-vision footage of her pulling a small suitcase down the steps and hailing a cab, and felt like his insides had been acid washed. By then, he'd been at the airport, about to take off for the island where he'd tried to forget about Annie, but all the while imagining her in his home, consoling himself that at least he could picture her going about her life there. That at least he'd given her that.

And now he had no idea where she'd gone.

Elliot had left the house, furious and scathing, blustering about filing a police report and Theo should consider the matter closed, seeing as he clearly didn't care for Annie anyway. Theo had wanted to shout at the older man to shut up, to stop saying things like that, but how could he deny it? If he'd cared for Annie, she'd have still been here. She'd have been safe in his house, safe with him, instead of God knew where.

He pushed up from his sofa, his heart thumping in his empty chest, as he paced the living room and tried to think. To imagine where she might go, where she could be living, who she'd be with. Friends? None that she was close to. She'd rarely travelled outside of Athens; as far as he knew there was nowhere she wanted to be, nowhere that called to her. Or if there was, he didn't know it. He didn't know where she'd turn to, in a dark moment of her life, and that gap in his knowledge physically hurt him. Suddenly, the idea that Annie was alive and he didn't know something so vital about her, didn't understand her well enough to know where she would flee to, was an impossible reality.

He couldn't live with it. He had to find her.

Theo reached for his phone and tried calling Annie. Again, and again, with no response. Then, with a sense of dread, he finally accepted that it was time to call the police himself, never mind that Elliot had already done so. He filed his own missing persons report, then he called a private security firm and enlisted their help, too. But even then, he just couldn't sit in his home, waiting for news. He had to do something, and so he went out on foot, scouring the city he knew so well, courtesy of having grown up in the back streets. He went to the restaurants they'd eaten at, the bars, hoping that he'd catch a glimpse of her, somewhere.

Anywhere.

Annie had barely left bed since checking herself into her hotel room. She couldn't say why she'd come back to it except that it had been the only thing she could think of, that awful night, when he'd ended their marriage. As though she could close this chapter of their lives just by coming back to where it had begun.

It hadn't worked.

The chapter was open. The wound, too, weeping and ghastly, so she'd climbed into bed and curled up in the fetal position, eyes squeezed shut. It hadn't helped to stem the tears, though. They'd fallen hard, almost saturating the pillow, but she'd just rolled over, onto the other side of the bed, and kept crying.

It was the most awful, heavy feeling, to finally have accepted how much she still loved Theo, and also accepting that he would never let himself feel that for her. Even if he did, in fact, love her, he wouldn't admit it, and he wouldn't act on it. It was futile and desperate.

Somewhere along the way, Annie lost track of the date. She eventually began to feel closer to human, to move from the bed to the small armchair and stare out at the city. To order room service that she would pick around the edges of, if not fully eat. At one point, she contemplated turning her phone on, but decided against it.

She didn't really expect to hear from Theo, but at the same time, it was possible he might reach out to her. Perhaps when he realised she was no longer at the house they'd shared? He'd no doubt be relieved she'd left quietly, without trying to revive their conversation. He'd finally pushed her away, and this time, it would be for good.

But the thought of her life, spanning before her without Theo in it, was its own form of torture. Annie's heart almost couldn't take it.

She moved back to the bed and curled beneath the covers, tears welling in her throat as she tried not to think about Theo: wanting him, needing him to reach for her and knowing he never would.

CHAPTER THIRTEEN

THE ROOM SERVICE came a little earlier than she'd expected, then again, she'd lost track of days and nights. It might have been a quiet Monday, for all she knew. She pushed out of bed, her limbs feeling heavy, and made her way down the carpeted corridor to the front door of her hotel room, pulling it inwards without noticing that the usual 'room service' announcement hadn't been made.

And stumbled backwards at the sight of Theo on the other side of the door, his face a mask of barely contained darkness. Anger? Fury? Worry? What? She didn't know. Only he was staring at her with those glittering eyes, his jaw clenched so tight it was practically squared off.

'Do you have any idea how worried we've been?' he demanded, striding through the open door and putting his hands on her forearms, holding her still so he could stare down at her face, as though needing to reassure himself that she was in fact standing right in front of him, alive and well.

Annie shook her head, shaking all over, unable to find any words.

'You disappeared, Annie. You disappeared. We had no idea where you were.'

She pulled away from him then. Moments earlier, she'd been facing the reality of how desperate she was to be held by him, to feel his strength one last time, but now, it was the cruellest thing, because it meant nothing.

'I'm fine,' she lied, moving into the hotel room and looking around with a grimace. At least it looked tidy—she'd barely unpacked, much less touched anything besides the bed.

'You look—'

She didn't want to think about how she looked. She whirled around, trying to cling to anger instead of the spasming pain inside of her. 'I wasn't exactly expecting company or I might have gone to a little more effort.'

'Annie,' he groaned, and he dropped his head, pressing his hands to his face, so she stopped whatever tirade she'd been about to dredge up and looked at him properly. Saw his stance for what it was—desperation. Misery. Relief.

With legs that were shaking, she moved to the bed and sat down, needing the support.

'I have spent the last week imagining you—I don't know. I had no clue. It was only that your father remembered an old credit card, thought you might have been using that, that led to you being discovered.'

Her stomach dropped. 'My father? Tell me he doesn't know about any of this.'

Theo strode towards her, crouching between her legs. 'Why did you run away, Annie? Why did you try to hide from me?'

'I didn't run away,' she said, hollow. 'You ended our marriage, I simply left, as I said I would.'

'But you didn't use normal bank accounts. You have been hiding here.'

'I have been taking some time,' she said, sniffling. 'And why is this your business? You made it very clear that you didn't want any part of this marriage.'

'Yes, I did,' he said, a muscle jerking in his jaw. 'And do you have any fucking idea how much I have wanted to take those words back ever since? How much I have wanted to fix what I broke? How much I have needed to see you to make this right?'

She sucked in an uneven breath.

'Annie, you were right. Everything you said was right. When I met Paul Georgiades, it felt like I knew him before, like I had no choice but to go with him, to keep going back to him, but it was never really about Paul and Stephanie, as much as I respected and cared for them. It was always about finding my way to you. My other half. My beautiful, perfect other half, my reason for being, my reason for everything.'

She shook her head then, tears slipping down her cheeks, landing heavily on her thighs.

'I spent a long awful week on the island, and you were there, in my bloodstream, whispering your love to me, making me wake up and realise what I wanted. And then, I knew I had to fix this. I had to start by facing up to my hatred for your father, by trying to fix that, because you cannot live in a marriage where your husband and your father are sworn enemies.'

She sucked in another breath, the sound a wrenching half sob.

'How did you try to fix it?'

'By admitting the truth to him. But a strange thing happened. In telling him what I thought was the truth, I realised I'd been wrong all along. All I wanted, from the minute you walked into my life, was to keep you right here, with me, where you belong. I made it sound like it was about revenge, when in reality, it's always been this. It's always been you.

'When we were seeing each other, before, I felt as though I had been given the greatest gift known to man. Losing you was agony. I suppose I have been trying to insulate myself from that risk, to handle this on my terms, but I've been so wrong. So wrong. Even now, I stand before you begging you to come home to me, to tell me I'm not too late, that you can still love me after what I've done, when there is a huge part of me that wants to let you go, because I don't deserve you. Because I could never deserve you.'

'You've always had to protect yourself, Theo. I know that.'

'Yes, but that's no excuse.'

'Isn't it?' She caught his face with both hands. 'I don't need you to be perfect, Theo. I don't need you to get it right all the time. I didn't.'

'You?'

'Do you think you're the only one with regrets? Breaking up with you was the worst decision I ever made. I know why I did it. At twenty-two, with my mother in hospital having suffered a heart attack, I was desperate to fix everything. That's how I'd been raised. But I was young, and I didn't understand the ramifications of that decision. It's not one I would make now.'

'You were acting out of love for your family. Your decision was born of decency and goodness, of caring for someone else. Mine was purely selfish.'

'You've been through more than one person should ever have to in a lifetime, Theo. It's okay to want to take care of yourself.'

'Please, don't be so forgiving. I deserve to feel this guilt.'

She laughed softly then, and the sound was such a surprise to her, that her heart seemed to bubble in answer. 'Theo, do you love me?'

He answered immediately. 'With absolutely the entirety of my heart.'

'Then can you do something for me?'

He hesitated longer then, though. 'Yes. Anything.' The second word was said with more conviction, and she knew he meant it. She knew that if she asked him to walk away, he would. But Annie had no intention of doing that.

'Would you just leave the past in the past, now? We both made mistakes. We've both been hurt. But there is no one else I want to be with, no one else I want to wake up next to, no one else I want to share my hopes and fears, and future, with than you. If you feel the same, don't we owe it to ourselves, and each other, to just...be happy?'

'Happy,' he repeated, like it hadn't really occurred to him. But then, slowly, a smile spread across his face, broad and genuine and so filled with hope that Annie's heart did thump almost out of her chest.

'Yes, happy,' she agreed, leaning forward, so her lips were just a hair's breadth from his. 'For as long as we both shall live.'

'Yes, my darling, my dearest, most beautiful Mrs Leonidas. For as long as we both shall live.'

Theo had not come to Sydney alone. He couldn't have, even if he'd wanted to. By that point, out of sheer necessity, he and Elliot Langley had become a unified force, focused solely on their shared need of finding Annie and knowing that she was safe.

When Theo got the call that Annie had been discovered, via a forgotten-about credit card, it was his private jet that had flown them halfway across the world. And locked in that plane together for twenty-four hours, Theo and Elliot had had very little option but to talk.

Theo had always found it hard to open up about his life, his childhood, and particularly with a man like Elliot, and yet, for Annie, he did so. He explained what his life had been like, why Elliot's insults had fundamentally changed him, had turned him so utterly bitter, had made him turn on Annie, too, to the point, and much to his shame, that when her mother died, he hadn't even reached out to her.

He'd been so angry, it was a miracle to think she'd found it in her heart to love him after that.

And yet she did, because she was Annie, full of light and love, full of compassion.

Elliot was an aristocrat to the core, and he found it hard to shake his views, but as he spoke about his daughter, who had died, and his and his late wife's hopes for Annie, Theo came to understand him better. To see that he'd been right about the older man. While his love for Annie was not as Theo would have wished, it was still love.

'I suppose even the royal family are allowed to marry commoners,' Elliot had conceded, as the plane came in over Sydney. And then, with a frown, as if he was reshaping his views of the world, bit by bit, 'Let's go find our girl, Theo.'

It was entirely surreal for Annie to be in Sydney, sitting beside her husband and opposite her father, over a high tea the following afternoon. Even stranger to hear her husband and father talk about the business, about the direction Theo was taking it in—and for Annie to see her father revitalised in those conversations, showing a genuine interest in the business for the first time in years.

By the time they finished tea, Annie felt almost as though she'd stepped into an alternate dimension—and she wasn't complaining.

* * *

They left Sydney the next morning, but almost as soon as touching down in Athens, and having Elliot disembark, Annie and Theo left once more, this time, returning to the island. Where their first trip there had been marked by long stretches of silence, this trip was the opposite. They talked the entire journey to the island, and once they arrived, instead of walking on eggshells, they were floating on air.

It was as though by finally accepting that he could love Annie, and accept that opening himself up to their relationship fully made him strong rather than weak, he stepped into a whole new reality. One in which he wanted her to understand everything about him, to know his entire truth, his childhood, the despair of it, because he was no longer grieving it—it was a part of him, and all those parts had led him to Annie, and the most all-consuming joy he could ever have imagined.

A year later, as they marked their first wedding anniversary, they were celebrating not only the fact that they'd found their way back to one another, but also the floating of the Langley company on the stock exchange as one of the highest offerings of all time, thanks to Theo's tireless efforts to turn it around. As for Annie, she was on the brink of opening her art gallery, and Theo was her biggest supporter and champion. His own achievements didn't get a look in: everything he said and did was about Annie, and how proud he was of her.

In its first year of operation, the gallery took the art world by storm, and though that brought Annie no small measure of joy, it was the discovery, three months after opening the doors, that their happy pairing was about to become a trio. Two years later, two more babies turned them into a five-person family, and five years after that, quite by surprise, another little Leonidas flew into their nest.

Though they loved and lived the rest of their lives in the fullness of those happy hearts, Annie and Theo devoted a lot of their time and money beyond their family, to street children. They raised money and awareness, built shelters, developed education programs, employment opportunities and therapy assistance.

From the wreckage of Theo's childhood had come something wonderful, and even as a very old man, Theo almost couldn't believe how rich and happy his life had become, all because he'd finally opened himself to love.

* * * * *

LET'S TALK
Romance

For exclusive extracts, competitions and special offers, find us online:

 MillsandBoon

 @MillsandBoon

 @MillsandBoonUK

 @MillsandBoonUK

Get in touch on 01413 063 232

For all the latest titles coming soon, visit
millsandboon.co.uk/nextmonth

www.ingramcontent.com/pod-product-compliance
Ingram Content Group UK Ltd.
Pitfield, Milton Keynes, MK11 3LW, UK
UKHW041827180426
470047UK00014B/87

9 780263 418163